THE BIG SWEDE

by

V. G. Hedner

Published by
Castle Publishing
Vicksburg Plaza, Suite 4
1115 Vicksburg Lane
Plymouth, MN 55447

ISBN: 0-9661383-1-7 (previously ISBN 1-878723-04-9)--Hard Cover
ISBN: 0-9661383-2-5--Soft Cover

Manufactured in the United States of America

Revised

October 1997

HISTORICAL CONTRIBUTORS

The Author acknowledges the contributions of historical societies and publishers providing historical background information for the historical novel, *The Big Swede*. Many episodes in the book, including the Sioux Uprising, are based on documented history.

The Minnesota Historical Society. General information. Also a modified map from the *Sioux Uprising of 1862*, Copyright 1961.

State Historical Society of North Dakota. General information.

South Dakota Historical Society. General information.

The Provincial Archives of Manitoba. Canadian History.

Roy Johnson's Red River Valley, Red River Valley Historical Society, 1982. The publication of a series of articles written by Roy Johnson for the Fargo Forum Newspaper, 1941 to 1965.

The Women of Red River, Willis J. Healey. Peguis Publishers, Winnipeg, Manitoba, 1923. Recollections from women who lived in Red River, Canada, in early 1800s.

In Dedication To:

MAUREEN LAJOY

Educator, Author, Publisher, Editor,
Advisor to a host of aspiring writers.

For many years she was my teacher, friend, and source of inspiration and encouragement. Maureen was my mentor. Ofttimes I could have abandoned the writing of *The Big Swede* had it not been for her generous support and direction.

Having nearly completed the book, my Guiding Angel took ill, finally succumbing to brain cancer on March 15, 1996. Developing writers, including this 'Old Timer Country Boy', will forever be grateful to her high professional and moral standards, and her unyielding friendship.

Rest in Peace! And - thank you, my friend, Maureen. I hold you in high esteem. I'll never forget you.

*   *   *   *   *   *

The Wednesday afternoon professional writer's critiquing group guided me when I meandered and went astray with "The Swede." These successful published writers are:

Bernie Becker	St. Louis Park, MN
Jim Brown	Minneapolis, MN
Marilyn Finnerty	Hopkins, MN
Al Mann	Roseville, MN
Dorothy Nordstrom	Brooklyn Park, MN
Joanne Reisberg	Minneapolis, MN
Sigurd Vikse	Brooklyn Park, MN
Tom Qualy	St. Louis Park, MN

THE BIG SWEDE

WATERWAYS AND OXCART TRAILS
OF THE FUR TRADE

Qu'Appelle Riv.

Assiniboine Riv.

Lake Winnipegosis

Lake Manitoba

Lake Winnipeg

Bas de la Riviere

ENGLISH R.

AL

lac St. Josep

PORTAGE

Ft. La Reine

PORTAGE LA PRAIRIE

Ft. Garry

Ft. St. Charles

Lake of the Woods

CHIPPEWA

lac

Souris R.

Ft. Union

Riviere Rouge

RAINY

Rainy Lake

Ft. St. Pierre

CHIPPEWA

PIDGEON Riv

GRAND PORTAGE

Ft. WIL

L.a. La Pointe

Ft. Clark

Ft. Mandan

SIOUX

SIOUX

Lake Amokan

Lac La Croix

Vermilion Riv.

SAVANAH PORTAGE

St. LOUIS RIV.

Boix Brule Ri.

PORTAGE

KETTLE PORTAGE

St. Croix RIV.

Lac Court Oreilles

LEGEND

Waterways:
the early
travel lanes.

Name changes:
Riviere Rouge
to Red River,
St. Peter to
Minnesota R.

Forts; trading posts.

. . . . Oxcart Trails

A quarter million natives populated the area
before the advent of contagious diseases.

Steamboats, not prairie schooners, brought immigrants to the Northwest.

Lake Traverse

Big Stone L.

Lac Qui Parle

Big Sioux Riv.

St. Anthony Falls

St. Peter

SIOUX

Ft. Miller

GERMAN

Chippeway Riv.

BEAUHARNOIS

Ouisconsin Riv.

LAKE PEPIN

TREMPEALEAU

Prairie du Chien

PORT.

Big Souix Riv.

MISSOURI RIVER

des Moines Riv.

Bellevue

MISSISSIPPI RIVER

Ft. Orleans

St. Louis

KASKASKIA

Ca

Lit

PROLOGUE - SHIPWRECK ON THE BALTIC

Olaf Olsson, a tall and gangly seventeen, already had completed two years of indentured service as a merchant sailor. Now, he and his mates were struggling to hold onto the decrepit Reliance, as the severe rocking and pitching threatened to thrust them into the brimey drink. The Baltic was a hellish sea churning from gale force winds, torrential rains, and thunder crashing relentlessly.

The aging Sloop had survived hundreds of violent storms while sailing the treacherous Baltic Sea, but never had it encountered the likes of the insidious tempest torturing her now. Sixty foot waves were tossing the beleaguered craft about like an errant piece of driftwood. The large square sails of the main mast, usually billowing gracefully in gentle breezes, were now tearing and shredding.

The antiquated wooden hull, with Olaf checking damage, met the wall of each powerful wave with a halting thump then, as if standing still, it raised to the top of the crest, the bow protruding thirty degrees upwards, out of the water, where she wrenched and shimmered, trying to break away from the angry sea's lecherous hold on her. The hull continued its repeated downward plunge, again--a halting jolt and a torrent of water cascading over the deck, ever threatening the hapless seaman with being washed overboard to an eternal watery grave.

Olaf, and his shipmates, had been saddened the night before when it became known that jovial Trigvie Bjornsson had lost his footing and gone overboard. Trigvie was Olaf's age, and the two were close friends, having spent many hours discussing their life's plans and whiling away the time playing cards and deck ball, or just sitting near the helm, listening to their friend, Kapten Krueger, spin yarns about the good old days in Stockholm.

Now the full force of Thor's anger and revenge struck the

fateful Reliance with one more resounding blow. The old hull echoed within from the crashing blast, repeating itself with each violent roll. As Olaf was descending the ladder to the lower hold, he froze in his tracks seeing tons of cargo flying toward him with deadly force. He leaped back up, barely avoiding being struck. Easing down again for a careful look, Olaf saw water shooting through several devastating breaks in the hull. Finally, shoving the hatch wide open, he focused on the tragic sight of old Solheim's smashed remains. The timeworn gentle mariner attempted to secure the loosened stowage, but had obviously slipped, and the tons of freight snuffed out his life instantaneously, no doubt. The young Swede, sickened, began crawling to the top deck.

Of the seven man crew, including Kapten Krueger, only five were left to control the battered sloop. Two young sailors were manning the riggings of the main mast. Brule Haugen, the First Mate, friend to no one, was busying himself on the small boat divots, and had the tiny craft hanging over the side, ready for lowering. It appeared he was about to abandon ship without consideration of the other sailors. He was a man born into hate and anger, it seemed to Olaf, who had no respect for his crewmates, even in the face of death.

The incessant pounding of the angry sea kept tearing at the rapidly deteriorating ship. As the main mast twisted and weakened, Olaf struggled against the wind and the violent thrusts of the ship to report the adverse developments to his friend, Kapten Krueger. Grasping firmly the cabin railing, he inched his way aft to the wheel.

He'd moved around the small foc's'l and looked on. "Kapten, Kapten," Olaf called. Though his efforts to manage the helm were growing futile, he continued diligently tending the wheel. His old legs had a seasoned rock to them, leaning to port when the ship rolled to starboard, then reversing when tilting the opposite way. Finally getting his attention, "First Mate Haugen has turned out the divots, and the whale boat is ready to be lowered. Don't ya think it's time to leave sir," he shouted over the whistling wind.

First, the Kapten looked solemnly serious, but a subtle smile came over his face. "Olaf, I know the old Reliance is at the end of the line." He paused for a moment, then spoke anxiously; "Olaf, you are young and strong. You can fight the sea, as I have twice before." He reached in his pocket, retrieving a small gold fob; the words 'Endearing Love - Hattie' were inscribed on it. "My heart will not allow another fight with the sea, Olaf. Find Frau Krueger, and give this to her." He said resolutely, "I will take the Reliance down to her final resting place." He quickly wiped his eye with his heavy helmsman's glove. "The old sloop is listing badly; the hold must be near full now." He said in finality.

"Ja Kapten, when the cargo broke loose, the pounding caused the hull to rupture very bad," Olaf reported.

A startling crash occurred as the main mast buckled and slammed down on the deck, severing a bulkhead from the foc's'l. Krueger didn't flinch. *"Har, mein freund,* you play the mouth harp much better than I. It was my good luck charm. When the water is dried from it, it will play good as ever. It has taken me through more than one encounter." Then, putting his hand on Olaf's shoulder, said, *"Gud* be with ya."

"Ja' and with you, Kapten Krueger, " Olaf said, trembling.

The kindly Skipper had one final word. "Olaf, fight the sea! You are a good swimmer, but you'll need help! Grab on to anything you can find, but fight the sea, Olaf! Fight the sea! And farewell."

The next monstrous wave cast the final blow, and the old sloop tilted to forty-five degrees. Olaf's feet went out from under, tossing him into the icy churning water.

He heard the desperate calls from the two other young seamen, *"Gud Hjalpa oss!"* one shouted. *"Brule, spara oss!"* another called to the first mate, trying to escape in the small whale boat. He heard them plead again, a time or two, but the fierce wind and heavy waves devoured their voices and no more cries were heard.

Tons of planks and debris tumbled all around Olaf. Pieces of the smashed Reliance whipped about like birch bark. Yet Olaf knew the heavy timbers could kill him instantly. As they reached the top of each wave, the violent wind flipped them out of the water and into the air. The whale boat, too, went tumbling out of sight.

The fierce murky waves pulled him down, but he tried to gasp for a quick breath in the short time his head bobbed above the surface. He sucked in some of the putrid salty water through his nose and mouth and flailed to keep afloat, instantly becoming nauseated. Coughing and struggling desperately, he knew he was nearing an all-too-close destiny with death. His eyes, too, were near blinded from the salt.

His thoughts become desperately reverent: Gud, if ever I needed a miracle it should be right now, he pleaded.

His shoulder took a heavy bump from one of the timbers. He grasped for it and had his hands on the thick plank, but his fingers, numbed from the icy water, were no match for the huge oak beam; it slipped away. In a sense of desperation he tried again, but the rough wood evaded him, leaving his fingers bleeding. Finally, getting close enough to throw his right arm across the full width, he held on, exerting his shrinking strength. Having broken wild horses for his family's landlord, he even tried throwing his legs around the tumbling plank, but the chafing and scrapping of the thorny edges shredded the skin from his chest, arms and legs.

Becoming exhausted and dazed, thoughts of giving in to the conquering sea were consuming him. His body could only take so much torture. He contemplated how short the pain of dying would be and then eternal rest at the placid bottom with Kapten Krueger.

"Fight the sea, Olaf! Fight the sea!" The words echoed in his head. Instilled with renewed energy, he looked around for the one speaking to him. Surely, it was the spirit of the Skipper, he told himself. Regaining his senses, he held on with renewed determination. The roughened board kept gnawing his flesh, causing severe pain, and his strength was being sapped to the hilt. How had he gotten into this mess? He had his whole life before him.

Confronted by still another mysterious object twisting around his submerged legs, he worried; could the tentacles of some sea monster be grabbing hold, ready to pull him below to devour him. He thrust his arm down to his ankles and snatched at it, but on pulling it out of the water, he was surprised to find a mass of snarled line. Rope from the ship's riggings he realized. With it, he could secure himself to the tumbling float he was clinging to. So, quickly looping a length around the timber, securing himself and leaving enough play for maneuvering, he was beginning to feel as though he could now fight the sea--and win. He decided at the moment if he survived this nightmare he'd leave this old world forever. He'd head for the new land, get himself some good ground for he and his loving Gerda.

It was still a worry with tons of debris tossing about threateningly. When floating high on the crest of a wave, Olaf, scanned around for a larger floating section that would allow for greater stability; something he could maneuver away from the dangerous wreckage.

But, pulling on the tangled rope, he realized another floating beam was closing in. It was the broken end of the rounded spar! Another huge wave signaled further danger; the pole tumbled uncomfortably close! The Swede was terrified! He leaned away to escape getting crushed, but his left leg was caught between the two heavy beams. Screaming from excruciating pain, Olaf sickened to see his leg was smashed!

His first thoughts were that the limb might have been severed completely. He tried to raise it, but there was no response. Nearing panic, he reached his right hand down to where the pain was most severe and knew immediately his leg had been broken. Worse, the shin bone dangled precariously.

Utter depression set in. What's the use of a half man, he thought. Not being able to walk! What could he do? He'd never make it to the new land now.

Still, the dangerous pole lurking threateningly close had to be controlled, his thoughts aside. The lines, part of the rigging, were attached to the menacing obstacle. He waited for the pole to drift closer, then pulled the line over the end, successfully securing it next to his timber. He managed to thrust himself out to slip a noose over the other end. Yanking with all his might, he forced the mast section tightly to his plank. It worked! He breathed a sigh of relief now the two large pieces were bound together. And taking no chances, he struggled to slide the line around and around many times so the two large members moved as one.

Though his broken leg pained him tremendously, and every second he was losing strength and ability to reason, Olaf Olsson acted instinctively to survive. Suddenly, he noticed the great waves with the towering tops had settled some, the wind not causing the same kind of havoc as earlier. And, though feeling faint, as if slipping out of consciousness, he struggled with the last ounce of energy. Now, for the first time, maybe he could hoist himself up on the flat timber and rest his fatigued body. The leg? That would have to trail along in the water. There was no way, in his condition, to garner up enough strength for retrieving the broken limb.

He groaned out in pain as he hoisted himself to the level board, and on reaching it, collapsed his battle-worn frame flat on his back. Giving a grateful sigh, he murmured thanks to his *Allsmaktig Gud,* who gave strength to persevere and fight the sea.

*   *   *

Olaf had no way of knowing exactly how long it had been since the Reliance plunged to the bottom. About mid day, he recollected--six or seven hours before, at least. The sky was dimming, and the heavy swells had worn themselves out, so finally he could rest his weary, mangled body for awhile. Drained, Olaf lay there in a semi-conscious state until sleep overtook him.

For many hours the bewildered Swede slowly rocked with the soothing movement of the Baltic Sea, fading in and out of consciousness. Sometimes the vision of land, endless stretches of land, entered his dreams. Once he saw a farmhouse, silhouetted in the sunset.

Eventually, in his more lucid moments, the realization of his smashed leg dangling in the water began to weigh heavily on his mind. He agonized over the possibility of dying if the lacerations brought on infection. Or, worse, the depressing thought of surviving as a worthless man incapable of working and supporting himself. And, there was dear loving Gerda who'd promised to marry him after serving his term at sea. Would she be satisfied with a cripple? He lamented, as he shivered violently.

I must get that leg out of the water, he decided. Maybe I can fix it. He raised painfully to a sitting position. He remembered when he and his brother Joel fixed Mutton Head's leg, which was good as new, almost. The brothers had often set broken bones on animals, including Mutton Head's, their pet sheep.

Olaf's stiff fingers unraveled some o f the line holding the two timers together. He didn't need them tied so tightly now, with the sea quiet. He made a slip knot on one end and dangled it down into the icy water and snared his flopping limb. Then he added a few loops further up the leg, so when pulling, it would all come together, he hoped.

But as he pulled the pain became unbearable. He gritted his teeth, getting the leg nearly to the surface on the next try, and heard himself let out a terrorizing scream from the horrendous pain. Too determined to yield, he cried out loud enough to be heard many *mils* away, but the leg was finally up on the plank. Now, to his horror, he could see the bone penetrating the blue mottle flesh about mid-point between the knee and ankle.

Resting a while to regain his strength, he contrived a way to reset the break. He untied the extra loops from the upper leg, leaving the one around the ankle. Sensing it had to be fixed immediately, he flipped the rope over the end of the board, below the foot and pulled away, stretching the leg in an attempt to set the broken pieces. Again, after three or four attempts, roaring and yelling violently, he felt the breaking parts snap agonizingly together. Crying and laughing at the same time, he knew he had been successful and cheered wildly in his triumph.

Pieces of debris came floating nearby. Looping the rope several times around his frozen hands, like readying to throw a lasso, he managed to drag some slats to the raft. Then he fashioned a tight splint. Now he felt confident there was a chance the leg might heal. Maybe, with the help of Thor, he would walk again.

He leaned back, and trembling with cold, rested. After all the grueling physical strain, his body dehydrated, his mouth and throat parched, he ached for some plain water. The putrid Baltic water would poison one's body in short order, he knew.

But, he slept most of the time, passing into the night and another day. the air was damp and the heavy fog prevented seeing anything beyond a stone's throw. Still he saw a future: grasses, trees, and wild flowers extending to a distant horizon.

The next day was the same. The sea became as smooth as glass, and the cold eerie setting brought on hallucinations. Much of the time he wondered if he wasn't out of this world altogether, or maybe somewhere between Heaven and Hell.

Visions of America still flashed through his crazed mind. While still a farmhand slave to Cronston, his cruel landlord, Olaf had read about the bountiful land where people could break away from the grips of poverty and become free and prosperous. Oh, how he dreamed of such a miracle...but would he survive and in what condition?

Choking from severe thirst, his eyes eventually blurred, and death seemed desperately close. Apparitions appear; a sandy beach, and partially tree covered cliff behind was closing in. He laughed insanely, thinking it to be only a delusion of grandeur flowing his mind.

But, focusing carefully on the sea gulls flying by, he soon came to the realization a miracle appeared to be happening! The sun suddenly came out in full glory and shone brightly on the coast-line and Olaf saw the mountain with two humps! He always thought of it as a giant camel. He knew for sure he had drifted onto his own Swedish shores!

He now found himself offering up a might prayer of thanks to Thor who saved him from the watery grave. Given another chance--this time he'd not waste it. He'd work like a madman to make the most of a new life.

Gud willing, if he can only mend himself, he'd break away from the grips of poverty and slavery, and go to America, his dream.

THE BIG SWEDE

UNTO A LAND MOST BEAUTIFUL

A LAND MOST BEAUTIFUL

The river steamer chugged on North, up the grand Mississippi River stretching a half mile wide at places. The beautiful breathtaking bluffs, covered by a continuous blanket of lush foliage were awe-inspiring to the newcomers. Eventually, just before dusk, the craft turned portside and the frontier settlement came into view.

"St. Paul! St. Paul, Minnesota Territory!" the Captain called out. The craft inched forward to the levee. The steam whistle sounded three loud blasts.

Very few of the forty passengers had ever been this far up the Mississippi River to the Northwest frontier. Now everyone was scurrying to disembark in hopes of meeting friends and seeing the promised country. Most were English speaking Easterners, except a few Germans and two Swede immigrants.

"*Kom med bror, detta är säkert det förlavade landet.*" The tall tow-headed Swede grabbed his young brother's collar and stepped off the boat. Once on land, they stood together viewing the stretch of landscape Olaf hoped to make his own. "We're here at last" he said in Swedish to Gustav. "It's even more spectacular than my dreams." He recalled so vividly the visions he'd had, as he survived the sinking of the Reliance.

It had also been a tedious and grueling year-long challenge for Olaf, nineteen, and little brother, Gustav, thirteen, who'd fled from indentured poverty in the old country. Laboring as deck hands for passage on a sailing vessel and crossing the treacherous Atlantic Ocean, they had arrived on the Eastern coast, penniless and near starvation.

Now as the two brothers stood on the shore of the Mississippi, Olaf's mind quickly recalled his recent life in the New Land. In New York, menial tasks had sustained them for months, but the dock managers soon learned the aggressive, hard-working Olaf could move more freight than two men. Not being able to speak English, better paying jobs evaded him. Gustav was too young to work and big brother's earnings barely kept them alive.

It was tough learning a whole new language, finding employment, and coping with an intimidating society, so the Olsson boys, Olaf and Gustav, went to *Sverige Hus* often, a social center in New York set up to help Swedish immigrants survive the first year.

Now, under a June sky in Minnesota Territory both grinned widely, gawking at the new settlement. A scattering of small new buildings -- dwellings and businesses -- sat along the river and spread out to the prairie. The river bluffs had impressed Olaf and now as he scanned the horizon he saw the sea of land -- his dream land -- spreading to the sunset. Piles of fresh-cut pine boards were stacked everywhere, ready to be put together for more construction. The smell of new lumber sweetened the air, and the sounds and sights of settlement indicated a hub-bub of activity going on; an encouraging sight to the boys.

Olaf, still limping slightly from his shipwreck survival two years before, stood a hand above six feet, drawing the attention of amused bystanders. Looking like outcasts from a desolate country, the two provoked frivolous remarks from a variety of frontier characters.

"Where ya from, big fella?" a paunchy, bearded, flannel-shirted lumberjack inquired.

"Vi är från Sverige. Kom for kusiner Rudolph och Marta Olsson. Känner ni dem?" Olaf couldn't find the English words to explain about his Swedish past or his search for his cousins, Rudolph and Marta.

The man, apparently a newcomer himself, laughed at their countrified appearance, making some fun of their inability to communicate. Though he must have understood Olaf, he exploited the situation for his amusement and three snoose-spewing characters near by. "No, don't know nobody by that name. Just walk around town. Somebody's sure to see ya."

"Kom bror, innan jag tappar humoret!" Olaf said disgustedly, pulling Gustav away from the group. He felt

dangerously close to losing his temper at their ridiculing.

"*Pojkar! Pojkar!*" a woman called the boys in Swedish, hearing the teasing. After giving the nasty jokester a stern look, she asked Olaf if she could help, then introduced herself. "*Jäg ar fru Moen.*"

"*Tack gode Gud,*" Olaf said, truly feeling the gratitude of those words. "*Vi kommer frán Sverige. Söka kusiner Rudolph och Marta Olsson. Kan du hjälpa oss?*" he repeated. He hoped she could help but he would find his cousins without help, if need be.

"*Ja,*" she laughed heartily, explaining she and the Olssons were good friends. "*Vi gár i samma kyrka.*" Looking out, Olaf wondered where the church they attended was located. Noticing Olaf's size, she was reminded that her husband, Sigfred, would like to see the young Swede for sure. "*Virk med hästar och vagnar,*" she explained to Olaf.

The thought of working with horses and wagons thrilled Olaf. Then suddenly he remembered to introduce himself and his brother. "*Olaf, mitt namn min lillebror, Gustav.*" He noticed his teasing welcoming group had walked down the dirt road to the saloon.

Mrs. Moen, a rosy-cheeked woman of thirty, hugged the two brothers and told them about their cousins being highly thought of in St. Paul. In fact, Cousin Rudy was a deacon in the Lutheran *Kyrka*. Then, realizing how anxious the brothers were to get going, she told them it would be easy to locate the Olsson cabin.

Pointing down the street they were to take, she explained that just past a mile they would see a log house with a rosemauling door. Since it was the only one of its kind, they wouldn't miss it, she assured.

"*En mil, engelsk, ja.*" Olaf repeated, translating the distance to make sure. "*Tack, tack, sá mycket. Adjö dä.*" Both, having said thanks, tipped their caps in additional gratitude.

Olaf's quick pace and long strides made brother Gustav force himself into a trot to keep up.

Olaf urged his *lillebror* to hurry, it being a bit farther, now. He thought about the recent-past, up to this moment. While the brothers had been saving money working on the coast, letters had been exchanged between the cousins. Marta had written,

3

promising that, even though it was a small cabin, they could all live together fine till Olaf got established. So, it was all arranged: Gustav would go along to help on the new farm the Olssons were setting up at Center City in the Spring. Three years had passed since Rudy and Marta had left Sweden, and there would be people and things to talk about, for sure.

Up ahead, Olaf saw the cabin Mrs. Moen had described. *"Titta! Titta! Med den målade dörren Fru Moen pratade om."*

"Himmel!" Gustav was excited, nearly jumping as he ran behind his brother. *"Och pinka igen, Olaf."* He'd always had a weak bladder, and now complained he had to pee again.

Picking up more speed, Olaf laughed, saying he thought he'd have to buy a string for that thing someday. Running now, the brothers snickered like little kids over the happy anticipation of meeting family and finally finding their new home.

The front door flew open; Marta and Rudolph calling greetings; *"Hej pojkar! Vi är här! Vi är här!"*

Everyone began to hug and kiss--all four Olssons. Marta and Rudolph had tears in their eyes as they laughed and called out pet names for their cousins. Gustav, still under pressure, was doing a little jig, not wanting to miss anything. When Marta understood his needs, she nearly split her sides, laughing at young cousin's problems. They showed him the little house in the back and Gustav ran like the wind.

Once the hugging and travel questions were finished, Marta suggested the boys and Rudy walk around and look at the livestock and property while she got a hearty supper ready. "You boys look good," she told them in Swedish, "but some more meat on your bones wouldn't hurt a thing." She'd just butchered an old hen that had quit laying, and they'd all celebrate with good soup and dumplings.

By the shed, Rudy proudly showed off his two draft horses, and the milk cow. Listening to his cousin, Olaf saw Rudy had done well in the few years here employed by the livestock company, first as helper, then--having learned English--working up to a trader of livestock. Rudy again told of his excitement about moving up to the farm he'd bought at Center City, forty miles North. He and Gustav discussed how to share the work

4

which they'd undoubtedly continue together for a few years, until the farm was properly set up.

As the three men sat on a bench next to the stock tank, Olaf described what he wanted to do; earn *pengar*, find some good land, send for his Gerda, and settle down in this long-awaited country.

Rudy was enthusiastic about the territory--ready to boom. "I'll take Gustav to the yards tomorrow," he said in Swedish; "they can use a stable boy." Then, Rudy mentioned his good friend Sig Moen was looking for a good man for the horse and wagon business at St. Anthony Falls.

"O Rudy, tack! Jag älskar hästar." he said excitedly. He really did love horses and this could be wonderful work.

* * *

The cousin's small cabin was a sight to behold with everybody wanting to talk at once. Marta, still busy cooking, interjected occasionally that they shouldn't forget the cook. "You men are raving like a bunch of Swedish hoot owls!" she told them, unable to get a word in crosswise. The little cabin nearly shook with Swedish stories, gossip and laughter.

After a while Rudy went to the cupboard and retrieved a jug of aquavit, strong Scandinavian liquor drunk at special occasions. This drink managed to loosen the tongue and activate the funny bone, hardly necessary with this convivial group of Swedish Immigrants.

At last, Marta brought out a big pot of chicken soup and dumplings, and the brothers gorged themselves as if they hadn't seen food for months. Hours were spent over the meal reminiscing about homeland and family.

The cousins reminded Olaf how they'd worried over the Reliance shipwreck. "Here I didn't think I'd ever see you walk again," Marta admitted. "And you hardly even limp."

Olaf acknowledged he was lucky to be alive, the pain slowly disappearing.

The Swedish jabbering went on late into the night. Marta and Rudy sat in rapt attention as Olaf told how, by a stoke of luck, the brothers had sat in a New York park one Sunday afternoon, lamenting their misery in not having *pengar* enough to come West. Olaf was playing his mouth harp when a lady with a toy poodle came by and dropped money in his hat which had accidentally fallen to the ground, thinking they were destitute beggars. Maybe they could make extra *pengar* that way, Olaf had hoped.

Marta and Rudy roared with laughter hearing how timid Gustav only whispered at first. "As more people came along and money was flying at them, he opened up, yodeling like somebody stuck him with a pitchfork! And, that's how, in two weeks, we had enough *pengar* to take the train and steamboat all the way to the territory," Olaf finished. Everybody laughed.

Finally Marta, whom Olaf thought wore the pants in the house, stood, clapped her hands, and commenced speaking English. "Now my good boys, ve do not speak any more Svedish in this house. Only on Sunday. It's the only vay to learn and get ahead."

"Aw...vas much fun," Olaf lamented, having to struggle with the new. Then, resigning himself to the reality, agreed. "Ve virk like Hell! Don't ve, bror?"

"Ja, sure, ve virk like Hell," Gustav echoed.

VORKING VIT HORSES

The lanky Swede walked briskly up the road to St. Anthony Falls in the early morning. A heavy dew on the grass, and a sweet smell of the meadow contributed to his feeling of excitement. It was a great day to be alive.

Suddenly ahead, the horse pastures appeared with as fine a display of horses as he'd ever seen. It was a sight to behold; one beautiful highly spirited silver-gray mare ran around as if she'd never be tamed. What a challenge she'd be, Olaf pondered. Farther along, several large sprawling buildings came into view as the sun was about to rise. Olaf walked faster. A man should be at work at daybreak if he expects to get on there, he thought.

The sun was just peeking over the horizon now, reflecting yellow-gold hues off the horse barn's recently milled vertical boards, and as he hurried closer, he detected the scent of cedar. He approached a small building next to the road with a sign painted in English across the front. Taking the paper on which Rudolph had written the name, he found the words matched perfectly; J. C. Burbank Co.

First, Olaf had in mind to survey the operation. Peeking in one large shed he was amazed to find dray wagons, carriages, and even several stage coaches, which intrigued him immensely. They were beauties, all right. What a thrill to drive one, he dreamed.

He hustled on to closely observe some of the horses at one of the corrals: bays, sorrels, blacks, whites, roans, buckskins; every imaginable color, and they were all large and beautiful beasts. Olaf loved horses, and he hoped he could get work here. Oh, glory be! he thought.

Seeing wagoners and teamsters hitching their horses and loading their rigs, he hustled over to inquire about getting work. Just about everybody stopped what they were doing and ogled the tall stranger, some showing amusement at his size.

"Lo, big fella, ya gonna be workin here?" one asked.

"*Ja*, vont yob. Virk like hell." Marta had helped coach Olaf with those two phrases before he left the house this morning. "Sig Moen har?"

"He's up front in the office," the helpful man pointed.

Young wiseacres always kidded the Swede about his size, and as he headed for the office one called out, "How's the weather up there, stretch? Freeze your ears off?" The crew was having a good laugh at his expense, but he just grinned back at them.

"*Ja*. Vont yob. Virk like hell."

Realizing he wasn't going to get work by lollygagging around the yard, he made tracks for the office up by the road. His eye was caught by two finely matched bays hitched to a fancy rig at the hitching post. Must be important people, he figured. He dashed through the front door, full of exuberance and eager to go to work. Sometimes the Swede didn't realize his overpowering strength, so it was unfortunate when barging in that he knocked one of the well-dressed business men rudely off his feet.

"*O, jag ar ledsen att jag knuffade omkull er,*" Olaf apologized.

The two important businessmen; one a dapper, slightly graying fiftyish, the other, a nattily dressed fellow in his late twenties, stood in shock at first and then exploded into laughter at the ridiculous turn of events. Brushing himself off, the older one looked up amusedly, "Say, young fella, haven't seen you around these parts before. New here?"

"Ja," Olaf grinned, answering in his sing-songy accent. "New." The Scandinavian and Germanic influence on speech heard in the territory was already apparent, even on those of English stock.

"Where ya come from?" asked the other.

"*Fran Sverige,*" near singing the words.

Oh, Sweden, the older one answered, becoming somewhat intrigued with this moose of a man showing a wide toothy smile as big as a horse's. He introduced himself. "Well, my friend, my name is Burbank, and this is my associate, Mr. Blakely. How can we help you?"

"*Vill traffa Sigfred Moen.* Vont yob. Virk like hell."

The two men glanced at each other in amusement, not

intending to embarrass the newcomer for his language difficulties. Mr. Burbank called out: "Sig? Sig, there's someone here you need to speak with." From another office came a man wearing a white shirt, arm bands holding his sleeves' high up his arms, and a pencil behind his ear. He smiled.

"Well, I'll be hanged. You must be Olaf Olsson, cousin of my good friend Rudolph in St. Paul. *God dag a dag, Olaf.*" He offered his hand.

"*God dag a dag,*" Olaf grinned, hearing Swedish, which was like music to his ears.

"See if ya can find a spot for this young man, Sig. Looks like he's got plenty of spunk in him." Mr. Burbank turned to Olaf. "Good luck my good man. You certainly started my day on a high note." Burbank chuckled with Blakely as they left Sig alone with Olaf.

Alone and recognizing Olaf's poor understanding of English, Sig tried to relax the eager Olaf by speaking Swedish. Sig, though pressed by business demands, took the time to apologize for not having a lot of time to visit about the homeland and mutual acquaintances. Next, he described to eager Olaf the possibilities of advancement in the rapidly expanding horse and wagon operation.

The more Olaf heard about driving wagons to new settlements, the wider his smile grew. Sig told him he'd have to start at the bottom, so he was destined to cleaning barns and tending horses and equipment. Learn English fast, and the sky's the limit, he was told.

"Vont yob, Sigfred. Learn Englisk fast. Virk like hell." Olaf begged, using a few more words he's learned.

"Start now?" Moen asked, impressed at his exuberance.

The aggressive young Swede jumped out of his chair. *"Tack. Tack sa mycket,"* he blurted out. *"Ja, start nu."*

Being warned about the foul language and brutal tactics of the yard foreman, one they called Scarface Williams (but not to his face), Olaf was told to comply with the man's orders, at least for the time being. New and better men were coming, Sig confided. Williams would be moved on West, soon.

Olaf, ready to tackle this challenge, made a beeline for the horse barns and found at the far end four workers who all stopped, leaned on their forks, and eyed the new recruit with interest.

"Boss Villiams?" He glanced from one to the other.

"I'm Williams," a rough looking character spoke up. "Yer sure a tall drink a water, fella. What's yer name?" There was a scar snaking across his right cheek.

"*Olaf Olsson fran Sverige.*" He smiled, hoping to establish a friendly association.

"So yer the new yard bird." Williams, frowning, sized him up and down in a belittling way. "Understand the goddam English?" he asked.

"*Ja, lite.*" Olaf answered, his smile contracting as he recognized the foreman's intimidating abruptness.

"Well, we start you greenhorns out all alike." With a sneer, Scarface picked up a pitchfork and stuck it in a pile of horse manure. "Know what this is?" he asked.

"Ja." Olaf said, getting flustered by being put to the test so bluntly. "*Det ar hastskit,*" he rattled off nervously in Swedish.

"No ya big dumb ox! That's horseshit! Horseshit!" Williams repeated.

"Horseshit?" Olaf copied, thinking that was probably what he said in Swedish.

"Ya, horseshit. Fill the wheelbarrow and haul it out. Walk up the pile and dump it on top. Then when it gets high enough, hitch up the horses, load it on a wagon and haul it out to the field." He sneered at his crew. "That makes the grass grow better, don't it, boys, so the horses got more to eat and make more horseshit." He broke out with a sardonic horse laugh.

The yard hands howled at the tomfoolery, but the big Swede just smiled and said, "*Ja tack.* I virk like hell, *Gud vet.*"

They stopped their snickering and watched as the big man immediately picked up the pitchfork, attacking the job, as he promised he would.

The first few hours, as Olaf pitched and hauled manure, he saw that Williams came across as a tyrant bully, ordering his nervous crew around with a never ending salvo of cuss words, and several times threatening to beat hell out of a couple of men who questioned him. His pet pal, Blacky, wore a permanent sneer on his face, supporting every move the boss made. Bull Houser, the second hand, never smiled and seldom talked. Then there was Mousey who tried to please everybody by his weird hiccuping laugh, going he-uh he-uh he-uh, like a sputtering steam engine. One thing was sure, Olaf saw the fear of Williams was in them all.

All morning, Olaf appreciated his uncanny luck of getting to work on the first day in the territory. The unique smell of old horse manure could be strong and burn the eyes at times, but there was nothing like it in the world. When teased, Olaf joked in return about it being good medicine, clearing a head cold faster than anything. One quick survey of the barn was assurance the work had been piling up for some time, and he could prove his worth right here by reducing the massive piles.

Scarface and his crew were working out of the barn, at the far end, where two year-olds were being harness-broken for dray duty. Olaf, who had worked with horses for his landlord in the old country, had never heard such miserable shouting and cussing in his life. Scarface was truly brutalizing these beautiful creatures. Olaf remembered Sig's warning about getting along with Williams, so he tried ignoring the horse whipping.

Morning ending, the newcomer was pleased with the dent he'd made in his work. Later, after everything quieted down at the other end, Olaf heard that weird he-uh he-uh he-uh laugh approaching. Finally, the little man, grinning, pulled up a pail and sat to eat the lunch he carried. Being a runt of a man, he seemed intrigued by Olaf's size.

As they kept smiling back and forth, Olaf was thinking of the small fellow in horse size. Fifteen hands sounded bigger than five feet. It's sad a man has to be so deprived, he thought.

"Here, have some lunch," the little fellow offered.

"*Nej Tack. Tack sa mycket.*" He went to his jacket to get the sandwich Marta fixed for him. Not many words were exchanged, but Mousey's friendly looks were self revealing and Olaf figured the measly man was reaching out for a pal. Olaf, himself, could sure use a friend now.

After several minutes of grinning, the two tried communicating: "Olaf got girl?" the older balding man, obviously inquisitive, asked.

11

"Jag forstar inte." Olaf didn't understand, and said so.

"Olaf got girl, Mousey repeated, cupping his hand in front of his chest to indicate a part of the feminine anatomy.

"Ja, ja." The Swede grinned in amusement. *"Ja,* Olaf got...girl. Flicka...girl. *Ja, ja."* he continued chuckling. Returning the question, "Mousey got...girl?" Olaf grinned.

"Naw," he answered, his face flushed in embarrassment.

"Awe, Mousey (need...) girl," Olaf kidded.

Raucous laughter announced the return of Williams and his crew, having taken an unusually long midday break. Mousy hurried back to his work.

Picking up where he left off, Olaf rigorously hauled manure up the ever growing mountain outside, wondering how high he could go. He liked to challenge himself that way.

The foreman was back at his violent horse lashing, this time trying to break the beautiful but feisty big silver-gray mare now tied up in a box stall. Earlier Olaf had seen this mare out in the horse pasture. Olaf felt sick to his stomach hearing Scarface beat hell out of the poor animal.

"I'll teach ya to settle down, ya damn wild bastard, or I'll put ya out of yer goddam misery!" Scarface stood high on the boards, whipping down at the frightfully neighing mare, screaming for her life.

His compassion for animals painfully strained, Olaf could stand it no longer. Taking his pitchfork he moved toward the wretched animal. He watched a moment longer. The stately mare stood a good seventeen hands, had long legs, a fine shaped body, and held her head high. What a fabulous riding horse she could be, he thought to himself. Oh, how he'd like to get that great dappled gray aside, and show that brute how to train and treat such a prized creature.

Williams kept lashing down upon the magnificent form. Olaf flinched with every smashing blow. Sweat rolled off his face and his heart pounded. He could see the frenzied horse's flank pulsate as it was whipped mercilessly into submission.

"Sluta! Sluta!" Olaf shouted, his anger no longer controllable, *"Sla inte hastar sa dar!"* Don't beat horses, he warned.

William's temper, already raging, was diverted from the horse and now directed to the young Swede. Jumping to the ground, the foreman clenched his fists, ready to swing, threatening Olaf as he had bullied every teamster in the yards.

Olaf stood tall, fire shooting from his eyes, ready for the challenge. Scarface nearly stopped dead in his tracks facing the Swedish monolith. Pretty soon the mad man backed down, having second thoughts about attacking the young upstart.

"*Du kan inte tamja hastar med piska.*" Olaf repeated, sticking to his guns of course, beating them was no way to train horses!

"God Damn green horn!" Scarface snarled from a safe distance. "Get the hell back to your shit pile, or you're a dead Swede!"

Olaf, too, had second thoughts. He'd promised Sig he'd try to get along with the wretched foreman. No sense of jeopardizing his chances now, so he backed away. Nevertheless, he felt hot and annoyed with himself.

Later, Williams could be heard shouting orders. Olaf could understand more English than either he or other people gave him credit for. At this moment, he understood the order that Mousey was to help clean the barns. Olaf shuddered at the rascals ranting. "We're going to shoot the goddam mare tomorrow." Scarface raged, as he and the crew left the barn.

Mousey was eager to help Olaf clean the barn. The simple minded, always cackling, little horseman looked on the newcomer for support and security.

Olaf welcomed his friendship, but wondered if Mousey had but a half-bag of oats in his granary, being a bit scatter brained.

An hour passed. The manager, Sig Moen, popped in the barn.

"Ho, Olaf, *hur gar det?*" Olaf was glad the boss was interested in his welfare.

"*O, fint tack,*" Olaf answered enthusiastically, but worried over the skirmish with this foreman on the first day.

Looking around at the manure piles, Sigfred complimented Olaf, saying he'd never seen so much done in such a short time.

"*Tack.*" Olaf smiled at the compliment.

Sig explained he had to leave for a meeting in St. Paul, but would have more time to visit tomorrow.

"*Fint.*" Olaf wanted to thank Sig for the great opportunity. "Sigfred, *tack sa mycket for jobb.* Virk like hell."

Sig laughed. "*Jag ar glad att du kom hit,*" he returned in Swedish, showing happiness Olaf had come to work for him.

Moen walked to the end of the barn and his laughter soon turned to shouting, "What the hell is this?" He was looking at the valuable gray mare strapped in the stall and not able to move, bleeding from flesh wounds.

Olaf walked brusquely to the box stalls, and told how he nearly hit Williams for beating the poor animal. 'Couldn't stand to see her whipped so viciously, like that, he said.

"Where the hell are those guys now?" Sig demanded of Mousey.

The small man hiccuped a couple of times, "Wooden Horse, I guess."

"Oh, that's what's been going on. I thought so, the way the place looks around here. They're taking off early and heading for the saloon. It makes me sick!" Sig said. "Cut the animal loose, Olaf."

Olaf cut ropes from every side of the box stall. The great mare reared up, trying to go over the six foot walls, and her rear legs kicking wildly struggling to free herself of the last of the ropes.

"Can I train, Mr. Moen?" Olaf begged in Swedish. "Please?" Olaf told of working with horses in the old country, and he knew he could do it, but it'd just take a little time.

Seeing Olaf's exuberance, Sig smiled, "I'll talk to Burbank about it."

After Sig left, Olaf flexed his muscles a few more hours on the pitchfork, his new little friend helping best he could. Mousey tried to talk him into hitting the saloon for some beer, but Olaf begged off, saying he'd do that another time. He was anxious to see how Gustav fared out.

Olaf's wide steps and fast pace covered the distance in less than an hour, but when he reached the river, the wide powerful Mississippi, his attention was drawn to a strange gathering of campers down the hill. Going closer he could see they were real Indians. He had read all about the fabulous natives living off the abundance of mother nature, and was intrigued at seeing a group of them.

He slipped as he lowered himself, afraid he'd disturbed them. He wouldn't have come so close had he seen how near naked they were. As he began withdrawing, a dusky brave came to the tree opposite him. Olaf held his breath, wondering if they might be hostile Indians. Then the Indian grunted, and a trickle found Olaf's boot sticking out the side. The Indian uttered a satisfying 'ah' and withdrew.

Backing away ever so quietly, Olaf crawled back up the bank and high-tailed it home to relate the exciting events of his first full day on the frontier.

❋　　❋　　❋　　❋　　❋

VICTORIOUS STRONG MAN

Walking the six miles to work in the early morning drizzle, Olaf was glad he wore the company-issue wide brimmed leather hat which shed water like a small umbrella. About half way to Burbank's, the new boss of the wagoners heard a single trotting horse and the grate of wheels coming up from behind. *"God morgon, Olaf."* a voice called. "Hop in my buggy and ride the rest of the way with me." Sig Moen, his boss of six months, gave him a hearty pat on the back as he climbed in next to him.

"Ja tack, Sig," Olaf grinned. As the new foreman of the St. Anthony yards, he was proud to ride along side Sig.

"Vell," Sig chuckled, *"hur gar det?"* There was a camaraderie in foreigners retaining their native greetings.

"O, tack bra," he returned light heartedly. "Tis a spinortin rig ya got, Sigfred. Top and sides, and ever-ting." He thought for a moment. "Some day, I get vun, maybe."

"Sure you will," Sig agreed, grinning widely. "I'm glad I caught up to you. Heard by the grapevine that you're in the finals of the Wooden Horse's 'Annual Arm Wrestling Contest'. It's tonight, right?"

"Ja, fer sure. I shoulda told ya, Sig. Not mad vit me?"

"Of course not. Olaf, would it bother you or anything if I come'n watch?"

"Nej, it vouldn't bodder me none, fer sure," Olaf assured.

"Good! I will, then. I'll drive my buggy over to the saloon, so if ya stop by my office after work, we'll go together." Then Sig registered a serious concern, "Oh ya, Olaf, I understand Scarface Williams is still hanging around town, and they say he's in the finals, too. He's got it in for ya, you know."

"Ja, I heard dat. No surprise after me takin avay Villiams' yob as yard's foreman. Hope I can get 'im and pin da foul mout rapscallion."

"Well, good luck. Watch the devil. Fights dirty," Sig warned as they approached the Burbank buildings.

"I know. I be careful. *Tack* fer da ride, Sigfred." The Swede stepped down, looking enviously at the wagoners getting their rigs ready for the open road. "Sig, I vont to be vogoner and travel da country, too, some. Is der chance?"

"I know. I know. You can always do plenty of that. Let's see. You drove a solo trip to Stillwater already, and two others there as a rider. And, you went along with Charlie Simpson all the way to LaCrosse to get that machinery. Frankly, friend, I've never known a newcomer catch on so doggoned fast as you. And you're learning the English pretty good, too."

"I been lucky, Sig. Cousin Marta good ta help. I learn ta read and write some too, now. I virk like hell."

"Let me tell you, Olaf," Sig said looking down from his buggy, "we're already talking about an expansion to new areas requiring over a thousand men, and a few thousand horses. I told you there's a great future here."

Olaf laughed, "I get excited yist tinkin about it."

"Oh, by the way, how are you coming along with the big gray mare?"

"She's goin to be da greatest horse ya ever seen, Sig. Vould ya believe it? Eatin oats out of my hands; betcha I'll be ridin her in two veeks."

"Burbank said the mare is yours, if you can break her."

"Na! Really?" Olaf couldn't believe it! That beautiful animal-- his?

"Olaf, you deserve her - if you can break her, remember. And to think Williams almost got her destroyed as an untrainable mad animal. There's been a lot less repair on harnesses and equipment since the men have been warned not to beat horses. We've got you to thank for that. Good riddance, that Scarface Williams."

"Vell, *tack,* Sig, but ya know, vas only plain sense." Olaf couldn't have felt happier. He already loved the horse.

The two friends sat visiting a while about their accomplishments in America, the opportunities ahead, and their mutual love of the horses, gathered all around them. Then both decided, they'd better hustle, so they could quit work early, and have a beer or two before the wrestling matches.

The mood of the wagoners and yard hands had improved greatly since Williams lost his authority to the big Swede, and grudgingly quit the J. C. Burbank Co. Olaf soon saw that decent men had no respect for that foul-mouthed ruffian. The only reason Sig Moen had put up with William's was because there just weren't enough good men around. More and better men would be coming, Olaf was sure of that.

Mousey was shuckin' corn near the barn when Olaf started work.

"*God Morgon*, Mousey. Hop on old Dan the svayback, and go fetch da horses virkin today. Ve git vagons rollin now," Olaf said. Then Olaf turned to another teamster, a man in his thirties and said, "*God Morgon*, Chester. Hope da sick boy's better."

"Thanks, Swede." Chester's youngest son had gotten the spotted measles. "Doin fine. Ate six buckwheats this morning." Everybody roared at the paunchy New Englander who joked about his two year-old boy already practicing to be a horseman, tangling with his wooden rocking horse.

Hubert, the old German blacksmith, was fixing a wagon outside the wagon shed and Olaf greeted him, as he'd done with all the crew each morning.

Harley Morse, already harnessing his team, yelled, "I'm planning to take in the arm wrestling match tonight, Swede!"

"I'll pin 'im down--whoever I tangle vit. Ha, Ha!" Olaf mocked. The others, joining in a chorus of guffaws.

As the new yard boss, Olaf was about as attentive to the teamsters as a cluck hen to a bunch of chicks; trying to help everybody - one way or another. He'd put on a collar or two for one, then, run over and help little Mousey throw a big heavy harness on a pair of tall horses. His optimism put the teamsters in a good mood.

"Big Ole, we're all betting big on ya tonight," gentle Nels Augustine said. "My wife's heavy with foal again, so with my winnings, I want to get her that new cook stove I promised before the last one was born."

"Aw, Nels, don't be countin too heavy on me," Olaf warned,

not wanting the worry of losing money for a friend.

At last, the rigs were all ready and began moving out in all directions. Olaf was particularly envious of Peter Dahlhiemer, dressed up 'fit to kill' in a neat suit with a black velvet collar, set off with a dapper top hat. Some day, I'll have a chance to ride on that shiny black coach with those bright yellow wheels, he thought. Some day...

"Swede? Oh, Swede?" Mousey was trying to get his attention.

"Ja? Ma mind voss somevere else. I s'pose ve better virk on da vagons. Grease da veels and stuff. You and Ole can start on dat. I go over clean up da horses fore tamorra. Need ta curry and brush em up. Der tails and manes lookin like mangy wolfhounds."

"Swede, do you mind if we watch the arm wrestlin match?" Mousey begged timidly, as if the big Swede might be opposed to the idea.

"*Nej*. Could use da eggin on, fer sure."

Olaf went over the horse barn to tend his pride and joy, the tall and feisty three year-old silver-gray mare. She was still plenty high strung, but not like when Scarface Williams was beating her six months ago.

"*God morgon,* Dancer Girl." He'd started calling her that soon after she'd taken little prancing steps when she'd felt uneasy. Obviously she didn't know whether or not she was scheduled for another violent lashing. "Nice girl," he continued talking low and easy. The beautiful horse turned her head directly back, and for a moment, her eyes widened showing fear.

The Swede kept talking gently. "How ya doin dis mornin, girl?" Vont a little breakfast, I betcha? Sure, sure." He put a measure of oats in her feedbox at the front of her stall, and then stepped back. Dancer Girl's eyes looked normal again, and she bobbed her head up and down and gave the low nickering sound which Olaf thought of a horse's purring; her way of expressing pleasure, he thought.

"Ve're not gonna do so much taday, girl," he said, practicing his English on someone who wouldn't know any better. "I yist vont ya ta settle down to da good life from now on. Besides, my friend, yer new master, dat's me, Olaf Olsson, gotta save strength fer a match vit dat awful Scarface Villiams. Dis guy ve don't much like, ya know. I'll beat'm. Don't vurry, Dancer Girl." Olaf laughed at his silly conversation. "Sure I vill."

As Olaf eagerly continued tending the horses with his usual enthusiasm, he saw that the other horses relaxed, not flinching when he curried out their mane and tails and brushed the loose hair from their bellies.

Today he had only one thing on his mind; to get that ten dollar prize for winning the arm wrestling match come evening. There was no sense of lollygagging.

Later, not wishing to be alone for any period of time, the Swede went back to the machine shed to see how Mousey and the other handy man were coming along with the wagon maintenance.

He was pleased with what he saw. The fellas worked real well even when joking and exchanging stories. Mousey and Pete hadn't traveled much, so they were all ears, when the Scandinavian told about his sea stories and travels.

* * *

Toward the end of the day, and this one being the last one of the week, most wagoners returned early to clean their neatly painted wagons. Burbank Company took a great deal of pride in the appearance of its equipment.

The teamsters joked and kidded around. Another hard week had ended, and an exciting evening at the Wooden Horse Saloon awaited them.

Jake Honnaker was holding his annual lamb oyster feed--always causing a ruckus with the ladies--after which the traditional arm wrestling championship would be held.

Hoards of characters showed up at the Wooden Horse for these special events; rogues from St. Paul, lumberjacks from Stillwater, gamblers, and gold prospectors heading for the goldfields of western Canada, were traveling as much as a hundred miles out of their way for another of Jake's extravaganzas. And, he really gave the entertainment. Some nights, even Madam Bourberay and her "Sunday School girls" came up from St. Louis; other nights there were special gambling and card games--if the Women's

Temperance Society hadn't managed to wreck the place with their pick-axes and hammers. Jake provided cock fights, horseshoe pitching and rifle shooting matches. A real promoter, Jake probably had it.

So, after everything around the yard was secured, Olaf anxiously dashed over to the office and found Sig ready to close shop.

"Well, Olaf, let's go over and win that sawbuck for you."

"Ja, if I vin, I send it to Gerda so she can come across, too. Gettin kind a lonely fer her, ya know." He really had been thinking about Gerda lately, hoping soon to get enough money for her passage.

Sig frowned a moment. "I heard that Scarface is madder than hell at you, Ole. That if you wrestle each other tonight, he's going to pay you back for the trouble you caused him at Burbank's."

"Dat so?" said Olaf, thinking of the beatings Scarface had mercilessly dealt Dancer Girl and the other horses. Scarface could be vicious, but it did no good to dwell on it.

The saloon was already crowded. The putrid smell of heavy smoking, kerosene lanterns and over a hundred sweaty men, many with shoes covered with horse manure, nearly overwhelmed Olaf. A layer of smoke shifted back and forth a few feet below the ceiling above his head.

His friend Sig grabbed one small table by the door for them both. "Now, we don't have to stand all night," Sig noted.

"My treat tonight. I fetch da beer," Olaf answered as he edged his way to the crowded bar. Of course, standing a head taller than just about everybody else, his loyal supporters called out encouragement for the contest; "We're bettin' on ya, man!" "You can do it! Good luck, pal."

"Hey, big fella. Glad to see ya,," Jake beckoned from behind the bar.

"Vell Jake. Ya got a big crowd," Olaf said with a confident smile, as he received slaps on the back from his well wishers.

"You bet!" Jake said, scanning the excited crowd. "It's gonna be great! What can I get you, Swede?"

"Oh, yist two beers, I guess," Olaf, trying to find Scarface in the crowd.

21

"What! No oysters?" Jake laughed heartily. "Puts fire in your muscles, Ole."

"I s'pose so," Olaf laughed. "Better have a couple, den."

Olaf took the beer mugs and the tin plate of delicacies back through the noisy crowd to the table and set them down. "Crazy. Dey call 'em oysters, here, Sig. Back home ve called em *kottbullar*."

"Ya, meat balls," Sig laughed. "The boys been castratin' lots a sheep.

Before long, Jake started ringing the big bell hanging over the bar. "Hear ye, hear ye! Let the matches start, everybody! The first team to battle tonight is," Jake read from a paper, "Bruno Buckhalter, the one armed lumberjack from Stillwater against the much-battered plainsman, J. K. Williams from the wild frontier."

A smattering of cheers for Bruno and boos for Scarface spread through the nearly packed room.

Jake then gave the ground rules. "The elbows of the battling arm cannot be raised off the table, or that competitor will be disqualified. Nor, can the left arm or hand, in any way, touch the other during the match. Get ready, gentlemen! When I ring the bell, the battle commences."

Olaf had been observing that the betting was heavy and figured most of the wagoners were betting against Williams just for spite.

The bell rang! Olaf stood up to see above the raucous crowd. Bruno and Scarface sat at the narrow table grimacing, grunting and groaning in an attempt to throw the opponent early.

Bruno's one arm had done all his work for many years and was developed to twice the size of an average arm. Williams' left arm managed to offset Bruno's level of balance, by throwing his arm up and out. Bruno struggled to hold his own as the bell rang one time at each minute interval, reaching six, and seven, and eight, and nine, and finally ten. By now, Bruno's face had turned blood red, and he let out a defeated yell, collapsing on the table. Williams was declared the victor.

Disappointment passed throughout the crowd.

"Who's your first opponent, Olaf?" Sig asked, taking a drink of beer during the break.

"I tink he's from St. Paul," Olaf said, looking for a likely opponent. "Peer Parrot, or sometin."

"You don't mean Pierre Parrant, the cock-eyed bootlegger, do you?"

"Vell, sometin like dat." Olaf hadn't had time to think much about anything except the money.

"Oh, my God! 'Old Pig's Eye,' they call him. He was last year's winner, Olaf, and many times through the years." Sig looked worried, even a little defeated.

Olaf answered as optimistically as he could; "Vell, maybe he's getting too old. But, I do da best I can, anyvey."

"Good luck, my friend," Sig said in the resigned tone Olaf had not heard before.

"*Tack.* I shoulda eaten a few more oysters, maybe."

Jake Honnaker rang the bell again and commenced reading from his paper, "The second match features Pierre Parrant, first settler in St. Paul. Parrant started his thriving business in Fountain Cave and was last year's winner right here. He will meet Big Swede, Olaf Olsson, recently from Sweden, now employed by the J. C. Burbank Wagon Freight Company of St. Anthony Falls." Honnaker took a breath. "Get ready men. Take your places."

Olaf left Sig's table and made his way through the crowd to sit on the stool at the competition table. He saddled up to the narrow table top, but as he looked up inquiringly at Parrant, he was met by the dead cold glare of a single crooked, marble-hued eye. A sinister white-ringed pupil gave a piggish expression to his sodden low features. Olaf glanced from the bad to the good eye and wondered which of the two was actually looking at him. The burly Parrant was most eerie to look at.

"Get set." Jake shouted. The bell rang. "Go!"

Immediately, Olaf realized the immense power in Parrant's right arm, and he knew, now, he was in for a desperate battle. Their heads were only a few inches apart, necessary to maintain maximum leverage. When Olaf glanced up at the gruesome face, the pupil in that devilish eye began dancing up and down so that Olaf felt the Devil, himself was draining his power away. To protect himself, Olaf turned away and refused to look at that face anymore. As the bell rang again repeatedly Olaf's muscles tired

23

and tightened. His blood rushed to his head, as his heart pumped heavily in his chest.

All too soon, the minute bell had reached thirteen and Swede, fearing he was about to lose his battle glanced up at his adversary. To his shock, he detected, even in that misty eye, the pain of defeat. Suddenly, Olaf became confident that his youth would sustain him, and with one last mighty lunge, folded back Parrant's arm flat on the table.

A cheer burst through the room, as Olaf Olsson won his first round. Olaf didn't dare consider the victory too much. The evening wasn't over yet.

Jake Honnaker called out, "There'll be a fifteen minute intermission before the final championship match between Scarface Williams and Olaf Olsson. Make your wagers, gentlemen...and we offer plenty oysters of the young at heart."

The wagoners were wild with excitement, cheering their Swedish comrade on. For the next few minutes, as the betting became heavy, Olaf felt himself gaining in confidence as he kept swinging his arms to get the circulation back. "I'll beat'm, fellas. I'll beat'm!" He told his supporters. He was as pumped up and invigorated as a fighting cock.

Williams, too, paced up and down in front of Olaf's supporter. Throwing his chest out, Williams puffed heavily in an attempt to intimidate the Swede. In response, Olaf clenched his fist and directing it at Scarface, showed no fear.

The bell rang, indicating time to begin the match. Olaf wondered where the fifteen minutes had disappeared. Hadn't it been only two or three minutes had elapsed since he beat the one called Pig's Eye?

Although there were already bad feelings between the finalists, the tension when they sat down to establish their positions in the match grew agonizing.

Williams mumbled, exuding a foul tobacco breath, "You haven't got a chance, green horn. I'll tear ya apart."

Olaf almost gagged at William's odor as they prepared to lock their hands together. He answered, "Vell, veel yist see about dat."

"Ready! Get set!" Jake called out, and then rang the bell.

A roar exploded from the crowd as the Swede heard his friends shouting, "Get'm, Swede. Get'm!"

Olaf suspected he should exert all his pressure right away, which he did. The struggle increased as the clenched fists tilted in his favor. Then Scarface gave a loud heave-ho and the hands tilted back to his favor.

Immediately it was obvious to the two combatants--and to everybody in the saloon--that this was going to be a bitter, grueling confrontation testing the limits of human power. Both men were already sweating heavily, and with their blood boiling, their faces had taken on a reddish glow. The table began to vibrate under the arm's muscular pressure. The combatants' grunts and groans became louder, in an attempt to give a boost of energy.

All the time, the crowd was getting wilder with excitement. Olaf could hear Scarface's cohorts, Blacky and Bull Houser, who'd elbowed to the front, cheering him and heckling Olaf, but most of the crowd yelled for Olaf.

At one point, the minute bell had rung seventeen times, and Honnaker grinned widely for he had never had a match go so long.

Olaf had heard that Williams was known for dirty tricks, and now when the Swede turned to look Williams in the eye, he was met with a splatter of slimy tobacco juice, half blinding him. Olaf's eyes burned painfully, but he would not yield. He blinked and blinked, his eyes watering profusely but Olaf never let up.

Some painful minutes later, Williams growled, "I'm gonna cut ya to pieces, ya bastard."

Olaf growled back. "Nobody ever insults ma Mudder and gets avay vit it!" He applied his total strength.

The excitement building, the crowd closed in.

Williams snarled, "I saved a surprise for ya, greenhorn. Take that!"

Suddenly Olaf felt an excruciating pain in his leg, and he raised his head in agony. Everybody in the saloon wondered what was going wrong that made the rugged Swede grimace so violently.

Olaf reacted by pulling his right leg back from whatever was gnawing at it under the table--only to feel the same tearing at his left. My God, the pain! he thought, feeling warm blood running down both legs now. Williams must have attached sharp knives to his boot, Olaf figured.

Desperate and wracked with pain, Olaf could hear his friends calling. "C'mon, Olaf, ya gotta win!" "Big Swede, don't fergit my wife needs the stove."

Olaf glared at Scarface. He separated his thoughts from his two legs and focused on his arm.

Even Williams was amazed at his determination. "For Christ's sake, yield, ya stubborn son of a bitch!" he snarled.

At the sound of Williams' cussing, Olaf straightened up on his stool as if he were inspired by divine powers. He muttered to Williams, "Nobody, but nobody, vill ever get avay vit calling my Mudder a sinful voman." And, suddenly growling like a mad dog, Olaf gave a final mighty thrust, and--pinned the villainous rogue.

A thunderous cheer went up as the big Swede stood up, but he stumbled his way toward the door where Sig was waiting, "Sig," he groaned, "I need a fast ride to da yards. I got good horse medicine der."

Sig looked down and saw the blood soaked trousers, as well as the two tracks of blood coming from the arm wrestling table. "My God! Let's go!" Sig urged. "You're going to bleed to death, man."

The noise level fairly shook the Wooden Horse Saloon that night. The folks had been treated to one of Jake's wild extravaganzas, and not a soul seemed disappointed. Once the crowd began to notice the trails of blood, the place grew quiet.

Reaching the door, Olaf turned, tipped his hat and smiled. "It's notting, folks. Yist a couple little scratches."

"Don't forget your sawbuck!" Jake came running after the two men. "God Swede, you made this one hell of a night!"

Sig was white as a ghost, probably thinking Olaf was in serious trouble, so he trotted his horses back. Olaf laughed wildly.

"What's the matter, Olaf? Are you becoming delirious from the shock?"

"Naw, I vas yis tinkin bout movin out to da vilderness. It vouldn't be as dangerous as living in town, I don't tink." He laughed more. "Besides, I vont ta git out and spread ma vings. It's gittin a little dull around da yards." He continued chuckling, as Sig shook his head in disbelief.

MAROONED PIONEERS

Proud of having become foreman of the St. Anthony yards, Olaf--still yearning for excitement and adventure--wanted to get out and see the countryside, and penetrate the unexplored frontier.

Olaf had noticed considerable action along the St. Croix River, with the lumbering industry going full swing at the falls near Stillwater. The Burbank Company, already impressed with the big Swede's progress, agreed he should become familiar with the territory, so willingly consented to give him a temporary transfer. Now, most of the lumber for the first houses and commercial buildings in St. Paul and St. Anthony Falls came from the St. Croix, so he'd be assured of continuous trips to the territorial Capital, St. Paul, just thirty miles away.

It was late September, and the northwesters were bringing on bone chilling cold. This particular day, with no jobs scheduled, Swede walked up the road to the two story Anson Northrop Hotel to see if he could drum up some business. The hotel was the center of social activity, especially at night when French fiddlers could be recruited for a long night's dance. Entire lumberjack families came, the little tykes put off in one room, leaving the revelers to high step it for hours.

The happy-go-lucky entrepreneur, Anson Northrop himself, was milling about the place. He, Olaf, and few assorted characters were carryin' on with swappin' stories of just about everything. Since Northrop had spent some time as a steamboat captain on the Great Lakes, sea tales dominated the joshing; and Olaf, with memories of the Reliance still fresh in his mind, contributed generously.

Talking about the weather invariably entered everyday conversation. It was mighty tough surviving on the frontier where winters were severe.

"They say it's goin' to be a long cold one," Northrop said.

"Even the muskrats are building bigger houses on the ponds this year, I see."

"Ja, doze little furry verms ver growin extra long fur dis year," Olaf agreed. "Da horses' hair is heavy, too."

With the casual bantering, Northrop put the question to a comical old Indian, his handyman, who was taking it all in, as they sat in the lobby. "What do ya think, Chief? Indians know better'n anyone about these things, they say."

"Huh," the Chief grunted, "Winter be bad."

"Why ya reason that? Medicine Man tell ya?" Anson joked.

"Huh," the Chief grunted again, a mischievous twinkle in his eye. "White man's wood pile, big pile. This year, much big!" Everybody roared. Then becoming serious, "But bones speak loud to me. Two moons bring hard wind and big snow."

"Aw, you're good, Chief, but the weather's too mild. You're off the track this time," Northrop laughed, and left to tend to business.

Olaf observed a smooth faced, clean cut gentleman of about thirty sitting nearby, smiling at the Indian's wit. The gentleman looked worried about the Chief's two moons forecast, then he returned to reading his book.

This man, with such smooth white hands, was no laborer or lumberjack, Olaf could tell, but he looked interesting, and the Swede was envious of anyone having the ability to read books. Olaf smiled at the gentleman. The man smiled back.

"How do, Sir? Olaf Olsson. Come from Sveden. I vish I could read English. 'Tryin to learn how Sir."

"How do you do. I'm Abner Goddard. Good for you. This happens to be Chaucer, early English poetry, I'm reading. It's good for the soul of man to absorb the beauty and charm of the written word," he said.

"Yes, Sir," Olaf agreed. "Are ya travelin troo, Sir? Do ya have business here?"

"Well, I'm rather distraught and frustrated, to be honest. You see, I came from the East to a new settlement down river, called Winona. Many of us came with promises of having shelter and some work, but when we arrived there we found only a few

28

shanties--over crowded to say the least. I came up here to buy lumber to build a small boarding house for my Catharine to operate."

"Catrin?" Olaf repeated.

"Catharine, my wife. That's all she's wanted to do ever since we lost our four children, three boys and a girl, to the scarlet fever."

"Oh, no!" Olaf reacted sympathetically.

"But, we've been blessed with three more since," he added. "Me? I'm a teacher, and I came along to educate the children."

"Oh, ja. I understand. I bet yer a good vun, too."

"Well, I'd like to think so. I've done it for years. Went to teacher's college one year back East."

"Vun can certnly see yer an edjacated man, fer sure."

"Well, anyway," Mr. Goddard continued, "I am kind of desperate. When we got off the steamer, like the others, we found everybody sleeping in the little shanties, or digging in the ground, like the gophers around here, in a feeble attempt to keep from the cold. People are going to die this winter, I fear."

"Vell, Mr. Goddard," Olaf pried, "did ya buy lumber?"

"No, not yet. You see, I have our total savings, and I didn't realize lumber prices have gone up so high. Catharine expects me to bring enough lumber to build a two story house-just a small house, mind you-sixteen by eighteen. Now I see I only have enough to buy lumber for one level, and pay the shipping cost. I may have to do that so we can keep warm, but then, she loses the income of the three small upper bedrooms, and we won't be able to live on my small salary," he explained.

"Dis may be a lucky day, Sir," Olaf smiled broadly. "If ya didn't have ta pay fer da haulin, vould ya have enough?"

"Well, yes. Yes. You talk in riddles, Mr. Olsson."

"No. Not really. By a stroke a luck, I'm headin sout vit empty vagon ta pick up stuff from LaCrosse ta haul back ta St. Paul. I vill be takin four horses and kin pull a big load."

"You don't understand, I said I didn't have money," the schoolmaster retorted in frustration.

"Now, Mr. Goddard, settle down. I vill haul it, and you pay me later. Vot ya say? Besides, I vill trade ya some buildin time--I'm a

29

good carpenter--if ya help teach me ta read."

"My God, man, I can't believe my ears! Would you really do that? I mean, haul all the lumber down without pay?"

"Dat's right, my friend, for a little book learnin. Ya looked purdy forlorn, and I tink ya needed a boost dis day," Olaf reassured the man.

Abner Goddard admitted he could hardly believe his luck. The two hustled over to the mill to negotiate for the original order so Catharine would have her three upstairs bedrooms to rent out. The Chief, Northrop's handyman, helped load the wagon quickly, and was happy at the two bits he earned.

When early morning came, three o'clock, and with Goddard's horse tied behind, the four large draft animals moved the huge three to four thousand pound load with relative ease. The ground was frozen for a fast pace.

As they drove along in the brisk morning air, Mr. Goddard turned to Olaf. "Well, my kind friend, let's get on with the reading lesson. May I call you Olaf, Sir? And, if so, I would like to be just plain Abner." The Swede watched as his rider removed a couple of small books from his pocket and handed one over. "Can you read the title on this book, Olaf?"

"Vel, let me see now. Da first verd is pomes, I know dat. I'll haf ta do a little tinkin on da next tree long vuns."

"It's the name of the author of the poems," Abner explained. "Henry Wadsworth Longfellow."

The eager student studied awhile, and then sounded the name as best he could, "He-nry Vods-vodsvert Long-feller."

"Excellent, Olaf. See, you've already learned to sound out words. It's just to get the meaning of new ones, and then practice, practice. You'll do just great, my friend."

The big adventurer continued working with the reading, with Abner's help, all the way to Red Wing where there was a change of horses to last the duration of the trip, and the men could catch a few hours sleep before completing the long journey.

Again, rising early, a clear sky with a shivering pale full moon shining on a thin layer of snow made it easy to focus on the trail ahead. A wagoner takes advantage of favorable weather, when he gets it, and Abner agreed, it was wise to leave early, especially recalling what the Indian had said.

Even while dark, the English lesson continued, mostly on vocabulary. After sunrise, still driving the wagon, Olaf took to reading poetry again. Stopped by unfamiliar words, Olaf found Abner always ready to help. The teacher complimented his student on his quick grasp of difficult words and was amazed at his innate intelligence.

Abner Goddard smiled. "You're a fine trustworthy man, my new friend," he said. "Please keep this book as a small token of my gratitude." Then, he brought out a second set of poems by Whittier, as an added gift, which thrilled Olaf beyond his wildest dreams.

Abner spotted a huge trophy deer near the road ahead. "Man alive, if I had my rifle, and if we were half the distance closer, I would try like the devil to get that meat for the folks at Winona."

Olaf grinned suddenly. Reaching for his rifle on the side rack, he handed over his reins to Abner, then aimed carefully, and fired. The deer moved forward a few steps, and then dropped. "I tink I got him clean in da heart. He din't struggle a bit!"

"Good Lord, man, I've never seen such spectacular shooting in all my life! I couldn't believe you'd even try it," Abner said.

Olaf smiled, "Vell, shootin is vun ting I'm good at." Reaching the spot, he jumped down, removed his knife from his sheath, and prepared the eight pointer for loading on top. Noticing how excited the professor had gotten over the venison, he pressed the issue further. "Mr. Goddard, uh, I mean Abner, do ya really need meat as bad as yer indicating ta me?"

"Oh yes, Olaf," he said emphatically, "Came too late to plant crops. Getting through winter without some provisions will be hard."

"Den, Professor, if ya don't mind, I tink ve take a break from readin, and I virk on gettin some game fer avile."

It was a mild day, having warmed up considerably. Now the animals were coming out of early winter's hiding to bask in the sun. Olaf Olsson, the student, could teach the teacher something about hunting game. The rest of the day he kept adding to the catch, and when reaching the shanties of the new settlement called

Winona, the men displayed a heap of game on top the load.

"Catharine! Oh, Catharine!" Abner called out excitedly.

Olaf was aghast at the dilapidated shacks people lived in. Many were nothing but holes in the ground with shabby lean-to roofs over them. Surely, he thought, a cold blast would be devastating. Some of the disillusioned pioneers had even moved in to abandoned Indian wickiups, whose previous occupants, no doubt, left in favor of more desirable conditions.

A short, bubbly woman, shouting greetings galore, came out of the small house. Then, she and Abner embraced. Several others, hearing the commotion, hustled over to investigate the goings on.

"My dear wife, I want you to meet one of the finest, kindest, gentlemen I have ever had the pleasure of knowing. This is Olaf Olsson; Olaf, my good wife, Catharine. Catharine, I don't know how I'll ever be able to repay this man for his trust and kindness, for had we not met, I would be without the lumber, and much less, the life saving supply of meat we have."

"How do you do, Mr. Olsson?" She looked in gratitude at the game and the lumber on the wagon. "Thank you for your goodness to Abner, and thus, to all of us," she nodded graciously.

"A pleasure, Mrs. Goddard," Olaf grinned and tipped his hat.

"Just look at that! Just look at that!" A desperate young man wearing a ragged gray cloth jacket exclaimed, seeing the life saving contents of the wagon load.

"Yes, Sam Hendrickson, and the rest of you Winona folks, this is Olaf Olsson from St. Anthony. He has made it possible for our new boarding house. Next, we need eight carpenters, since Mr. Olsson promises he will stay tomorrow. Listen! By nightfall we will have warm sleeping space for eighteen people."

"God knows how worried I am for my Jeannie. If the baby comes tonight, they may both die," Sam Hendrickson admitted in a quivering voice.

Olaf had a whopper of a lump in his throat, such as he hadn't had the likes of before, and he heard Catharine whisper to Abner, "Tell them--if you can do what you say you can and have the boarding house totally finished by night--I'll prepare the finest dinner of my life. Yes, and tell poor Sam not to worry for Jeannie will have a small bedroom for her laboring, and I will see that she's cared for properly."

It was decided that the little shack the Goddard's called home would become an adequate horse barn, but for tonight, the small house would have to hold Abner, Catherine, their three children and Olaf, who'd be fine under the small table on his animal robes. After hanging the deer in the tiny pantry and stacking the five coons, nine large white jack-rabbits, and five prairie chickens on the floor, there was hardly room to move in the place.

Later that night, the remote community was filled with expectation, as most of the men had volunteered lending a hand for the next day's work. Catharine Goddard promised a good rabbit stew for all the workers, and plenty of coffee and coon grease donuts during the building of her boarding house tomorrow.

When all had settled down, Abner, worn out from the emotional stress of finally getting the lumber home, fell quickly asleep.

Olaf, a light sleeper, and worrying about the Chief's weather prognostication, was up before everyone else. Figuring the time moving on to six, still a while before sunrise, there had to be something he could do to get organized for the big crew. He lit the lantern, keeping it low. Maybe he could get out of the house without waking everybody, he hoped. From his lowly position under the table, he soon saw a ghostly figure with a long floor-length nightgown whisk by him. The apparition stopped at the little iron stove and added wood to the glowing embers. Then the figure filled a tin pot from a pitcher of water and placed it on the stove. Soon the nightgown disappeared into the small bedroom.

Quickly slipping on his boots, Olaf grabbed his heavy leather jacket, and eased out the door. The winds, which had been balmy and warm from the Southwest last night had switched to the Northwest and felt damp. An eerie whistling whined from the sky. How prophetic of the Chief, he thought. With anxiety, Olaf recognized the signs.

Checking the future structure's corner markers, he found Abner had laid out the plan square and the land had been properly leveled. Everything seemed perfect. With such confining space inside, it appeared Abner and Catharine had been doing a lot of cooking in the outside earthen fireplace, which happened to be directly in line with the south wall of the planned building.

Whacking at the clay chimney and finding it to be as hard as rock, Olaf smiled to himself, thinking how perfectly detailed they had been in their planing, and how much fun it would be to place the small boarding house around the fireplace.

The tall Swede had a glint in his eye as he gathered twigs and kindling, placing a pile right in the center of the planned walls. He picked up larger chunks of logs and built a stack as high as his shoulders. In only a few minutes, that bonfire blazed as a roaring inferno and lit up the sky as if it were high noon. The light reflected the ominous crystals in the sky.

Townsfolk, among them the volunteer carpenters, came running from all directions to see whose shack was burning up. Olaf laughed at the hasty response he'd gotten, and soon all spirits were high.

Then, Abner and Catharine came out with a steaming pot of coffee for anyone planing to work, and Catharine promised plenty of coon grease donuts after the first framed wall was standing. Olaf had never seen so many happy-go-lucky carpenters attack their work. By ten o'clock the entire two-by-four framework was completed for the first level. Although it had turned bitter cold, that huge fire kept the men warm; in fact, there was some concern the new walls might burn down before finishing, so when the foot-wide vertical sideboards were being nailed, only the hot embers were used to heat the interior. Catharine frequently brought out coffee.

Light sleet had begun falling, and a sense of urgency induced the men to work at a hectic pace.

While a crew finished the siding and nailed the battens over every crack, Olaf and a few of the better carpenters built the inside wall down the center, and immediately, a couple of young fellows nailed rafters in place. Abner's plan called for the upper rooms to measure only six feet high at the outer walls, with the roof tapering up to the center, reaching seven and a half feet. Not spacious, but adequate, Olaf agreed.

When the flooring was partially completed on the upstairs level, Catharine, and a few of the women came with a hot steaming kettle of rabbit stew, as promised. The carpenters, whose clothing was soaked from the sleet, nearly devoured it, as they sat near the hot embers of Olaf's huge early morning fire trying to warm up and dry their clothes, even though sleet continued to drizzle. Sensing the possibility of the approaching winter storm, all were eager to get back to the task of finishing their work.

Sam Hendrickson was a good carpenter, Olaf could see. As they worked side by side, Abner hoisted two by fours to the second level. Two of the men began putting the sheeting over the frame. Right on schedule. Within minutes, the snow was coming down heavier than before, and the wind was churning up.

"How will we ever get the roof covered?" Abner worried, snow flying in his face.

"I don't know fer sure, but dey say dat ver der's a vill der's a vey," Olaf said with determination.

Just at that time, Sam took a break and ran across the road to check on his laboring wife. Moments later, he came running back, his face, ashen. "Abner, Jeannie is in a bad way, and the pain comes quite often, now!" His voice carried the helpless agony his face presented.

"Abner, you'd better run and get Catrin!" Olaf urged.

"Don't worry so much, my friend!" My wife will be the finest midwife you could possibly have," Abner said, leaving them to go back in the little house.

"Is it varm enough for her now?" Olaf asked Sam. "Ve have lots a lumber scraps for the fire."

"Yes. Yes, it is for now, but only the good Lord knows what it will be when this storm hits."

The whole sky had turned a dusky white and a distant whine warned of the approaching winds. The menfolk of Winona didn't need more motivation for getting that house completed in the few hours before dark.

The wailing wind when it arrived was ferocious, and at the time when the most dangerous work had to be completed: putting the sheeting on the roof. Olaf figured much could be done from inside with men standing on the saw horses he'd put together. The one-by-twelve's would be slipped through the rafters and nailed from above. Then, after three rows of boards had been secured, a row of tar paper would be placed over and battens tacked over that to keep the paper from tearing.

The howling and bitterness of the storm, and Sam Hendrickson's wife's cries of laboring, kept everyone emotionally on edge. Every once in a while Sam came running with progress reports.

"Settle yerself down, Sam," Olaf, who'd just come down from the roof for some nails, patted him on the back. "Vere gonna be done vit dis yob in anudder hour or so. Soon as ve can, ve'll get her over in dis varm house, yu'll see."

The last boards at the ridge of the roof had to be done from standing on top of the roof and now the blizzard of snow was heavy; densely cold. With the wind raging at gale force on his already wet and cold body, the big Swede got some ropes from his wagon, tied them together, and securing one end to a tree, tossed the other over the building. Hoisting himself up onto the roof from the upstairs floor, he tied the rope around his waist to keep himself from being blown off.

A sudden powerful blast of wind whipped him off balance from the start, and his body skidded down the slippery snow-covered roof's surface! With the rope and his feet catching the toe cleat, he was able to regain his position, straddling the ridge.

Abner, and the others, shouted up words of encouragement. "Careful, Swede!" many voices called anxiously, but the blizzard absorbed the sound.

Up on the roof, Olaf saw only blankets of freezing white snow. He could see nothing! Oof-ta! I may yist be meetin da end here, he thought. Still, he had to do his best. Grabbing the first board coming through the rafters, he could only feel how the pieces should fit, as the blinding snow and freezing wind made his eyes water. Soon his tears were freezing his eye lids together. Putting the wind at his back, he continued nailing the second board. That went better. The final board would be toughest to secure, for no longer could he reach one arm inside to hold on to a rafter. In an awkward attempt to balance his nearly numb body, control his hammer and the board; catching in the violent wind, the big man shuddered at the consequences to him, should the storm win the battle. Nevertheless he managed to nail the last wide board in place, and breathed a sigh of relief.

Still, getting down was not going to be any picnic, he knew, but having done a lot of climbing with ropes as a sailor, he felt confident of getting down. While fighting the blizzard, Olaf tied knots on the free end of the rope on which he was able to catch his hands and feet at the protrusions, lowering himself to the ground.

The men below, who looked out, couldn't see two feet into the blizzard, and had been worrying he'd fallen off, when the new door just put in place suddenly flew open, and the tall Swede, looking like a sculpture in ice, stood there with a huge grin of accomplishment on his face.

The men exploded with cheers of praise. "My God, Olaf, you'll never know how indebted we are to you," Abner said, "I just ran in and got..." his voice cracked with feeling, "the little bottle I keep mostly for medicinal purposes, I figured you'd need something to warm you after such an ordeal." He offered the bottle to the big Swede.

Olaf smiled through his snow frosted face. "Ah," he said, "I had visions of such a revord, but I din't spect da miracle at dis time."

As Olaf crouched close to the embers, the ten men grew wildly jubilant, complimenting themselves on a job well done.

Later, the door flew open again. "Holy Moses, I got a baby boy!" Sam screamed and jigged about like he was on the hot coals.

"Yeay! Yeay! Yeay!" A boisterous chorus of congratulations erupted.

Like ve told ya, Sam, vee'll get some bedding and tings in here, and vee'll have yer Yeannie and da new baby boy in dis varm house in turdy minutes. I guarantee dat." Olaf grinned. Maybe someday he and Gerda would be experiencing the joys of life like Sam and Jeannie were: a home and family, Olaf envisioned.

Catharine and the women joined the celebration, dancing around their menfolk, as if they were heroes of war.

Olaf, knowing how severe the winter could be, felt relieved.

Having seen other scenes of winter devastation, he knew many would not have made it through this night.

* * *

The winter of 1852 turned out to be downright violent; fierce cold and heavy snows raged for days on end. Building construction was at a stand still and not much was going on in wagon freight. For a while, Olaf spent a lot of time reading Whittier and Longfellow in his cabin - or at the Burbank Company.

Soon a devastating measles epidemic swooped down on settlements throughout the region. Olaf ended up transporting doctors Thane and Thompson, the area's only physicians, to remote areas for treating the deadly disease. Hundreds died anyway.

Penetrating the huge snow drifts, many times through fierce blizzards, could only be done with wide runner bob sleds and the largest and strongest draft horses. Olaf, considered the most competent of bobsled drivers, was frequently called.

* * *

Even through the winter, J. C. Burbank continued his optimistic expansion of the wagon business. Olaf was mighty proud to be included in the day's meeting with the likes of Mr. Burbank, John Blakely and Sig Moen. It sure felt good to be appreciated for all the hard work he'd done.

J. C. commenced, "Gentlemen, I want to discuss the status of the company, and to explain where I think we're heading in the transportation business. Frankly, the whole country's in a financial mess, fellas, and there's no credit to be had. The railroad building has shut down completely. That's good for our side, for we know the German and Scandinavian immigrants are coming by the thousands next summer, and," smiling broadly to emphasize his point, "we'll have the lion's share of the total business."

J. C. pointed at a hand drawn chart showing where new

installations would be constructed. "As soon as the winter breaks, we'll build four major stations at these sites indicated by a star. The circle indicates twenty-six smaller horse exchange posts. All this must be done by June."

"Holy Cow!" Olaf blurted out accidentally in excitement.

The others broke out in laughter at the big fellow's outburst.

"Yah, Swede," J. C. quipped, "We've got plenty to keep you out of mischief for a long time." He saluted his trusted employee.

"So, Blakely and I plan to head down to St. Louis to buy about two hundred horses, twenty dray wagons, and some new concord stages. We're planning to take the new enclosed coach with the wood heater for a test run day after tomorrow. Swede, we'd like you to drive us down. Could you get away?"

Olaf was flattered. "Vell, yentlemen, I never seen St. Louis. Sure, I vill. I'll hurry and get everting ready, den, if y'll excuse me."

"Oh," John Blakely spoke up. "Swede, I think there's a letter for you; from those people you helped in Winona early this winter."

Olaf was tickled to hear from Abner and Catharine, and hurried into the waiting room to read it. His excitement faded to an expression of disbelief as he read the message, not from Abner, but from Catharine.

"January 2, Winona, Minnesota Territory.

With a heavy heart I relate the sadness that has befallen the Goddard family since your benevolent help in constructing our fine boarding house.

My beloved Abner succumbed to the epidemic of measles which struck our community the day you left Winona. Abner was stricken and passed away two weeks later. Bless their innocent souls, two children went with him."

At last, Olaf choked and couldn't suppress his sobs. He covered his face with his huge hands, the ones that had nailed that final roof board down on the Goddard house in the violent winter storm of late September.

Betsy, the Burbank secretary, seeing his sorrow, rushed over from behind her desk. "Olaf, is there anything we can do to help?"

"Nay, not really." Olaf wiped his face with the back of his

hand, "I yist lost vun fine friend. He taught me to read poetry and then, he gave me two books, vun by Longfeller and vun by Vittier. I have read each of dem many times," he smiled, reflectively.

Pulling himself together, he continued, "No, I vill alvays have vonderful toughts of dat man. I'll never fergit 'im, fer sure."

❋   ❋   ❋   ❋   ❋

GOING FARMING

The sweet smell of Spring air was breathtaking and exhilarating to the immigrants, especially those like Rudolph and Marta Olsson heading out to challenge the untamed land by establishing homesteads. Having been St. Paul residents for two and a half years, and so involved in the Mission Church, Rudolph and Marta had a lot of friends grieving their departure.

These Olssons were lucky, or perhaps more prudent, for they weren't heading out to the treeless tundra to dig in like gophers, as many were doing, ill prepared. The Olssons were heading up north, where a few other Swedes preceded them in settling the scenic woods and lake country. Rudy had already gone up there to grub out trees, and frame a small log cabin amongst a heavy stand of oaks and maples, and pillars of birch, all perfect for erecting walls, roof timbers, and stock fencing. Better yet, the abundance of maples would ensure a bonanza in maple sugar. There were still a thousand hours of grubbing out trees for fields and pastures, and that is why they needed Gustav's help so much.

Olaf wouldn't miss the event, especially with little brother leaving his protective care for the first time in years. He knew he'd miss Gustav, and their shared memories of the dismal times in Sweden.

When Olaf arrived at Rudy's cabin in the early morning, Rudy was already out in the stock pen currying his horses, the milk cow and the young heifer. All must be well groomed for leaving town.

"*Hur gar det, kusin?*" Olaf called, inquiring how things were going, a standard Swedish greeting.

"*Bara bra, tack,*" Rudy grinned, excited to move out.

The exit parade was soon to begin. It would take two days to reach the farm, forty miles north. With a good team of horses one could make it in a day, but the pace of the milk cow and heifer would slow the progress.

"Maybe ya can help Gustav crate the chickens, Olaf. I locked em in the coop this mornin' so ve vouldn't have ta chase em all over kingdom come."

"*God dag bror,*" Gustav called, coming from helping Marta load the wagon with household goods and food stuff to take along.

"*Vell, lillebror,* yer set ta go farmin, I spose." Olaf joked, giving a brotherly hug.

"Ja. Ya betcha, I'm excited enough!"

The brothers went into the chicken coop and closed the door, knowing once they started snaggng the flighty fowl with the long hooked pole, feathers would be flying as if a whirlwind had hit. With thirteen good laying hens and two roosters there would be plenty of eggs to eat, and extra for hatching. Older hens were good eating, too.

Sig Moen then stopped by a few minutes to bid farewell to his best friend, Rudy. He ended up assisting Rudy in tying the plow on the back of the wagon. After a bear-hug, Sig left for a Burbank Company meeting.

Everyone was packing the wagon, which was filling up fast. Lots of laughing and tomfoolery went on while Rudy used a few Swedish cuss words in his frustration, trying to fit everything in. Marta, showing several months of pregnancy, came running out with more boxes of preserves. "*Min Gud i himlen,* Marta, ya be careful liftin like dat!" Rudy scolded. "How many more hundred boxes ya comin vit? I already took up two loads before, ya know."

Marta, looking healthy and happy, just reared back and giggled. "Vell, I know how ya like ta eat, ya boys, so I fixed a lot of good food ta take along; a big smoke ham, a sack of turnips, and two sacks of potatoes - some for seed - still good from the root cellar."

"Ja, ve vont go hungry up der, dat's fer sure," Rudy quipped to the menfolk. "I got a good garden spot and she'll be rootin in dat as soon as ve get der, I know!"

The crate of chickens took up a lot of room on the wagon. Rudy removed the end gate, allowing half of the birds to stick out the back.

"Gus, vould ya hand up dat big can a molasses, so I can set it right in da corner, here?"

Gustav was distracted some, as the little sweetheart he'd met in church, Jenny, had come over to see him off. They ogled each other sadly, like a couple of orphaned hound puppies being separated.

"Ver ya vant dis sack a flour, and da oat seed." Olaf asked Rudy trying to be helpful.

"Ai, yie, yie," Rudy scratched his head. "Is der no end?"

The gathered menfolk began offering suggestions, and for a time, a dozen arms were all hanging over the sideboard shifting things back and forth. Gustav came out with several armloads of bedding and goose down feather ticks the crew packed in between the chairs and small folding table Rudy made.

It was impossible to get everything on, so Olaf took several nonessentials in his rig to keep at his cabin until they could find a way to move them up later.

Finally, everything found a place. The women helping Marta came out, all sniffling in their handkerchiefs. It was time to say good-bye.

Olaf had traveled all directions a hundred miles, and he couldn't figure out all the gloom and doom. "My goodness, folks, one'd tink da cousins ver goin ta China! Ya know, I drive up der vit good horses in vun day. I'm sure Rudy and Marta vould like it if yu'd go up and stay vun night after dey git settled in."

Marta dried her eyes, agreeing, "Oh, it vould be vunderful if you'd come. All of ya. Vouldn't it, Rudy and Gustav?"

"I should say so," Rudy said, shaking hands with all the men gathered around. Gustav grinned, nodding in agreement.

Marta, always the sensitive one, had been showing considerable concern for Olaf's welfare, took him aside for a private chat. "Olaf, ve're gonna miss ya, but I swear, your little brodder will be well cared for."

"Marta, yu've been a blessing to da bote of us, and I am so tankful for all da Englisk ya taut me. I owe ya a lot, fer sure."

She reached up and hugged him. "Nonsense, ya big clown. Ya know, you boys brought a lot of joy to our little household." She also mentioned with concern Gerda's long silence. "I just hope Gerda gets here pretty quick so you two can begin to get settled down to farming like the rest of us."

"Ya know vot might happen, Marta?" Olaf said with a wink. "Maybe she got on a ship and will come chuggin up da river before her letter gits here. Did ya ever tink a dat?"

"Oh, glory be! I hope so." Marta gave him one last hug.

Some of the men helped hitch Prince, the white horse, and Tom, the black one. The others tied the milk cow and the heifer behind the wagon. The family was ready to move on, finally.

Olaf gave Gustav, whose eyes were wet, a big bear hug. "Don't vurry, I'll come up often," he assured him.

"Ve go now. *Tack fer hjalpen,*" Rudolph called out to everyone, as he assisted Marta up on the spring seat. "Ve really appreciated it."

"*Ingen orsak. Adjo,*" the folks called out, saying they were glad to lend a hand and bid them good-bye.

Marta waved her handkerchief as the wagon rolled away. "*Tack sa Mycket. Adjo, adjo,*" she kept calling back. Rudy turned once, giving a hearty wave.

Sitting on the back of the wagon, Gustav waved at the crowd who followed them for a hundred yards giving a final salute..

* * *

Once the wagon was out of sight, Olaf high-tailed it for the Burbank office to continue planning for bridge and road improvements northwest to Sauk Rapids. From all indications, Northern Europeans were expected to immigrate by larger numbers in the coming years, and J. C. was anxious to get a head start on the dray business. He was eager to place a major station in the heart of the Sauk River Valley which had some excellent farm land waiting for German families with an envious eye on the West.

"Good mornin, Mr. Burbank," Olaf greeted enthusiastically, after racing past Betsy, the secretary.

"Good morning, Olaf," the big boss returned. "My, you look like you're full of piss and vinegar today, my boy." He chuckled at his young field manager whom he favored and treated somewhat like a son.

"Ja, vell, I'm ready ta hit da trail to-morra--vit a good crew, I tink."

"Good. Grab a cup of Betsy's 'sheep dip' and we'll join the others in the meeting room and talk about it." He went in.

Olaf winked. "Mornin Betsy," he said again. "How ya been behavin? Were ya good last night?" He filled his mug with coffee from the steaming pot at the space heater.

"Don't know fer sure, Swede. You'll have to ask Bill how good I was!" She gave a bawdy wink, sending Olaf into a fit of laughter. "Ya know, Swede, I can't wait for ya forever." Betsy was a spitfire who always came back with a sharp answer, but was as good as gold, and would do anything to help out wherever she was needed.

"Mornin' gentlemen," Olaf greeted Senior Associate, Bill Blakely and Sig Moen, now the St. Anthony Falls area manager, both of whom returned high spirited hellos, as he entered the meeting room.

"I beg yer pardon fer bein so late dis mornin, but I vonted ta make sure da folks got off fer der new farm, ya know."

"Don't be concerned about it, Olaf. As a matter of fact we didn't expect you this soon. They must've been ready to roll out bright and early, though, according to Sig," J. C. stated.

"Ja, that they ver. That cousin is a good organizer. Ven he gets done he'll have a show place up der, no doubt 'bout dat."

Olaf always felt mighty proud to be included with the top brass in planning the expansion of the freight company. Lately, he'd continued to prove himself as an impressive foreman of small field crews, constructing well-built bridges over streams along the new trails. Burbank frequently raved over the Swede's ability to design log structures with angle bracing he considered to be masterful engineering. Olaf always shrugged the compliments off in suggesting his work was just a result of using common sense.

Another quality the young aggressive Swede possessed was his innate ability to handle men. Just about everybody liked Olaf, except of course, foul-mouth unscrupulous, lazy bums like Scarface Williams. Most workers, however, strived to please him.

"How about your crew for tomorrow? Did you put on extra

men?" Mr. Burbank questioned.

"Dat I did, Sir. Der'll be nine of us, includin da two young Therault fellers, not qvite ready to move on der land yet. Den I hired a youngster from Mendota, a seventeen-year-old mulatto, I tink dey call him. He speaks some Englisk, and is eager ta virk. Name is Joe Godfrey."

"I don't know the Therault boys, but I know of the Godfreys," John Blakely added. "The father is Joseph, a French Canadian voyageur and the mother is a fine Negro woman. Good family."

"So, ve'll be headin out at six in da morning, and vill be gone four, five days I expect."

The remainder of the time was spent going over charts and maps and discussions on building the new terminal at the end of the line, the stepping stone to the western prairie.

It was an all-day business session. Unlike earlier meetings nobody asked Olaf about his sweetheart from Sweden, and this time he was glad he didn't have to come up with the same old feeble excuses for her not coming. Though worried inside, Olaf never let on his concerns to anybody.

The meeting adjourned, the men extended well wishes; "See you in the morning." Olaf mounted his buckboard for the long ride back to his cabin.

Riding by the small main street stores, he heard a voice calling loudly from in front of the apothecary-post office. It was Doc Shellum.

"Hey, Olaf! Olaf! I got good news! The steamer brought in a letter for ya today from Sweden. Knew how anxious you've been waiting, so was watching for you," Doc said.

Stopping his horses and jumping off his buckboard, Olaf dashed in to get the letter. Thanking the postmaster for being so accommodating, but nervous about its contents, Olaf pocketed the enveloped and proceeded up the trail. Out of town, he pulled off in a secluded spot to read what excuses Gerda had for not coming, this time.

Being mighty nervous, his hands shook as he opened the letter. He saw it was not a long letter, which could be good, or bad news. His throat got dry and his chest tightened as he read the miserable message.

"*Min kare Olaf, Jag ar ledsen,*" his voice choked as he read on quietly. Tears came to his eyes, as he read the message she'd not be coming. Ever!

"Aie, yie, yie, yie," he bellowed out loud. "Now vot da hell vill I do? And I sent all dat *pengar* so she cud come over!' His savings were gone--for nothing!

Getting himself under control, he read on. It got worse as she explained her reason. *Manson's pojka* would be the father of her baby, already fussing to get out.

Olaf was bristling now, and getting hot under his collar as he responded to the letter. "Ja, some friend *Kalle Mansson vaz*! He took care of my Flicka all right! 'Jist having a little fun, she says, and Kalle vosen't careful! But Gerda, I vooden't have you now fer anything!" he yelled out loud, pounding the buckboard seat with his fist.

The trip home was a nightmare. First, he felt sorry for himself, and then, downright anger overtook him, as he cussed his old friend Kalle Mansson, and his childhood sweetheart Gerda Johannesson.

The question that pained him most deeply was, now what would he do for the future? He thought, thank the Lord for the St. Louis trip coming up; that would relieve him of his miseries some, anyway.

Nonetheless, the big Swede's pride had been temporality shattered.

RED RIVER OXCARTS.

SMITTEN BY THE OXCART GIRL

The trip to St. Louis along the mighty Mississippi had been an awesome experience for the big Swede, and diverted his attention from personal set-backs to the great opportunities his new country offered. Olaf wasn't sure, exactly, how he'd fit in, but the lure of the mysterious frontier seemed to be calling him, and that pretty much dominated his thoughts.

At week's end, the teamsters hit the saloon. Olaf stared out over his beer, half-listening to some of the silliness and the big talk of these frontier characters. Oh, he figured, maybe one or two might find skirts, but with an average of one woman for every twenty men in the territory, the odds weren't too good. Most of the jokers had gone, now.

"Well, Swede, what ya got up your sleeve for the weekend?" Jake Honnaker asked.

"Oh, nottin so great." Swede attempted a smile. "Yist going up to ma cabin, enyoy da peace and qviet, tussle vit Spot, da black and vite springer Rudolph left in my care. Den Dancer Girl and me, ve'll take a ride along da river, like ve alvays do, and look at the scenery. It's so purdy der."

"Well, Olaf, I'm proud of ya, the way ya bounced back from your siege of miseries over that girl from back home that cheated on ya. Good thing ya found out 'for too late."

"Ja, who vant ta drink da skimmed milk after da cream's been taken off da top? I alvays say."

Jake howled, then said, in a serious vein, "But, Swede, we were sure worried about you' hidin out and bein alone all the time like that? It's not good, ya know."

"Aw, ya don't have to vurry a bit about dat no more, friend. I got lots a new dreams now, ya see." He'd had enough to drink to loosen his tongue plenty, and was jabbering like a penned rooster. Olaf rattled on like somebody'd wound him up. First, he talked about his little brother finding a sweetheart, the Swedish girl brought over from the Old country by the rich childless Mrs. Washburn. The wealthy woman had handed the girl a silver spoon to hold: a fine wardrobe, tutors, music lessons, and all. "Dose pups, Gustav and Jenny, aren't even fourteen yet," Olaf said, "and are already talkin marriage. Not even dry behind da ears, so dey say. Vimen! Dey only cause trouble." A sorrowful look filled Olaf's blue eyes.

Jake kept washing mugs, hearing little of what the Swede was saying, but kept answering 'yeah, yeah', anyway.

"But, me," he kept chattering, "vot I'm tryin ta tell ya is, I vont ta live a little bit; I vont ta see a little more of dis great territory before dey put shackles on me. Ya unerstand, Yake?"

Jake's fat belly shook with amusement. "Settle down, big Swede! Come on down off that soap box! Ya know, I never heard ya rattle on so much. 'Think you better plan on being a politician the way you can talk."

Olaf hadn't realized he was getting carried away. Feeling sheepish, he apologized. "Oh, I'm sorry, Yake, I didn't mean to run off at da mout like dat. Guess maybe I had vun more beer den I needed."

"Well, it's good to see ya got all yer horses back in the barn, for sure, but I'll bet ya - two ta one - the next sweety eyes you, the big Swede'll fall like a ton a bricks!"

Olaf smirked. "Not a chance! I'm tru vit vimen!" Then, pondering some, a bright idea came to mind. "Yake, I feel so damn good, tink I'm gonna buy me a yug a rum, go home, nip a little more, and have a relaxin night." He stood, putting his jacket on. "Git me a small vun, Yake."

The jolly Dutchman fetched the bottle but cautioned Olaf about the chilly fall nights. "Better wait til ya get to the cabin before poppin the cork, pal. It's sixty-five cents."

Digging for pocket money, "Aw, don't vurry. I be fine. I enyoyed da visit, Yake. See ya Monday," he said, whistling his way out the door.

No doubt about it, Olaf had found peace of mind again. While walking home he kept thinking about getting back to Spot and Dancer Girl. Caring for them required some responsibility now, and that meant a lot to him.

Not paying attention to Jake's warning, Olaf popped the bottle for a nip, or two, on reaching the woods.

He imagined he was handling himself pretty well, and even though he felt himself staggering, he didn't suspect he was walking on pretty thin ice. Suddenly he was stumbling on a tree stump negotiated hundreds of times before, and tumbled helter-skelter down the river bank. Finally landing flat on his back side next to the water, he began to laugh. Sitting up next to the river, Olaf noticed his mouth harp had fallen out of his pocket, so he amused himself by playing old Swedish folk tunes as he staggered the rest of the way home.

Once at his quaint little cabin three miles north of St. Anthony Falls, he was met by Spot, who circled playfully around his master's legs trying to bite his pantlegs off. The five-month-old pup was in that chewing anything and everything stage. Master and dog went out to greet Dancer Girl who neighed for some attention, not having seen her keeper all day long. It was also well past feeding time. After getting a fork of prairie hay, some oats, affectionate patting, and a lot of extra conversation by the loose-tongued, tipsy Swede, she responded with the usual soft mellow whinnying, Olaf always thought of as 'horse purring'.

Stumbling into the log cabin, his fumbling hands lit the oil lamp. This was a major task, trying to manipulate the wick with one hand and the match with the other. Next, after lighting the kindling in the small iron stove to take the chill off the air, Olaf removed his boots and sat down on the big soft chair Mr. Burbank had hauled up for Olaf when he moved in.

The Swede grinned to himself as he picked up his favorite pipe, leaned back to enjoy a relaxing smoke, and dream about the future plans for his big farm. He figured he'd more than likely sit there an hour or so, and scratch Spot's belly as the dog lay on the old bear rug, gazing obediently, somewhat quizzically, at his fuzzy-headed master.

Before long, Swede Olsson conked out, being more tired than he thought. He didn't feel a thing as Spot turned about, licking his master's hand when it stopped petting.

Later, Olaf's deadened body started twisting, turning, and jerking from a wild nightmare aggravating him. He woke himself up shouting, "Stop dat racket! Stop dat noise, I tell ya! Stop it! Stop it! Stop it!"

Stumbling to the washstand, he splashed water on his face in an attempt to clear his head of the irritating dream. Spot followed, looking up in confusion.

"Vell, I don't spose ya heard dat, puppy, huh? I tink yud a been yappin yer head off at da sqveeling! Like a bunch a pigs, it vas. Still hear it some," he said, tapping his ears.

Spot cocked his head sideways, but didn't come up with any answers for the confused Swede.

"Damn stuff, dat rum! My head's spinnin like a top. Nay, I better get inta bed and sleep dis off as fast as I can. Crazy! Terble dreams like dat!"

As night wore on, his dreaming continued. The last one, was at the gates of hell, and the devil was playing a fiery welcome on his violin, Olaf's punishment for drunken carousing. It got louder and louder! He shouted, "No! No! No!" Spot crawled under the bed to hide.

Olaf couldn't understand what was happening! When he opened the door for a breath of fresh air, the violin music became louder than ever, and now he could hear people laughing and singing! Realizing the sounds were real--hung over or not--Olaf decided to get to the bottom of those rapscallions invading his quiet world.

Jumping into his pants and slipping his boots on, he grabbed his jacket with the rum bottle still in the pocket and tore out the door.

The sound echoed through the woods, getting louder as he got closer. When he saw the trees above the hill casting a reddish glow at their tops, Olaf stood baffled. It seemed the whole woods were on fire ahead. Running the last fifty yards to the crest, an awesome sight took his breath away!

The entire valley, over a half mile across, was mysteriously encircled with hundreds of two wheeled carts, with oxen and horses grazing by them. People, in large numbers, were celebrating around a huge bonfire in the center, with musicians playing those devilish violins, and gaudily dressed revelers dancing furiously.

"*Min Gud I himlen*! Vot can dis be?" Olaf gasped.

At first he thought they were Indians, but their clothing was not native dress by any stretch of the imagination. Men and women, alike, wore colorful shirts and blouses, but oddly enough, they also sported leggings and moccasins like Indians. Then, he noticed the quick-step jig dancing of bearded men. It was a cinch, Indians had no face hair! The ornaments, with many strings of beads jingling and flying in the air was most entertaining, but confounding, defying any reasonable explanation to the bewildered Swede.

A chilling thought entered Olaf's mind. Could this strange army have come to invade St. Paul and the other settlements? He moved cautiously to the last clump of trees, for a closer look.

Suddenly, something flushed out of the thicket! At first, he thought it an animal, but the moonlight revealed a person darting away. Then, it fell to the ground, as if being shot. He listened! A muffled moan followed, sounding like the whimpering of a young girl.

In his delirium, he moved quickly, but cautiously toward the sound, not wanting to frighten the creature anymore than he already had. He stumbled on the prairie dog mound, the same that caused the initial accident, he thought. Now, he realized it really was a girl whimpering in pain.

Her frightened eyes stared up at him, as he towered over her. She was pleading for help, but the words were of a strange language he couldn't understand. Kneeling down slowly, he struck a match for a better look at the injury, and saw the upper part of her leg bleeding badly. She continued pleading something unintelligible.

Olaf felt terrible, his presence frightening her and causing the accident! He realized she'd not be able to understand him any more than he could her, but by talking gently it might have a soothing effect, the same as he'd done to help injured animals. He smiled. "Oh my, dat is a purdy bad cut, fer sure." He lit a second match and held it up at chin level, promising to help her.

He observed that her fearful look was changing to one of

52

guarded curiosity, as she seemed to stare up at his blond hair with interest. Olaf was surprised in finding not merely a girl, but a pretty, fully developed, young woman. Her wide dark eyes sparkled, and when she feigned a smile, two lovely dimples graced her beauty.

He continued talking to her in a soft and easy way and her fear appeared to be lessening.

"Ja, yer sure a purdy von, I tell ya." Olaf was enjoying this knowing she didn't understand his words. "My, how I'd like to have vun like you ta take home fer keeps." Then, he winked and laughed.

He now saw that the ugly cut had come from scraping against a sharp rock near by. The incident sobered Olaf, who was now questioning whether rum might be a helpful disinfectant for such a wound since the dirt must be washed off. Then it must be wrapped to stop the bleeding.

Taking the huge handkerchief he always carried, and thankful it had just been washed, he began cleaning her wound. At first hesitant and nervous about touching her delicate soft leg, and not being the least experienced in these matters, he proceeded tenderly. He moistened the corner of the cloth with rum, glancing up to calm his patient. "Could ya hold dis?" He placed the open bottle in her hand. Smiling at her again, he talked softly. "If ya ver a man, ya cud take a little nip. Good medicine," he chuckled. "Kills da pain," He joked, knowing she wouldn't understand and he was pretty grateful she wasn't a man!

"O-o-o!" she whimpered some at the sting.

"Dat's it now. I'll wrap it and it'll be all better," he assured. Ripping off a piece of the cloth, he bandaged the wound as carefully as his unsteady hands would allow. Glancing up at her face, he noticed a quizzical smirk."

"You -- medicine man?" she said coyly.

Olaf was stunned! "Vot? Ya talk English?"

"Hm," she grinned, realizing she'd been caught off guard. "Talk some English." Then, she said brightly, "You good man."

"Ah, ya fooled me. Didn't tink ya cud understand." So, realizing she'd understood some of his earlier comments, Olaf reddened at the thought. "Vot language ya talk before, den?"

"Talk *Francais*, most time."

"Ah, I'm sorry fer da foolish tings I said. I cud cut ma tongue off fer sayin dem."

She laughed, then looked at her leg. "Cut much better now."

"Ja," he agreed, now admiring her pretty face. "So, vot is yer name, den?"

"*Je M'appelle Marianne*. Marianne LaMond."

"Marie..." He tried again. "Marie -- ann. My dat's a pretty name, I tink. Mine is Olaf. Sometimes called Ole, or Svede. I come from far avay, across ocean, from Sveden."

"Olaf, real name, *oui*? Ole, nicky name? I call you that some. Good friends call me Marie some. You can, too, *s'il vous plait*."

There was a pause as the two became more and more engrossed in each other, a mutual attraction evolving.

"You said beautiful words and did not think I understand, *non? Moi,* I can trust you, now," she assured him. "Olaf," she repeated his name, giving him an endearing smile.

Intrigued, Olaf wanted to know more. He pointed to the valley. "You have family down there? Maybe boy friend?"

"*Mon cher Papa,* only. Mama die when I was *enfant*."

"Ah, dat's a shame. Did Papa raise ya den?"

"*Non!*" Papa, he is voyageur, go on river, go far North for furs to sell. Gray Nuns, Sister of Holy Roman Church at St. Boniface take me, give me good home, teach me of God, teach me a little English, and teach me to read and write." She paused for a moment, recalling his other question. "No, *Monsieur le Swede*, with so many mothers, I never have time for boy friend. Besides, my mothers discourage them."

Olaf grinned. So far, this is good, he thought, becoming infatuated with the sun-kissed beauty.

He tried helping her stand, but the pain caused her to crumple. She'd obviously sustained further damage in her fall.

"O-o-o my foot! Maybe broke," she whimpered.

"Better sit again," he suggested. He knelt down and removed her moccasin, and lightly massaged her foot. The pain was bad, she complained, so taking the rest of his big handkerchief, he wrapped it around her ankle a few times, bringing the ends under her foot, and tied them on the top, making a firm bind. Glancing up, he caught her taking another sip of the rum.

"Never had medicine like this before," she whispered, a cute expression on her face. "Make nose tingle."

"Hey! Be careful! Too much makes vun dizzy," Olaf cautioned, restraining her hand with the bottle in it.

"Eh, *Monsieur*," she laughed provocatively, now intrigued over her fortunate meeting of the overwhelmingly kind stranger. "You are good doctor, *bien sur.*"

"Aw," he smiled modestly, "I've helped lame horses and fixed broken bones on small animals and birds. Dat's all." He stood, reaching down and putting his hands under her arms for support, again and gently lifted her.

"*Oui, non gentile homme.* Feels much better!" She studied his gentle smile, and added, touching her nose. "But, *le nez* tickles from medicine, I think." She giggled foolishly.

The contrast of their sizes was striking. The huge blond Swede and the petite dark woman. She continued holding on to him, probably more as a thank-you embrace than to merely support her foot. He gazed at her sparkling eyes. Whenever she smiled, two enchanting dimples graced her cheeks.

They remained close, as if some unexplainable force held them together. Olaf was clearly struck by her dark exotic beauty, and she, reaching up to stroke his golden blond hair was intrigued by the strong, pale image he presented -- so different from that of her people.

"You like great white Prince I read about," she said, looking up at him with wide eyes.

Olaf, embarrassed said, "Awe." Gaining confidence, he blurted, "I tink yer da purdiest vomin I ever saw, Marie - Marianne." Their faces moved closer and closer, Olaf bending down and Marianne on tip toes, and finally their lips touched.

The diminutive dark-eyed beauty had a worried look on her face. "I will never want you go. My heart hurts when I think you leave me. Oh, Monsieur, *C'est l'amour* - for first time."

They kissed again, and again, and again, totally oblivious of the celebration taking place down the hill, and of everything else.

Coming to the realization the hour was getting late, a look of concern came over Marianne. "Papa will worry I am in trouble! *Cher* Olaf, will you help me back to my people, *sil vous plait?*" she pleaded.

Olaf, glancing down the hill into the vale below, studied the wild crowd in their merry-making, still dancing and singing at a frenzied pace. Unsteady himself from the long night of drinking, he couldn't turn down the invitation, and allow this romantic moment to end just yet. He downed the last drops in his bottle to fortify himself, starting to feel apprehensive about meeting so many strangers. What if they were angered by his keeping their beautiful Marianne out in the darkness so long?

"Olaf, please do not leave! we just be *les amis* friends."

The starry-eyed Swede put his arms around her to support her injured foot and leg and headed down the hill, hoping for a friendly reception.

When Marianne and Olaf approached, the singing and laughing ceased abruptly and a deathly quiet came over the valley. The men and women of the gathering looked shocked once they caught sight of the tall blond man standing head and shoulders above his tiny partner. As the pair walked cautiously toward the center of the crowd, some of the young men looked most unfriendly to Olaf. The young girls, however, tittered, appearing surprised by Marianne's obvious catch.

Marianne directed Olaf toward a group of older men, and stopped in front of a short, stout, bearded gent wearing a red plaid jacket with a little black visored cap tilted on the back of his head. She gave the old fellow, seated on a stool, a kiss on the cheek, and spoke the foreign language in a most animated way for what seemed to be an eternity. Olaf felt uncomfortable after a while, not knowing what was being discussed.

Then, the music started again, and everybody returned to their merrymaking, satisfied the stranger was no threat. Eventually, Marianne said to the Swede: "Ole, this is my Papa, Pierre LaMond. Papa, friend Ole. Talk English."

Though he'd glanced at Olaf before, now Pierre looked around to the side from his lowly position, his eyes moved up, up, and up, until he focused on the tall light-complected moose of a man above him. Amused at the size of the Swede, Pierre howled in laughter and immediately fell off his stool. Then, quickly jumping back up he extended his hand.

"Hello, Ole. Marianne say you fix hurt leg. Thank you. Where you come from, big white friend?" He grinned.

"Live down river. Not even half mile."

"Marianne, she says you good man. Here, have drink. We celebrate end of our people's long journey to St. Paul."

Olaf accepted his friendly gesture, but choked some at the taste of the proffered drink.

Pierre LaMond kept Olaf in conversation for a considerable time. LaMond talked excitedly of his experiences as a voyageur in the Canadian wilds, and extolling the virtues of his beloved daughter.

Any fears the Swede had concerning the threatening presence of the colorful folks from the far North were soon laid to rest. He was quickly convinced they were honorable hard working men like himself.

"You are most fine gentleman," Pierre LaMond raved, patting Olaf on the back like an old friend. "I like you. Marianne, she is fine judge of character. She want you as friend." LaMond winked at Olaf, then added: "I approve. She is smart daughter." The old voyageur was elated at the match he'd approved and wanted everybody to know. "Hey, hey everybody! Come meet Marianne's new friend," he roared.

"Monsieur! Monsieur! Drink," they coaxed playfully, all intrigued with the fair-haired giant, towered over the much shorter, black-bearded cart people.

Soon, the whole valley echoed the spirited music and singing, and dancing of the quick-step jig. After obligingly taking drinks from every person, Olaf's inhibitions completely left him. Feeling no pain from drinking the fire water, as they called it, his huge frame began to pulsate to the rapid tempo. Taking his mouth harp he began playing with the musicians, and doing a little dance of his own. The musicians, in turn, stopped to applaud this humorous behavior.

Marianne, pulling at his shirt sleeve, finally pulled Olaf from the men who were engrossed in the Swedish-laden version of his sea stories. "Come, Ole, dance Red River Jig with me now. Ankle much better," she explained.

"Nay, nay, no can dance, Marie," he winced helplessly. Once she got him up on his long rubbery legs, he let loose like a wildcat with a burr under his tail, and everybody cheered with delight. In response, a huge ear-to-ear smile spread across his face.

As the night wore on the drinking spree began taking its toll. After most of the weary travelers had retired to their tents, the two infatuated lovers stood in the shadows, kissing and holding each other as if the world was about to end.

"Olaf, don't go!" she begged, though he had no intentions of leaving yet. "Just learned miracle of love with you on hill. Never had such feeling. Your eyes-they have kindness and love in them, like magic spell. I overcome with excitement and need for you."

Drunk from the night's excesses, and uninhibited, he poured out his love for her. "I vas hopin some vun like you vud come along, Marie, but I never in my vildest dreams expected such perfection." He wished his head were clearer. How would he ever remember the magic of the moment, he wondered.

"Olaf, I ask Papa, you stay the night. He say me old enough now to decide myself. With Papa only in summer, rest of time back at convent, where it be different. Want to share miracle of love with only you - ever."

Olaf was overwhelmed and anxious. They both were, he was sure. They walked arm-in-arm to Marianne's tent, where her longing to hold the big man, and his to hold her, would extend their ecstasy for a while longer.

* * *

Bewildering hours passed. The dazed Swede, having been transported to heaven the previous night, was harboring a hangover such as he'd never had in all his life. He groaned, "Oh, my head! My head! I tink it's split vide open." Barely conscious that someone was with him, he was trying to sort out the circumstances of the night before.

He looked up to see the lovely Marianne. No, that part hadn't

58

been a dream; the expression on her face said that.

Marianne felt sorry for him. She was muttering something half in English and half in French about the way the men duped him with firewater. "Does that help, love, cool wet cloth to head?"

"Ja. Ja. Don't stop, please," he pleaded. "Ma head's on fire, fer sure." He tried to get up but the tent kept spinning, so he flopped back on the robes.

"Stay quiet, nice Swede. I nurse ya back to good health."

She was trying to feed him some strange tasting elixir. "Tis *un peu* bitter, but will give clear head," she insisted. "Papa swear by it."

The ailing Swede finally relented. Soon his senses returned and he tried to sort out the strange twist of events leading to the unbelievable night. Again, as his eyes focused on the beautiful girl smiling and fussing over him the mystery of the night haunted him.

Confused, he asked, "Who are ya?"

"I, Marianne your friend," she pouted, "You do not remember me?" She continued massaging his forehead.

"Ja, Ja, Ja, but **who** are ya? And all da udders vit ya, who are dey?" He asked, trying to satisfy his curiosity.

Again, she looked hurt. "We cart people. Don't remember?"

"But, I never hear of ya before. Vare ya come from?"

"From far North. Red River. Land of Northern lights."

"Vut ya haul on all da two veeled vagons I saw, den?"

"My big friend, every year we come. Bring furs, other things for Hudson Bay Company. Furs from far North," she explained.

The cobwebs in the Swede's confused mind were clearing now. What she just related was beginning to make sense. He recalled his employer, Mr. Burbank, contemplating a far-fledged plan to extend stage and freight transportation clear up into Canada, five hundred miles to the North. The arrangements were with the same company Marianne mentioned, Hudson Bay Co. It was all adding up. As a matter of fact, he recalled being asked to think about establishing a wagon trail west to the Red River.

The attentive angel of mercy softly sang a tune in French, trying to soothe her confused patient.

His thoughts kept turning. "Marie, I'm confused. How did so

many French people get up to Red River? They didn't come by treacherous Indian country, I'm sure."

"Papa's ancestors, French fur traders, came from the east by way of lakes and rivers in Indian birch canoes to trade with the natives who hunted and trapped the animals," she told Olaf, still wiping his face with the cool cloth. She told how Frenchmen married local women and had big families. All such children were called *Métis* (maytee'), or *Bois Brules*, meaning of burnt wood color, which they were proud of, she said.

Ja, ja," Olaf listened, his mind now quite alert.

Marianne explained that the native people learned French through trade. Then, later, the English came by way of Hudson Bay, defeated the French, she explained, so it became necessary to learn English, as well. "You understand, *cher* Olaf?"

"Ja, ja," he answered, reminding her he was still attentive.

She had his undivided attention, even though she kept dabbing his weary head, as she related the story of her people.

"Bois Brules, part French - part Indian, then. They are best boatmen, called Voyageurs. Best buffalo hunters, too." Obviously enjoying her caretaking, she hummed occasionally. Then, she'd start explaining again. "We not farm much though. Scots came to Lord Selkirk's colonies many years ago. They are great farmers in Red River." Marianne's eyes sparkled, as she glamorized her mystical homeland.

As for Olaf, he was in a dream world, as his new love lavished her care on him.

Marianne paused long enough to plant a tender but demanding kiss on Olaf's lips, making his flesh tingle as the warmness overcame him. Nurturing turned to lovemaking as they enjoyed each other completely for a while.

Finally, she leaned back. "Olaf, I never even kissed man, ever. And God is my witness to that."

He grinned, "Dat's good, but da kisses sure full of fire, fer sure. Make me sqvirm plenty ven ya plant a big vun."

She blushed, "Only do that when you touch me that way."

"Uh ha!" he kidded, tickling her; time for a little horse play. She tickled back, and both snickered, letting off steam.

After some time of reflective quiet, contemplating their thoughts, Marianne became serious. "My gentle Olaf, you have lover?" She asked, her face even more beautiful, with worry.

He raised himself up on his elbow. What should he say? Visions of Gerda came to mind.

"You have lover?" she repeated.

"Nay! I have no vun now," he decided to answer the truth. "Only you."

Marianne's expression showed her struggling with her thought and what she really wanted to say. Finally she whispered. "You go home with me, my love, Olaf?"

He was flabbergasted at her proposal! What could he say? Finally he stammered, "I-I-I go home vit ya?"

"Will you?" She pleaded softly. "In only few hours we move carts to St. Paul. We must arrive early morning, then unload carts. When finished, then we take long journey back home."

Putting his arms around her, Olaf held her tightly. He was still at a loss for words. Though he'd fallen desperately in love with Marie, he couldn't just up and leave his job, and family, and revert to becoming a nomad of the plains. The cart people seemed like wanderers; people without a care in the world. On the other hand, here was a chance to be with this beautiful creature forever, and he'd never been happier.

"I love you, Olaf." she pressed.

"Oh, Marie, Marie. Ya are da loveliest girl I ever met, but...but, vud ve get married den? Live togetter?"

"You are my new life, Olaf." Being inspired by a thought, she said, "Sister Laurent told me I know when man right for me. You are man," she insisted affectionately.

"You have a sister named Laurent?" he asked curiously.

"Non!" she said, becoming flustered. "Sister Laurent is Gray Nun in Holy Roman Church where I study." Suddenly she looked as if she didn't wish to speak anymore.

He observed her face as she quieted herself. She folded her hands as if in prayer. Glancing up, Olaf saw a tear trail down her cheek.

"Vie! Hey! Marianne. Ya ver veepin! Vie?" he asked.

"Oh, *Cher amie*, I have broken a sacred vow. I have given

promise to Sisters and the good Bishop to not drink like other *Bois Brules*. And I not be held by man yet." She glanced up into his eyes and smiled feebly. "I am sorry, my big Ole. I should have waited. Sister Laurent will be disappointed; until now I hoped to become nun like her." Pausing in thought for a moment, she added, "You see, in few days I be old enough to make vows to Church." She held back her tears, though her face showed the pain.

Olaf was taken back by this information, but felt sorry for her suffering. Suggesting an alternative, "Marianne, maybe it vas meant dat ve should be togetter. Vould that be so bad?"

Thinking he was making a strong commitment, she asked again: "You go home with me then?" She smiled anxiously.

"Marie, Marie, vot vould I do now? I don't know anyting about trappin and huntin buffalo." He noticed how downcast and unhappy she looked in response. Still, he had no desire to end their beautiful relationship so, recalling his dream of America, he countered, "Marianne, I am a good farmer though! I come to America to be a farmer. Now I have a fine yob and earn good money. Soon I'll have enough to buy my own farm." He took hold of both her arms, "Marie, do ya tink yu'd ever vant to be a farmer's vife?"

"Oh, *oui! oui!*" she smiled brightly, "Like Scotty farmers with real big house, many sheep, and cattle, and horses, and everything!" She almost saddened as quickly. "That is too great a dream, monsieur, for a poor métis girl to have."

"*Nej*, Marie, if ve really vant it bad enough, ve can have it," he reassured her. "Nuttin is impossible in dis great vorld ve live in." Suddenly a new idea was out of his mouth. "Maybe I get land in Red River country!"

The two lovers agreed how wonderful life would be if it continued as of the moment, but realized common sense dictated their parting for the time being. They made a serious pledge to be true until they could be together again.

A disheartening voice called from outside the tent. "Marianne! Marianne! *C'est le moment de partir.*"

Marianne answered, "*Oui* Papa." She looked sadly at Olaf. "I knew the time was close. The thought is so sad. Come, *mon amour,* I drive you to cabin. I can catch others easy," she said.

The Swede stepped out of the tent into the sunlight, shielding his eyes. There was a spontaneous din of greetings from the happy cart people; "Hey, hey, Ole! You funny man," said one. "Monsieur, you come with us," invited another.

Papa had already hitched the pony to her cart, so Marianne helped Olaf onto the bales. He waved good bye to Pierre LaMond, and the others, as they headed to his cabin.

The excruciating screeching of wooden wheels on ungreased wooden axles brought back thoughts of his dream about pigs squealing the night before. Had it only been a night? --It felt like a lifetime. He gave an amused chuckle at the thought, but kept holding his weary aching head.

When they finally reached the cabin, neither wanted to let go. "I will think of only you while I'm with the sisters at school," she bemoaned.

"I vil virk hard and save money to buy our farm," Olaf promised. "Some day, soon, I vill get to yer country; ya kin bet on dat." He put his arm around her. "I know I vil miss yer cheerful and vunderful smile. I'll never forgit ya, Marianne. I svear ve'll be togetter - sometime."

She playfully reached up and tousled his blond hair. "You one big handsome man, Olaf. My heart breaks to leave you." Her eyes grew damp as she grabbed and gave him a tender kiss he'd never forget. "Don't want to cry," she said, quickly hopping on her cart and driving off. Then, she called back, "Come again in spring when trees and flowers live again. Wait for me."

Olaf jogged after her a ways. "I vill vait fer ya! I promise dat! Maybe I get to Red River country soon," he kept calling and waving until the pretty dark-eyed, brown skinned girl, her shiny black hair blowing in the wind, disappeared down the trail.

CAPTURED BY CHIPPEWA

The Big Swede couldn't get the exotic métis girl out of his mind...the agony of being without her pulled at his heartstrings. Yet, life must go on, he knew. He would work desperately to earn enough for their small farm while breaking trails to new settlements, helping the pioneers, and striving to protect the rights of his new-found Indian friends.

Recognizing Olaf's interest in the native cause, his boss, along with Indian Agent Harriman, and Commander Jones from Fort Snelling, came to depend on the Swede's skills as a trail boss. He was contracted for hauling goods into the wilderness reservations, to the Indians who soon grew to trust him.

The starving, disgruntled Chippewa were getting restless, so a plan was set to haul four wagon loads of annuities to the new town of Duluth, close to the Fond du Lac reservation. Olaf was to take four of his best teamsters; the wagons to be escorted by four sharp-shooters from the Fort. A métis by the name of Claude La Fontaine would serve as guide.

Olaf had a problem. The family planned a thanksgiving get together at Cousin Rudy's farm at the same time. After much arm twisting, the Swede reconsidered. The agents had put a guilt trip on him. Olaf knew he would blame himself if even one Chippewa Indian would die because of his inattention to their needs, so he yielded.

* * *

The train of four wagons, and four guards had left two days earlier than planned. Olaf insisted on that so he could stop at Rudy's farm on the return trip - in just five days. Affable guide La Fontaine delighted Olaf on the grueling trip up the untraveled Indian trail along the St. Croix river. Clearing the brush was tedious and time-consuming, though.

Further, a Chippewa war party threatened them near the Rum River, but La Fontaine, their half blood-brother, convinced the Indians the freight was heading for Fond du Lac. They had other ideas, La Fontaine said, maybe seeking out enemy Sioux.

Though Olaf was intrigued by the giant white pine forest grandeur, he was worried. The trip was falling behind schedule.

Then, like magic, reaching the top of a hill, an awesome great lake came into view. La Fontaine laughed and shouted, "There she is! Kitchigami! Worshipped by Chippewa for ages."

"Dat's da purdiest sight I ever saw. Reminds me of Sveden; like standing on da banks overlookin da Baltic," Olaf raved.

The horses, tired from the grueling trip, eased down the long hill to the new town of Duluth. They'd get a well-earned rest before returning the next day, Olaf thoughtfully promised.

A large number of Indians camped on the hill, above town. The Swede was appalled at the sight of the gaunt and raggedly dressed Chippewa. He hoped his wagons contained warm clothing as well as food.

That evening, Olaf's crew bunked in the new barracks next to the lumber mill. It would house lumberjacks soon to invade the great pine forests of the northland. La Fontaine spent long hours talking about the ways of the Chippewa, which was illuminating to Olaf, who knew of Dakota life, but little of this northern tribe. Afterwards, a restful night was most welcome to the tired trailmen.

* * *

Many Tears, the Indian cook, served buckwheat cakes and maple syrup and her zesty hot coffee the next morning. Claude introduced Olaf to the cheerful, squat woman who had unique spiritual powers, as he had informed Olaf. She communicated with the spirits of the wind each night as she strolled along the great inland sea. Claude asked her of her latest contacts. "Many Tears, is the world at peace?"

"Winds of death cry much past moon. Some of brothers taken by Great Spirit," she said, noticeably trembling.

"Later," Claude advised, "One never questions her visions, my friend. Could be danger ahead. Be cautious, and farewell."

Olaf thanked the congenial guide, who said he would be heading north to his home at Grand Portage the same day.

* * *

It was nearing mid morning. The wagons, loaded with a small amount of freight from the trader were exerting little strain on horses, allowing for a fast trip home for Thanksgiving. The teamsters and cavalry were horsing it up, having a good time.

Having traveled about thirty minutes, one of the riders called back: "Looks like a small bunch of Indians didn't make it to the reservation last night, Swede."

Olaf then noticed the five Indians huddled together on the side of the trail. Closing in, he could see an old woman lying flat on the ground. He impulsively pulled off the trail and stopped his wagon to offer a hand, if he could.

He called back to the men, "You fellas keep on goin. I can catch up later."

"Swede, there's nothing ya can do. They're all in the same shape, the poor devils." Dutch yelled back.

"De old lady looks half dead. Maybe I can git dem ta ride in my vagon box, and I'll take em home. You keep goin, Dutch."

A young man and woman, and two children, about eight and ten, stood around the sickly woman who was perspiring profusely and shaking from the chills. They all had looks of desperation on their faces.

Olaf tried communicating with them. "Talk English?" He asked. Looking bewildered, they obviously did not understand. Olaf tried again, but the couple looked at each other and spoke in Chippewan. The young man whiffed longingly at Olaf's pipe, it appeared, so Olaf presented his tobacco pouch, but the young Indian shook his hands side to side, indicating he had no pipe.

The Swede gave a reassuring smile as he returned to his wagon tool box and found an old pipe he'd half chewed the stem off from thousands of hours of pleasurable smoking. The man literally shook in response to the gift, and inhaling deeply and filling his lungs, gave a gratifying nod, exhaling slowly.

Then, the old lady gave out a startling cry. The man got down on his knees, as if to comfort her, but after exchanging words Olaf couldn't understand, the young Indian finally raised the old broken stem to the old lady's anciently wrinkled and toothless mouth. Her eyes brightened, and a puff or two seemed to perk her up some.

Noticing how emaciated the children appeared - as well as the older ones - Olaf opened his food box and gave each some hard tack and beef jerky, and found the family to be most receptive.

Now was the time to get their cooperation, Olaf figured. Depending on the sign language he'd learned from the Dakota, he pointed to the wagon, repeating, "ride...ride." They seemed inquisitive when he pantomimed picking the old lady up, carrying her to the wagon, and unfolding a buffalo robe for her to rest on. He was sure they got the message by their humorous response, all mimicking his actions perfectly.

As he headed along the trail, the entire family sat together in the wagon box, indulging in the pipe.

Exchanging hand signals with the man, Olaf assumed he'd arrive at Fond du Lac in time to discharge the Chippewa family, and head south to Cousin Rudoph's. The Swede smiled to himself, anticipating the fun of the family reunion. Two hours passed, and the sun was slipping ever so close to the horizon. Had he misread the directions?

"Hoiga! Hoiga!" The Chippewa man grunted and pointed to the right. Olaf was certain he never could have found the trail had the young man not guided him.

Heading toward the west, Olaf saw the last glimpse of the sun fade as small trees and shrubbery gave way to a darkened forest of giant pines. The trail snaked in and out and around the towering trees and sudden darkness eliminated the possibility of seeing the evening departure, so Olaf resigned himself to hopefully finding a receptive welcome at the Fond du Lac Village.

Feeling a quick shaking of the wagon, followed by a strong jolt, Olaf glanced back in time to see a shadow leap over the edge! The young man had disappeared into the darkness, perhaps heading for some faint flickering lights just coming into view to the right of the path.

The horses made an abrupt turn to the right, as well, though they were not guided that way. One does not question the innate keen sense of direction the horse possesses, so Olaf didn't become alarmed.

Suddenly, as though a curtain had been raised, a grand natural panoramic spectacle presented itself before him. A tremendous fire burned in the center of this panorama. Olaf discovered that the path led straight into the village where white smoke billowed up through the tall pines. The surprised Swede quickly focused on the mass celebration taking place around that fire, surrounded by a circle of dome-shaped wigwams.

As he drove on, the wild movements of the dancers came into view a quarter of a mile ahead. Olaf could see that the faces of some were grotesquely painted. Many wore headpieces of numerous feathers. When he stopped momentarily, Olaf heard the beating of the tom-toms, and the scratching of the rattles. What chilled his spine was the eerie falsetto yelping of the revelers. This was one time the brazen Swede wished he'd not intruded.

Abruptly a violent thud rocked Olaf's head, inducing immediate disorientation! Vague senses returned to him gradually, only to realize that angry warriors were mauling him on the ground. Olaf was terrified! Hammers, hatchets and clubs flew by so close he could feel the air wisp by. Seconds later he felt a sting to his cheek, his warm blood dripped from it. Olaf couldn't breathe yet his heart pounded as loudly as the drumming of the tom-tom drums. His captors were torturing him like a cat with its prey before the kill.

Coming to his senses, he called out, "Friend! Friend! Friend of Chippewas!" Paying him no heed, they tied him to a tree and continued flogging him. The pain was excruciating, and several times he passed out for a moment. He finally realized his captors were mere young boys, probably vying for status of brave, but they came on like a fierce war party, he thought.

Then, a strong voice called out something that sounded like "Kwahinto! Kwahinto!" An old Chief in full war dress came forward, accompanied by the young man whose family Olaf assisted back to the reservation. A Chippewa girl dressed neatly in doeskin followed and became involved in the three way conversation taking place. It seemed the young man was pleading for leniency, and proceeded to untie Olaf's hands from behind the tree, leaving him bound by the waist and legs.

"Wasichu not honored guest of Anishinabi! Disrupt ceremony of Anishinabi!" The Chief spoke gruffly.

Olaf was relieved to hear English, but not too comforted by the tone. The three continued their discussion in Chippewan, after which, the girl spoke in fairly good English.

"My father, Chief Nug-aun-ub. Speak for Fond du Lac people. Will not harm more," she assured him.

"Tank God!" Olaf gasped. "I'm friend of Chippewa. Yist helped da family vit sick old lady get home," he nervously explained. He'd been watching the young juveniles unhitching his horses, and feared never seeing them again. Fortunately, the Chief scolded the boys and made them rehitch the horses to his wagon.

The young girl retrieved Olaf's pipe from one of the 'would be warriors' and returned it to him. She asked, "Have tobacco for Chief?"

"Ja. A bag in my box under da seat. I'd like some, too, please."

She came back with two small cloth sacks. Thankfully, he traveled with a good tobacco supply, his usual gifts to the natives. "You will please the Chief with fine smelling smoke."

The old fellow didn't say another word, but gave a grunt of approval for the tobacco, filled his long stemmed piece and turned his back to enjoy his treat.

"Lakoma, my name," she said. "Daughter of Nug-aun-ub. Learn English at mission on Madeline Island in Kitchigami. Teach Chief words to talk to Great White Fathers." She paused for a moment, then added, "who we learn to distrust for taking away Kitchigami."

"I am sorry, and feel bad fer dat. I plead for native people to da Agent, and da Governor. Der's plenty room for all, I tink."

"Then, speak more as Anishinabi than white man," she said. "Not good time friendly Wasichu come. Celebrate victory with

'Snakes in Grass' -- known as Sioux," she boasted. "Can see by trophies of their scalps." She pointed at the scalps hanging from a post nearby.

Olaf swallowed hard, having glanced up at the gruesome sight, hoping what he was seeing was only a figment of his imagination. Now, she had verified it and it sickened him. He feared the Chippewa were already considering displaying his blond scalp along side the others.

Lakoma was talking to her father again. It seemed she was pleading his defense, Olaf guessed. Once the old Chief finally nodded in agreement, the stoic old man returned to the celebration.

"I beg you stay since never find way at night. Father warn you remain at tree which holds you. Close eyes and ears to what you see and hear this night."

"Tanks fer helpin me. I vill obey him fer sure," nodding in gratitude. For a moment, she ogled him curiously, then backed away slowly, and returned to her father's side.

The frenzied dancing and yelping of the revelers continued as he remained at the rim of darkness. The fire raged brightly and reflected on the intense faces of the revelers, their bodies turning in a huge circle around the fire. It was an awesome experience for the frightened Swede. His throat had never been so dry. It hurt to swallow which he did repeatedly, as he stared at the hideous faceless Sioux atop the poles. The fire reflected the blood-red flesh beneath the black hair. One appeared much smaller, like that of a young boy. Could it be from one of the bands of Sioux he'd become friendly with this past summer? Olaf prayed it wasn't Wowinapi whom he'd fished with many times.

Olaf knew of the Sioux-Chippewa warfare dating back hundreds of years. He'd seen many Chippewa scalps displayed and prized by the plains' people. Olaf knew the vicious hatred between the two tribes, as decreed by their Great Spirit, would continue to the end of time. An old Indian Shaman once told him how the older men would talk to the young boys about previous atrocities by the enemy, how their grandfathers and uncles, and other family members had been mercilessly tortured and butchered. The Indian children learned to hate early, and while growing up, were told they'd later have their chance at revenge.

Three young braves in the center of the circle were getting much attention from the young women. Olaf figured they to be the warriors being honored for taking the scalps in battle. He was troubled, not understanding how these bronze skinned people, sharing their possessions in common, having a genuine respect for the sun, earth and water, and revering the creatures of the world, could hate their blood brothers so vehemently.

The incessant beating of the drum and the scratching of the rattles--accompanied by the piercing howling of the stomping braves--went on, and on, and on, till Olaf's head throbbed with pain. Dancing as though in a deep trance, the revelers' heads jerked and bobbed erratically, their bodies bent and their toes tapped the ground like puppets on a string.

Eventually, Lakoma left her father's side, moving close to where a sizable animal was being roasted. The starved Swede watched intently. In addition to terror, he was suffering hunger pangs, not having eaten since leaving Duluth over twelve hours before. Finally, Lakoma came toward him with some pieces of venison on a tray of bark, and some water.

"Father said thank you bring Fond du Lac family. Said was bad unruly boys welcome you unkindly. Here, have meat of deer. Is good--was young tender buck."

"Oh, tank ya, tank ya, La...La..." he said, attempting to foster more friendly relations, but her name escaped him.

"Lakoma," she repeated.

"Hm," he smiled. "Lakoma is a purdy name, I tink." He munched on the succulent roast venison, talking with his mouth full. "Most people dat like me call me Svede."

She tried it. "Sss..Suu.." But, couldn't pronounce it.

"Svede," he said slowly. She looked confused, so Olaf tried to break the sounds out for her. "Su..vee..d. SuVeeed."

"Su-Veed. Su-veed." She copied him.

Olaf chuckled. It wasn't exactly right, but he was satisfied.

"Is good?" she asked, referring to the treat she brought.

Still talking with a full mouth, "Ya, tis vunderful, fer sure."

"We lucky today. Deer all gone -- almost," she said, ogling his

71

tall frame with interest. "I better go now." She looked a bit apprehensive.

Having felt a rather urgent nature call for some time now, he desperately pleaded, "Lakoma, I vill not run avay, but need to go to bush a minute. I promise."

She giggled, and went back to loosen the bindings. "I trust you big man, but please fly like wind before someone comes."

And fly he did. When he was finished he rushed back to the tree he was getting attached to. "Tank ya. Tank ya. Yer very kind to troublesome stranger," he said.

"Put ties back now, as Chief ordered." She looked sorry to have to do this to him.

"I know. Ya have ta obey yer fodder," he sympathized.

"Su-veed, you are funny big man. Lakoma like. I go now before asked to explain suspicious talk." She hurried back to her father's side.

Olaf was somewhat relaxed after the friendly chat with Lakoma, but he wished the irritating wailing and the monotonous beating of the drums would end. His legs felt like two dead tree stumps from lack of circulation.

Oh, how he hoped the Chief would let him go by morning so he could get to Rudy's and Marta's farm for the family celebration.

Suddenly, the most heinous and ear piercing scream interrupted the proceedings, sending a chill through the alarmed Swede.

The drumming ceased! Dancers halted in their steps! Everyone sat in the huge circle, as if the occasion had been rehearsed. Only the rattles kept scratching as the tragedy unfolded.

Yet, another scream rang out! A horrifying sight followed: a woman raced from her wigwam, her face totally blackened, her arms, legs and body slashed and mangled with cuts and wounds, blood oozing from every part of her. Even her hair had been whacked off at her skull.

When Olaf saw her wielding her own knife, it became clear all the mutilation had been self inflicted. Then, in one grand flourish, she flung her garment to the ground, drew the knife across the top of her breast and shrieked in excruciating agony. The blood did

72

not just ooze now, as crimson streams were draining from her body.

Olaf yanked desperately at his ropes, and with little effort, freed himself. Someone had to help the poor creature, he felt. But his eyes met Lakoma near the circle, who held a restraining hand up, indicating he had no business interfering. He couldn't watch any more! His eyes watered in anguish, and still shaking from the chills, with his heart pounding in sympathy for her, he tried not to look.

Still, she was not finished. She stepped into the fire! An ear-piercing scream faded as she fell away from the fire, unconscious and quivering.

A slow drumbeat began. The Chief stepped forward and signaled several young women who then approached. They slowly and tenderly raised her to a sitting position, though her head drooped like that of a broken doll. They cleaned the wounds and treated the cuts with a black substance. Though moaning in obvious pain, her recovery was incredibly hastened, and the attendants placed a clean new shawl over her.

The Chief signaled the young braves honored earlier, who went to another wigwam and returned with two young children, about seven or eight, Olaf thought. The distraught woman held out her lacerated arm, accepting them. Then, from an open wound she took some blood on her finger and made a mark on the forehead of each. Holding them affectionately, she stopped her soft wailing and began singing a slow mournful song, like a lullaby, Olaf thought.

The assemblage, apparently moved by the ceremony, slowly rose and quietly retreated to the wigwams, leaving a most terrifying memory to be replayed in the Swede's mind for the rest of his life.

The Chief and Lakoma remained outside their lodge. The fire, now smoldering, gave way to a pale moon waxing above the lake.

Olaf again felt the pains of standing the long night. The wind whistled softly through the tall pines. There was an occasional call of a wolf, mysteriously howling from afar.

Lakoma approached and spoke somberly. "What you saw here, we celebrate often; glorifying our heroes, grieving the lost."

73

"I know of the vorring traditions with the Sioux, but I feel so sorry for families of doze dead, as I feel sad ven Anishinabi dead are displayed. Be good to end da vore, da Government vould look kindly on bote yer nations," he pleaded.

"We no question your ways. Why you speak of the Great Spirit that we war?" she said. "All we have left is small honor to win battle, now and then. This brings honor to once proud warriors. Su-veed, your soldiers are honored for killing Indians. What is difference?"

"I know. I know," he admitted. "I yist don't understand vie anyvun has ta kill, or be killed." Then the violent self-mutilation by the woman confounded him; "Vie da voman try to kill herself? And da children? Ver dey hers?"

Lakoma looked downcast, "Woman was squaw of fallen brave this day. It is custom she takes away some of dead warrior's pain. She suffers and family of Fond du Lac make honor. It may be hard to understand, but these, our ways."

"Make honor? But how?" He asked.

"Children taken from enemy in war. Chief awarded them to appease her sadness. She will attend them well. They become Anishinabi; become strong braves, and bring much honor," she explained.

Olaf finally apologized for questioning their ways, saying; "Lakoma, I am sorry I intruded. I shouldn't have."

She smiled. "I know, and I trust you." Trying to explain her personal feelings, she added, "This I say; I learn white man ways and tongue at Madeline Island form priests with long coats. I, too, grieve for families of fallen Sioux. This is my Catholic teaching. But, I pray to both your God and our Great Spirit for mercy and understanding." She paused, smiling slightly. "How can I not be on winning side big Su-veed?"

Olaf smiled at her compassionately.

"The Chief says you must leave before first morning bird sings. Go quietly. We don't know what Anishinbi will do in these times of distress."

"I vill. And I'll alvays be tankful to ya and yer fodder fer saving me from young eager vorriors."

"Good friend, remember. We will need food and clothing which treaty promised for hunting and fishing lands. I pray you will help us Ju-veed. Soon, many will die of cold and hunger, I fear. Our number grows smaller much too fast," she said.

Hearing her father calling, Lakoma grew fidgety and knew she could not stay, though Olaf sensed she wanted to.

"Lakoma, I vish you and yer people vell. I vould like ta be yer friend." She seemed to be taken with his broad smile and, giving her farewell hand signal, moved back to her wigwam.

Later, Olaf sat quietly on his high wagon seat and shivered from the chill of the night--and the memory of the awesome ceremonial. Watching the eastern sky for daybreak, he wasn't sure, but if his mind was not playing tricks, the time had come.

Checking his hitch and mounting his wagon again, he slowly eased the horses around and moved down the trail. Making his first turn to the East, a bird chirped from its lofty perch high in the pines.

Another few miles down the road Olaf let out a loud, "Whoo-pee! Better have goose and plum puddin fer me. I'm hungry as a bear, Marta! Ha, ha," he laughed. "And Gus and Rudy, I yist decided, I'm gonna stay anudder day so ve Olssons can spend a little time togedder, for a change. Ha, ha, ha," he roared. The horses were so startled by his shouting that they took off like scared jackrabbits.

Breathing a sigh of relief, he would soon be with his family, now realizing he had plenty to be thankful for. The big Swede was relieved that the Chippewa let him go on his merry way.

❋ ❋ ❋ ❋ ❋

ENTERTAINING COACHMAN

It was February. The congenial Swede whistled as he walked out of the Northrop Hotel in rapidly growing St. Anthony Falls, and headed for the big coach waiting out front. He had finally talked boss Burbank into relieving him of some of his more arduous tasks. Finally, he'd been given an easier assignment, driving the stage to St. Paul.

In St. Anthony Falls the new mills were sawing lumber in ever-increasing amounts, thanks to the perpetual power of the falls and the unlimited white pine floating down the Rum River. The population of the new town had exploded to fifteen hundred in a few years, necessitating transportation service between the two towns.

Olaf had worked hard for the wagon outfit, first confined in the St. Anthony Falls' yards as forman for six months, then field manager at Stillwater for a while. As an occasional wagon master on jaunts out in the dangerous wilderness, including horrendous trips north with supplies for the starving Chippewa; Olaf figured he deserved something a little more glamorous in his life.

Luckily for Olaf, Kingpin J. C. Burbank, building his horse and wagon empire, found in the ambitious Swede a capable general field manager; his right hand so to speak. But, Olaf's luck went deeper than that. Burbank showed affection for the young bruiser as if Olaf were his own, the son he'd never had. Olaf, for his part, admired and respected Burbank, so it had become a most compatible association.

The Territorial legislature was about to convene for the February session in St. Paul, and the gregarious, sometimes outspoken, Swedish-American wasn't all too pleased with the way the politicians were treating the displaced Indians. He felt remorse for these real Americans, who'd managed the land well for centuries. Now Olaf was determined to speak to the legislators on their behalf.

Another political issue was taking place. The Friends of Temperance, a bunch of ax-wielding, hymn singing women, part of the national movement, was raising Hell with sporting saloons, trying to abolish pleasure drinking forever.

Having quickly become a heroic frontiersman by his daring exploits and accomplishments, Olaf was anxious to face the situation.

This being his fourth day, and starting his regular morning run from St. Anthony Falls, he wasn't surprised to find the usual patrons waiting to ride over to St. Paul and cause some chaos. The women wearing black, street-length skirts and capes, and round flat hats decorated with tiny white and pink imitation flowers were ready to board. Olaf wondered which saloon was destined to suffer the wrath of the Friends of Temperance this time.

"How do, ladies. Now, vare are ya headin taday? Da Territorial Capitol in St. Paul, I'spect?"

"Yes, Mr. Olsson, we're going to do the Lord's work, again. The West is full of wickedness, and we're determined to clean it up," Mrs. Higginbottom proclaimed.

Olaf knew they wore those black, full skirts especially for a purpose, because underneath them, they were concealing the clanking weapons: hatchets, pokers, and pipes.

Olaf was quite startled to see a fourth member today, but this one was no prune-faced old lady like the others. She was as pretty as a picture; appearing to be about seventeen or eighteen. When she smiled, Olaf could see that her sparkly eyes could ignite any moment. Lord a mighty, he thought, she's sure a purdy vun.

The Swede, standing next to the carriage, tried to assist the women up the high step by taking their arms, but each pulled away, not wanting to be touched by such a man, it seemed. But the young beauty smiled and leaned her arm out, hoping she'd get a lift from the big smiling coachman. Mrs. Higginbottom reached back, and grabbing her ear, pulled her in. "You naughty girl," she scolded.

Olaf at last mounted the high seat, took the lines and moved out with one of the finest quartets of horses in the Burbank stables. Standing about sixteen hands, they were of golden buckskin color:

authentic show horses.

This February day, a heavy snow covered the landscape, which had necessitated the removal of wheels for sliders. Now, with Olaf high in the driver's seat, that big coach just glided along smoothly and quietly, except for the bright tingling of the Swiss bells adorning the harnesses.

Tuning up for their rally downtown, the good ladies belted out a noisy rendition of "The Battle Hymn of the Republic." Olaf shook his head at the screeching. He thought it sounded more like a bunch of métis' ox-carts with ungreased wheels. Thank goodness they were still in the country, he thought. It could have been downright embarrassing in town.

He lit his pipe for a pleasurable smoke. The heat from the pipe also warmed his hands enough so he wouldn't have to wear clumsy gloves.

Feeling a bit guilty about lusting for the sweet thing in the coach, he quickly forced his thoughts to Marianne, and got his wandering mind back on the right road again.

About half way to St. Paul, the old drunkard, Sam Skinner, stood on the road in front of his small cabin, wanting to hitch a ride into town. He'd gone in with Olaf many times before, so Olaf pulled over to let him come aboard. However, even at a distance, he smelled pretty ripe, and was wearing that old moth eaten bear coat of his. Sam's first impulse was to stagger toward the coach, but on meeting the flurry of flying brick bats coming out the window, he went sprawling backwards to the ground.

Olaf chuckled under his breath. "If yer goin in today, ya gotta ride up here vit me, Sam." So, the old timer struggled to keep his footing, finally climbed to the top.

"Holy mountain cats, Swede! A man's not safe in this here country no more. Ten year's prospectin' in the mountains, fightin off lions, and all. Never seen nothin like that."

Awe, settle down, Sam," Olaf snickered, "better days ahead."

A half hour drive brought them to the outskirts of the town. St. Paul, now three thousand souls, was well spread out with a combination of one-and two-story frame houses. There was no need to crowd together, Olaf agreed. There's still a lot of room in the territory.

By now, Olaf knew most of the townsfolk, so he called out greetings to just about everybody. St. Peter, and some of the other streets downtown were shaping up to create a typical booming western town. A bustling excitement filled the air, with folks eager to get a piece of the dream.

Always admiring the dramatic flare of the stage and hack drivers in New York, the Swede tried his best to emulate them in maintaining the romantic image beholding the profession. One showy trick these heroes of the coaches contrived was to send the steeds in at full gate, using the long rawhide whip in splitting the air in a most rip roaring way. So, Olaf seemed to have put wings on his horses, as they flew into town that last half mile. Then he swung into the usual spot, pulling the brake lever with tremendous force, creating a small cloud of snow, before skidding to a stop. It was even more fun in summer when dirt flew better.

Sam half slid off the top in his excitement to get the word to the saloon keepers, figuring he'd get a good hefty glow on from free drinks for his efforts.

The womenfolk disembarked quickly when Olaf opened their door, and the pretty young one ogled the big Swede with interest. But, Mrs. Higginbottom came back, grabbing her, "C'mon, Nettie, we've got lots of work to do." Olaf gave Nettie a teasing wink; she returned a flirtatious smile. All in a day's work, Olaf figured.

The lead buckskin was tied to the hitching post, allowing the gregarious Swede to mingle with the fairly large gathering outside the Central House, the two-story hotel where the territorial legislature would soon go into session. It'd be fifteen minutes before the stage was due to return to St. Anthony Falls. He had plenty of time to chat with acquaintances.

Sighting Governor Ramsey and Representative Rice, the delegate of the territory to Congress, smoking their imported cigars, and waving, he returned a friendly salute and ambled over. The two politicians greeted Olaf most courteously, respecting his imposing position as one of the important personages of the community. After all, even though everybody knew Swede Olsson, few recognized the politicians, or even knew them by their first name.

Olaf took the opportunity, cold as it was, to press for some considerations of his cause; improving the lot of the Dakota people. Both men, not too encouraging, stated that Congress was not sympathetic. Congress wanted the country to be opened up to settlement by Europeans, they explained.

"Ve are only being greedy! Der's plenty room fer everybody," Olaf lashed out, his breath shooting across the winter air. "If I ver in Voshington, I'd ring some tail fetters! Dey got no Conscience! Da land belonged to da Indians in da first place."

Governor Ramsey did seem to sympathize, but felt there was little to be done. The committee on Indian affairs would meet one evening during the legislative session, and Olaf would be welcome to sit in with the Chiefs at that time, Representative Rice agreed, admitting the territory had some say in regulating Indians.

"Now I learn to talk English better, I yist might do dat," Olaf said, checking his new company issued pocket watch, realizing it was time to move out.

Mrs. Higginbottom's black garbed angels joined the St. Paul supporters; the group now numbered about twenty. They marched down the snow covered street - the bang of pots and pans accompanied the usual singing of some forty or fifty hymns deploring the evils of drinking and carousing.

Olaf, now heading back to St. Anthony Falls moved his horses slowly so he could sneak a peek at the flirtatious Nettie Higginbottom, who beat away on her wash pan. Glancing up at the tall driver, she quickly dropped her wooden spoon, embarrassed at the stage driver's ogling. Mrs. Higginbottom, noticing her lolligaging, reached over, pinched her on the back side, and the poor little imp commenced beating that pan like the devil had stuck her with his fork.

* * *

On the final trip to St. Paul that day, Olaf saw the women warriors' success. When Olaf passed Buddy George's Town Pump, a favorite hangout for lumberjacks and teamsters, he noticed it looked like a tornado had wiped Buddy out. Broken jugs, bottles, chairs and bar stools were strewn all over kingdom come.

"Holy heifer dust! What a shambles!" Olaf yelled out at the town sports standing with their heads hanging low. Buddy sat on the boardwalk in misery over the attack, and old Sam Skinner was trying to console him.

* * *

Not every day was filled with exciting events, but Olaf didn't mind. Happiness was greeting people and informing newcomers all about the fabulous frontier.

The legislators were eager to go into session, but everybody was looking for the evasive Jolly Joe Rolette from Pembina, the largest county in the new Minnesota territory, reaching from the Red River to the rim of the Western mountains. Rolette held a good handful of métis half-breed votes, so the Governor and Congressman Rice depended on his support.

One afternoon, a few days later, riding in from St. Paul the Swede was surprised at the excitement brewing in St. Anthony Falls. On the corner by the livery gathered a large crowd of town folk, mostly women and kids. Their attention was drawn to a bunch of harnessed dogs hitched to a sled. Olaf hopped down.

"My golly, doze are some nice lookin pups, I tell ya. Who's da fella vit dis outfit?" he asked the spectators.

"Jolly Joe Rolette just came on it! Can you imagine, Swede, lovey, that dignitary came four hundred miles that way." Dolly, the respected hotel Madam, raved.

"Dat is somtin. Vare is he now, fer cat's sake? And vare are all da men?" Olaf scratched his head. "I vud like to talk vit him bout some urgent problems of dis country."

"Oh, you'll always find the jolly Frenchman behind a mug of beer. Try the saloon next door," she suggested.

Dashing next door in hopes of finding support for assisting the Dakota, Olaf bolted into the smoke-filled saloon finding a bunch of characters rollicking in mild hysterics. Though tall enough, he still couldn't focus on the center of attraction.

Anson Northrop, the hotel owner, whom Olaf had met earlier at his Stillwater establishment, caught sight of him. He called, "Swede! Oh Swede, c'mon up here and meet the finest politician this country ever had, the Honorable Joe Rolette." The crowd parted, allowing Olaf to elbow up to the bar. There was no doubt in his mind the short black-bearded gent with a face many shades darker than the rest in the room was the wind-burned driver of that dog sled. Realizing the comedy in their differences, the pudgy northerner doubled up in boisterous laughter as he greeted the big man who stood a shoulder higher than his head.

"Joe Rolette, this is one of our great men about these parts, Swede Olsson," Northrup blurted. The rotund comic insisted the Swede hold his arms out to the side, level with the floor. Taking his fiddle, Rolette played away, at the same time, jigging. His legs tapped the floor faster than a woodpecker hammers a hollow tree as he danced around and under Swede's arms. The gathering cheered his antics as if he were a showman from the circus.

Finally, the crowd settled down, and Olaf got a chance to explain his concerns. Rolette's face became as somber as a bull ox, and they found a place for a serious man-to-man conversation in a private nook behind the bar.

"You don't know how delighted I am to meet another good white man with the gumption you have," Rolette asserted. "It might be interesting to know that my wife is a half breed; part French and part Chippewa," he revealed. "Raised fifteen children with me."

Olaf was eager enough to bend the Frenchman's ear. When telling of his stage coach driving, Rolette showed delight.

"Have you a place to keep my huskies, friend?"

"Ja, I can keep dem over at da Burbank barns."

"Non, Non!" the northerner chuckled. Those dogs would die inside. An open air shelter would be better," he insisted.

The deal was made. Olaf offered to board the huskies, and then take Rolette over to the Central House Hotel in St. Paul. On the way, the two discussed the degrading treatment of the Dakota, about to be evicted from their great hunting grounds. Olaf realized he'd have to do some arm twisting, especially after Rolette revealed most métis were allies of the Chippewa, and detested the Dakota. But, the affable Frenchman was somewhat sympathetic, finally agreeing to do what he could.

Suddenly, bells started ringing in the Swede's head! Pembina!

Marianne! The cart people! "Mr. Rolette, ya vouldn't happen to know Pierre LaMond, vould ya? And Marianne, his daughter?"

Rolette roared. "You bet, big fella! Aha! Oh, so you're the one she pines for. Won't eat! LaMond, my friend, told me all. What a coincidence to run across you. Small world, isn't it?"

Olaf felt like he'd been hit on the head with a scoop shovel. He was amazed the Frenchman knew the LaMonds, but he was happy to hear Marianne missed him. She'd really meant her faithful pledge. He knew now.

Rolette, always a prankster, thanked him when parting, saying, "Tomorrow I will shed these skins of a voyageur and call on the local tailor to fit me with a gentleman's suit, for which, I will send the bill to Representative Rice." He laughed slyly. "And he'll pay it too, after all the favors I've done him."

* * *

How sweet it is to be a carefree stage driver, Olaf thought while making his daily rounds at hotel stops in the two towns. But the call of the wild had grown more alluring, and with spring breaking soon, he was getting anxious to move out on the wilderness again.

In a few weeks the legislature would be over. Hopefully, hunting rights would be restored for the Dakota. Olaf was working hard lobbying for that to happen. The likable and popular Swede only laughed when frontier folks urged him to become a politician. "Why," they said, "if you'd run for Governor, you'd win hands down."

This particular day he was heading to St. Paul with a solitary rider. As usual, he smoked his pipe for awhile, then played the German mouth harp Cap'n Krueger had given him. Those melodies brought memories of his old friend now resting at the bottom of the Baltic, and Olaf's own miraculous escape from a watery grave.

It was a windy, blustery day. Anybody out in this kind of weather ought to be horsewhipped, he thought to himself, giving his thigh a slap. Eventually, more than the wind and the cold was nipping at his right ear. Something else was irritating him. Was it his collar? he wondered, reaching up with his hand. The irksome tickling continued. "Damn it!" he yelled, swatting at it. "Whoa," he hollered, stopping the rig to resolve the mystery. Looking back, he finally saw the culprit pestering him!

Little Crow, whose Indian name was Taoyateduta, the Chief from Kaposia was doing a war dance on top of the stage, above and behind him, laughing as Olaf had never heard an Indian laugh before, and holding a feather in his hand.

"Damn ya, Taoyateduta," Olaf howled, actually amused at the Indian's trickery.

Little Crow, dressed in deer skins and a coon hat, came up behind him. "No see Tall Like Oak some time. Wawinape ask for Tall Like Oak."

"Aw, Chief, been busy," Olaf apologized.

"Huh?" Little Crow grunted, not understanding.

"Busy," he repeated. "Virk." He held his lines up. "Drive horses all da time."

Little Crow looked downcast. "Tall Like Oak turn back on Chief. Tall Like Oak turn back on Wowinapi. Tall Like Oak turn back on Dakota."

"No. No." Olaf protested. "Tall Like Oak friend of Taoyateduta. Friend of Wowinapi and Dakota. Soon spring comes, and Tall Like Oak can fish vit liddle Chief anudder time. Like Wowinapi," Olaf chuckled. "He caught da biggest fish ever seen."

Olaf was recalling the time he took Wowinapi down to the river to fish, and the six year-old, trying to throw his line far out, hooked himself in his own behind, and Olaf had a devil of a time getting the hook out. The two men always bantered about that.

The Chief had learned some English at the mission school he attended at Kaposia, just a stone's throw below St. Paul. After being away to the West a few years and marrying several daughters of a western Wahpeton Chief, he had returned to re-establish himself as Chief of all the Mdewakanton Dakota living in and around the juncture of the Mississippi and Minnesota rivers.

Olaf kidded. "Vie ya come out in a snow storm, anyvay? Should be home in tepee vit all yer sqvaws ta keep ya varm!"

"No worry. Taoyateduta not neglect squaws." He scratched his head, answering, "If that happen, would call Tall Like Oak to tepee for help," he grunted jokingly, and winked. They laughed.

Little Crow had a reputation of being a rounder. He was considered a gambler and womanizer, though he was truly a fearless warrior, having a hefty number of eagle feathers from battles with the Chippewa. He had abided by the dictates of the two-year old treaty, but he and other Mdewakanton Chiefs had been tricked, unaware that their cherished hunting and fishing rights had been taken away.

"Tall Like Oak come to hearing on Indian matters and speak for Dakota," the Chief begged.

Olaf nodded agreeably, and added, "But I hear dat greatest orator of yer people is Taoyateduta. Vite law makers respect and have some fear of Chief."

The Chief grunted, "But more warriors win biggest battles. Being the humorist again, "Besides, Tall Like Oak shoot off mouth good as anyone."

Olaf chuckled. "Don't vurry, I vill be der."

"Tall Like Oak best white friend Indian ever have."

After a moment of quiet, Olaf, looking back, was surprised to find him gone. He obviously moved back and slid down the back boot, disappearing into the woods before the rig reached St. Paul.

* * *

As he rode atop his coach, the Swede kept thinking about how rapidly the wilderness was being settled. The territory called Minnesota in 1853 had accumulated the five thousand residents required by congress to eventually qualify for statehood. With representation of delegates to the national government, and with an allocation of federal funds for development, many local decisions had to be made for establishing institutions and laws.

Olaf learned about politics while driving the representatives to and from the different towns. He'd hit it off favorably with Rolette and Rice, as well as the Governor. Whenever he could, he tried to influence some action to help the natives survive acculturation. The joking little black bearded representative from Pembina, along with Olaf, was the driving force in getting the law reinstated. This law restored to the Indians, the hunting and fishing rights in all lakes and woods, and freedom of passage through settled land, as agreed in the treaty of 1835.

Olaf could see how soon the wild country was changing. After much debate, the law makers decided the capitol would remain at St. Paul, the penitentiary would go to Stillwater; and the university to St. Anthony Falls. The fledgling towns were becoming cities.

For all the mischief by the Friends of Temperance, the prohibition bill that had passed, was annulled. The court had given the law-making power to the legislature and they weren't about to give up the privilege of sporting and liquor for its energetic settlers.

Now, the big Swede looked to the West, intrigued by the mystery of the wilderness. He'd worked hard for the Burbank horse and wagon outfit, clearing trails, heading up dangerous missions, improving wagon transportation, and then he satisfied his longing to drive the stage coach.

It had been nearly two years since the romantic encounter on the prairie with his beautiful métis. Now, he longed for her and was mystified why she never returned with the cart trains as he met them, every one. These friendly métis assured him Marianne was being true, but it wasn't convenient for her to come just yet. Maybe, by going northwest, Olaf contemplated, he might be able to find her.

* * *

When Spring broke, the various bands of Dakota were gratified by the return of their fishing and hunting privileges, and attributed this miracle to their great Swedish spokesman at the legislature.

Taoyateduta, whom the settlers called Little Crow, had both wrists deformed from stopping a gunshot by his half brother in a show-down for leadership of all the eastern Dakota. This only enhanced his authority.

Olaf met Little Crow his first year in the territory when the Chief invited him to Kaposia to go fishing with the Chief and his son, Wowinapi, about eight. Wowinapi was intrigued by the guest's size and gave him his Indian name, Tall Like Oak. It so happened a huge oak tree towered above many smaller ones, and the bright-eyed boy chuckled and pointed, first at Olaf, and then to the tree, saying, "Tall Like Oak." Little Crow howled, "Tall Like Oak. Good Indian name. That's it then."

With weather warming, a pow-wow was held in Olaf's honor. All the Chiefs came: Big Eagle, Traveling Hail, Wabasha--from Winona, Shakopee, Chaska, and many lesser chiefs, all dressed in their feathers and finest regalia.

Olaf was prepared. He brought a large amount of good tobacco - the Indians cherished the pleasant taste and aroma of his over their own - and the traditional pipe of peace was handed back and forth. Soon, the great skin-covered drum began thundering as young men started beating on it, accompanied by a high falsetto song. The older men, including the chiefs, commenced dancing in a slow rhythmic motion. Their heads were bent down toward the ground, then they looked up to the sky, as if communicating with a great spirit in a most serious and somber way.

Olaf found himself caught in the spirit of the dance. Little Crow edged his way over and sat on the ground next to him.

"The song tells of sadness when we have to leave these great happy hunting grounds. Old Chiefs beg for Great Spirit to hear their prayers. To take their souls, so their bones can stay and become a part of this world; that their blood and flesh may nurture the earth forever."

Next, Chief Wabasha came to have a philosophical talk with Olaf. With hand signals and Indian words he'd learned, Olaf understood the elder Wabasha to infer he was favorable to Tall Like Oak's kind treatment to the Dakota. The Chief from the father of rivers told how he did not wish to sign the treaties two summers ago, giving up their rights. With the signing done, he would honor it and become a *wazuwicasta,* a farmer, like the white *wasicung.*

Having spoken, Wabasha puffed the long-stemmed pipe. Then he passed it to Olaf, who smoked it too.

The spiritual dancing ended at dusk. The Chiefs, and their followers greeted Olaf a final time, then slowly meandered away, not jubilant, for they would be leaving this sacred land soon.

ROMANTIC BUFFALO HUNT

Olaf was traveling to the Red River through 'no man's land', as early white arrivals called the age-old battle grounds dividing the Chippewa of the north woods and the fierce Sioux of adjacent prairies. The two tribes had warred here for two hundred years.

Since leaving the Sauk Rapids trading post at the Mississippi River, Olaf found the trip most exhilarating, heading northwest through the wilderness on Dancer Girl. He had traveled three days, following the métis' cart trail. With the ruts deep and profound, it would be near impossible to lose one's way, Olaf found.

The awesome beauty of the tree-covered hills, which set off innumerable lakes between, almost took Olaf's breath away. The Dakota called it the finest work of *Wakantanka*, their great spirit. The métis cart people described it the same way, crediting their Almighty God for its grandeur.

Boss Burbank was leery of sending his favorite field manager on the dangerous mission, but Olaf was anxious to go. With the Mdewakanton Indians being relocated to the southwest, along the old St. Peter River--now renamed the Minnesota--it couldn't be long before immigrants would be flooding the area for choice land, free for the taking at this time. Transportation routes needed to be planned early, Burbank had asserted.

So far, Olaf had met no resistance or threat along the way. In fact, the previous night he'd camped with a hunting party of twelve Indians, whom he knew from Chaska's band from back at the big rivers.

Now that it was spring, Olaf was anticipating meeting the first métis cart train of the year. Maybe they'd have some word from his elusive lover, who mysteriously had become involved with the Roman Church. The Swede hadn't told his employer, Mr. Burbank

- although a tolerant man - about falling in love with a dark-eyed French-Indian. Most early white settlers looked askance at such behavior, so Olaf thought it better not to say anything. Maybe later.

The woods abruptly ended as Olaf rode on into the fading sun and he was amazed at the sight before him. As if overlooking a vast placid sea, he saw the horizon become a straight line, void of trees or hills. The wonder of it all was startling and caused the Swede some anxieties about his venture yet, he rode on for miles and miles, glancing back to see the great hills disappear.

Finally, scanning the horizon through his telescope, he saw a new line of trees running north and south. That must be the Red River, he said to himself. So he hurried on as daylight was fading fast. He glanced through his scope again, and was surprised to see small camp fires illuminating the trees ahead. He hurried, but was fearful of possibly heading into a camp of unfriendly Indians.

Being cautious, he paused again; this time hearing the lowing of cattle, he thought. He continued on alertly.

A gunshot rang out! A bullet singed overhead! A voice called out: "Halt, Monsieur!"

Olaf's fears were put to rest. He knew immediately it was a métis camp. They always guarded their camps against the enemy, the Sioux.

"It is Olaf Olsson from St. Paul. I intend no harm," he shouted.

"Monsieur Ole!" the lead man called. "Welcome to Red River."

As Olaf walked around the camp, he was thrilled to find several acquaintances from the first night he spent with the *Bois Brules*, the people of burnt wood color, and they had a delightful time joking at Olaf's antics from over imbibing that night.

Finally, the old gent called Pascal cornered Olaf. "Monsieur, before we left, I saw Pierre LaMond. He told me his daughter, Marianne, would be going on the spring buffalo hunt to commence first Monday in April. Marianne has told everyone she longed to see you. It would be the last chance for a long time, Ole,

89

but she thought it impossible for us to get word to you in St. Paul in time."

"First Monday," Olaf shouted. "Vie dat's four days avay! My God, man, could I get der in time?"

"Aw, Monsieur, I fear not. Since leaving Pembina, we travel sixteen days. It is very long way, my friend."

But Olaf would not be denied. He couldn't sleep. Would Mr. Burbank understand his being gone so long, he wondered. He could send word back with Pascal informing his boss that he wouldn't return for many weeks, so at least, Mr. Burbank would not worry that Olaf had been killed by hostile Indians, or the like. He tossed and turned in his bed roll. Finally, Olaf decided to put his rangy great mare to the task of traveling two hundred miles in four days. Maybe he could catch up to them.

More motivated than ever, Olaf rode hard, day and night. The two hundred miles was exhausting to both he and Dancer Girl. He rested her when he could, but he worried, for the last day, after all this hard running, she was coming up slightly lame.

The cart trail led right to Pembina. As soon as Olaf saw small houses and birch shacks, his excitement grew. But, on closer scrutiny, he found little to cheer about. The buffalo shelters were gone; the place was deserted!

Olaf was devastated! Had he still been struck another blow, arriving too late to find Marianne and all his métis friends for the hunt? He shouted desperately, "Marianne! Marianne! Vare is everybody?" He laughed out of frustration. "C'mon now, yer yist playin tricks on big Ole, aren't ya?" Then, angrily, "Damn it! Vare da hell is everybody?" he shouted.

Finally, a lone hunter came from the North with a gun on his shoulder and a rabbit dangling from his belt. "Hi! Hi!" he called. It was none other than affable Joe Rolette, his legislative friend.

"Joe Rolette! Is Marianne LaMond here! Has she been here! Have you see her?" he pressed with questions. "And vie da hell are you here?"

"Take it easy Swede." Noticing Olaf's horse limping "You

can't ride your good horse anymore. She needs a rest, man," Rolette cautioned.

"Are dey gone? Did I miss da buffalo hunt--and Marianne?"

"Aw, settle down, big fellow," Joe laughed. "You'll be able to catch them easy enough. They only travel twelve or fourteen miles a day with the slow oxen. You'll reach them before Pembina Mountain."

Without another word, the lanky Swede set off running for the West, calling back, "I'll find em! I'll find em!" He shouted back, "take care of my horse, Joe."

The Frenchman doubled up, entertained over Olaf's impulsiveness. "Don't be a fool, man, you'll get yourself lost in the dark. Come back here and I'll help you out. I owe you a favor or two, remember."

Turning back, resigned and dejected, Olaf pleaded, "Vot vill I do?"

"Big friend, if you'll settle down, I'll tell you. Don't worry. I promise you'll be with her tomorrow night. Besides," the Frenchman grinned, "I have an excellent buffalo horse--Wild Fire's his name. He can outrun and quick turn faster than any buffalo pony in the country."

Olaf relaxed, knowing not all was lost. Rolette, sitting down on a boulder to catch his breath complained, "My lumbago is acting up, so I am forced to miss my first buffalo hunt in twenty years." Having convinced Olaf to stay the night, the two soon were engrossed in conversation which was always entertaining with the happy-go-lucky legislator whose district covered the huge area from the Red River to the Missouri, a few hundred miles west.

Heading out at daybreak, Olaf held the rangy gelding back, for with his weight and over forty miles to travel, Wild Fire would be put well to the task. It was a cool clear morning and the trail along the Pembina River was fast. Plenty of time to anticipate the thrill of being with the beauty he'd fallen in love with and he wondered how the bright-eyed, spirited and uninhibited lass might have changed the past two years.

To rest Wild Fire, Olaf stopped. Dismounting, he pulled out a handful of the rich coarse grass and found it had a good clean smell to it. Chewing on the stem end, he detected a pleasant sweet taste. Due to a rainy spring the prairie grass stood full and tall, nearly up to his waist. Prairie grass, or buffalo grass, was an unending source of food for the millions of buffalo through the ages.

The rolling land was void of trees, except along the rivers and streams where foliage was abundant. Wild flowers, especially wild roses, filled the air with a pleasant fragrance, enhancing romantic desires in the Swede's mind. How exciting, and how desirable, he thought, to share this spacious openness with the one you love.

Getting more and more anxious as he rode on ever closer to his destination, the flat topped Pembina Mountain came into view just like Rolette had described it. Eventually, a section of the western sky became hazy, and excitement building, Olaf started tickling Wild Fire's ribs with his heels, encouraging a speedier gate. His anxieties were stirring within. It was only a matter of time and he would be with her again.

Moving his horse to the right, he headed up a gradual rise to the top of a ridge paralleling the cloud of dust to his North. The cart train, miles long, came into view, so he stopped momentarily. A wide grin came over his face on hearing the ever present squealing of the ungreased wooden wheels. He remembered how the screeching had driven him crazy. Now it was like music to his ears. There were hundreds of people, mostly walking alongside, but a few older ones and the children were allowed to ride on the two wheeled carts. If Olaf hadn't known better, he would have thought an invading enemy was slicing through the prairie.

But, this was no invasion! These people were part of the land. Olaf stood on the highest point and observed the happy singers of French ballads, their strains echoing over the hills. He noticed first one cart, and then others halting to observe the intruder. The métis were always on the alert for the enemy Sioux. Once Olaf rode closer to the group, those he knew best let out a cheer: "Ole! Ole!"

they shouted.

Taking his field glasses for a closer look, he was surprised to see a black spotted pinto pony break away from the line and dash towards him. It was Marianne! He turned Wild Fire and headed down the hill to the river to meet her. They nearly collided in the middle of the stream! Marianne literally threw her arms out and flew right into his. They embraced most spontaneously. Olaf swung his leg over his horse, dropped to the ground, and helped Marianne, whose eyes brimmed with tears, down from her pony. They embraced again and again.

Olaf grinned and held her back at arm's length; "Let me look at ya! Marianne, oh Marianne!" he exclaimed. "You're even more beautiful den I ever imagined!"

Her shiny black hair was pulled back in a pony tail, a brimmed tan hat hung behind her head held by the string under her chin. She wore a plain white blouse tucked in her deer-skin breeches. Olaf chuckled to himself, looking down and seeing the familiar moccasins all métis wore.

Olaf kissed her again, and he felt her heart racing against his.

She leaned back, breathlessly revealing, "There are two years which have passed. Olaf, I never violated trust. How beautiful to be in your embrace, *mon amour*."

Marianne looked down, slightly flushed. Then, studying Olaf's face again, a look of quizzical intrigue filled her dark eyes as she tickled and stroked his blond beard. Olaf had forgotten he'd grown a beard. She giggled, admitting she liked it.

She had become a more mature young woman. Though her dazzling eyes still showed the excitement of their initial romance, Olaf noticed a subtle change--a more contemplative and serious expression.

Marianne turned away pensively. Olaf noticed she automatically crossed herself, like he'd seen the nuns do. Then, he heard her say under her breath, "God forgive me."

Her serious thoughts repressed, she became excited again. "My good prince Ole, remember my love, when I call you that?" she smiled, reflectively. "*Mon amour,* you so helpful and kind to fix injured leg." Suddenly a challenge twinkled in her eyes, "Come, now," she coaxed, "I race you back to hunting party?" She jumped on her black and white pinto pony and was soon flying off at a quick gallop.

Olaf was hot for the challenge. "I tink I can beat ya, young lady." He jumped on Wild Fire, yelling, "Giddy-up! Move out!"

"Don't think so! Hi! Hi! Hi! Blazer," she yelled.

"C'mon Vild Fire," Olaf shouted, more than tickling her ribs, now.

The two were out in the open, and the whole party knew what was going on; some cheering Marianne on, others - older men mostly - were giving the Swede some encouragement. "Yea, Yea, beat 'm, Marianne," the women and the children cheered. The men shouted "quit draggin yer feet, Big Ole," and everybody got a hilarious kick out of it as Olaf trailed in -- second best.

Marianne said she'd have to care for the children now, so he could greet and visit with the others. They would be together later. She quickly joined several six to ten year old children as they walked along, keeping abreast of the slow moving Oxen train.

Olaf thought he would break with anticipation but made himself calm down. The black bearded métis men dropped back for an excited greeting. He was then reminded it would be time for dancing and singing, and telling stories. Several asked Olaf if he'd brought his mouth harp along. They would enjoy that, they laughed, recalling the first night he met Marianne and entertained them.

Marianne's métis' sisters approached Olaf on foot. He stopped Wild Fire long enough to talk. "We not tease you with sexy looks anymore," they giggled. "Our men be jealous." Cecille introduced her husband Francois, who had ridden up on his pony; Josette, her man, LaRoque; and Angele, her Louis, all riding their buffalo horses along side the train.

Father Foshet had accompanied the groups as the spiritual leader, there always being one along, Olaf learned. Marcell had been elected le Capitain of the hunt, and informed Olaf he would certainly hear his share of "Hail Marys and Our Fathers" for the duration of the trip. The métis loved their partying, singing and dancing, but were devout in their religious and spiritual life. It seemed like Father Foshet was around Marianne at all times.

The frustrated Swede, after several days, was getting downright irked over the complete dominance of Marianne's time in caring for the children. If she walked away from her charges for even a moment, the good Father was right there reminding her of her duties. Olaf was frustrated with too little time alone with Marianne, by the church's control over her.

The Swede soon discovered the trip had become tedious, constant work. He was spending much time away from the cart train--and even the sight of Marianne--in search of food for the multitude. And, if the hunt was bad, some of the hundreds might have to go hungry. Olaf, an excellent shot and hunter, always seemed to come up with a few elk or deer - sometimes a stray buffalo - to supplement the small game usually prevalent.

The women and older children searched the draws and bushes for berries and plums along the streams. Some would be eaten each day, but most of the choke cherries were to be saved for adding flavor to buffalo meat when pounded into pemmican. Olaf watched with keen interest as the older women dug wild prairie potatoes, and turnips. He was getting a good lesson in survival techniques, and these *Bois Brules* lived it most every day.

Marianne and Olaf were desperate and frustrated in the few moments spent together each evening. But, Marianne kept reminding her Olaf how briefly they had really known each other, and that this physical distance would be worthwhile, allowing time to understand each other's inner thoughts and concerns for life. Obviously, Marianne put high significance on a spiritual commitment, and promised it would only be a matter of days and she would reveal her complete arrangement with the Mother Church. Clearly the agreement caused her some personal anguish.

Olaf tried not to seethe, knowing he was ready to make a

pledge of marriage. How fair was it--for a man who'd waited two years--to be put off indefinitely? But, on the other hand, he admired Marianne for being so kind and sensitive, dedicated to working with the orphaned métis children. Through the church, she could do many kind and good things for her people. He could understand that.

Marcell, le Capitain of the hunt, and his lieutenants met regularly, the hunting party always functioning as a military unit. There had to be a line of authority with so many involved. The mood of the métis had become exhilarating, for fresh buffalo droppings were dotting the landscape in large amounts. Olaf's heart, too, began to race. The buffalo hunt was close at hand!

There would be no singing and dancing, or reveling of any kind tonight; nothing to disturb the sought after beasts of the plains. Excitement filled the hunters' faces. There was an agitation as the men were feeling jubilant in anticipation of a successful hunt -- maybe tomorrow. Even though the largest herds were diminishing, there were still some that numbered in the thousands in the Northern plains where the white man had not dared to decimate their numbers, fearing the savage Sioux.

Le Capitain Marcell gave the order to set up camp. Even though an hour of daylight remained, Marcell didn't want to take a chance on spooking the great buffalo herd.

Olaf observed the métis men watching a small band of plains Indians approaching from the West. The métis went out to meet the sixteen hunters. Olaf soon learned that these men were Mandan and Arikara Indians, whom his friend, Mr. Peltier explained, were friendlies they had traded with for generations. The skins of crushed corn and grain they brought were traded for manufactured goods the hunters had procured from Hudson Bay Company: pots and pans, knives, and a few rifles.

Olaf was intrigued at their appearance--physically tall and muscular, unlike any of the Indians he'd seen before. And most unique was their light complexion. The one, nearly as tall as the big Swede, was amused, as were the métis, by the comical likeness to the Swede; both were fair haired and had blue eyes. Olaf would later learn from Marianne the legend of the white women of the Northern lights, who some believed were Nordics who came many centuries ago, down the same route the English took through Hudson Bay. The métis joked that Olaf was probably seeing his long lost cousins for the first time. He was as amused as they.

But, the congenial exchange between the two groups soon turned somber, though Olaf could not understand what was said. Marcell and his men registered concern on their faces, then mounted their horses in haste, and followed the Indians to the southwest. Louis Peltier gave Olaf the sign to come along to see what the Mandan and Arikaras had to show. Peltier also asked Father Foshet to come. All of a sudden everyone was looking grim.

The sun rested on the western horizon as the considerable group rode over the hill. And there, stretched out before them, was a most dastardly sight anyone had ever seen! Spread out for miles were slaughtered buffalo, and soon on a breeze came the stench, as repulsive as the murderous sight; hundreds and hundreds of rotting carcasses. A few hides had been removed, but only a few. Then Louis and Olaf dismounted near a dozen slaughtered buffalo and examined them. Louis made a rather ironic statement when he said, "Well, my friends, no one will probably ever know who did this; every blasted tongue has been taken." Olaf, though in pain over the horrendous waste, understood. Buffalo tongue was a sought after delicacy.

The métis, and the Arikara and Mandans, alike, agonized over the sight, the Indians raced off to the distance howling in grief at the tragedy.

Father Foshet prayed, "Lord, have mercy on their miserable souls." Those of French blood, giving private prayers, crossed themselves more than once.

Olaf, his insides broiling, now remembered meeting a large number of Eastern hunters camping by the Red River, en route to

Pembina. They had displayed an awesome variety of high-powered weapons. He'd barely heard them making bets on who would shoot the most. As he grew more and more angry to think that humanity could be so devastatingly reckless, he pledged he'd hurry back to put pressure on the Government to stop the slaughter before the Indians' sole source of food and clothing would be wiped out in a few years. But, he wondered, would anyone listen?

The visiting Indians from the upper Missouri River would stay with the métis, welcoming the security of the larger force. Though a few carried old rifles, most sported their conventional bows and arrows. La Roque and Marcell reminded Swede he would be surprised to see how effective they'd be in the hunt.

Finally, at night, Olaf was waiting for Marianne to get her little ones tucked away for the evening, so they could resume their 'orderly' courtship. Olaf was clearly fed up with the good Father's interference, and the once cloistered beauty was mellowing out some, and not feeling quite so guilty when she felt a burning need to be held by her *mon amour*. Marianne pressed Father Foshet for some private time with her big friend, promising she would not indulge in intimate pleasures.

So, this was the night Pierre LaMond's daughter decided to discuss her commitment to the Holy Roman Church. Her eyes moist, she admitted how torn she was, but she'd made a sacred vow to the Sisters in the Order of the Gray Nuns at Montreal. She'd received the support of those around her; those who thought Marianne to be divinely inspired and filled with heroic virtue.

"Oh, Olaf," she confessed, her eyes pleading for his understanding, "I have had dreams -- visions, my love, that may come to be. I must do this, though it separates us once again." Tears trailed down her cheeks.

The big Swede was feeling most disturbed at her revelations, but sympathized for her, knowing how she suffered.

"I am here," she continued, "because my visions say if Marianne not come, bad things happen to children." Glancing toward the sleeping children, she paused for a few moments, then reached up and gave Olaf a tender kiss. "I regret to share burden with you," she spoke sadly, her lips trembling. "But all will go well," she added.

That night Olaf tossed and turned, trying to get to sleep. His mind spun with dissatisfaction. There were the religious problems with Marianne; there had been the horrible slaughter of the buffalo; and finally the worry of finding a live herd so the métis could have the harvest to see them through the next winter.

The search for buffalo went on the next day in earnest. Marcell told his men to fan out in all directions and return immediately with news of sightings, for he warned, the animals would be spooked after the slaughter of recent days. Olaf rode along with Jean Baptiste and Antoine. Louis Pettier and La Roque were to the right, on the next hill. Then Marcell signaled Olaf and the others to their positions, and as they peeked over the ridge, a never ending herd of buffalo stretched out before them.

Olaf took his field glass for a close look. "My God, I'm sure glad I got ta see dis vun time! It is truly a vonder!" he said. "Louis, and den you odders, take a qvick look, if ya like," handing his glasses over. Louis let out a muffled laugh, "Ah, huh, huh, huh, there he is again! The great white one!" And everybody had to take a quick look, for there was a large bonus to the hunter to bring him down.

The Swede took another sighting. "Lord, he is a big vun, isn't he? Vot a beauty!"

Louis confided, "Big Ole, that white giant has more shot in him, more broken arrows rubbed out of the wounds than ya can imagine. Have seen him for many years, but is faster than any horse and has more stamina and elusiveness than the devil, himself."

The huge herd of buffalo--with the one white--was an awesome sight. Olaf was tense and breathless, anticipating the ensuing hunt. But then, the whole party was, he knew.

There would be about three hundred hunters, and the Capitain wasted little time in drawing out the plan of attack. If all went well, in two hours, the air would be filled with the thundering of thousands of hoofs, and the ringing out of gunfire so intense the rampaging buffalo herd would charge violently at anything and everything in its path. Louis warned them, to get caught up in the stampede could be certain death.

Before the hunters could get completely in place, the animals started shifting nervously. The hunt began immediately! The hunters were given the go-ahead by three rapid shots, and the fleet-footed ponies sped down in the valley from all directions. Suddenly the confused buffalo were going back and forth, looking for an escape route. The great white buffalo lowered his head and tore through the line with lightning speed, and Olaf watched him angle back toward the east, and disappear behind the hill. Many hunters took shots at the trophy, but he went unscathed, it seemed.

Olaf watched the big Mandan Indian release his arrow, in chase of the remaining herd, and when the Indian had shot the arrow, Olaf saw the projectile go clear through a huge bull, and it dropped! It suffered little. When he watched the other Indians shoot with the same keen marksmanship, Olaf smiled to himself at their proficiency.

The horse Joe Rolette loaned the big Swede was overly anxious and pursued a huge animal. Wild Fire turned the buffalo around and around so quickly it took no great shot to drop the monster practically in his tracks. Shooting these docile creatures was easier than taking sitting ducks, he thought, but it was a matter of self preservation for the métis and the Indians, so the big Swede was glad he could help out.

When Olaf had dropped two of the bulls, he'd reached his quota. These bulls would provide one winter's supply of meat and robes for the métis' and Indians' own use. Perhaps they'd even get a little cash income from extra hides and pemmican from Hudson Bay Co. The hunt was good.

Still curious about any wounds suffered by the legendary great white buffalo, Olaf rode up the hill to investigate. He was shocked seeing the animal, enraged by the wounds to its flank and belly, kicking up dust, as it pawed with its front feet! A feeling of anxiety came over the Swede, as he noticed the bull's proximity to the métis camp. Olaf then moved around the back side of the hill in hopes of cutting off the infuriated buffalo before it reached the circle of carts where the women and children remained. Olaf suddenly noticed that Marianne had left the protection of the carts and had taken the children to the creek. Now the huge animal had moved between the children and the carts! The wounded creature bellowed and bawled in severe pain and anger--at those who tormented him, it seemed. The bull looked as if it might charge Marianne and the children at any moment!

Olaf stopped Wild Fire in his tracks! He aimed his rifle! But, still a hundred yards away, he dared not move closer for fear the bull would get confused and charge Marianne and her little ones, less than twenty steps away. He was stunned to see the tremendous discipline Marianne and the children showed, for there wasn't an iota of movement, except for Marianne looking unswervingly at the bull, and consoling the four-to-ten year old children, all holding fast like statues in stone.

The white bull continued holding his head low to the ground, as if he were to charge at any moment, and his low painful bawling thundered frighteningly. He stood there, Olaf thought, complaining 'See what they have done to me with all the wounds and barbs penetrating my hide?'

A most amazing phenomenon then occurred! The big bull began withdrawing slowly -- ever so slowly -- gradually backing away to the thickets on the other side of the creek.

Once the bull was at a safe distance, Olaf rode cautiously toward Marianne and her children, wondering if they'd turned to stone. He noticed how Marianne projected an ethereal glow in reverent prayer, and then, she smiled slightly as if giving thanks for the answer to that prayer.

Speaking slowly, but firmly, Olaf said, "Marianne, take da little children and valk slowly back to da carts--ever so slowly, and I vill follow and vatch behind."

The youngsters clung to Marianne and moved to the carts slowly. Half way, they left their guardian angel and darted back to their mothers who'd been watching desperately through the whole ordeal.

Olaf dismounted slowly, keeping an eye peeled for the buffalo who had now disappeared in the thickets of the creek. Marianne and Olaf held each other tightly for a few moments. Olaf said, "Damned if I understand it, but I tink I vitnessed a small miracle yist now, my love."

Marianne crossed herself. "It was good to have you there, my dear Olaf," she said.

"How did you manage such behavior, Marie? So brave?" Olaf asked.

"I just told the little tots a story from the Bible about the lions, and I told them to have faith, and pray hard." She smiled tenderly at her big man. "Thank you, my love, for not shooting the great white bull. He was terribly injured, yet he walked away and left the children unharmed." Olaf didn't say anything, but he thanked God in his thoughts for saving his Marianne from death.

* * *

The hunt had been successful. It would take several days to process the meat and hides. Stripping of the hides was done by the men. The women and younger children would all help in the scraping the flesh away from the skins and preparing it for drying. Everybody helped by cutting the meat in long strips, pounding, drying it, and pounding berries into the meat to enhance its flavor before being placed into the tallow pouches. It was hard work, taking several days.

When the carts were filled with the pemmican and hides, the *Bois Brules* grew festive again, and there was much laughter, joking and singing. Louis Marcell, the Capitain of the hunt, brought out a generous regale of rum to highlight the festivities.

During the evenings, on the way back to the Red River Valley,

Olaf and Marie at last had time to be together alone. The good Holy Father did like his rum and had taken to imbibing at night. The bonds of love grew deeper and stronger between Olaf and Marie, their last evening together being filled with poignancy.

"Olaf, God willing, I be back in a year, and then can be together forever. Nothing ever tear us apart again," she promised.

"I'll be very happy ven dat time comes, my love, believe me," he assured, "and I'll be vaitin yer return."

But, Marianne turned weepy and troubled. "My big lovable Olaf, hope you'll one day forgive for the mistakes in my life. I am filled with sadness right now, that I shall not speak of. Some things are done in childish innocence sometimes."

Olaf wondered what she'd meant and had trouble sleeping that night. The mystery of Marianne's responsibilities to her church was still most baffling to him.

The cart train reached Pembina early one afternoon. A big homecoming celebration commenced immediately. The women prepared a huge feast of buffalo meat. The men began toasting their successful hunt with rum and spirits. Fiddles played with gusto, and singing and dancing started, and would continue on far into the night, as was the tradition after every hunt. The two lovers, their faces beaming in the fire light, danced the jig as wildly as anyone, making it an even more jubilant occasion.

Marianne finally stood on a rock and whispered to her man. "Olaf, let us be alone for while. We have so little time."

"Ja," he agreed, "but der's no privacy to love, some, huh?"

"When I was little girl," she continued, "we children played under wooden arched bridge over there, on trail to St. Boniface. There is a small cave that goes back into rock bank. Was children's castle, where could pretend we be noble in beautiful world of make-believe."

She glanced around to see where the ever alert Father Foshet was, but the Father was dozing with his head against a cart wheel. "Olaf, come quick!" She took his hand and led him around the bushes, and down the bank by the side of the bridge, and there was her castle.

Olaf laughed. "Ah, a perfect hideaway," he agreed, somewhat sarcastically having delusions of a more romantic encounter. They crowded into the cave.

Then, Marianne reached up, put her arms around her tall man's neck and pulled him down for a long warm embrace. "Oh, I have loved our time together, my love, Swede Ole. Needed more time to be held, and to hold, though."

"Ja, seems like notting should ever be able to pull us apart again. Let's stay here all night long, my beautiful Marianne. Let us forget everyting else."

"Oh, my darling," she sighed, kissing him.

There was a sudden rumble from the bridge above, and the clip-clop of horses' hooves thundered over them.

"Vot is dat, fer Heaven's sake?" Olaf asked.

"I'll look." Marianne moved over to the cave opening to look out and up.

Olaf followed her, repeating, "Vot is it? Vot is it?"

She began trembling, catching sight of the conveyance. "Oh, no! Oh, no!" Her face filled with disappointment. "It's the St. Boniface carriage!" She suddenly lunged for Olaf and fell in his arms, and clung to him so tightly he could feel her pounding heart.

"Vot is happening?" He begged her.

"Sh!" she said. "Listen!"

Men's voices could be heard. "Father Foshet, please. Is he here?"

"Yes. Yes, your Holiness. I will inform him you're waiting."

"Please hurry. We have precious little time."

"Who is it?" Olaf demanded. He could see her eyes filled with tears.

"My dear, Olaf, our beautiful tryst is coming to hasty conclusion, I fear. Hold me tight, my love! Hold me tight!"

The voice of Father Foshet could be overheard. "Bishop, Your Holiness, we didn't expect you till morning." Though he'd been drinking, the father seemed to have pulled himself together, now.

"Governor Simpson's fast brigade leaves when the bells toll at St. Boniface. It is the only way we have to get her back to Montreal. Did you observe any unusual signs, Father?"

Father Foshet expounded. "Oh yes, Your Holiness, as God is my witness, to that I will attest. It was a maddened and injured monstrous white buffalo that charged Novice Marianne and the children at the creek! It tore at the earth with its front hoofs so that a cloud of dust near blackened the heavens, but still our Novice held firm like an impenetrable force and prayed til the beast withdrew and no harm came to the children. There was no doubt in my mind she was in a State of Grace, Your Holiness."

"And her virtue?" the Bishop asked. "Was she challenged?"

"It was somewhat threatened by the coming together of an old friend, Your Holiness, but I kept constant vigil."

"Then, it is imperative we leave immediately, Father Foshet."

A call for Marianne left the religious group and soon the air was filled with shouts for Marianne. In a moment it seemed as thought the whole village had truned to the search.

"Oh, my love," Marianne sobbed, her body shaking violently. "I am so frightened at the seclusion facing me, now."

Olaf was emboldened by her distress and said: "Marianne! Marianne! Come now! You do not have ta go back. Come vit me now. Ve'll be happy togetter."

She sobbed for a moment onto his shoulders. "My dear Olaf, I made a vow to return another year, and to defy the Holy Church is to defy God, I am told. My vow to God is as sacred as my vow to you. My love, believe me, you will always be in my heart. Remember that and remember we will be together."

"If ya must, den dat's it. I'll be vaitin fer ya, Marianne."

"One more beautiful parting kiss, and I'll be gone, then." The kiss was unlike any Olaf had ever experienced.

Later, Olaf and the others watched the black carriage, from St. Boniface disappear to the North. There would be another day when no one would ever come between them again. Olaf would bet on that.

MOUSEY'S INDIAN LOVE CALL

"Swede, I know how excited you were after that trip west on the buffalo hunt," Mr. Burbank said, "but I must tell you we were mighty concerned knowing how dangerous the wilderness can be-- Indians and all. Now you're back, the sparkle in your eyes, and the spring in your walk shows how damned exhilarating it must have been."

Olaf twitched, slightly self-conscious for not being able to reveal the true reason for his exuberance. It might have been a tinge of shyness holding him back, but on the other hand, Olaf wondered if folks would really understand his infatuation with a mixed-blood maiden.

"Vell, it's a big country out der, Mr. Burbank." He cleared his throat, trying to suppress his romantic thoughts in favor of a more practical description of his venture. Olaf stood tall and confident. "Y'know, doze tree tracks made by da métis' oxcarts troo da years packed da ground so hard vit deep ruts dat notting grows on it now. It's like a vide street runnin all da vey ta Canada. And dat rich soil in da Red River valley--I dug in it--it's richer den anyting I ever seen. Da prairie grass come up to my shoulders; vavin like an ocean, I kept tinkin." He paused a moment, then added, "and I'll never fergit da yoy of da buffalo hunt vit doze tousand fun lovin métis."

Burbank smiled, impressed with his young adventurer. "You've sure got a whale of a lot of courage, young man. You know, I've come to think very highly of you. I want you to know that, Olaf."

"Tank ya, sir. You've been awful good ta me, Mr. Burbank."

"Well, son, some folks are looking northwest for a substantial pioneer settlement, and I'm depending on you to set the wheels in motion."

Olaf's ears perked up. "I'm lookin forward to it, sir. Ven do ve start?"

"The only thing going up the Mississippi to Sauk Rapids when it's navigable is the steamer Governor Ramsey. Southern plantation folks--rich ones--like that area for hunting and fishing, and they want reliable transportation. Then, too, a promoter is looking at the Sauk River Valley for farm development and is about to have it plotted. Pioneers will sure be eyeing that area, don't you think?"

"Ja, sure. I tink I'm readin yer mind, sir. A trail fer vagon and maybe stage service later." This was a challenge Olaf liked. He wondered if it would be a commitment longer than a year.

"That's right. We're on the right track, Swede. A day's trip each way with a change station in between."

Olaf described his passage through Sauk Rapids on the way to the prairie hunt, where the métis trail crossed the river. He'd met trader Joe Chambois and his Indian wife, a congenial couple.

"How many other people live around the area, Swede?"

"Chambois lives above da store, and der are two log lean-to qvarters fer sleepin. I saw several hunters' tents close by, like ya said, and den, furder up da hill a hundred yards, or so, der ver a half dozen birch vigvams da Indians lived in. Besides dat, not very many, yist a few characters - huntin guides, and da like."

"Good. I rode a steamer up there once," Burbank admitted, lighting up a cheroot, "but I'd like you to take a man or two along and start clearing the trail. Maybe we could dig in a few logs across some of the ravines for temporary bridges. Spend a week setting up the project. What do you say?"

"Ja, it sounds excitin. I rode Dancer Girl across da ravines and creeks vit little effort." Olaf pondered a moment, then added, "I tink I'd like ta take Mousey Michaels along. He'd like to go, I'm sure."

Burbank chuckled, amused at the choice. "He sure won't be much help lifting huge logs, being such a skinny little fellow," he cautioned.

"Naw, but I like 'im. Den he cood get outta da barns fer a vile. Besides, he's got a heart bigger dan himself. He'll do yist fine, Sir."

* * *

Olaf felt beholden to his little friend, Mousey, for agreeing to go on the assignment. They were heading north to where the Crow River joins the Mississippi from the west side, and the Elk River joins from the North. As they rode in the wagon, Mousey, though much older than Olaf, idolized the big wagonmaster. Now he jabbered like a chipmunk along the way.

Olaf realized the little fellow felt seriously inferior, having taken constant insults from boisterous bullies on the frontier. Now, Olaf wanted to bolster his confidence. Mousey's eyes brightened when nice things were said about him and he always acted like a real man with the Swede. Olaf knew the good Lord had given Mousey a meager measure of size and brain power, but the smile on his face was genuine, and he wouldn't hurt a fly.

On reaching a deep but narrow ravine Olaf suggested, "Here ve can lay a couple big long logs, pardner." He made a large circle with his arms to show how round. "Den, on top of doze ve'll lay smaller posts acrost, pardner, about dis size." He made a circle with his fingers and thumb touching, so his partner would understand. Mousey beamed when Olaf called him partner, and soon he remembered to call Olaf partner, too.

"Wow, that'll be durn fun," Mousey said in his squeaky voice.

The wagon trip up to Sauk Rapids was rough, but except for stopping to remove some undesirable rocks, Olaf moved his big black team, Tom and Daisy, along at a brisk pace. He'd left Dancer home to rest this time.

Olaf reached the trading post before dark. Trader Chambois greeted him with enthusiasm. "Ah, *Monsieur, quel plaisir!*" This time come with four wheels instead of big horse like last time."

"Dat's right, Mr. Chambois. My outfit, da Burbank Vagon and Stage Company vants a land trail improved soon. Me'n my pardner planned to stay up here a vile fixin vauter crossins and da like," Olaf explained.

"*C'est bien,*" the trader exclaimed. Then, noticing Olaf's half pint friend, chuckled. "That one--a lumberjack?" he joked whimsically.

"Dis is Mousey, my helper," Olaf added seriously.

"Oh, excuse me. Yes," more amused, "Hello, Monsieur Mousey."

"How do." The little beady-eyed man gloated at being called Monsieur.

Chambois enthusiastically welcomed his visitors. "This trail will be good for business," he admitted. He then called Muhoni, his wife, and asked if she'd fix supper for the guests. She said she would gladly fix venison knowing how pleasant it had been to feed the big Swede the last time he'd eaten with them.

After they had eaten, Olaf thanked Mrs. Chambois for her fine meal, which included potatoes, parsnips and corn she'd gotten from the Winnebago Indian gardens. Olaf was impressed when he learned the Winnebago people were such fine growers. Though her English was far from fluent, Mrs. Chambois had learned enough from frequent visitors, and could be understood if Olaf listened carefully.

The men returned to the porch, continuing their discussion about the trail. "Chambois, if ya ask me, I tink your young vife is a most attractive and charming voman," Olaf complimented. "You're vun lucky man, sir."

"Lucky, you say! You know, I had to give her old man a fine horse to get her. But," stroking his beard, he added, "she proved to be a very good woman."

Seeing Mousey enviously eyeing the river, Olaf suggested he fetch a fishing line and try his hand at catching a 'lunker' probably. Much of what was being discussed was going over the little fellow's head, anyway, so he eagerly went down to the river.

Chambois and Olaf discussed the agricultural potential of the picturesque landscape along the Sauk River valley above the west bank. The trader told how more and more southern plantation owners were coming for sporting activities, but he disapproved of the ugly way they treated their slaves, he confessed.

An hour or two later, dusk setting in, Olaf watched Mousey land the sizable pike he proudly held up for display from a hundred yards away. The men waved in acknowledgment of his good fortune. A young Indian maiden was fishing up-stream about fifty paces from Mousey, and watching the two had made some real entertainment. The two people fishing had been ogling each other more than watching their corks.

"Mousey and Little Singing Bird seem to be flirting some," the trader chuckled.

"Ja, I noticed dat. Bote too shy ta git closer doe," Olaf agreed.

More amusing, Mousey laid his five pounder on a big rock between them, then backed away, obviously wanting her to take it. Some time passed as he continued withdrawing. Finally, the Indian lass ran over to the big fish, took it and darted most enthusiastically up to her wigwam. When Olaf's partner returned to the trading post, a smile of ecstasy spread on his face.

"Vell pardner, you done real good getting dat big fish, but I tink ve best hit da hay. Ve've got a big day ahead fer to-morra," Olaf reminded Mousey. That night they occupied one side of the lean-to shelters attached to the trading post. Olaf lit an oil lamp so they could see to spread their bedrolls over the hay-filled box bunks the trading post provided. That done, he immediately blew out the lamp, and bid his partner good night. After Mousey tossed and turned noisily for awhile Olaf presumed his right-hand man was preoccupied with his fishing episode, so he lit the lamp again to settle the little man down.

"Dat vas mighty kind a ya to give yer fish to the Indian girl, pardner," Olaf said.

"Yah," Mousey snickered once, then later giggled. "Pardner, I think she was purdy. Cute as a lady bug, I keep thinken."

"Hm. Ja taught she was da razberries, huh?" Olaf joshed along.

"Vell, good night pardner. Pleasant dreams." He blew out the lamp.

Olaf was about to doze off, but Mousey continued, "Pardner, we gonna be here a few days?"

"Ja, pardner, maybe four, five." Olaf yawned loudly. "Best get yer rest now."

"I'm glad we be stayin here a while. Good night my friend, Swede."

"Good night, Mousey."

An hour later, the wildest ruckus broke the night's silence. The trading post sounded like a battle ground, and there was screaming as though someone was being murdered. Frenzied dogs barked and howled in agitation. Mousey jumped up in deathly fear.

"Sh!" Olaf urged. The two listened to the sounds of violent cursing followed by what sounded like several cracks of a whip-- and more cries continued.

Mousey shook and whined in sympathy for whoever was being threshed so violently. Finally, all quieted down, except for howling dogs.

Olaf attempted to explain about the southern slaves, asking Mousey to try to forget it and get some sleep. But Olaf tossed, too, recalling such floggings he'd received from a tyrant landlord for the least unprovoked reasons back in the old country.

* * *

Olaf and Mousey rose early in the morning, neither having slept very well because of the racket in the camp last night. But, the little pardner was thinking about getting back to that fishing spot in hopes of having even better luck tonight, he confided to Olaf.

Leaving their shack, the men were horrified to see a wretched Negro stretched out in a standing position through the night. Olaf's anger raged within, seeing such violence going on in America. It made his blood boil! Slaves came to the North with their southern owners quite regularly now, and many owners were promoting expansion of such barbaric behavior in the whole country.

Mousey looked up at his big friend as if to say - certainly, you won't let that happen. Do something. Swede could not interfere.

"Mousey, dat's da law vare dese men come from. Negroes are slaves, and dey are owned - like a man buys a horse from anudder. Someday, good vite folks are gonna stand up and do vots right fer all people, maybe."

Olaf was prepared to head out early, planning to eat their victuals later, along with hot coffee they'd make. While they were hitching the horses, Muhoni called.

"Monsieur! Monsieur! Come! Falppajacks." She waved them in.

Muhoni showed delight when Olaf gave her a sack of flour in

111

return for breakfast. Olaf grinned, while Mousey snickered at the most welcome invitation to a fine breakfast of fried fish and pancakes, with hot steaming coffee. She explained her trader had left on business to the saw mill down the river, obviously to share the exciting news of Burbank's plan for land travel. Olaf and Muhoni tried to discuss the previous night's flogging. Though Olaf shared her pain, he couldn't really understand what she was saying.

The men worked up a sweat that first day cutting tall straight white pine, trimming the branches, and floating them down river to the desired site. The dray wagon was also filled with eight foot lengths of six inch logs for the surface of the short bridges the men planned for construction.

Olaf was eager to get one bridge started, so he pulled the king-pin, releasing the double-trees from his wagon. After attaching a heavy log chain from it to a large log in the stream, the strong horses were put to the task of pulling it out of the water and into position on the bank. From there, the ends were set down into the bank, leveling the bridge with the ground from opposite sides. The smaller eight-inch logs were laid across the top, after being sheared on two sides with the broad ax, so horses and wagon wheels could cross over that surface with relative ease.

Satisfied with their accomplishments, the two men headed back to the trading post. Mousey admitted being all tuckered out, but he'd have enough energy for fishing again, he assured Olaf.

Reaching the post, they found the southern men had already left camp. Chambois told of selling them a raft that was taking them down to St. Anthony Falls to catch a steamer south. They were angry over their slave attempting an escape into the north woods. The trader apologized for the ugly scene of last night. Olaf said he was equally unhappy of having to hear of such devilish behavior again.

"Come Monsieur, I have someone you must meet in the post," said the trader eagerly. Olaf followed with hesitation.

"Monsieur Wilson, meet Monsieur Olsson." Chambois introduced the two men.

"How do you do, Swede Olsson. I heard all about you down at St. Paul when I was talking with Burbank. He spoke very highly of you, so I presume you and I have got lots to talk about," he said.

Olaf was a little confused, but he soon learned who Wilson was. Mr. Wilson, an affable, energetic gentleman, not unlike Mr. Burbank himself, had bought a piece of choice land just south a couple miles of the post, and was having that area platted for a town and residential lots. No doubt it would become the center serving the farmers in the Sauk Valley. Wilson said he already had dozens of German families from the East organized to move out in the spring. Olaf assured him there'd be reliable transportation ready for freight and passenger travel by then.

Enthused about Mr. Wilson's ambitious project, Olaf forgot about Mousey. Finishing his business with Wilson, Olaf walked down the bank a ways, but suddenly stopped at the most unexpected sight. There, a few hundred yards up-stream, sat Mousey at arm's-length with the Indian maiden he'd given the fish to last night. Olaf, astounded, stopped to watch the amazing scene, for his partner, a plain simple little boy in mind, had found someone to be with. Oh, it wouldn't be easy for the little man and the maiden to communicate by words, the Swede knew. Mousey couldn't read or write, much less understand the Indian language. But there they were, two of God's creatures totally absorbed with each other, and Olaf marveled at the miracle of human companionship.

Feeling guilty for intruding on Mousey's special moment, Olaf withdrew to his shelter. If last night's distant encounter tickled the little man's heartstrings, what on earth will it be like tonight, Olaf mused.

About a half hour past dark, Mousey came running, giggling and babbling so wildly Olaf could hardly understand a word he was trying to say.

"Settle down pardner, or yer gonna split yer ribs vide open, laughin dat vay," Olaf joked, glad to see his partner's display of happiness. He lit the lamp to get a full view of Mousey's excitement.

"Vell, vot happened, pardner? Did you talk to her?"

Mousey looked confused. "No. I couldn't." Mousey tried explaining. "I say one thing, she say other. We can't understand either one." His eyes looked sad suddenly. "I want to talk with her. How can I, big friend?"

Grasping for a way to help his frustrated friend, Olaf kept prying; "Tell me, vot else did ya do vile ya sat der so long?"

"Ah," he sighed. "She smiled at me...and...and...I smiled back. We did that for a long time. Then, pardner, know what?"

"No, vot?" Olaf urged encouragingly.

"She play music on a wood stick. Purdy, purdy, music." He was reliving his magic moment all over again.

"Oh, it's an Indian flute she played, I'm sure. Dey sound purdy," Olaf agreed. "So, dat's da vey ya have ta show how ya care. Ya smile, and give tings." He began recalling last night; "like the nice fish you gave her. She played purdy music for ya, and vell, someday maybe yu'll vant ta listen to her music all da time, and she'll be happy if ya can provide, like catching fish fer her." Mousey's eyes were fixed on space as he obviously pondered such a happy life for himself. "How did ya feel ven she smiled at ya like ya said, pardner?"

"Oh, I broke out with goose bumps, big friend Olaf. I had goose bumps where I never had em before," he grinned shyly.

Olaf chuckled, patting him on the back. "I tink da love bug bit ya, dat's vot I tink. But I yist remembered someting. Mr. Chambois mentioned her name. I tink he said, 'dat is Little Singin Bird fishing by Mousey.' Ja, Ja, dat's it - Little Singin Bird."

"That's good name for her," Mousey's smile was huge. He started humming, and then singing as if in a dream world, oblivious of Olaf's presence. "Singing Bird up high in a tree, I think she's singing just for me." Repeating those words over and over again, he drifted off in a dreamland of love and make believe.

* * *

Muhoni was calling the men before the horses were harnessed the next morning. She was ecstatic over the growing infatuation between Mousey and Singing Bird and wanted to talk to Olaf about it. She said the young Indian maiden had hounded her all day yesterday with the same concerns Mousey had mentioned to Olaf, not being able to converse with her newfound kind friend.

Singing Bird had asked Muhoni to talk to Mousey about her feelings.

Unfortunately, Mousey couldn't understand Muhoni either but Olaf caught the meaning and explained, which elated the little fellow. Mousey asked Olaf to tell Muhoni that he couldn't wait to see Singing Bird again, and catch more fish for her, and listen to her play her flute, if she would. Muhoni laughed, assuring Mousey she'd tell Singing Bird all he'd said. Muhoni appeared most exuberant in her role of playing the part of matchmaker.

Breakfast was to become a daily courtesy of the jovial Mrs. Chambois, but Olaf always reciprocated with a gift in return, the way folks usually did on the frontier.

Now, it was time to head out and set more large logs across three more creeks today. The one began the day before needed finishing, so that would be the starting point as they headed downstream. When they reached the site, Olaf's mouth dropped open in shock! The cross pieces had been torn off! Something or somebody was opposed to a permanent bridge no doubt, and Olaf wondered, at first, if the Indians had done the damage.

"Holy horse feathers!" Mousey blurted out. "I'd hate to see the size of the beavers could do that!"

"Vell, I doubt dat vuz done by busy veavers, Mousey," Olaf explained, unable to keep a straight face at Mousey's observation. "Dey do tings in an orderly vey. No doubt der's some rascal vite people doin dis kind a dirty virk, I tink." He scratched his head in utter outrage. "Vell let's put it back tagetter agin, and finish da utters like ve planned. Tonight, I guess ve come out here and votch; try ta ketch da culprits in da act."

Finishing the day by completing all log crossings, the men knocked off early and returned to the trading post for some rest and relaxation, knowing tonight they'd have to try to catch the culprit sabotaging their work.

* * *

"Mousey, I'm damned sorry ya had ta leave little Singing Bird so early dis evenin. I told ya, ya didn't have to come, ya know?" Olaf said as they headed four miles down river where they had built the last two bridges.

"I think she'll wait for me, pardner. I don't know how, but I'm starting to understand some of the things she tells me. You know, the way her face and hands talk. When I say, 'Mousey go, Mousey come back' she understood me, I'm sure as horses don't fly."

Olaf, feeling delight over the little fellow's thrilling brush with love, chuckled. Then he noticed that Mousey became very quiet, showing a concerned expression on his face. "Vell, vot's eatin at ya now, pardner?"

"Mousey's worried some. Tonight Singing Bird's father came. Looking and sounding gruff, he took her back to her home. I don't know what he said, but Singing Bird looked sad when she left. I could not understand what the old man said to me, either."

"Hm." Olaf tried to reason such a reaction by her father. "Mousey, know vot I tink?" he concluded. "I tink it's yist possible her fatter is vorried he's not gonna git anyting for her. They sell their daughters for someting."

"Aw pardner, I have tiny little money, ya know," Mousey moaned.

"Naw, it doesn't alvays mean a lot a money." Olaf had another idea. "Tell ya vot, to-morra ve'll git Muhoni to talk to da chief. Ya vant ta do dat?"

The little handyman had never had such emotional problems in his life! He'd never had a girlfriend before, especially one who talked to him.

It couldn't be all that serious, Olaf reassured his partner, as they reached their work site well after dark. He could see clearly in the full moonlight that their earlier work was left undisturbed

Two of the bridges were very close together; only a couple hundred yards apart. Olaf had reservations about leaving his friend, but Mousey insisted he wanted the responsibility of guarding one bridge himself. If trouble came he would call Olaf who could run that short distance in a hurry.

The sky was filled with a multitude of stars this clear night; many more than usual, it seemed to the cautious Swede. As he hid in wait behind some bushes he was feeling compassion for Mousey and his quest for the romance which had evaded him for so long. Then, he considered his own precarious romantic life with

Marianne - she a thousand miles away. His mind filled with pleasant memories--and worries--and he hoped first that he'd receive a letter from her soon, and second, that the year would go fast so she'd come back to him.

Hours passed waiting, and it looked like the watch was for naught. Maybe the culprit would never come back, Olaf hoped.

Suddenly, Olaf thought he heard a weak cry! He jumped up! It could have been a small screech owl, he figured. After a moment, the cry came again, more distinct this time! Olaf quickly dashed through the trees, his heart pounding in concern for little Mousey, who'd been caught off guard before he could call for help, most likely.

Olaf could see the shadow of a man beating Mousey mercilessly and that the little victim had no voice left to cry out. With one desperate leap, Olaf threw himself down the bank and knocked the violent attacker off his fragile victim! Who was this dirty scoundrel? The moonlight revealed immediately that it was his enemy, Scarface Williams. Williams now charged and momentarily stunned Olaf with a rock to the side of the head. The big Swede's eyes blurred, but cleared in time to see Williams coming at him again with one of the eight foot cross rails, raised for a deathly blow. At the last second Olaf jerked away as the timber came crashing next to his head. With Olaf's senses quickly restored, his pulse pounded in a rage that anyone would mangle such a harmless little man as Mousey, and for no reason whatsoever. But now, even Olaf's life was threatened. He ducked from Williams' blow and sent his own right fist with the power of his immense body behind, connecting solidly to Williams' jaw. Olaf heard a cracking! He had broken the jaw clean! Still the violent devil kept coming. Olaf, showing mercy, landed blows only to his body until Williams too, lay lifeless, just as Mousey now lay.

Olaf feared the worst. He knelt down pleading: "Mousey, Mousey, can ya hear me? It's Olaf, yer pardner. Please, Mousey, move some." Olaf took his large red handkerchief, soaked it in the river, and ran back to clean Mousey's bloody swollen face. One eye had completely swelled closed. Still, he lay motionless. Olaf near desperation, leaned down and listened for a meager breath.

Then touching Mousey's neck, he felt a weak pulse. He soaked his handkerchief several times, squeezing the water so it dripped on Mousey's face and forehead, flushing the blood, still spewing from his nose and mouth. It appeared Mousey was dying.

Olaf couldn't help it. He began to sob. Why had this happened to his harmless little partner? Then, Olaf heard one weak moan, then another. Mousey was responding! At least he wasn't dead as first thought.

"Mousey, my good friend! Mousey, can you hear me now?" Olaf wiped tears from his face with his sleeve. "It's Olaf, and you'll be safe now. Mousey, can ya hear me?" he tried again.

"Ya, Olaf," Mousey mumbled ever so weakly. More bathing of his mutilated face gradually restored his consciousness. After awhile Mousey began whimpering and speaking more words. "Olaf, Mousey sorry. Mousey not watch close enough," he muttered, blaming himself for the tragedy.

"Awe, c'mon pardner, don't tink about it. Ya did everyting ya could," Olaf let one last sob go. "Rest quietly for a few minutes, and I'll take ya back to Singin Bird, and she'll get ya back to good health in nuttin flat. You'll see."

Olaf looked over at Mousey's attacker. Scarface Williams was writhing around on the ground like a snake ready to strike again. Olaf planted his size twelve foot on Williams' back with the full weight of his body behind it, disabling him agin. "Lay still, ya devil or I'll knock the rest of your teeth out a yer miserable mouth."

Getting a rope from the wagon, he tied Scarface securely with knots he knew from his sailing days that could never be pulled loose. He was not gentle in throwing the rascal over the wagon's end gate. Then, laying a buffalo robe on the front of the box, he carried Mousey up and gently placed him close to the spring seat so he could keep an eye on his suffering friend who still coughed blood into Olaf's wet handkerchief.

Dawn was breaking when Olaf's wagon rolled into the trading post. Chambois was readying his boat to head north to Crow Wing with a priest, Father Pierz, who had been a missionary to the natives up there for the past ten years. Muhoni was fixing the food box for their journey.

118

Not seeing Mousey riding on the spring seat with Olaf, all came hurriedly to see what had happened. Everyone, including the Priest, was devastated at the sight of the mutilated, swollen and bleeding face of the little near lifeless body lying on the animal robe. Olaf carried his partner up to his bunk where all stood around in shock. Father Pierz introduced himself to Olaf. Being moved by Mousey's condition, the priest offered a prayer asking the Lord to ease Mousey's pain and grant him speedy recovery.

Mousey, who hadn't said a word, suddenly turned his head. Then a weak smile came over him, with only one eye opening slightly, he whispered, "Thank you, Father, for the prayer." Then he passed out in sleep.

Singing Bird, noticing the concerned gathering, came running. Seeing Mousey badly bruised and suffering, she stood next to his bunk weeping, her tears rolling down her cheeks in near streams. Muhoni consoled her in the native tongue, then brought a basin of water and toweling, with which the Indian maiden tenderly commenced cleaning Mousey with loving tenderness.

The men withdrew to talk amongst themselves about the dangers of the wilderness now that more and more people were coming.

Before Chambois left, he and Muhoni told Olaf they had had a talk with Singing Bird's father, Rocks Falling in Water - Falling Rocks, they called him for short - about *Oo Wing Yon Zitkadong*, Little Singing Bird and Mousey's romantic cooing. Falling Rocks was worried for fear Singing Bird would get caught and have a baby like her older sister and he wouldn't get anything for her. Nobody would pay for two mouths to feed so he was only watching out for his self interests, he said. Both Muhoni and Joe assured the father that Olaf and Mousey were honorable people and would no doubt pay handsomely for Singing Bird. It was decided that the parties concerned would talk when Mousy felt better.

As luck would have it, the day Olaf brought Scarface Williams in, a paddle wheeler happened to be scheduled to go to the John Wilson's landing down river a couple miles. Olaf took the broken mouthed ruffian to the boat pilot who agreed to deliver him to Sheriff Sam Sullivan down at St. Paul. Olaf scribbled his grievances against Williams and said he hoped to have the rascal put away for awhile. Besides, with his dangling two halves of a lower jaw, he'd need to be wired up by Doc Farmer, the horse doctor, who patched up broken bones on animals and derelicts like Williams.

While Mousey recuperated under the tender care of Muhoni and Singing Bird, Olaf spent some time down at John Wilson's settlement, helping Wilson and three young farmers from Indiana. This group had come as an advance party to make their claims and build a few temporary log cabins to house incoming families until more permanent housing could be built. Olaf picked out a piece of acreage for a prospective horse and wagon station, convinced the men were serious about settling the area by springtime.

After two days of pampering, Mousey was looking fairly good, his one eye near normal, the other still black and swollen. Olaf was relieved that Mousey could at least see shadows with the battered eye. Perhaps a full recovery was possible.

"Pardner, I vas really scared fer ya. Taught ya ver dead, fer sure," Olaf confided as they hit the hay on the fourth night.

"Ya, me too, pardner." The little fellow was still dazed from the pounding, and was trying to sort out what had happened. "Pardner, I think God came and said a prayer over me."

"Vell, dat's possible I s'pose," Olaf agreed, but wondered if Mousey was somewhat confused, having heard Father Pierz's prayer that first night.

After a few moments, Mousey started chattering about his infatuation with Singing Bird. "Pardner, I'm scared her Papa be unreasonable, and I won't be able to have Singing Bird then."

"Vell, to-morra mornin ve meet vit Fallin Rocks and ve'll see. Ya know, her Papa's a good carpenter. He vas helpin build da cabins down stream dese last days." Olaf chuckled. "I gave him a bunch of tobacco smoke, and he hung on me like a cockleburr. Gotta try to tink hopeful pal."

After a bit, Mousey started giggling.

"Vell, don't treat yer pardner like an orphan, Mousey," Olaf grinned. "Vot's ticklin yer funny bone now?"

The little fella continued to laugh, apparently out of embarrassment, but finally tried to explain what delighted him so.

He started in a serious vein: "Well, ya know my friend Swede, I never touched a woman before, and when little Singing Bird held me to make me feel good--well--" He started such giggling again that he couldn't talk.

"Hey, yer pardner's a big boy, Mousey." Olaf chuckled at his little friend's behavior. "Vot'd ya do? Kiss her?"

"Aw, I couldn't do that yet," Mousey snickered. "Promise me you won't laugh, Olaf, and I'll tell ya."

Olaf was biting his lip, trying to control himself. "I svear."

"Well, then, Singing Bird held me like I remember as a little baby, my head right next to her--her--ya know." He put his hands up to his chest.

"Ja, Ja, Ja," Olaf responded, eager to know more of Mousey's first romantic encounter. "Den vot?"

"Well, she had very loose dress on, and--and--aw, this is tough, pardner."

"Go ahead, ya gotta tell somebody. I'm your friend, ya know." Olaf was relishing the moment.

"Well, ya, then. I saw her--the whole thing--right next to my face as she held me. It was her, her soft--her pretty soft t - t - titty!" He giggled, feeling foolish like a little boy who'd wet his pants.

"So, vot'd ya do about dat?"

"I - I - I looked on those soft pillows a long time, then I couldn't help myself, I--I reached up and touched her there."

"Vot'd she do then?" Olaf kept prying.

"She held me tighter and rocked me faster. So, I think we both liked it, pardner. Never, never had such a thing happen in all my life."

Olaf chuckled in sympathy with Mousey. "Vell, Mousey, yer all man, ya know. Tomorra ve'll see vot her Papa says. Have pleasant dreams, now." The little fellow, though nearly twice Olaf's age, started humming, and soon singing about his fabulous romantic encounter. Olaf pondered how a man nearly four score years could have been so sheltered from life's normal blessings.

This time Olaf interrupted: "Pardner, how'd ya like to move up here next spring and care for the horses and vagons at the new station ve'll be building here?"

"Really, Olaf? You're not kidding me?" Mousey squeaked, thrilled by the thought. "Then I would be close to her always! Oh, my, I've got a lot to think about, haven't I?" He began humming again. Olaf chuckled to himself, out of happiness for Mousey.

* * *

It was the last day of the week, and Olaf and Mousey would be heading back to St. Anthony Falls. But not until after Falling Rocks gave his decision on what his price would be for Singing Bird. Mousey was nervous as a bear cat in a trap. He wanted his little Indian maiden more than anything in the world.

Chambois and Muhoni came over to help interpret for the two sides in the negotiations, as Falling Rocks marched forward with an air of importance about him and his delicate anxious daughter by his side.

Olaf was confident an amicable agreement could be reached, but Mousey already looked skeptical and dejected.

Falling Rocks eyed each present, to show the importance of the occasion, and then spoke firmly: "*Oo Wing Yong Zitkadong Ong Ska Sungktonka.*"

Chambois translated. "Singing Bird's father will give his favorite daughter for a white horse. A reasonable price, he thinks."

Mousey looked even more devastated. Where in the world would he ever come up with such an expensive barter for the precious maiden?

Olaf thought about what he'd do to have Marianne - give everything. "Mousey, don't give up hope, now," Olaf cautioned. "Fer such a prized gem, it sounds purdy reasonable ta me." He took Mousey aside. "Pardner, ve got some good vite horses dat vont cost too much, I'm sure. Besides, I promise ta help ya get vun from our stables. Ve'll strike a deal, and yu'll have Singing Bird ta share yer life vit forever."

The little fella smiled and went to Singing Bird. They looked at each other adoringly, while Olaf, Falling Rocks and Chambois worked out the details for an exchange of the properties agreed on.

"Mousey, it's all arranged! I tink ya better seal da agreement vit a kiss, don't ya?" Olaf proclaimed.

Muhoni laughed, and told Singing Bird what Olaf had suggested. Singing Bird glowed shyly, looked at her father who nodded, then smiled at Mousey, waiting for the token of endearment. Mousey puckered up and confronted Singing Bird with a kiss. She reciprocated in kind to the delight of the folks witnessing, who all cheered the happy occasion.

GUEST OF LITTLE CROW

"Well, Olaf, my Ada is certainly impressed the way you present yourself in our circle of friends--your fine manners, and all. It's a pleasure having you join us for the concerts and immigrant benefits."

"Tanks, Mr. Burbank, I enyoy doze tings. You and da Missus have been more den kind ta me, fer sure, deze four years."

More and more time was being spent in casual conversations now that the Swede had learned to speak a fair English. Olaf wondered, too, if his boss wasn't trying to encourage his wooing one or more of the young eligible sophisticated women of town. Perhaps Mr. Burbank felt bad about Olaf's Swedish flicka messing up his life's plans. Olaf had purged Gerda from his mind long ago, especially after meeting the dazzling métis who sparked a love he'd never known.

"What do you think of the Whipple girls, my boy? Either would make a fine catch, if you ask me."

"Oh," Olaf chuckled, "der certnly fine and lovely ladies." He chuckled again, probably more out of embarrassment than anything. Now, he wished he could reveal his true feelings about Marianne LaMond, but on the other hand, he wondered if anyone would understand, her being part Indian.

Obviously sensing Olaf's mild discomfort, Burbank quickly changed the subject to business matters.

"Swede," --now, at work everybody called him Swede-- "with the settlement well under way eighty miles up the Mississippi at Sauk Rapids, and people flocking in that valley in less than a year, we need to set our sights on helping other budding settlements, as well." He paused in thought, "Oh, again I say you did a hell of a job improving the road and bridges. You've set up a prize area for us," Burbank praised.

"Vell, I had good help vit Mousey." Olaf chuckled. "It vas a small miracle dat Mousey found his Singin Bird, and he's settin up a fine vagon station der fer us, fer sure. Guess vot? Mousey's soon gonna be a Papa! Vould ya believe it?"

"That's great! Olaf. All because you had confidence in him," Burbank smiled. He paused, lighting his cheroot again. "Swede, I'd like you to go on another rather important fact finding trip."

"Sure, Mr. Burbank. Vot is it?" Olaf's ears perked up.

"You know, Parsons Johnson and his wife settled down the Minnesota, where the river makes a sharp right turn and heads northwest. It's about eighty miles from here. Several folks had joined him the last week."

"Ja. Ja. I've been down der once, but I usually cut off at St. Peter village and turn straight vest. It's faster to Fort Ridgely and da Lower Indian Agency dat vay."

"I know. But, there's an eager bunch of people beginning to settle that area, and I think we'd better keep our eyes open before anyone else gets the idea to open up wagon services there."

"Fer sure. Mr.Yohnson let me stay in da unfinished big vooden building vit an upstairs, and everyting. He vas goin to call it da Mankato House, he said. Same as da town to be named fer Chief Mankato, I s'pose. Mrs. Yohnson fixed a very good meal, I member."

"That right? Well, anyway, more and more folks are heading down there on steam boats. And further up stream, the settlement of New Ulm is taking off too."

Liking what he was hearing, Olaf leaned forward in his chair.

"The steamboat's been getting the lion's share of the business. Even the lumber for that Mankato House you speak of, went up river by boat from St. Paul, I understand," Burbank added.

"Ja, but steamers can't alvays make it ven da vauter's low," Olaf noted, "and it's froze over fer six monts." He scratched his head, contemplating such a venture, and a chance for some pleasure.

"I see you've got your thinking wheels turning. What do you say, son?"

"Vell, I vundered, it bein close, if I could take an extra day; go up river ta da Lower Indian Agency ta see how der fairin?"

Burbank laughed impulsively. "Of course, my boy. I kind of thought you'd more than likely want to do that. And Olaf, if you say so, we'll start wagon and stage service there on a scheduled basis."

"Ja." Olaf grinned, knocking the ashes from his pipe bowl. "I'll take da military trail, as bad as it is, to Mankato to-morra. Ya know, ve might haf ta improve some of da river crossins, and do a little corduroyin of some soft spots before settin a schedule."

Burbank grinned, knowing the job was in reliable hands, again.

*   *   *

Riding along on his rangy dappled gray mare, Olaf headed Southwest along the Minnesota. Breathing in the early morning fall air with its cool damp meadow freshness, the trees turning reds, yellows, and browns was invigorating to both him and the faithful steed under him. The pastoral setting of grassy rolling hills along the placid river inspired thoughts of the sea when large swells of water-not prairie-dominated; reaching out to the horizon. The river woods were the ocean's islands in this rolling terrain. Farther down, the valley widened to a mile or two of trees and foliage on either side of the river. Olaf saw that in some places bluffs dropped down in steps from two hundred feet to the bottom land. Travel by wagon or horseback was fast and easy away from the river, but the thoroughfare from place to place was always the waterways for early settlers.

Olaf had seen many a steamboat carrying supplies for the relocated Indians chugging ninety miles southwest against the current of the Minnesota river, where it made an abrupt right turn, then headed northwest to its source, the Big Stone Lake. Just below a high coteau the meandering River Rouge - now the Red River - headed north three hundred miles toward Hudson Bay. Someday I'd like to go there, he thought.

Olaf stopped only long enough to fill his pipe, and allow Dancer Girl time to graze, drink and rest.

Parsons Johnson had picked a grand site at the river's bend for his town of Mankato. A dozen or so modest frame cabins already dotted the landscape and several more were under construction. Up on the bluffs, a few eager farmers were staking out farm land not yet surveyed.

Reaching the new settlement, Olaf proceeded to the large two-story Mankato House, dominating the landscape. Anticipating a night's lodging, and an opportunity to discuss transportation with Mr. Johnson, Olaf found the host most enthusiastic and cordial.

"Hello, Swede Olsson," the Mr. Parsons Johnson called out, sighting the strapping visitor riding up. "My Lord, you're our first two-time visitor!" he laughed congenially. "With such traffic, we'll soon be competing with St. Paul."

Olaf laughed over Parsons Johnson's humor. "Vit yer optimistic tinken, ya yist might do dat, Sir."

"Come now, it'll soon be dark. I know we'll have more guests eventually, more than you can imagine, Swede. But right now, it does get a bit lonesome around here. You wouldn't deny my invitation to stay the night. Mrs. Johnson makes the best beef stew this side of Chicago and we'd both be delighted if you'd join us."

"Vit dat generous invite, who could turn ya down. Mr. Yohnson?"

Mrs. Johnson was most excited having the frontiersman for dinner and an evening of conversation. The Swede always had entertaining tales to tell about the frontier, and his infatuation with the Indians.

"Mr. Yohnson, yu've got da town goin good vit all da buildin," Olaf complimented.

"Mr. Olsson, this country is going to boom like crazy in the next few years. I'll bet my life on it," he practically exploded.

"Oh, and please call me Parsons, and do away with the formalities, if you don't mind."

"Dat I like. And folks in my business usually call me Svede."

Well, the town founder soon brought out some grape wine, apologizing for it being only homemade from local wild grapes, and bragged that some day his community would draw high class people who'd require fine wines imported from Europe. Mr. Johnson was a dreamer, but men like that were the builders of this country, Olaf had concluded.

The town king pin was ecstatic at Olaf's proposition to set up two regularly scheduled stagecoach runs each week. With horse changing stations every fifteen miles, the entire trip to St. Paul would take only one day, Olaf explained. Parsons Johnson was a bright promoter, offering free lodging for Burbank drivers making the return trip to St. Paul the following day.

The two shook hands and the deal was struck. The congenial talks ending, Olaf retired early, anticipating the rest of his trip.

* * *

The Swede whistled his delight as he and Dancer Girl moved on to New Ulm, twenty-five miles west and further up river. The scenic beauty of this new town intrigued Olaf with its level approach from the North and the wide valley quickly rising in a series of wooded bluffs and hills on the South.

Advance settlers were industriously building a town with preplanned character, it appeared. A misty fog set the tiny village off like something out of a fairyland, Olaf thought. The style of a few quaint houses indicated these pioneers were going to be different. More than simple cabins, some of the roofs were steep and the structures were artistic in design. A few had dormers, some had little outcroppings of carpenter's lace, and one of several first homes sported an open turret on its upper level.

Olaf, scratching his head with tingling curiosity, hurried to the north bank of the river where he found a rope ferry in place, but in his excitement and with Dancer Girl's long legs, he was able to ford the river with ease.

A colorful and cheerful man wearing wide red suspenders and a short brimmed hat with a decorated band met Olaf.

"*Gut Morgan*, stranger, I am Frederick Beinhorn, and you are in New Ulm. *Villkomen* to the new city of charm and tradition."

"Good mornin, Sir. Pleased ta meet ya. I'm trilled ta see vot's happenin in dis beautiful valley. I'm Olaf Olsson--or Svede, dey call me--Mr. Meinhorn."

The dapper greeter about popped his suspenders, laughing at Olaf's mispronouncing his name. "*Nein, nein, nein!* Not Meinhorn! Beinhorn. B-e-i-n, Beinhorn. Call me Frederick."

"Oh," Olaf chuckled, embarrassed. "I'm sorry, sir."

"Don't let it bother you, my friend. We are from Wurttemberg, Germany. Most of us anyway are of the Turner society. We plan to bring hundreds of our countrymen to this beautiful valley in the next few years."

As they stood visiting on the river bank, Olaf was impressed with the vivacious town founder explaining his Turners as being culturally consumed, loving their music, drama, and dancing. With a glint in his eye, "Yes, and we love our beer and polka dancing, Swedish friend." Pausing, he asked, "Will you stay the night?"

"Vell, I certnly spect to pay if der's room fer hire."

"Nonsense! You'll be my guest! Frau Beinhorn will treat ya to some fine German food; sausage makers and beer brewer along, we have the essentials of life," he winked warmly. Then, taking Olaf by the arm, he led him to his home - the neat house with the turret on the upper level.

Olaf was flabbergasted. Here, this friendly immigrant invited him to stay and share their hospitality yet never asked of his business. He could have been a scoundrel crook, for that matter. That's trust.

Frederick admitted later that he was a fine judge of character and didn't have to be told of someone's background. He continued relating the virtues of his people, and explained they were social revolutionaries.

"How did you find this charming place?" Olaf asked.

Frederick said he'd been here back in 1852, three years before, and selected this spot. Then, returning to Chicago, he organized the "Chicago Land Society" which recruited pioneers, and his pure society of Turners from the city of Ulm, Germany, to the enchanted valley of this northwestern territory.

Olaf was so overwhelmed with Frederick Beinhorn's enthusiasm for his new town, that not until a delicious German meal, as promised, did the conversation turn to Olaf's business. After Olaf had described his company's proposal for regular stage service to Mankato for the near future, Frau Beinhorn, was especially delighted.

"Ach, it will be good to know there'll be safe travel for the women and children coming soon," she beamed. "We few women are getting worn out from dancing with all these men all the time." She wiped her brow humorously with her hand.

Olaf soon found out what Frau Beinhorn was talking about, for less than a half hour after eating, the total population of the village had descended on the household for an evening of music, dancing and fun. One man played a concertina, they called it, and another a played a fiddle. The brewer came with a huge jug of cooled beer from his deep well. Before long, all nineteen neighbors-four women, the rest men-arrived for the buoyant fellowship. The men wore vests and knee length britches, and the women, bright full length skirts. *Gemuetlichkeit*, they called it.

The big Swede soon learned what these Turners were all about, and he liked what he saw. For instance, he learned how to polka, since none of the women would let him be without at least one dance. He knew he'd look forward to coming back here many times in the future.

What a thrill, Olaf thought. All these new settlers were of high character, people with a vision of creating a new home for themselves. Throngs like them would be coming from the old world of confinement and age old rules of behavior which discouraged self-expression and freedom. Olaf could envision the great valley ready to burst with eager settlers from all parts of the old world, and he liked what was already happening.

* * *

The following day the anxious Swede headed west, away from New Ulm. Now, he would have a chance to see some of his Dakota friends beyond Fort Ridgely, farther up the valley of the Minnesota River.

Having started early, Olaf planned reaching the fort by noon. With a distance of about twenty miles he'd be able to make a courtesy call to the company of men stationed there. Though most of the supplies had come up river on steam boats where the camp was constructed the last two years, Olaf had hauled a few loads overland during the past winter and made friends with some of the happy-go-lucky sergeants on duty.

After enjoying Fort Ridgely hospitality, he hastened on toward the Lower Sioux Agency, still several miles west. Olaf spotted the chiefs' villages along the river. The villages were usually only a few miles apart, a good distance so that the bands could retain their community identity.

Olaf stopped to exchange greetings with Chief Wabasha and his orderly community of Dakota farmers who, though not experienced, were trying to adjust to white man's ways. Olaf shared a smoke with the respected leader, and praised him for his efforts.

The Swede felt compassion for the struggling Dakota, taken from their hunting grounds of vast woods embracing the Mississippi and the St. Croix rivers. The Dakota had been generous to the white man, Olaf knew. The Swedish settlers up north in Center City nearly starved to death, and would have, had the Indians not brought in game and wild rice to help sustain them. My, how soon we forget, the big Swede thought to himself. His eyes moistened, thinking about the horrible life now imposed on the humble nature-loving natives.

Excitement stirred within, as Olaf neared Taoyateduta's village. They hadn't seen each other for a long spell. Approaching the village, Olaf saw the bark lodges constructed for those Dakota showing willingness to pursue the ways of the white man; the less cooperative being satisfied living, as before, in animal hide tepees.

One substantial house stood out, Little Crow's place, which Olaf had visited before. On this warm summer day, most of the squaws and some of their braves sat idly under the shade trees. A few of the lethargic bucks recognized Olaf, and raised their hands in greeting.

Closing in, Olaf caught sight of the chief, himself, tossing his tomahawk at a large tree trunk west of his house. The two had always played tricks on each other, so Olaf got an idea to sneak around the house to surprise the chief.

The idlers watched with interest as the strapping Swede took his rope off Dancer Girl and stole around the corner. On closer scrutiny, Olaf noticed the chief was dissecting a rat he'd pinned to the tree, tossing his tomahawk at it from thirty feet away. Taking dead aim, Little Crow reared back to let his weapon fly, but at that exact moment Olaf threw his lasso, catching the Chief's arm on the back swing and the tomahawk went sailing straight up in the air, above the trees. Little Crow, displaying the shocked expression of his life swung around. Upon seeing Olaf, he let loose a huge howl of delight and then went into minor convulsions. The other Dakota watching, laughed and applauded the silliness, as their chief rolled on the ground in hysterics.

"Damn you, Tall Like Oak!" he roared, catching his breath.

"Got even vith Taoyateduta for de last trick pulled on Tall Like Oak," Olaf admitted, joining in a harmony of guffaws.

The tomfoolery over, the trickster friends exchanged warm greetings, giving each other a huge bear hug. Little Crow invited Olaf into his new cozy house. It was well built with planked flooring. Clearly more substantial than the common bark lodges of the others, Olaf was impressed with the neatness, and noticed certain pictures on one wall that intrigued him.

"This picture from Washington--earlier times," Little Crow explained. "This one father Taoyateduta. The next grandfather, also named Taoyateduta, great chiefs of Dakota. Both go to great Father in Washington," he boasted.

"Chief, you and yer fotter and yer grandfotter have done much in leading yer people - specially in dese times of cruel and unfair treatment," Olaf acknowledged.

"Now, I am invited to go to Washington to speak for my people, even though these trips have little to show done much good," Little Crow said. As if wanting to avoid the subject, he called to a young woman. "Nawki, make strong black coffee for Tall Like Oak." He reminded Olaf that it was he who introduced the Chief to coffee drinking, which Little Crow said he liked as much as the hairy people now. He always saved enough coffee to share with his tall friend.

The Chief moved over to a small wooden crate in the corner and took out a container. "But first have small treat;" he winked at Olaf; "Good corn spirits," he said. Olaf took a gulp, but had all he could do to keep from up-chucking from the potent substance.

Holding up his pipe, Olaf nodded at the Chief, who grunted his pleasure and retrieved his own. He filled both pipes with his fine tobacco and lit them. Both puffed pleasurably for some time.

Once they got to discussing political issues, Little Crow reminded Olaf that the Dakota were angered over the greedy traders taking their government land pay for clearing trader debts, which were greatly exaggerated.

Wowinape ended the discussion by barging in, thrilled having seen his big friend's horse tied to the post. "Tall Like Oak! Tall Like Oak!" he shouted, excited finding his old fishing companion from Kaposia.

"Sufferin vild cats, Vowinape! Look at ya!" Olaf near shouted. "Yu've grown half a foot!" He noticed the youngster, now nine, had successfully snared some game. "Vot ya got der? Vow! Dat's a vopper of a yack rabbit, if ya ask me."

Wowinape looked admiringly up at his friend. Olaf stood over him with his great paw on the youngster's shoulder and kept squeezing it, showing his affection for the lad.

"Good see, Tall Like Oak," Wowinape grinned, using a little English he'd learned back at Kaposia.

"Nawki!" The Chief called the youngest of his wives, demanding she skin the rabbit, Olaf noticed. His fat wives sauntered around like queen bees, not called on to do any tasks.

The three males were content, for now, exchanging hunting and fishing tales while Olaf and Little Crow smoked their pipes.

Little Crow's Nawki prepared a fine supper. She cooked a prairie chicken the Chief had shot that morning, along with Wowinape's rabbit. The potatoes were a gift from Chief Wabasha, he admitted, explaining they did not always eat so well.

Nawki had fixed a fine meal and Olaf complimented her to Little Crow. The Chief had many wives. Three were daughters of a western Wahpeton Chief and could not speak English at all. So when the chief relayed Olaf's compliments, he did so to the fat ones, who responded with typical womanish giggles, but he did not look at Nawki who did all the work.

The two men continued their discussion for several hours while gazing into the fireplace. Little Crow's two favorite wives fussed, arranging robes and blankets near where the men visited.

Olaf finally stood. "Vell, my friend, I tink I'd better get movin' down da road. I can reach Fort Ridgely in an hour. Then tomorra morning I'll head north fer St. Paul."

"No, no, no, no," Little Crow insisted. "Stay here tonight! We never know how many times have left together. Sleep on robes women have laid out. I plan to stay by fire, too. Don't like to sleep in bed boxes upstairs. Indians like to stay close to Mother Earth. This time stay. Make Taoyateduta happy."

"Vell, it is very peaceful here. But I don't vant ta put ya to any trouble."

Little Crow grunted, "Huh," poking his pipe stem into Olaf's ribs playfully. "You stay. Two wives and children gone west to visit Wahpeton family. Much room here."

"Vell, ja. I'll stay den. Yer a kind man, Taoyateduta."

Again, they sat quietly for a time, gazing at the glowing embers and smoking their pipes - contemplating. Olaf watched the two older wives with interest, for they worked together as a team while arranging the beds for the night. They seemed to be making a game of their task. But his eyes were drawn more to the thin, but well-proportioned woman. She could have been Little Crow's daughter rather than wife, Olaf thought. She was obviously cast off for some reason and appeared sad not being included in family activities.

Little Crow always spoke harshly to her. "Nawki, put more logs on fire," he ordered. She jumped up, hurrying to the task, eager to please him.

The warmer the house got, the more clothes were being shed by the Chief. The others also undressed. The big fellow had witnessed naked Indians before, as in the summer time. That was their custom. But, for some reason, in the confines of the house, nudity seemed a little threatening to the Swede's Scandinavian modesty.

"Tall Like Oak, take off clothes and let skin breathe like it is meant to. Dakota never got sick until given your tight clinging things. Now our numbers grow fewer by getting white man's diseases. You can be natural here, while at Taoyateduta's house. Only wear clothes to keep warm, and small cloth for modesty, if you like."

Olaf agreed to removing his shirt, but that was where he'd draw the line. The two older fat wives flaunted teasingly around Little Crow indicating the hour was getting late and they had needs too.

Little Crow laughed. "See, my friend, my two favorite cuddly bears. They are nice and soft to lay on. Little scrawny wife need to put on some flesh on her bones, pointing to Nawki, then she will be good to take to bed."

Now, Olaf certainly could have taken issue with the Chief on his choosing the voluptuous females to such a pretty young woman with a willowy body and well-developed breasts. Prettier than a picture, he thought. It was not his place to complain, so decided he best keep his thoughts to himself.

"I am sure you are tired after long ride, my friend," Little Crow said, "and I am ready to lay with my doting wives. You will be comfortable on those robes laid out for you."

The big Swede thanked the Chief for his kindness, and at Little Crow's suggestion, decided to smoke his pipe a while longer. His host said he would enjoy the tobacco smell all night if Olaf wanted to smoke.

It was quiet for a few moments. But, eventually, the big fellow's attention was drawn to Little Crow's big bed where his two wives lay, one on either side of the Chief. The gradual movements, and finally, the wild undulation of the buffalo robes was more than slightly distracting. All that came to mind was the herd of buffalo stampeding when he was on the hunt with the métis out on the Dakota territory.

It was not the easiest thing to be a lonely bachelor in a family oriented world. So, to keep his sanity, Olaf knew he'd have to turn away. His eyes then became fixed on the poor disgraced young woman who sat on the far edge of the big earthen fireplace. The room was almost dark, but with the reflection of the fire on her beautiful body she seemed to be glowing from within. It caused a most sensual feeling in the big Swede. He smiled to himself, and felt no guilt at all for his lustfulness. My God, he thought, they can't deprive a poor man of everything. And he began drawing heavily on his pipe. The young woman began massaging herself in a most rapturous way, having to be content, more than likely, with providing her own stimulation, thought Olaf.

The Scandinavian was exhausted from observing the goings on, and was feeling somewhat guilty thinking of the pledge he had made with his lovely métis, Marianne LaMond, that they'd be true to each other until they could be joined forever. He pulled the cover over his head, not wishing to be teased any longer. Finally, he was able to shut out the local distractions and concentrated on the first time he'd met the alluring beauty from the land of the Northern Lights. Then, he remembered the last time they were together on the buffalo hunt, over a year ago.

The big Swede tossed and turned, still frustrated. But, finally he was able to drift off to sleep.

Later, he began dreaming, aroused by the night's activities. Like magic, Marianne appeared in his dream. "Oh, my dear prince Olaf! How I have missed you, and longed for you. I will never leave you ever again. Isn't it wonderful! We can be together for ever more." In his dream Marianne leaned her body next to him. He could feel her heart racing, and the enticing thrill of her hot breath on his neck. He rolled over to take her in his arms. But, the dream quickly ended! Olaf let out a weak cry. "Aie yie!" He jumped up. Nawki had dared come into his bed! Startled by his outburst, she quickly crawled along the floor to her own, obviously lonely, cot.

Little Crow came half awake. "Huh, is there something wrong Tall Like Oak," he mumbled.

"*Nej*, Taoyateduta, I yist had a little dream, dat's all." The room became quiet, again.

The big Swede grabbed for his pipe and started smoking again and again. More frustrated, he knew the only sensual stimulation he'd get the rest of the night would be from sucking on his pipe.

* * *

As in any rural setting, the morning rooster crowed rambunctiously. Little Crow was back at ordering Nawki to make coffee. Olaf noticed Nawki's obvious embarrassment over her alluring aggressiveness during the night, and the big frontiersman had nothing but sympathy for her, as he too, had been deprived for a long time.

Finishing his coffee, Olaf went out to saddle Dancer Girl while host Taoyateduta and his wives watched. The beautiful, youthful Nawki waited in the distance, still attracted to Olaf. He went to his saddle bag where he carried his sundries and found some sweets which he gave to the Chief and his wives. When approaching and giving sad Nawki hers, he also slipped a delicate colorful brooch in her hand. On discovering it, her eyes brightened gloriously, he noticed. She closed her hand, quickly concealing it, and displayed a most endearing expression.

As he trotted down the road, the Swede called out, "Thank you, Taoyateduta. You ver a most gracious host, my friend."

The Chief held his arm up, palm forward in a friendly farewell.

* * *

Olaf was lonely not hearing from his betrothed métis who'd promised to write often from her remote sanctuary in the far northeast of Canada. It usually took a year for a letter to travel that far in the early times, but with greater numbers of pioneers moving west, parcel delivery had been speeded up substantially. After two years, Olaf quit running to the post office every day-- just once a week. Now, after three years, he had about given up hope, but--not totally.

Steamboats were traveling up the Mississippi in greater number. They were bringing more-and-more eager German and Scandinavian immigrants seeking land and population centers to establish a better life for themselves. It was exciting to watch each town grow from a handful of adventurers to solid communities of a few hundred. Brand new towns were springing up overnight; as fast as Dakota hunting villages on the open prairie. The only difference, these towns would not be moving on.

As field manager for the Burbank Stage and Wagon Company, Olaf had exerted his full energies toward moving the frontier farther west. Though a humble man, he gloated plenty when folks recognized him for his heroic virtues, and he liked it when everybody befriended him. So, to ward off the doldrums, he thrived on work and doing good deeds.

STAGE ROBBERS AND POLKAS

Tragedy struck the Stage line to the Southwest between St. Peter and New Ulm. Young Tim Hinks, one of Olaf's trusted drivers, tried to apprehend the masked bandits, but was shot in the back in cold blood.

Highwaymen were plaguing stagecoach drivers and settlers regularly, holding them up and heisting money and jewelry, what little the foreigners had brought with them. It was darned embarrassing to the Swede and the Burbank organization. They prided themselves in safe transportation from anywhere to everywhere.

An earlier rider recognized the culprits as the dangerous Stimler brothers, Two Finger Fritz and his little brother Hairless Harry who were forced out of St. Louis. With a large price on their heads, they figured it would be easier to steal and avoid the law in this less densely populated northland. They were not only thieves, but were dreaded for their heinous reputation of deflowering young unsuspecting women, and therefore, terrorized everyone wherever they roamed.

Olaf was determined to clean out these parasites, but whenever a sharp shooter rode the stage, the cowards lay low. Olaf sought out Sheriff Boardman, his respected friend from St. Peter. The sheriff agreed to work with him to snuff them out once and for all. Alone, Olaf would drive the coach as a decoy, and lure the thieves out in the open. After making a half dozen trips between St. Peter and New Ulm, hide nor hair of the bandits had been seen. Olaf was frustrated and lonely hauling his load of dummies dressed like tourists.

* * *

During his venture Olaf decided to ease his loneliness. The

Swede got involved in plenty of tomfoolery each night as he returned to New Ulm, the most rip-roaring hamlet in the territory. Luckily for Olaf, this settlement of a hundred families was blessed with an abundance of pretty girls, most of whom were taken with the tall handsome Swede who'd been starved for female companionship for what seemed to be an eternity, and felt it was time to have some fun.

In addition to his three years of faithfulness, and his vanished black-eyed treasure away on a sojourn to a Montreal nunnery had not answered even one of his dozens of love letters, Olaf decided to try to forget her for new romance. It wouldn't be easy he knew, but a man can't be a lone wolf forever, he figured.

Now bunking at the Dakota house and looking forward to good times, he climbed the wooden staircase to the second floor, and walked to the end of the hall towards his room - the last one on the floor. Looking out the window, he grinned at the excitement taking place, people laughing and gallivanting about everywhere. The carefree lifestyle of these folks hailing from Ulm, Bavaria was intriguing for they seemed to be less God-fearing than most other European settlers. Folks of neighboring towns, St. Peter and Henderson, raised eyebrows over these nonconforming free thinkers. Some claimed they were plain social revolutionaries.

These free thinkers called themselves Turners; the name being indicative of their physical and athletic prowess. Cultural expressions also consumed them. Singing and performing Shakespeare plays were high on the social agenda. Turner Hall was the "spiritual" place of this clan, where concertinas set a hectic pace for polkas, and beer drinking lasted till the late hours.

A sweet voice called as he approached his room. "Swede! Wait, Swede!" a pretty flaxen-haired chambermaid called, as she came down the hall toward him.

"Fraulein Marlena, my favorite cuddly polka dancer!" Olaf answered the girl with the hour glass figure. Though his fingers could link around her waist, his arms could barely make it around her bosom. She was sweet and soft as a kitten to hold when dancing. Olaf liked her a lot, thinking she could help him forget his old flame.

True to Turner clan spirit, Marlena went up on her toes and

pulled her fair haired idol down for a powerful kiss, making Olaf's knees wobble.

"Coming to Turner Hall tonight, Swede? Hope so. Love to dance the way you hold me so tight," she giggled. "And, Swede, you can walk me home afterwards." The sweet chambermaid was giddy -- "Only, I hope you'll stay a bit longer this time. You know how I love you."

"Ja," Olaf chuckled, wondering why in blazes he never had stayed longer in past visits. "Yer sure purdy, Marlena. Lookin forward to da dance. See ya tonight," he grinned and slipped into his room.

Olaf tidied up a bit, changing into his dressy shirt and arrowhead string tie Chief Little Crow had given him. Next, he donned his buckskin jacket and matching wide brimmed hat. He felt great. As he opened the window, an irresistible aroma from Heidner's Sausage Shop came in, encouraging him to slip out the door to buy some of the spicy delicacy.

At the sausage shop, Fraulein Gretchen was tending her father's meat counter. She was another one of his favorite polka partners whom he'd escorted home several times. Spotting Olaf, the tall seductive redhead yelled, "*Ach, mein Gott in Himmel,* Olaf." She ran around the counter and flew into his arms as if to devour him.

"Good day, Fraulein Heidner," Olaf greeted the saucy flame haired lass with a warm hug. As they embraced, she chewed on his left ear which sent a sensuous chill down his spine.

"Polka with me, you naughty Swede?" she teased in her husky voice, stroking his biceps. "You know we're the best looking couple on the floor; we're such a match!"

Olaf began sweating, having already promised Fraulein Marlena a fair share of his attention tonight. What bad luck! The two usually danced different nights which had been a perfect arrangement for him.

Like Fraulein Schnitzler, Fraulein Heidner was nineteen, and Olaf recognized the jealousy between them. But Gretchen Heidner's fiery red hair set her off from other town beauties, and he just couldn't turn her down. A man's pulse raced just gazing at her, Olaf only knew too well. Olaf and Gretchen had often made an imposing couple dancing the double-quick step polka, delighting other dancers who usually formed a large circle, to applaud their act. Olaf had also learned the métis' Red River Jig and by mixing it up with the polka, it made for an entertaining innovation.

"Gretchen, I'll be lookin forward to da dance," Olaf agreed, somewhat concerned about Marlena's presence. "But, I have an early evening appointment so it'll be qvite late for me."

"I'll come later myself, then. But plan to spend a little more time with me when we go home tonight. Papa will be going over to visit the Frau Gutzman. He's been doing that lately since she came out of her mourning. Now," she winked, "he sometimes stays till morning."

Olaf swallowed hard. She was irresistible, but he wondered if he was ready to be hog-tied yet.

"Olaf," Gretchen's father called from his workroom. "Come a minute."

"Ja, Herr Heidner." Olaf started to the back of the store.

"Gretchen, my dear, you go now. We have some man talk to make."

Olaf went back to the work room and watched the butcher. "It's sure interstin da vey ya make sausage, Herr Heidner. It's da best in da vorld. I sure vould like to buy some."

"Ach, I give you some." Herr Heidner scratched his hind end. "I like you, Big Swede." Scratching more, "You like my daughter, ay vot?"

Olaf grinned, "Ja, yer daughter's a purdy vun, fer sure."

Heidner placed a stack of pig intestines on the wooden block. Putting his butcher knife blade against the table, he pulled several casings under it, removing all but the tough thin skin for his sausages.

"Doze skins sure make vunderful sausage," said Olaf. "The flavor stays in, and da meat don't dry out, Herr Heidner."

Olaf wondered what the butcher would say next about his daughter, but the butcher continued fussing with the skins, cutting several shorter pieces about hand length. Then, he tied a tight knot at one end of each. After rolling them, he placed several in Olaf's hand, talking low so Gretchen couldn't hear. "I've been using them for years, so I'm not overrun with mouths to feed."

Olaf couldn't believe what the butcher had confessed.

Then, confidentially, Heidner whispered, "I know Gretchen is hot-blooded like her mother was and she's after you, I can tell. I would like her to marry the young banker who's coming from the Fatherland this fall. He has his eyes set on her. If she marries him, maybe I wouldn't have to work so hard. Ya understand?"

Embarrassed, Olaf snickered. "Herr Heidner, nay, I don't tink..."

"Nonsense! Don't forget about those skins. We Turners got some damn good ideas," he chuckled. "Now, I must be off to see my dear Frau. If she makes me a good dinner, I will probably thank her appropriately." His pot belly giggled as he walked away.

Olaf was flabbergasted at the education Turner Heidner had given. But, worse, he worried about having two beauties for the night. How would he stand the pressure? Polka dancing with two tireless dancers, each alone practically did him in. A great worry was that they both planned to be taken home, expecting him to stay longer.

He paced the floor nervously with his hands in his pockets, and discovered Heidner's romantic sausages. He laughed at such a thing, "Vell, maybe da damn ting virks, but it sure vould be aggravatin, if ya ask me."

Finally it was time for the concertina music to start at Turner Hall, so Olaf hightailed it over.

Olaf immediately saw that Fraulein Schnitzler was wound up. Her face red with excitement as she anticipated the Swede's holding her tightly for another thrilling moment she'd have dancing the Polka, his style

"Like to dance, Marlena?" Big Olaf bowed.

"Gut," she swooned, fanning her face with her bare hand as if she might faint right there on the dance floor.

They danced and danced, and danced some more. Olaf enjoyed the racing polka with his voluptuous sweet flaxen haired Fraulein Schnitzler, who literally floated in air, so light and delicate.

Fraulein Heidner wouldn't be coming to the dance until late, but Olaf worried about a confrontation and Gretchen's pledge to save her energy exclusively for Olaf. He swallowed with difficulty, recalling her wish to share a long night of undisturbed loving in her father's absence.

Feeling self assured again, Olaf and Marlena laughed and danced throughout the evening. Between dances, they refreshed themselves with a big stein of dark German beer. With polka dancing one needs beer, and that makes one perspire. It's part of the polka. The longer one dances and the more one drinks, it's natural to be full of happiness by three in the morning.

Drinking also makes one forget! Suddenly, Olaf noticed Gretchen! There was a disturbed look on her face as she watched Olaf swinging Marlena! Olaf's face got hot, his knees weakened as the dance ended.

"Marlena, my dear, I promised Fraulein Heidner a dance or two," he said feebly. "You wouldn't mind, vould you?" Olaf pleaded innocently.

"Oh no. Not her again," Marlena moaned. "She wants everybody."

"Ah, just a couple dances. Ve've danced before a few times."

"Well, you know I love you." The chambermaid promised. "I'll miss you."

The band struck up a fast paced polka, perfect for the double-quick step dance the tall red-head and Olaf perfected. Smiling solicitously, he walked over to Fraulein Heidner and held out his hand. She smirked at Marlena and stepped out on the floor.

"Big Swede, I have been resting and I'm bursting with excitement. I relish the idea of spending the rest of the night with you," she smiled invitingly.

"You're beautiful, Fraulein Heidner," Olaf drooled. But his voice quivered hearing her threaten a long night together, her inviting smile, husky voice and red hair revealing the intense passion within her.

The two exploded into the double step rhythm, making an awesome display. Thirty to forty dancers stopped to applaud the amazing speed of their stepping. When the dance ended, the crowd cheered.

Sweat poured off the Swede, who'd danced long with Marlena before. "Some beer..." he gasped. How dramatic and glamorous the Sausage maker's daughter looked tonight, he thought.

There was little time to rest. The concertinas began playing again and Gretchen grabbed him. The exhausted frontiersman polkaed one dance after another. Olaf was getting desperate. He longed for a smooth, easy polka with Marlena, whose ire was beginning to flare. When the music stopped, she came between Olaf and Gretchen.

"Olaf, you said a few dances. It's already been eight. I counted."

Infuriated, Gretchen stormed to the beer barrel. She glared at Marlena who held her ground for the next dance. Marlena's timidity had left after eight beers, one for each dance as a wall flower. As Olaf felt the tension build, he cursed himself for getting in such a mess. Nevertheless, he now favored the slower pace with Marlena. Gretchen cut in at the break, ready to take back what was hers, but Marlena was not to be bullied. When Gretchen grabbed a handful of Marlena's flaxen hair, Marlena retaliated by pulling two long red braids, side to side, as if ringing Gretchen's bell.

The crowd of German settlers stopped dancing and gathered around. Being taller, Gretchen had the upper hand from the start, but her blows bounced off Marlena like water off a duck.

Olaf, feeling responsible, tried stopping the silly spat, but the crowd booed him for interfering, so he withdrew and let the two fight their battle with honor. First, they clawed and scratched each other, and then Marlena dumped the feisty Gretchen right on her keister, throwing her twin howitzers on top, and urging her adversary to cry defeat.

The Turners enjoyed it. Some cheered for the sweet hotel chambermaid, others sided with the sausage maker's saucy daughter. Everyone knew they'd more than likely be walking arm in arm tomorrow. This was just a little town of free independent thinkers, where folks polka danced and drank beer with the background of sweet concertina music until the cows came home.

Sheriff Boardman showed up after midnight looking for the big Swede. Said he knew it was a damned good chance of finding him grazing around a dance floor with a pretty filly hanging on his arm these days. "What happened with those felines?" spotting the tired women. He pressed Olaf, whose face reacted with guilt for causing the ruckus. The crowd laughed.

The Sheriff told Olaf the bandits were holed up in Swan Lake Ravine, and he was needed in the morning to help capture them. Olaf grinned, appreciating this excuse to knock off early tonight.

The girls figured they'd scrapped to a draw so were ready to compromise with Olaf and each other. The two laughing frauleins hugged one another, asked if he'd take them both home tonight. He happily agreed. They were a tired and affable trio strolling home.

As they walked, both Gretchen and Marlena suggested he come into the Sausage Maker's house for a little group cuddling. Olaf was flabbergasted. Although he was broad minded, this Turner society of free thinkers just might be getting carried too far away, he figured.

"Sorry, my lovely ladies, but duty calls. I face danger at sun up. Best get me a little rest." He gave each a tender kiss, knowing that each had a future which wouldn't include him.

The Big Swede needed to get back to the hard work of building a decent world from this territory of wilderness and lawlessness. The stage robbers needed to be apprehended, Olaf thought, as he headed toward the Sheriff's office.

* * *

Olaf, fuzzy headed from the previous night's carousing, filled his jug at Mable's Kaffee Haus. He didn't want to be half asleep when meeting with those gun slinging Stimler brothers, should he be lucky enough to flush them out of hiding.

As planned, Sheriff Boardman and two of his deputies had taken positions about the ravine before sun-up. At 7 a.m. Olaf would ride by the target area with his stage full of mannequins and the top rack bulging with fake cargo. Nearing the place, he felt a tense chill running down his spine, realizing how damnably vulnerable he felt on this high seat. A well placed shot from the brush only thirty feet away could strike, ending his life as it did his friend, Tim Hinks. Closing in, Olaf's throat felt dry. He reached down slowly for his big mug of coffee, keeping his head erect and watching. His eyes scanned the woods for the least movement.

146

The Big Swede

"Zing!" A bullet whizzed by his ear. Olaf ducked. Another shot went over his head! In one movement he stopped and tied off his lines to keep his four horses from stampeding. Swiftly, he dropped to the ground away from the direction of the shooting. Several shots smashed through the coach, but his fake passengers didn't bat an eyelash.

Reaching around the stage, Olaf unhooked Dancer Girl who'd been trailing behind, and pulled her next to the coach. Hoisting himself onto her back, he raced to the front for the deathly confrontation, risking his life in the name of his departed friend.

The culprits, realizing the dummy passengers were a set-up, rode out from their hiding place in the bushes and galloped down the wooded hollow. Dancer Girl was rapidly advancing toward the get-a-ways and Olaf shot at them. They fired in retreat, but Olaf's second shot found its mark, knocking one of the culprits off his horse. He rolled into the brush! The other bandit rode on.

Cautiously dismounting, Olaf dashed into the brush behind him and shouted, "Yer surrounded Stimler boys! A sheriff's pose got ya surrounded. Ya got no vey out!"

Olaf listened. With no immediate response, he wondered if he'd killed the man.

Finally, a husky voice called out. "Ya got me! I'm shot bad." The hoodlum didn't show himself, so Olaf took extreme caution.

"Come out of there with your hands up. No tricks!" Olaf warned.

"My leg's shot bad. Can't stand. I'm in here," the raspy voice responded from the bull rushes.

Being careful, Olaf inched his way toward the cornered fugitive. Suddenly, a bulky form flew out of the brush, freezing Olaf momentarily. The thug had played possum, his leg not shot at all. Olaf dove behind some bushes. He peered out and spotted the one who'd been hit. His right arm hung as if broken, his shoulder bloody from the hit. Olaf tackled the ruffian from behind and quickly subdued him. Noticing the missing fingers on his right hand, Olaf immediately knew he had captured Two Finger Fritz.

Sheriff Boardman and his deputies eventually came up with Hairless Harry, the other notorious brother. His identity was unmistakable; his head as bald as a baby's hind end.

147

"Goddamn sun-a-bitch! Dey got us Fritz," he babbled. "Da big Swede got us!"

"Shut up, Harry! There ain't no jail made'll hold us! We'll git back and take care of this long drink a water in no time!"

Olaf smirked. "Dat's vot you tink, Stimler boys! Ve got a new big penitentiary at Stillvoter, and dey've got a pile a big rocks need bustin up. Varden Jim Gunderson knows how to tame blowhards like you two."

The Sheriff took the highwaymen away. Though Olaf had had a close brush with his maker, he was relieved the trail was again safe for travelers.

While returning to his home base, Olaf started whistling. The danger of capturing the bandits soon left his mind. He turned his thoughts to the pretty girls in New Ulm; the sweet voluptuous Fraulein Marlena Schnitzler, so cuddly and soft; and the butcher's saucy red-headed daughter, Fraulein Gretchen Heidner, who's hair could set off a spark in a man at ten feet. Aw Hell, there was no harm in having a little fun. Maybe I'll stop in and dance vith some others next time, he thought. He started laughing so loudly he spooked a herd of deer who took off as if a bunch of hornets were stinging their hind ends.

❋   ❋   ❋   ❋   ❋

RED RIVER VALLEY

TO CANADA

Olaf was impressed with George Simpson who came to St. Paul by boat and oxcart a year ago. The eager Swede had sat spellbound listening to the negotiations for a joint transportation partnership between the Hudson Bay Company and the Burbank enterprise. Hudson Bay was trying to get permission to transport its furs, duty free, through the United States, and then ship them by steamer to England and Europe.

The "Emperor," as he was called, was the managing executive of the vast Hudson Bay Company in Canada, and the governor of all territory draining to the Hudson Bay. The Red River, with head waters two hundred miles into the United States, flowed north toward the Bay, becoming a main avenue of commerce between the two countries.

The flamboyant Simpson traveled from his home in Montreal to the arctic in the North, and four thousand miles west to the Pacific Ocean. He managed the tremendous network of forts and trading posts for the giant corporation. His highways were the swift rivers traveled by brigades of boats propelled by his revered motley dressed Algonquin Indians.

"Gold" was the valuable beaver pelts collected by thousands of Indians and Frenchmen since the 1600s. The English took over the land at the turn of the nineteenth century and expanded the huge industry to the maximum.

Olaf was getting a burr in his britches to travel to Fort Garry, and was being encouraged by Burbank and the St. Paul business community, who were anxious for the increased commerce to bolster its sagging economy. The entire nation was in a dreary depression in 1857.

Soon, the frontiersman found himself riding north on Dancer

Girl. This time he opted for the more hazardous wood's trail, which travelers found to be safer from hostile Indians. Maybe the road could be improved for stage service going west from the Crow Wing trading post. He would find out.

Olaf spent his first night in the Sauk Rapids area. He had a chance to visit his old side-kick, Mousey Michaels, and new wife Singing Bird and little baby Meadowlark. Olaf was humored by Mousey's tale of how he named the baby. When she cooed, she sounded like a meadowlark.

Measly Mousey had become a ball of fire. He managed the Burbank station with thirty-two horses and several wagons and three coaches. A few months after opening his yards, stages were heading as far as fifty miles north with mail and passengers to Fort Ripley, which was established in 1848 to maintain peace among the Winnebego, Ojibway, and the Dakota of the south.

The old trading post of Crow Wing had also become a thriving town a few miles North of the fort. To Olaf the territory rapidly expanded with new settlements in all directions.

After leaving Wilson's settlement at Sauk Rapids, the Swede enjoyed the fast ride on the straight sandy road the government had built from St. Paul to Crow Wing. Olaf, a farm boy at heart, shook his head and frowned at the sandy hills and scrubby grass as he headed north. Not worth piddly jack-straws in hell for farming, he thought.

As a covering of leaf woods and scattered pine appeared, he knew he was closing in on Fort Ripley. Having stopped there before, the gregarious frontiersman had already made friends with the troops. He halted long enough to beg for a cup of coffee and jabber with the ofttimes bored servicemen. Keeping a fast pace, Olaf approached the Crow Wing trading post as darkness neared. My Lord, he thought, this town has increased by one hundred or more. This rapid growth in population was exciting, for Crow Wing was now a paradise for trappers, traders and lumbermen. He looked forward to a visit at the Woods Tavern where more tall stories were told than there were trees in the forest.

Looking west across the Mississippi to the north side of the Crow Wing River, he was surprised to see dozens of tents and birch wigwams. The Red Lake Indians had made their four day trek south to trade with Allen Morrison, Olaf figured. He'd never seen so many Chippewa at one time. Only about two dozen made Crow Wing their home.

The Swede was thrilled to be back in this bustling business community, with its small frame and log cabins, shops, hotels, boarding houses, brothels, and warehouses. It had become the dominating town of the North. The darkened streets were filled with a conglomeration of mixed races and tongues as Olaf headed for the livery behind the neatly painted hotel where he'd bunk tonight. It sounded like everybody was celebrating. Boisterous talking and laugher delighted the Swede.

"Evening, Collette," Olaf greeted the hotel clerk, who happened to be one of the attractive métis daughters of Allen Morrison. All seven of Morrison's dashing black-eyed daughters, well respected, did much to enhance the town's glamorous image.

"Ah, Monsieur, Olafson. Happy to see good big man from St. Paul."

"Nice ta be here! Yer smile alvays brightens von, Collette."

She snickered, "Oh, you always big joker, Olaf."

"How's Papa Morrison? Must visit with him 'for leavin tomorra."

"He's good. But you have leave so soon? Usually stay couple days?" She reminded him.

Olaf explained he had to head west on business. Collette wanted to know everything about her admired guest, aware that he was responsible for setting up the stage service to Crow Wing. She wondered if he had plans to extend such service on the trail along the Crow Wing River, because of the increased cart travel along the Woods Trail. Olaf admitted hearing the path was somewhat treacherous for wheeled equipment at this time. It would definitely need work, he thought.

After a cordial visit with the dark-eyed beauty, he quickly

stowed his saddle bags in his room, doused his face at the washstand and ventured out. On his way to the Woods Tavern, the gregarious Olaf greeted the town's folks with his infectious smile and hearty hellos. In turn, they cheerfully reciprocated his enthusiasm. Farther down, turning the corner, he passed some small shacks only a few yards back from the dirt road. Out of each window sat the bawdy wenches of the night, enticingly and scantily clad, pitching their wares as energetically as any street huckster he'd seen in New York.

"Come, long fellow, I please you tonight. Be happy here."

Olaf, never rude, always greeted them respectfully. "Thank you, ma'am. Have a nice evening." And he'd pass by, chuckling to himself.

"Ooo, you handsome one, Monsieur," the second one leaned three fourths of her body out her window, revealing her voluptuous bosom.

"Sorry ma'am. Little tired from traveling. Pleasant evening." He tipped his hat in tribute to her being so graciously endowed.

He passed a few others, but the last one on the block caught his attention, a dark complected little waif - still in her teens - said she'd sell her wares for half the going price. He heard a baby crying in the background. Said she'd do anything to please him to get food for her baby. Her sincerity moved Olaf. He walked to the window and she tittered in obvious delight. Olaf handed her two bits. "Here, take dis and get food fer you and the baby." He wished her well, and moved across the Woods Tavern.

The tipplers of the evening were having a rollicking time. Olaf was entertained by a group of characters from Maine. Their accents revealed a mix of English, Irish, Scottish, and French. Most exciting for Olaf was the presence of three Swedes, boasting of being the strongest axmen in the woods. Every ruffian bragged about his women back home; their beauty, brains, and lusciousness. Olaf knew this spirit of jovial horseplay helped overcome loneliness.

The Swede didn't stay at the Woods Tavern long. He wanted to chat with trader Morrison, if time permitted, and then have an opportunity to mingle with the Chippewa of the north woods.

Olaf was surprised to learn that some of the Red Lakers were antagonized with his playing favorites with the Sioux. Some showed downright anger over his associating with their prime enemy, Taoyataduta, who'd taken too many Chippewa scalps through the years. But there were those who knew the big Swede championed the red man's cause, and much of the negative grumbling soon quieted.

* * *

The métis and whites traveling in smaller cart trains, found the treacherous east-west woods trail safer than on the prairie. A finer element of trust prevailed between the whites and Chippewa, for through the ages they were more dependent partners in the fur trade. The Chippewa got more guns and goods for the greater numbers of furs they traded. But traveling through the woods was tedious and slow.

Olaf rode the five miles to the mouth of the Gull River where he found over a thousand north woods Indians still waiting to receive annuities and payment from the Chippewa Indian Agency located there. His stay was brief, the time for the Canadian trip was limited.

Soon he encountered fir trees covering the steep hills. Olaf could see that the cart trail crossed through tamarack swamps, as tamarack posts lay side-by-side for considerable distances in a corduroying support. Seeing broken axles and wheels strewn at many swamp crossings, he found the method had been dangerous. The bark had scraped off many of the posts, making them extremely slippery. Olaf knew this would cause damage to animals and wheels trying to negotiate such construction. Dancer Girl treaded these timidly and her leg thrust through the posts once, causing Olaf concern for her possibly breaking a leg. So, with his long legged steed, he found it much more sensible to ride around these swamps, or cross on the edges of the treacherous corduroys. He felt his anxieties build as he traveled.

Farther down, his fears were soon substantiated, as two oxen carcasses lay in the dangerous passage ways. Investigating, the Swede found that one of the critter's leg bones had been completely severed. The animals were obviously destroyed right on the trail.

In another place, a cart lay completely smashed at the bottom of a steep hill. The unfortunate driver obviously believed it safer choosing the hill rather than the floating tamarack reinforced trail. Olaf recalled his earlier trip through the Red River Valley where the road was level and fast; the feared Sioux had forced much hardship on the wayfarers to and from the North.

He continued down the trail, anxious to reach another new settlement called Wadena. An enterprising adventurer had set up a well-stocked store, catering to the Red River traveler in this forested setting, containing beautiful stands of stately White and Norway pine covering the majestic hills. Olaf was inspired by these grandiose pillars and smiled in delight at the invigorating pine aroma permeating the woods. Reaching the quaint settlement at the juncture of the Partridge and Leaf Rivers was a welcomed sight to the lone horseman. In addition to the general store, a rather impressive structure drew Olaf's attention. The sign on the front read "Halfway House." What the devil is that? He wondered. More impressing, a convenient livery was attached to it. Olaf dismounted and stretched his arms. A young man wearing a bright red vest came out of the establishment and introduced himself.

"I'm Peter Roy. Welcome to the Halfway House, half way between Crow Wing and Ottertail City, the finest on this side of heaven."

Olaf grinned. "Yes sir. I'm Olaf Olsson; dey call me Svede, and I'd be most beholden ta find a bunk fer da night."

The man gave a hearty laugh. "Ah ha. That we have, traveler. We serve the most mouth-watering roast duck nesting on a bed of wild rice, and all the trimmings to quell your hunger pangs, too."

Peter Roy suddenly looked surprised. "Say! You can't be! But, by George, you are!" He called out to the men leaning on the horse rail; "Hey fellas, look who's come to our town! The great frontiersman, the Big Swede is here!"

Those in ear shot hurried over to greet the visitor, all explaining new faces were a most welcomed sight in this remote village, and they felt real honored that he came. Everyone wanted to hear about some of the Swede's famous exploits.

Olaf, always modest, tried playing them down. "Der yist blown out a proportion." he said.

One braggart, an excellent shot himself, challenged Olaf to target shooting. Legend had it, the Swede could shoot the eyes out of a rattle snake at fifty paces. The man insisted seeing it first hand. Olaf shied away at first, but anticipating an exciting match, the innkeeper and the storekeeper egged him on. They seemed pretty confident that the tales were true. Olaf finally consented.

Five one-inch pine cones were placed on a rail fifty yards away. The braggart, called Lucious, shot five times knocking all but two off the rail. The townsfolk were impressed and applauded him.

By this time the entire village population of seventy-five gathered. Olaf was worried. He hadn't shot for a while and was tired from the ride. But, he raised his rifle, aimed and fired.

"Yeah," the crowd shouted. The first target had gone down.

Then, the second and the third shattered from his direct hits. Olaf only needed one more so he braced himself and shot again. "Zing" went the bullet. But...Olaf missed! Right before the last shot one could have heard an ant breathe, it was so quiet. The Swede steadied his arm, a bit nervous, and finally pulled the trigger. This time, a direct hit! The spectators cheered their hero.

Olaf modestly bowed. The instigators of this frolic were not finished though. Both the innkeeper and the storekeeper were making a side bet of their own. The innkeeper wagered that Olaf could hit a ten dollar gold piece at a hundred yards. Olaf was tense and edgy now, for he disliked having friends bet on him, and he liked these men.

The dramatic tension was nerve wracking to Olaf as he raised the rifle and aimed again. The crowd grew quiet. Many whispered that this tiny target about a half inch wide, could never be hit.

Olaf bit his lip; took a deep breath and leveled his sight on that minute speck in the distance. He paused, blinked his eyes and aimed again. Finally, "Zing" the bullet whistled.

No one stirred. The crowd leered toward the top of the post which held the nearly invisible disc. At once a delighted cheer went up; the ten dollar gold piece was no longer there. "Yeah, Swede!" they roared.

The storekeeper who offered the use of his coin for the target, said jokingly, "Well, Mr. Roy, it looks like you win. The ten spot is yours, if you can find it." Everyone searched high and low for the gold piece, anxious to see what damage was done by the bullet, but no one found it, or at least admitted finding it. Being good friends, the two businessmen guffawed over the ordeal, and tried to figure out who really won and who really lost the bet.

* * *

The Wadena stop was most enjoyable. The lodging and victuals were as fine as anything he'd experienced. When leaving in the morning, he asked the innkeeper why he had made such a foolish bet after his missing one of the targets. Peter Roy snickered and admitted to having seen Olaf close his eyes on the missed shot. The Swede reluctantly said he hadn't wanted to embarrass Mr. Lucious too much. They both chuckled over the incident.

The terrain continued much as it was the previous day; hilly, laden with more tamarack swamps, making it rugged. The trail, still heading west, followed the south side of the shallow, but dangerous Leaf River, which before had meandered along the north of the Crow Wing. More and more broad leaf trees appeared: oak, ash, maple, birch and poplars now replaced the towering pine. Olaf noticed that the water flowed the opposite direction, away from the Mississippi watershed. The sandy soil, too, was replaced by a blacker loam.

Ah, what luck! The Swede was glad to see people again. Up ahead a small cart train was laid up, and the occupants yelled halloos, greeting the lone rider. Another casualty had interrupted their progress. A cart was on its side and the métis were busy chopping a tree from which a new part would be made. The dangerous stumps had broken still another axle. The available hard wood would soon be hewed into the proper shape so the cart could proceed with it's thousand pound load.

Olaf knew some of the drivers from previous meetings, and enjoyed visiting with Henry Sibley, the prominent fur dealer who was traveling with the cart train. Usually moving in families, the métis women busied themselves cooking and mending clothing, while the children laughed, sang and frolicked about happily. Olaf enjoyed his treat of pemmican stew.

Aiming to reach the Leaf Mountains by dusk, Olaf's visit was short. Though it was a thrill meeting people on the Woods Trail, he had two hundred miles to go, and knew that fewer and fewer whites or mixed bloods would be encountered before reaching Pembina, and finally, Ft. Garry, Canada. There was little time to dally if the anticipated meeting with the "Emperor," George Simpson, was to happen. The Governor of the great territory called Rupertsland would be moving farther north to Norway House, which accommodated the giant annual meeting of factors, managers, and voyageurs of the Hudson Bay Company,

Finally, the exhausting day's trek was completed. The full beauty of the fabulous Leaf Mountains, with its mass of lakes had been reached. Olaf loved this wonderland he remembered so well from traveling through to the buffalo hunt, and he was anxious to penetrate the wooded hills looming up in the north. Occasionally, from a high point, he gazed west and saw the endless level valley cradling the Red River, most of the time the hills obstructed any view of the plains.

Olaf spent the night at Ottertail City, once a thriving fur trading post. However, with the continuous depletion of beaver, the one log building was now the home to an elderly trader and his wife, content to live out their days in the land of lakes, bountiful fish and water fowl to supply their needs. The old trader told Olaf he did enough business in muskrat furs to maintain a small cash flow for a comfortable life.

Still hurrying along, the fresh smells of the lakes and ponds were invigorating through the scenic hills of the Leaf Mountains. After riding up and down the steep hills, Olaf finally met small hunting parties of Chippewa, none of which caused any disturbance to his travel. The hunters found this strapping white man most entertaining, as he conveyed his friendship through hand signals, a compassionate smile, and a gift of tobacco. He ofttimes played a couple of tunes on the mouth harp given to him by his old German Kapten, and the Chippewa were enthralled by his musical renditions, not wanting him to stop playing so soon.

Continuing on his journey, the woods and lakes were soon left behind replaced by barren ground. Sand and gravel ridges appeared, generally lying in a north-south direction. These beach-like ridges boggled Olaf's mind, as he kept watching for a sea of water. But, none was found. Ah, the mysteries of time overwhelm one's mind, Olaf reflected.

Riding on for two days showed little change. Then, a profound cloud of dust loomed up in the direction he was going. Excitement egged him on; his map showed he'd soon cross Sand Hill River. One only needed to scan the terrain to realize the river was properly named. Olaf estimated the giant sand hills rose to two hundred feet.

Some forty carts returning to the northland were finally overtaken, as Dancer traveled at four times the speed of oxen. It was an enthusiastic meeting with the métis cart people. An added treat was a visit with a German and Scottish family accompanying them. They told of their ancestors coming to Lord Selkirk's colonies over forty years before through Hudson Bay, and happily revealed their delight for the advent of the cart trains, which opened up the world for them.

Olaf was excited in staying with the caravan that evening, but rose early and continued on the trail before sunrise. He would have to ride hard to reach his destination in time to meet with George Simpson, who'd be leaving for Hudson Bay's annual meeting at the remote Norway House. His boss, Burbank, would be most disappointed if Olaf hadn't successfully firmed up plans for the proposed joint transportation venture.

With the majestic forests to the east, Olaf continued along the gravel ridges occasionally flanked by stands of willow, aspen and balsam poplar. To the west lay the great expanse of grassy plains, a soil-rich savanna. He wondered why mankind had evaded such a promising land, recalling the arid, worn-out ground on which his ancestors had toiled.

* * *

As Olaf hurried north along the stony ridge trail, nearing his final destination, he became more and more bewildered over the disappearance of Marianne LaMond, the woman he loved. Her commitment to spend one year at a Montreal nunnery began four years ago.

He would soon be approaching St. Boniface village. There would be a large Roman cathedral, a nunnery, and a church school where she'd received her religious training. Marianne admitted she was devoted to the nuns, and the Holy Bishop, and had a devout spiritual commitment to the place.

Olaf recalled the last time they parted after the buffalo hunt, the Bishop's coach came to Pembina to whisk her away to a Montreal convent. Knowing she'd be cloistered for a year and isolated from the world, a desperate fear had come into her eyes. She had consented to that for the privilege of going on the buffalo hunt.

It is not good to question the church, Olaf thought, but maybe somewhere at St. Boniface he might find a clue as to what happened to Marianne. They had made a sincere pledge to marry. Not knowing if they would ever see each other again was agonizing to the forlorn Swede.

Suddenly, Olaf was excited to see small farms along the Seine River which he now followed. The farmsteads were hugging the water, a common sight when traveling in the north country. These rural people huddled together; their farmland trailed in long narrow strips away from the river. In such an isolated country, farmers need to group together, he thought, otherwise life could be desperately lonely. Personal contemplation's aside, Olaf was filled with enthusiasm and anticipation of reaching his destination before total darkness.

In the distance, two spires atop lofty turrets caught Olaf's attention. After such a long trip, it was a most welcomed sight. Entering the age old settlement from east of the Red River, more small farms appeared; always close to the river. Riding on, he observed that most of the homes were made of logs, but several bright whitewashed sandstone buildings enhanced the unique pastoral setting along the road leading to the cathedral. Red River carts dotted the landscape.

Several children came running to greet the unusual sight of a lone rider, particularly one on such a magnificent horse.

"Monsieur Ole! Come for buffalo hunt?" a black bearded métis called out from where he was repairing his cart.

Olaf, recognizing the man from the hunt four years before answered, "I'd sure like ta, but have utter business dis time. Sorry, must go to da fort now. Maybe tomorrow I'll come visit. I'll try."

"Come, if can. Good to see you, big Ole," the jovial man shouted.

Olaf moved ahead towards the great Cathedral. He was impressed by its dominance on the east bank of the Red River, across from where the Assiniboine River joins the Red. The large arched stone structure was awe inspiring, but it was mystifying for Olaf to ponder the tremendous influence the church had over the

French métis.

The brazen Swede, with a sudden dryness in his throat, passed the walled-in St. Boniface complex and wondered if there could be a clue to the mystery hidden there. He would seek out more information later.

Equally grand, the gigantic citadel of the Hudson Bay Company, Fort Garry, caught his eye. With its commanding position on the western bluff overlooking the two rivers, the walled fort with rounded bastion-like towers on each corner loomed most impressively. Olaf stopped on the bluff, observing the giant complex. His eyes quickly focused on a mass of carts assembled outside the fortification, and he saw people scurrying about; many carrying bales on their shoulders down to the water's edge. At the base of the fort, he saw the boats, small and large. He assumed they were being readied for the voyage to Norway House.

Had he arrived too late for a meeting with Simpson, the "Emperor?" A sense of urgency overcame him. Seeing the ferry up river, Olaf quickly guided Dancer down to the crossing. Having come all this way, he thought, it would be a crying shame not to meet with Simpson. Finally reaching the fortress, Olaf learned the flotilla would be moving seven hundred miles north toward Hudson Bay at sunrise. Would the canny, energetic Governor Simpson take time for him, he worried. In haste, he tied Dancer Girl to the officer's rail nearest the entry and dashed into the courtyard.

Olaf gawked at the dozen or more buildings: the stately headquarters, a three-story block building stood in the center; several residences, warehouses, and a retail store filled the complex. Here in this bustling community, Olaf had no idea where to find the "Great One." He entered the store, filled with general merchandise: guns, traps, clothing and produce, tea and sugar-everything.

It was a strange crowd: brightly clothed voyageurs, Indians adorned in feathers, fur-clad traders, and numerous Hudson Bay officials in their tailored suits. Olaf's huge presence drew immediate attention. It seemed to him all eyes were suddenly staring at this burly visitor. Aware of the scrutiny, Olaf removed his trail hat, and even looked down, checking to see if he'd left his barn door open, or something.

Two dapper gentlemen finally approached, chuckling. "Stranga, I say, you look rathah lost. You must be from down below."

"Ja, da States."

"May we be of assistance in some way, friend?"

Olaf relaxed, being called a friend he smiled broadly, explaining the purpose of his trip. The astute company officials, having had some knowledge of pending negotiations with Olaf's enterprise quickly whisked him up to George Simpson's private chambers.

"Swede Olsson from St. Paul! Glad to see you!" Simpson bellowed, remembering him from the meeting with Burbank a year before. He got up and shook Olaf's hand.

"I high-tailed, sir. Do ve have a few minutes ta talk, maybe?"

"Well, we leave at six a.m. But for you there's plenty of time," the energetic Governor of Rupertsland assured. "We will dine together and discuss the proposed partnership, which is looking favorable, I might say."

Olaf was most impressed with the kind reception he'd received. Having been provided a fine bed in the officer's bachelor quarters, he had a chance to freshen up, change shirts, and don his favorite buckskin jacket.

The Swede felt like royalty at the executive's table where he was treated to imported wines and a spread of elegant baron of roast beef.

"Swede," Simpson beamed, "my New York agent reports getting final approval from your Treasury Department for transporting Hudson Bay furs through the United States-duty free. We need dependable passage."

"Dat's good news, Sir. It's all comin togeter den. My government is yist startin ta build a military base at da source of

Red River. Vee can build roads and guarantee fast haulin to da steamers at da Mississippi, fer sure. I vouch fer dat, Mr. Simpson."

"Great," the dynamic executive responded. "After dining, we'll retire to my office to firm up plans and set a timetable."

Olaf gave a grateful sigh of relief, knowing his trip was not in vain, and now looked forward to his return with the good news for his boss, Mr. Burbank.

Simpson, was most hospitable for he knew the economic gains from the new travel routes would be most lucrative to his company.

Olaf was introduced to several local business men, including Andrew McDermot, the leading independent fur dealer and retailer. These merchants were most enthusiastic about expansion of trade to the United States. McDermot begged Olaf to be his guest on a morning tour of the expanding Red River Community.

These boys sure know how to live, Olaf thought, impressed as he collapsed his weary bones on the softest mattress he'd ever stretched on. He chuckled, finding that his feet didn't stick out at the end of the blankets as happened in every other place he'd slept. Thankful the trip had gone so well, he went to sleep with a smile on his face.

The restful sleep was short lived. "Boom!" A loud blast vibrated the fort! Olaf was catapulted out of bed. "Vot! Vot! Vot!" The befuddled Swede shouted, grabbing his watch. "Holy heifer dust, it's only five-tirty," he mumbled to himself.

"Hey travelah, that's George Simpson's alahm clock," a gent called out, humored at Olaf's outburst. "Want to see something spectaculah? Get your oss up on the obsavation towah at six for the graund affaya."

Olaf stumbled around in a foggy daze, but finally gathered his wits, dressed and stepped out into a pandemonious confusion. Men were running helter-skelter, like a bunch of stampeding cattle, he thought.

From the tower, flares lighted the otherwise pitch dark setting.

The voyageurs worked in desperation, readying their boats for the final departure. People everywhere! Hundreds of them!

Local folks were crowding the observation area for a bird's eye view of the Emperor's departing brigades. Olaf's eyes focused on the large York boats, now being secured by voyageurs, and the colorful Algonquin Indians appeared in full color and feathers in tribute to their esteemed "Emperor." Olaf was intrigued with the pageantry unfolding, characters in motley dress and flamboyant activity. Surely soon there would be a spectacular production.

It was mind-boggling to witness so many diverse people working together--like ants--in their preparation for departure to Norway House. Executives toiled hand-in-hand with traders and voyageurs; métis of French, Scottish and English mix. Then, the Algonquin Indians added a romantic ingredient of fantastical proportions to the extravaganza.

Finally the great one appeared wearing his dashing white capote and took his place in the lead sea-going York boat, like an admiral leading his flotilla in battle. A smaller man stood behind him.

"It's always the same, travelah," an eager observer verified, "But, we'd nevah miss these expositions, his coming and going."

"That so?" The Swede acknowledged, his eyes glued to the drama.

"Sir. He always wears a white capote. It's tradition, ya know."

"Den, who's da smaller man standin next to him?" Olaf asked.

"Most delightful, mah friend, he's the fifah. They say he stirs the oarsmen with such inspirational music that their ahms churn fastah than birds' wings in flight. The men know their rewaud will be a regale of rum at the end of a long day."

Olaf chuckled.

Alas! Roman candles -- flares -- filled the sky with glowing lights. Boom! The canons fired from the bastions. Boom! Boom! Boom! The blast echoed down the river. A wild cheer rose from the boatmen as their vessels veered away from the moorings. The fifer struck up a fiery cadence, establishing a vigorous pace for the oarsmen, hundreds of oars stroking as one. Simpson's brilliantly painted boat brigade streaked away with amazing speed.

The local citizens cheered, waving farewell to friends and loved ones, none to return for over a month, and those leaving for the frigid northland would not be back until next year at this same time.

As the noise of the crowd lingered, several onlookers shouted "Quiet!" "Quiet!" And the well wishers stood in silence, waiting.

Olaf's ears perked up hearing the voyageurs singing their robust French ballads. Hundreds of men harmonizing in the distance made Olaf's flesh tingle. It was an experience the big Swede was certain he'd never forget. In half an hour the voices gradually faded away.

Later, after breakfast, Andrew McDermot came by with his carriage. He'd invited Olaf to join him the previous night. The men rode along the Assiniboine River so Olaf could see the stately homes of the wealthy retired company officers, McDermot explaining they chose to remain with their Indian wives and English-speaking métis families. These retirees were the aristocracy of the community.

Next, the tour headed north of the fort along the west side of the Red River. Here were the farmers of Selkirk Colonies, Highland Scots, who came in 1812. Their simplistic, but orderly narrow farms trailed some two miles back from the river. Fine substantial houses with lush landscaped yards and deep green lawns reached out to the river. Olaf was intrigued by the old world appearance, particularly the numerous wind mills, with huge sails turning gracefully far above the tree line at every river's bend, supplying the power for grinding grain into flour.

"Dis is qvite a trill to dis farm boy, Mr. McDermot," Olaf said.

"Yes, isn't it now? They have survived nobly, but lived frugally, my friend. See what I mean by saying what it could have been for them if they'd had available markets?" He smiled as he pointed ahead, "Here are more of the retired company residences up ahead. Some of those wealthy officers own as much as three thousand acres, would you believe?"

"Wow." Olaf reacted, "Dat vill be virt tousands ven steamboats and da rail reaches here. It'll all come sooner den vun tinks."

"Some day. Some day." The prosperous merchant nodded in agreement.

The tour ending, Olaf thanked Andrew McDermot for the enjoyable scenic tour of the unique Red River, and apologized for having to move on.

Friendly residents gathered around Olaf as if he were some prominent dignitary from afar when he said his good-byes. They showed sincere sadness that he was leaving. He thanked them for their congeniality, promising he'd be back soon to this world few outsiders had ever visited.

* * *

One more stop was to be made. It had been lingering in Olaf's mind, even during the pomp and ceremony at the fort. He was hopeful some small thread of information could be found, a clue, to shed light on the long, long disappearance of his precious one.

Faithful Dancer Girl was ready to trot. Whinnying and snorting, she tossed her head up and down while eating her morning oats.

"Ve'll soon be headin home to da pasture and a much deserved rest, Dancer," Olaf promised. She nodded approvingly, Olaf understood that.

Crossing the Red River instilled a sense of anxiety in the Swede's mind. The privacy and isolation of these Roman Catholics behind foreboding walls was troubling to Olaf, but having waited and worried so long, he'd confront those who might help solve the agonizing mystery.

Olaf reached the great arched door at the front of the towering St. Boniface Cathedral. He entered apprehensively. The high ceilinged entry was dimly lit. Having just left bright sunlight outside, it took several moments for his eyes to adjust. Candles highlighted the stature of the baby Jesus and other religious symbols he recognized. The profound smell of incense suggested a spiritual presence, and the Swedish Lutheran felt like he was being a transgressor.

Then, two shadowy objects moved about, spooking Olaf momentarily. As they took candles from a table, he realized they were nuns. Two glowing white faces came floating eerily toward him.

"Bonjour, Monsieur? Qu'est-ce? Qu'est-ce? que c'est?" One asked accommodatingly.

"I speak only English, sisters. I come ta ask about somevun I knew from here about four years ago. Could ya help me?" Olaf asked.

The nuns shook their heads. *"Nous non comprenons pas, Monsieur."* They bowed, motioned he should stay, then, departed hastily as if going to seek assistance.

The determined Swede was relieved he'd broken the ice. His curiosity focused on the large arched doors leading into the sanctuary of the big Cathedral. He shuffled over and slipped inside for a quick view, aware he was probably snooping where he shouldn't. The awesome grandeur of the place was breathtaking! He looked at the altar and saw a most life-like statue of Jesus knocking at a door, and another of the Virgin Mary kneeling in prayer. Then, he saw the vivid paintings of the stations of the cross elaborately displayed on the church walls. Glancing upwards, the entire domed arch was filled with heavenly angels. The magnificent array was mind boggling, and he became weak-kneed.

Abruptly, every figure seemed to come alive, and the astounded Swede froze in his tracks! The fear of God shot through his veins! Finally, regaining his senses, he glanced up for one last look, but this time he could have sworn Jesus waved back! He stumbled out quickly! Once in the foyer he shook his head at such elusive affects the life-like biblical images projected. "Vell, I had no business goin in der, anyvey," he mumbled, while gradually getting hold of himself.

The two nuns returned with a young handsome bearded man wearing a black cape of sorts. He had a distinct swagger in his walk. The olive-toned, black-eyed man had the distinguishing hue of a métis, Olaf thought.

"Greetings, Monsieur. Speak fair English. Can help you?"

"Oh, tank ya, sir. I vas hopin ta see da Bishop, if possible."

"Very well, big man. Follow me. Bishop Tache will see you in the sacristy." He smiled most congenially. "I, Louis Riel, assist good Bishop when home from Christian studies in Montreal. God willing, hope to become priest one day."

"I bet you'd be a good vun too. Ya have a friendly vay about ya."

Upon reaching the door to the Bishop's quarters, Louis Riel paused, "By way, how I present you to Bishop Tache?"

"Oh, I beg yer pardon. My name is Olaf Olsson from St. Paul, in the States."

Abruptly, Riel stopped in his tracks. His friendly smile transformed into an angry glaring stare. Olaf was shocked at this sudden display of resentment, wondering what he'd done to anger the man.

Opening the door unceremoniously, Riel's anger reflected in an icy introduction. "This is Olaf Olsson," Riel blurted, and then abruptly stormed away.

Bishop Tache sat behind a rustic desk, amongst a stack of papers he'd been reading. He looked shocked at the rude introduction by his young assistant. The Bishop then eyed Olaf curiously. Olaf's nerves were now frayed. All he wanted was a bit of information, never expecting such an antagonistic reception. He looked pleadingly at the Holy Father, then forced a smile, hoping to melt the icy stare.

Bishop Tache finally gave a thin smile and spoke. "The Bois Brules tell of many happy tales of cart travels; tell of many happy occasions with great sandy topped comrade below the border." He smirked. "So, what brings you to the Northland to honor us so, Mr. Olsson?"

Olaf wasn't convinced the Bishop was receiving him as an honored guest, but at least he was willing to listen, Olaf thought. "Vell, I met vit da governor last night - my official reason. Da unofficial part is personal, yer Holiness."

"Personal? In what way, may I ask?" He sounded challenging.

"Vell, ah, I ah," Olaf was all flustered in confronting the Bishop. All of a sudden he closed up like a clam, wishing he hadn't come at all.

"Might as well settle down, Big Ole. I knew of your joining the buffalo hunt and your attraction to Marianne, Pierre LaMond's daughter." He paused a long time, staring at his visitor. "Incidentally, Louis Riel and Marianne were childhood playmates and Louis was upset when she lost interest in him after meeting you that time. That may explained his behavior."

He might as well have hit Olaf between the eyes with a brick bat. Olaf's thoughts turned and he started thinking - Big Olaf, da guy says. Seems he knows everyting. But vut business is it of anybody to make fun of my romantic affairs, anyvay, Olaf thought.

"Fatter, Marianne LaMond and I made a firm pledge to be faithful to each utter ferever. Now I have lost her and need help," he said desperately.

"Yes, but Marianne made a pledge to the church, too," the Bishop reminded him in evenly measured words.

"I know dat. Marianne vould not lie to me. She said she'd come back in vun year, after serving da church, as promised!" Olaf stormed.

The Bishop gave a quizzical look. "She told you that! I did not know," he said, showing more concern than Olaf had expected. Pacing the floor in silence for some time, the Father continued reflectively, "I like that beautiful child and I like her father, Pierre. He is not well, now." The Bishop palmed his forehead as though he were troubled.

The frustrated Swede just kept quiet and waited.

"Pierre told me he wrote his daughter last year, saying he

wanted to see her, but when the boats came down river, there was no word. It takes a year to get an answer by boats, Mr. Olsson."

"A year?"

"*Oui.*" He sat again. "The sisters had such high regard and aspirations for Marianne who showed exceptional signs of being in a state of grace, and they thought her residing at the Montreal Monastery was what God wanted." He was speaking introspectively, it seemed. Now, looking directly at his visitor, he pontificated, "Mr. Olsson, if she had decided to pursue a life of dedication and poverty, she would be in her own cubicle, praying. Visitors are rarely allowed, but when they are, they must speak to her through curtains. She could be praying continuously for years," he explained the traditional novitiate commitment.

Olaf had lost his power of speech, and sat in a dumbfounded fog.

Bishop Tache continued, "Marianne would have written her father, I'm sure. Or if what you say is true, and I have no reason to doubt that...All that I hear about you is honorable, and now that I've met you, I find you to be a sincere and likable person. I am sorry for your tragic dilemma, Mr. Olsson" He smiled sympathetically.

"But, it all sounds kind a fishy. Is der notting to be done? I must know, Bishop Tache. Marianne told me she had high regard for you and Bishop Provincher, and the nuns, so I come to you for help."

"Big Swede, I'll tell you what I'll do. I'll send an epistle with the returning boats to Montreal. I can't promise anything for certain, you understand." He stood, formulating his final thoughts. "If what you say about Marianne's wish to be true, I pray she was not unjustly influenced. That is not the intent of the Catholic Church."

Olaf, realizing the interview had ended, stood, and prepared to leave. For a moment he saw a ray of hope, but at the earliest, it would be another long year before any answer could be expected. He thanked the good Bishop for his time and compassionate understanding and headed back home.

The Red River Voyageur

"The voyageur smiles as he listens
To the sound that grows apace;
Well he knows the vesper ringing
Of the bells of St. Boniface.

"The bells of the Roman Mission,
That call from their turrets twain,
To the boatman on the river,
To the hunter on the plain.

John Greenleaf Whittier

POOR MATILDA

"Ho, ho, Gustav, I'm back," Olaf yelled while pounding on the door of Gustav's little log cabin in St. Paul. Olaf had just returned from a long stint in the wilderness and was anxious to find out how young brother was getting along.

The door flew open! "Olaf! God, man, good to see ya!" Gustav exclaimed. The two exchanged their usual rowdy Olsson bear hug. "Holy Cow, ya don't know how I've vurried about ya out dere in Injun country. Yeesus, I vunder if sometimes I'll never git to see ya again, Olaf," he said in a concerned voice. "Come in, bror."

The adventurous older brother held up a sack, and winked. "But can talk better after ve have a little snort, or two," he grinned, taking out a jug of rum, some beef jerky and pretzels. Olaf tossed them on the table. "Hey boy, git da cups, and ve'll celebrate--yist da two of us--huh?" They laughed and sparred about, slugging each other playfully, like they'd done since small boys back in Sweden.

"My God, man, ya must be doin good vit dat Burbank outfit, buyin expensive stuff like dis," Gustav raved.

"Oh ya," Olaf shrugged his shoulders flippantly. "Doin all right -- all right fer a big dumb Svede, I spose." They pounded on each other again, so the cabin timbers shook from the rowdiness.

Gustav had gotten his job back at the stock yards. They were eager to take him back as he'd established himself as a hard worker that first year where Cousin Rudolph was a trader. Then Rudolph went into farming, and Gustav went along and spent four years helping his cousins grub out trees and build the farm up north. Now at sixteen the strapping young lad had grown about a foot and was ready to take out on his own.

"Bet der glad to have ya back, da vey ya hustle, Gustav."

"Ja, sure seem satisfied vit me. But, brudder, I'm awful tickled

Hedner - The Big Swede

Jenny vaited fer me." Being excited, he flew into a wild jig and spilled some of his drink from his cup. "Oops!" he said. They laughed.

"Man, yer grinnin like a hog in the feed trough. Out vit it, Gus."

"I've been vaitin so I could tell ya da excitin news! Ya see, vun night Vashburns ver gone, and ve sat by da fire in da mansion, yist talkin like people do, ya know. Somehow, I asked Jenny if she'd ever consider farmin. 'Didn't mean to corner her like dat, but she yumped up and down, sayin she'd marry me as soon as Mrs. Vashburn vould release her from her services." The two then tipped their cups jubilantly.

Jenny and Gustav met at a church social for Swedish immigrants those first weeks in America, and their affections had been growing since, though Gustav managed to get to St. Paul to see her only a few times each year.

"Ah, hah, Gustav! By God, man dat sure calls fer anudder bump," Olaf roared as he filled the cups.

The noisy jostling came to a sudden halt by a tap on the door.

Little brother looked startled. "Oh, Holy Cow, Olaf, I almost fergot! Dat's Jenny, I betcha!" Gustav stashed the jug and cups up in the cupboard and tried tidying up a bit. "Comin, dear! I'm coming Jenny!" Gustav called out. Young brother looked as innocent as a lamb opening the door. "My sveet Jenny, nice to see you," he greeted her.

"Hello, Gustav," Jenny giggled, giving him a kiss on the cheek. Glancing over his shoulder, she spotted the visitor right away. "Olaf! What a surprise! When did you come?" she yelled happily.

Jumping up to greet her, Olaf accidentally bumped his head on the kerosene lamp hanging over the table, making it rock back and forth, casting shadow waves up and down the walls. Always the clown, Olaf put on an act of being knocked coo-coo and fell to the floor with his long legs sticking straight up.

Jenny giggled, applauding his act. She carried a basket of freshly baked blueberry muffins. "I'm glad I brought extra tonight, I had a strange inkling you might come, Olaf." She went directly to the stove to make coffee. Olaf could tell the two young romantics had been playing house regularly, because she knew where things were.

The three jabbered and joked as she worked, but when Jenny reached for the cupboard, Gustav popped out of his chair to intercept. Thinking Gustav offering to be helpful, she pushed him aside playfully, "No, I can do it, silly."

Well Jenny's face turned about as flush as a red hot stove when she laid eyes on that liquor bottle and the half filled cups. Turning back slowly with an accusing smirk on her face, she declared somberly, "Hm, boys will be boys, I guess."

"Awe, Jenny, I yist brought a little drink so ve could enjoy our visit a little more. Ve don't do dis much," Olaf assured her.

Jenny finally admitted she wasn't totally opposed to a social glass now and then, as long as they only drink to moderation.

Olaf dramatized the exciting high points of his trail blazing for the two. Jenny's eyes were big as saucers, taking it all in; his escapades with the Indians, and the frightening scare to his partner, Mousey, when he was nearly killed by Scarface Williams. Jenny and Gustav smiled over Mousey's touching romance with the Indian maiden, Singing Bird.

"Oh what a delightfully happy ending to that story, Olaf." Seeming somewhat pensive, she added, "but I can't stay long tonight. Olaf, I planned to give Gustav an elocution lesson. You should improve some more too. Goodness, it's been a long time since you studied with us, Olaf," she reminded. "You boys want to sound like real Americans, don't you?"

"Awe, ve don't need it," Olaf quipped. "Vee talk *Svenske.*" The two big strappers started acting up again: *"Hur some gjorda, Gus?"*

"Oh, bradda bra, bror," Gustav answered.

Jenny snickered at the tomfoolery, and poured the coffee.

"Tack fer motten," Olaf jibed, thanking her for the coffee.

"Ja, tack sa mycket, Gustav mocked, thanking her.

She continued giggling, but was getting slightly irritated, wanting the boys to get serious about the lesson. Tonight they'd work on the th sounds. Jenny was a good teacher. Having had the best tutors in town, she could show them how to say the th sounds, which Swedes had trouble with. When concentrating, saying 'these' and 'those' were easy for the boys to pronounce, but away

174

at work, they slipped into their bad habits of saying deze and doze.

"Deze -- these," Olaf corrected himself, "are sure good muffins, Jenny, I tell ya." Olaf praised.

"Have another. Clean the plate and we'll have good weather tomorrow," she joked. "My Papa always said that."

"Ja, whose didn't? Papa Olsson said that, too." Olaf drew chuckles.

The boys did well on their th sounds, but the lesson was short. Jenny was a tad nervous, saying "I must get back to Mrs. Washburn, she's not doing too well right now." Jenny hurried cleaning the dishes.

"Vot's wrong vit her, den -- then?" Olaf corrected himself again.

"Oh, nothing too serious, I guess. It's quite personal. Gustav can tell you about it sometime," Jenny said, evading the question.

Because it was dark, Gustav insisted he'd walk Jenny home.

Olaf's rig was standing out front, and he made a big production of offering it to the kids, pronouncing the th sounds slowly and with emphasis. "Those horses of mine are hitched to the buckboard. You take them Gustav, and drive her home. Then, I vill vait fer ya here."

Jenny giggled. "You got it right, Olaf! Keep working, and you'll soon say it right all the time." The ecstatic couple then left.

It didn't take long at all for his kid brother to return. But Olaf noticed Gustav's looking rather gloomy. He interceded. "Lill bror, a vile ago ya ver all vound up like a spinnin top, but now ya look as sad as a hound dog vit a bad cold. Vot' troublin ya, anyhow? Better tell me da whole virks."

Gustav finally admitted having an appointment with Pastor Tolickson tomorrow, to seek his counsel and blessings on their desired marriage. He felt bad because neither Jenny's or his parents were in this country to present them. He guessed they might as well forget it altogether.

"Vait a minute, Gustav. I got a letter from papa making me your legal guardian. I vould go vit the two of ya," Olaf proudly vowed.

"Vould ya, Olaf? Vould ya really do dat--I mean...that?"

"Sure I vill. I'd be honored to vouch fer the two a ya."

Their plans were to get married and then farm as soon as possible. They'd known each other over four years, Gustav pointed out.

But, there was more to it than that. The kids wondered if Olaf might talk to Matilda Washburn, in as much as she was so taken with the big frontiersman. Maybe he could talk some sense into her, so she'd agree to release Jenny from her obligation of two more years, her payment for Matilda's bringing Jenny to America.

Olaf leaned back chuckling. "Vot else ya vont me to do? Part the vaters so ya can git across vit out gettin vet? Holy Moses, boy, dat's vun big order." He continued snickering, then suddenly stopped. "Of course I vill try to talk to her. It may do no good, though. But...first things first. Vot time ya sposed ta meet da preacher?"

"Ten o'clock ve're sposed to be dere. Will you really do that for us?" Gustav grinned like one battle was being won, anyway.

"Sure. Glad to." He looked at his new big pocket watch Burbanks had given him. "Have to go take care of some late vagon business now. I'll pick you up early, at nine. Ve'll talk about Mrs. Vashburn. _That_ might be tougher _than_ partin vater," Olaf accentuated Jenny's lesson.

* * *

The day was bright and sunny.

"Giddy up, ponies," Olaf yelled, splitting the air with the crack of his buggy ship. "I'm glad ya vanted me to go vit the two of ya. Yer lucky to find such a purdy vun," Olaf confided. He glanced over at his little brother. Detecting a troublesome expression, he forced the issue about Gustav's long face until he finally let the 'cat out of the bag'.

"I didn't vant ta tell everything, but I'm vurried, brudder. Ya see, goin in to da mansion is like stickin yer head in a hornet's nest."

"Vell, Gustav, I tink ya better tell me da whole story. I know her pretty good; rubbed elbows vit her several times ven I was a guest of Burbanks and Blakelys. Maybe I can help some vey."

"It's Mrs. Vashburn's mental condition dat's on da rocks. At

176

first I thought maybe she yist didn't like me, ya know, but Jenny explained how completely mixed up she is. Goin tru life's doldrums," she says. "I never knew vomen got so crazy in da head ven dey cross over from young to old. Vie, she'd next ta takin her own life sometimes, Jenny says."

"Ah, vell, I know about dat stuff, boy. Dere nerves go to pieces; but dey get over dat in time," he assured. "Not all vomen go tru dat."

"I hope she feels better soon. It's sure hard on Jenny seein her veep all da time. Mrs. Vashburn hasn't gone out of the house fer monts. Tinks, I mean <u>thinks</u>, she's gettin old and ugly, ya know."

"Holy cow, brudder, I never seen anyone more sharmin," Olaf raved.

"Ja, but it's in her head, ya know, and she's gone to see doctors vey down in St. Louis, and everything. God, I feel sorry fer her. Olaf, ya have to be careful vot ya say; she might go off da deep end anytime."

"Vell, thank ya fer tellin me. I'll be careful not to upset her. Don't vurry," he assured Gustav confidently.

They rode through the huge brick archway and headed up the curved cobble stone drive to the side entry next to the carriage house. Gustav jumped down and jogged up to the service entry. Jenny popped out, still in her house coat, her flaxen hair still wrapped in curling ribbons. Olaf smiled to himself as the two infatuated love birds romantically nuzzled each other. Then, they went into the mansion.

It was a gorgeous place, such as few immigrants had ever seen. The garden displayed flowers of every color; red, yellow, gold and russet fall blooms. It must be heavenly to live in such an exotic place, Olaf thought. He watched a small water wheel in the stream carry water up to the top where it poured out to form a small falls over a picturesque rock garden. So peaceful and serene, he thought.

Suddenly, the scene was interrupted by the appearance of none other than Mrs. Washburn, herself. She left the verandah and strolled through the flowery path. She walked slowly, as if without purpose or destination in her strolling. Reaching down, she plucked a flower, but didn't as much as examine or admire its beauty. Olaf could see how troubled she appeared, and wondered if he shouldn't try to cheer her up a bit, if he could.

Hopping to the ground, he moved ever so cautiously, not wanting to frighten her. Still at a distance, he greeted, "Hello, Mrs. Vashburn. It's such a lovely day, isn't it?"

Turning quickly, Olaf saw a startled look on her face! "Oh, I didn't hear you," she said under her breath, and stared for a long time. It seemed as if she didn't recognize the big Swede. Then she looked at the flower she was holding; her eye brows lowered and came together, revealing deep fear or worry lines, then again, she focused on her visitor.

It was shocking to see her ashen white face; her hair hanging lifeless, in long strands like a mad woman, he thought. Not believing his eyes, he wondered how this attractive socialite he had known, looked so bedraggled. Rarely was the big Swede short on words, but now he grasped for some way to express himself. He finally stammered timidly, "Mrs. Vashburn, I...I haven't seen ya for many monts...months," he corrected, trying to speak his new proper English.

Returning a glance, she finally mustered a weak smile, which evaporated quickly. She folded her arms in front of her and turned away, as if realizing her wild, disheveled appearance.

"Ja...you have the prettiest flowers in the vorld, Mrs. Vashburn," he said, trying to flatter and relax her.

Finally, speaking weakly. "Thank you, Olaf. I thought you were someone else at first."

There was not a more compassionate soul than the tall Swede, and his heart ached for the suffering lady standing there, agonizing amongst her lovely flowers. He recalled little brother's remarks about her feeling old, ugly and unwanted. So he put on his best smile and said, "Mrs. Vashburn, I vas at the concert last Saturday evening with Burbanks and Blakelys. I missed you."

She looked up, smiling dryly as if to imply that no one in the world could care the least. "You missed me, Mr. Olsson?" Then, under her breath, she added, "How nice of you to say that." her smile transformed into a look of pain and wretchedness.

Perhaps he should have stayed at the surrey, he wondered, leaving the troubled lady to resolve her own dilemma.

But, momentarily coming out of the apparent trance, it seemed she'd returned to the present, becoming rational again. "I heard of your promotions with Burbanks," she half whispered. "You've brought some excitement to this remote territory with your daring escapades on the frontier." She scanned his face, saying, "It's easy to see why local women admire you so."

"Oh, tank, -- thank ya," he smiled broadly, "I haven't done anything so unusual; yist love the country and the adventure this yob gives." He was shocked he'd broken the seemingly impenetrable shell.

Jenny and Gustav popped out the side door. "Hurry, Olaf, or ve'll be late for the appointment," Gustav urged.

Matilda started trembling, as if going into shock. She put her hands up to her face, and turning away, she began sobbing.

Olaf sympathized, but feeling helpless he bid farewell. "Mrs. Vashburn, I...enjoyed the visit." He stood there for a time, wondering what more he could have done to ease her mind.

Turning quickly to see if he had left, she began rambling in a desperate, cracked voice, "Oh, Olaf, my whole world's falling apart, and now I'm about to lose the only thing I have left - my little girl." She shook her head in desperation. Her eyes, full of pain, she stopped sobbing, and pleaded, "Olaf, I'm so desperate! I have no one to talk to like this. It helps! It really helps talking to someone about my melancholy -- and my condition." She looked up pleadingly. "Olaf, could we talk again? Oh, please? she begged. "Please?"

"Ja -- Ja, sure Mrs. Vashburn. Anytime. Anything I can do. Please tell me ven," he said.

Through her sniffling and choking, she whispered, "Tomorrow, early afternoon. Would you come? Jenny has her music lesson, and then plans to visit her friend the rest of the afternoon. I would be so grateful if you would," she gasped desperately.

"Sure. Sure," he smiled reassuringly. "I promise I'll be here. Try to get some rest now, Mrs. Vashburn."

She gave a weak smile. He backed away and returned to the surrey, full of anguish and concern for the poor suffering soul.

* * *

The kids were starry eyed, deeply in love and eager to discuss their engagement with Pastor Tolickson.

Olaf was preoccupied over his planned meeting with the emotionally troubled Matilda Washburn, but wasn't about to put a damper on the kid's thrilling moments. He'd do the best he could in his private meeting tomorrow, but knew it wouldn't be easy convincing Matilda to cut the apron strings. Olaf reflected on his own precarious romantic situation. It would sure be nice to be in Gustav's boots, he thought, with a planned future well in hand and starting his own family. Memories of Marianne lingered in his mind, but with each passing year without her, he had all but resigned himself to a lonely life of bachelorhood.

* * *

The great oak door opened abruptly! The startled Swede was taken back by the amazing sight, for Matilda Washburn had been transformed into an astonishing apparition, he thought. Though her face was stoic and expressionless, her physical appearance was ravishing. She was dressed in a spectacular floor length silver-gray robe trimmed about the collar and down the folded edge with a white feathery down which rippled from the doorway breeze. Her hair, combed straight back, joined in a natty pug over her left shoulder. Olaf was puzzled; in a way, she looked stern and threatening, but in another, he saw a mysteriously inviting woman, painfully crying out for attention.

His power of speech totally vanished being entranced by two large dangling diamond earrings, and the even larger gems in the necklace embracing her low cut neckline. They sent back sparks of fire from the sun beating down over his shoulder. He became desperately weak in his knees.

"The cat got my tongue, Mrs. Vashburn," he confessed. She remained silent, giving a slightly noticeable closed-lipped smile, waiting for a more profound greeting. Olaf stammered clumsily, "Ya...ya are the most beautiful voman...uh...I, I ever seen in all my livin days." He bit his tongue again, thinking, that was sure a dumb thing to say.

Finally, with an intimidating smile and a hollow voice, she said, "Come in, Mr. Olsson." She moved as if floating on clouds, he thought.

Olaf gawked at the high ceilings and the huge center candelabra hanging from it. He strode across the thick Oriental rugs, as she led him to a room for her desired meeting. She said, "Sit, Mr. Olsson."

Nervous as a kitten in water, he eyed the plush ruby upholstered furniture she wanted him to sit on, not sure if it was supposed to be chair or half bed. He hesitated.

"Sit, Mr. Olsson! This is just a King Louis chaise lounge."

"But, it's so purdy, I might soil it," he said weakly.

"Nonsense! Sit, Olaf," she said firmly.

He was shaking in his boots plenty, for Jenny had warned that Matilda could become confused at the least provocation, so decided he'd better cooperate with her on every turn. He sat. She moved to a small serving table, and poured two glasses of wine from a fancy crystal decanter.

"Here, Mr. Olsson, have this. It is the only thing that settles my nerves these days," she smiled. "It's amontillado wine, it eases my pain."

"Thank ya," he mumbled, trying to control his shaking hands.

"Now then, Mr. Olsson," she began pacing the floor, becoming more fidgety, constantly twisting her glass. "I suppose you wonder why I needed someone to talk to. I'll be straight forward." Taking another sip, she continued pacing. "I have been living in a hellish prison, Mr. Olsson!" Then, as though she intended pouring out her soul, she went back in time, "Oh, I have money, position, influence--everything!" She poured another glass for herself, took another sip before completing her sentence. "Everything, but nothing, Mr. Olsson." She mellowed. "I mean Olaf. After all, we are friends, aren't we?"

"Ja, ja, Mrs. Vashburn," Olaf responded, but he had no idea what she was driving at, and tried being careful not to upset her.

She paced back and forth several times, without saying a word, and as if arranging her thoughts, she proceeded. "Olaf, I asked you here for the purpose of convincing you to discourage your brother and my Jenny from getting married. I have a contract for her services for two more years." He detected a harshness in her voice which, he thought, could easily culminate into a violent outburst, but she seemed to catch herself. Studying him, she sighed, and became strangely emotionless again and merely dropped the subject, Olaf noticed.

Slipping back in the past, a near smile came over her face as she began dreamily, near whining, "Mr. Olsson, I came from Boston, was married to a fine young man who had a great promising career in finance. Michael was so tall, handsome and successful." She paused, and looked at Olaf somewhat enviously, as if appealing for understanding. She emptied her wine glass. Her voice again became dry and harsh as she continued. "There was a financial crisis, and the market crashed!" She finally turned directly to the Swede, who was beginning to feel left out of the conversation. Her voice dropped down to a raspy whisper. "We lost everything!" She paused, poured another drink and said in finality; "Michael took his own life!"

"My God, I'm sorry, Mrs. Vashburn," Olaf gasped.

"Then, I had nothing," she said coldly, as if seeking sympathy. "I never told anyone before, but I felt a need to finally tell someone. It happens to be you." The rest of her revelation was unemotional. "At one point Mr. Washburn came East, and I met him at a social function. He was a successful business man from Chicago. Though older, he offered the security of a privileged life to which I had become accustomed," she said.

Breaking her train of thought she stopped. Going to Olaf, she put her hand on his arm, and revealed, "Oh God, Olaf, you cannot imagine how comforting it is having you to confide in. This has helped me immensely."

She visited the wine table again, but noticing that Olaf's glass was not empty, by-passed him. Olaf worried, aware that excessive drinking was bound to effect her behavior and became concerned for the immediate consequences.

Matilda meandered again, slipping into despondency and talking under her breath. She turned quickly towards him, and most maudlinly pleaded, "I'm getting old now! And Mr. Washburn, twenty-six years my senior has become decrepit, nearly blind, and is almost stone deaf." Refilling her glass, and sipping constantly, she came directly to Olaf and confided, "He is unable to hold his bowels!"

"What," Olaf blurted, not knowing what she said which sounded awful!

Whispering, she confided, "He shits in his pants!"

Olaf started laughing in an emotional release, then turned red in embarrassment. "Oh, I'm sorry. I didn't mean to laugh. It's sad."

She smiled in sympathy for her guest's blunder, but continued, wanting more compassion, "And he has not been a husband for most of our married years. What do you think of that?"

Uneasy, Olaf felt he had to flatter and help boost her confidence, so he praised her. "Mrs. Vashburn, if it pleases you, I think you're beautiful; certainly a young and vital voman."

Stopping in her tracks, she stared at the big fellow for what seemed to be an eternity, showing appreciation at such flattery.

He squirmed for fear he'd said the wrong thing, ever aware of her precarious state of mind.

Whimpering in self pity, the dramatics continued. "Four years ago the light of my life came in the form of a poor immigrant girl who became a vital part of my very existence." She choked back her tears. "Now, Mr. Olsson - Olaf - I selfishly want to keep her."

Olaf stiffened at her remarks. Lord, he thought, how would he ever get such a troubled woman's approval for Jenny and Gustav's wedding plans. He pondered the likelihood of having to tell the love struck kids he'd failed, but mentioning it now might bring on a violent outburst.

Matilda quickly dropped the subject and altered her train of thought, and became somewhat intimidating. "I was doing quite well with the mental stress, Mr. Olsson - Olaf - and then, yesterday in the garden, you came. I turned, and in my confusion, I looked up and thought my first husband had returned from the dead." She came to Olaf and sat next to him. With a child-like innocence she said, "Olaf, you look so much like Michael. You have such warm comforting eyes, and such a kind way about you."

Olaf squirmed. Was she cozying up to him, he wondered?

She uttered, "Yes, I can understand why the women in the guild are so taken with their big idol of the frontier, and rave over his escapades of daring," she smiled at him with envy. He fidgeted.

How would he ever get out of this, he worried. He tried to stand, indicating it was time to leave, fearing Matilda would go into another seige of despondency, but she grasped him tightly.

She whimpered again. "Now I'm getting old, my head aches, and I burn up in anxieties. Oh! I don't want to be old!" She kept shaking and sobbing to herself. It was the wine, Olaf figured she'd had too much.

Olaf tried comforting her, but each time he'd repeat how sorry he was, she'd sob more and more. Finally, reaching up, he patted her arm and said. "You poor soul, I feel awful bad for you."

The much older Mr. Washburn hadn't shown such caring tenderness, Matilda confided. He hadn't touched her in many years. She said her husband had been too engrossed in counting money, working in his mills during the day. He then spent the evenings catching butterflies in the flower garden. Olaf was sad that Washburn ignored this beautiful woman.

She continued shaking and weeping, and Olaf put his hand on her shoulder, patting her sympathetically. She leaned on him and confessed, "Oh, Olaf, I looked at your warm comforting eyes in the garden, and I hoped I could talk to you like this! I've never been able to reveal my frustrations to anyone in town, not the strong influential community leader people think I am. Then the word would quickly circulate how weak and disorganized I am, and what a nervous wretch I've become." She was mellowing a lot, Olaf saw.

"No, no, Mrs. Vashburn. You are such a fine, vell respected voman." He now felt responsible to hold her, soothe her and comfort her the best he knew how.

She got into such a sobbing spell. Olaf didn't know what to do. He was plenty nervous, feeling so clumsy in such a delicate situation. When she got control of herself and eased up on the crying, Olaf tried withdrawing his arm, being the gentleman he was. But, like a small infant, she needed coddling, so she just turned on the weeping and lay her head on his chest, begging for tender affection.

The big Swede was downright flustered. She would only quiet

herself when he held her tightly and comforted her the way she wanted. Her over-indulgence of wine had obviously altered her desires from a need for sympathy and understanding, to a desperate ache for physical gratification. She put her hand directly on Olaf.

"Mrs. Vashburn! Matilda!" he said. "Are ya sure?"

She, in her satiable desires, assured him. "Oh, Yes! Oh, yes, Olaf." She leaned back in her passion. Olaf's eyes gazed on her feminine softness, her robe parting, showing a most revealing firm breast, which suddenly seemed inviting.

Olaf was shocked at first. He thought of reaching over and pulling her robe over her bosom. But he didn't. He was aroused at the sight. She nestled closely.

"You are so gentle and warm," Matilda whispered.

Now, Olaf wouldn't argue with that as little drops of perspiration popped out on his forehead. Each time he suggested he better go home now, she'd moan and tremble, giving him no recourse.

She finally said, "Michael. Please hold me tighter, Michael."

Olaf was overwhelmed by Matilda's passionate desires, and she settled down like a purring kitten. He comforted her in the best way he knew how. When it comes right down to it, Olaf grinned to himself, it's awfully nice holding onto such a glamorous lady. It didn't seem exactly right, but on the other hand, it sure felt good. Seeing how Matilda had settled down, now relaxed and tenseness gone; it all seemed so natural.

"Olaf," she begged, "please help me to the bedroom it's much more comfortable for us in there."

The hours flew by, and Matilda's highly emotional situation drastically changed. The anxiety had left her. The worry and pain wrinkles disappeared from around her eyes, as she eventually slept in his arms. After all, she'd had a lot of wine.

Late afternoon shadows were darkening the room. Jenny would certainly be along soon to check on her adopted mother, and Old Man Washburn would be trotting up the cobblestone path in his old one-horsed carriage. Though Olaf worried over the consequences of waking the peaceful lady, he had no choice but to do so as tenderly as possible.

"Matilda. Matilda," he repeated softly. She sighed, "Mmmm," a relaxed smile on her face. "Matilda," he whispered, "It is getting late. Everybody will be coming home now," he anxiously reminded her.

She seemed confused at first and looked about the room to see where she was. "Oh, dear, maybe I had more wine than I should have." She smiled again. "No, I had just the right amount. Yes," she kissed Olaf tenderly, "it's getting late."

It seemed as though Matilda had come back from a fantastic venture into a dreamland of grand expectations. It seemed she was happily at peace with herself. Neither spoke for several moments.

"Olaf," she finally said, "I want you to know how grand this tryst was for me. I know this must sound crazy, but I suddenly feel a new breath of life. Once again, I'm a new vibrant woman."

Olaf smiled, "Ya look vunderful, Matilda; yist like the pretty, and strong villed voman I've alvays known."

"Hm," she smiled, "It's strange the way a person can allow oneself to become confused. It's as though every day storm clouds churn and never let the sun shine through." She smiled, "Now, the sky is clear blue, and the sun is warm." She continued, "Olaf, will your forgive me for my unnatural behavior?" She smiled softly, "Thank you, Olaf, for helping me through the storm."

"Matilda, I've alvays had the greatest respect and admiration for ya. Certainly, nothing has changed, my friend," he said assuredly.

"You are a most unusual and wonderful man, Olaf." She smirked a bit teasingly, "Please forgive me for intruding on your life."

Matilda never knew Olaf had any romantic ties, so she probably felt the great charming frontiersman needed this moment of rapturous love, especially after fortifying herself with ample wine. On the other hand, Olaf had lost nearly all hope of ever seeing his alluring métis again, it being four years, and no answer to his letters.

Olaf chuckled, amusedly, "I really better go now, the hour is late."

"Yes, yes, Olaf, I'll see you to the door." She said while slipping into her exotic silver-gray robe with the rippling feathers.

Olaf gazed at the radiantly charming lady, and gave her a tender supportive embrace.

"You know what, Olaf?" She had a pixie-like twinkle in her eye.

"Vot? Vot?" He urged, wanting to know what excited her so.

"I'm thinking this town is about to have the biggest and fanciest wedding they've ever seen."

"Ah, ha," Olaf laughed, giving a spontaneous hug. "The kids vill be very happy!" he assured her, and then left to tell them of her strange change of heart. But, he would never, ever tell anything else about the day when Matilda Washburn crossed over the bridge, to a new happy life.

Olaf grinned while riding away. Standing at the end of the cobblestone driveway was none other than Mrs. Higgenbottom and her temperance friends shaking their 'naughty, naughty' index fingers at him.

"Lovely day, ladies," Olaf nodded, tipping his hat most respectfully.

❄   ❄   ❄   ❄   ❄

A DELIGHTFUL VEDDING

Olaf felt so damned disoriented he didn't know east from west, riding Dancer Girl through the blinding blizzard. His big sheepskin mackinaw was pulled up tight and the flaps of his furry beaver hat were pulled down over his ears and forehead. The strings were tied under his chin to keep the driving snow out. The steam from his breath frosted his mustache. His eyelids, frozen together, pulled as he blinked.

Had he not stayed to help locate the stranded Wilber Barfnechts west of St. Cloud, he could have made Gustav's wedding in time to enjoy the pre-nuptial hoopla, visit with Cousin Rudy and the others. On the other hand, if he hadn't rescued the German family, Mrs. Barfnecht, who was sick, would have died of exposure. There was nothing else he could have done.

He checked his new big pocket watch. "C'mon, babe girl, it all depends on you now," he urged Dancer Girl along. Raising his shoulders and lowering his head into his coat, he lit his pipe again. Smoking was relaxing and the warming of the bowl felt good.

What a hell of a time to get married anyway, he thought; even a squirrel knows enough to stay in its den and sleep it out. But, those young ones are so in love ... I s'pose it makes sense.

Suddenly a dark shadowy object appeared ahead. He rode up to the lee side, away from the wind, and found himself next to the big barn at the St. Anthony Falls stables. He burst out in haughty laughter at the amazing miracle!

"Good girl, Dancer," he shouted wildly. "Good girl!" Hopping off, he kicked the double door open and led his amazing big gray mare into the warm barn. Dancer whinnied, greeting her stable companions. A chorus of whinnies erupted from the others.

Martin, the stable boy, came running. "Swede! Swede! Everybody's been lookin' fer ya. Yer brother's gittin married today!"

"Ja, Ja. I know. I can yist make it I think. Get the halter on Dancer and put her in her stall, vill ya? Hitch up Bessie and Bell to the bobsled vile I run in to change my duds," He babbled, then raced over to the headquarters.

Johnny Bizby, the office boy, was the only one on hand. "Vare in the hell is everybody?" Olaf asked, tearing into the closet to retrieve some dressy trousers and a clean shirt.

"They're all over in the Hall for Gustav's wedding. Didn't ya know?" he asked.

"Gustav's vedding?" Olaf blurted. "But I thought it vas going to be such a small affair."

"No. Mrs. Washburn decided otherwise, I guess. Mr. Burbank, Mr. Blakely and Mr. Moen all took the afternoon off, Swede. It's big doings, I tell ya," he related excitedly.

"Holy heifer dust," the big fella grunted. After he put on his dressy clothes, he splashed some water on his face, and ran his wet hand through his hair. He was having a little trouble trying to get his waves managed. Finally he said, "Oh hell vit it! That's good enough."

Olaf trotted the little bays, Bessie and Bell, at full gate, crossed the new suspension bridge, not even pausing to throw Captain Tapper, gatekeeper, the nickel toll. "Get ya double next time," he yelled, "got ta git to my brudder's veddin."

"Go, Swede, go!" The gatekeeper roared, then added, "I won't even fine ya the sawbuck for racin' across this time, ya rascal."

Olaf glanced at his watch and grinned broadly. There will be some surprised faces when they see this old reprobate pop up, he laughed boisterously.

Pulling up to the hall and seeing the large assortment of buggies, spring board, and carriages, it was easy to guess there would be a big to-do after all. Mrs. Washburn's regal white carriage stood out amongst a half dozen fancy rigs, even ahead of J.C.'s classy coach. Olaf was glad to see some -- not so fancy -- oxen and wagons tied over yonder. Matilda was kind enough to include some of their poor Swede immigrant friends.

"*God dag*, Olaf. Come in this way," Cousin Rudolph called.

Olaf made a dash for the door. "*God dag*, Rudy, I'm glad to see you could come down. You must have beat the storm." He gave the usual bear hug greeting. *"Hur som gjorda, kusin?"*

"That we did. Wouldn't have missed it fer nothin! But, get inside fast. Your brother's fit to be tied, fer sure," he urged.

Olaf laughed, and entered. It was bedlam in that little room, and sparks began flying as Gustav vented his ire.

"Vare the hell have ya been, Bror? I been vorryin' so, thinkin' you'd never make it." He was near breaking down.

"Awe, c'mon Gus, no horse marbles now! Here, how about an old fashioned Olsson greeting?" He gave Gustav an exuberant hug.

"You're my only real family, ya know, and I was vorried sick ya mightn't make it, " Gustav lamented.

The boy's friends: Mr. Moen, Rudy, and a few of Gustav's pals from the stockyards, were trying to get everybody organized. It was time to start. Reverend Tolickson came out with a black dress coat for Olaf, like the one Gus had on. These coats were used for young immigrants wanting a dressy wedding to look like important people.

Olaf donned his coat, put his arm around his brother's shoulders, and they admired themselves in the looking glass. "Ve look like a couple a preachers, Gustav," Olaf said as they guffawed playfully.

Everyone was settled down now, and it seemed the obvious tensions of the bridegroom were under control. Soon, strains of the pump organ could be heard playing introductory music. The gangly Gustav, only an inch shorter than his big brother, began pacing the floor. Cousin Rudolph, Olaf and the others chuckled at his nervous behavior. Lining up to enter the auditorium, Gus suddenly took on a sickly pallor, showing a look of desperation.

"Vot's the matter now, Bror?" Olaf asked.

Gustav groaned, "Olaf, I gotta pee, vouldn't ya know it."

Cousin Rudy overhead the urgent plea. "Over there behind the screen there's a commode. You've got time, but hurry." The snickering was contagious, even Reverend Tolickson bent over with laughter.

Gustav gave a hefty gasp of relief from behind the curtain and returned. Unfortunately, Olaf had missed rehearsal so the parson told him where to stand by pointing through the open door. The music began again and the big Swede was pushed out to take his place. There was a chorus of "ahs" filtering through the crowd on seeing Olaf, for just about everybody thought the frontiersman had not made it. Olaf gave a sly smirk to Mr. Burbank and the others which brought on amusing chuckles from the gathering.

Glancing to the other side, and directly in the front pew, Olaf sobered seeing Matilda Washburn, Jenny's beautiful and stately American mother. She smiled weakly and looked down, but shyly peered up again. It was the first time they'd seen each other since that fateful day at the mansion several months ago. Olaf fixed his eyes on her and gave a strong smile of assurance; she straightened herself, and returned a nod of appreciation.

Gustav, ashen and noticeably nervous, came out and assumed his place next to his brother. Bridegroom and best man made an impressive appearance. Both standing, tall, with wavy blonde hair, they looked like they'd come out of the same mold.

Few had ever heard Lohengrin's Wedding March before in this frontier land, but Matilda Washburn, who'd seen a lot of opera in New York, knew it was the right music for her dear Jenny.

Madam Persoens, a recent transfer to the western frontier from the New York Opera House, and Jenny's music teacher played on the little pump organ with gusto. She had a typical operatic demeanor, along with an hour glass figure and a set of lungs defying the laws of human dimension. Her body pitched from side to side, her feet pumping vigorously. Olaf always joked, it looked like she was sitting on a hotplate and couldn't take the heat too long in one place.

The musical interlude ended. There was the usual tense excitement of anticipation for the grand entrance of the bride. Pastor Tolickson came out and took center stage. Gustav stepped down to his position right behind the parson. The Madam Persoens' hand flew in the air as she punched those foot pedals, starting the wedding march. Everybody stood, in eager expectation.

Donna Jean Moen, Sig Moen's daughter, who was Jenny's best

friend and the bridesmaid, began the walk down the aisle amid 'Oohs' and 'Ahs'. Matilda's seamstress had made her pretty dress to blend and to complement Jenny's. It was floor length, full-skirted knit costume covered by a sheer pink overlay.

Reaching the front, she took her place next to Olaf, who winked and whispered, "Ya look so pretty, maybe ve should have a double vedding, huh?" She blushed in embarrassment, of course.

The music reached a crescendo, the grand entrance at hand. And magnificent it was, as the lovely, dazzling Jenny stepped forward and beamed a smile so radiant the guests gave a gratifying expression of approval. Her exotic presence lit up the room as she stepped, paused, and proceeded down the aisle in a state of sheer ecstasy. Her stunning gown was of white fine imported lace, covered by a soft powder blue veil, in addition she wore a tiara of silk lavender and pink flowers.

Olaf noticed when Gustav stepped down and took Jenny's hand, he had suddenly transformed from a shy insecure brother to a man of pride and confidence, as though he'd just been given the whole world.

Pastor Tolickson gave an inspiring sermon, reminding that if they take the Lord with them, they'd be sure to have a happy and prosperous life; then he declared Gustav Olsson and Jenny Lindberg husband and wife. Everybody snickered, it seemed, when the two kissed - something that wasn't done often - but Matilda thought it would be an endearing touch.

Deprived and privileged alike were treated to an ostentatious ceremony. Matilda Washburn left no stone unturned in making this the most gala event. She also arranged a reception at the Nicollet House private party room. The reception line was a mix of the well-to-do and plain down-to-earth common folks, many newcomers to the land in the last year. Fine proper English with broken smatterings of Scandinavian and German filled the reception room.

Matilda was in her glory seeing that everything proceeded with the most impressive aplomb. Hosting the reception line, she greeted all most graciously.

"So pleased you and Mr. Burbank could honor us with your

presence, Mrs. Burbank," she said as they came through the line.

"My, it was such a beautiful ceremony, Matilda. Jenny and Gustav make such a handsome couple," Mrs. Burbank praised. "Thank you for including us."

Jenny, radiating her usual charm, occasionally giggled in mild embarrassment at some of the over generous flattery about her beauty. Gustav grinned broadly and confidently, displaying some of big brother's suaveness.

Olaf noticed Matilda struggling with some of the non-English speaking Swedes, waiting for their chance to congratulate the newlyweds. Leaving his place in the line, Olaf moved to assist her.

Looking mildly relieved, she whispered, "Oh, Olaf, thank you."

"Happy to lend a hand," he said. "Mrs. Vashburn, these are some old friends ve knew in Sveden. They just arrived a few months ago and haven't really learned English yet." He took the lady's arm, saying, *"De forstar inte svenska. Far Jag presentera Matilda Vashburn, Jennie's American mor.* Mrs. Vashburn, Jenny's friends, Hilda and Ragnar Holmgren."

"So pleased to meet you Mrs. and Mr. Holmgren. I'm delighted you could be with us."

"Tack. Hur star det till? Det har ar ett fint brollop." The Holmgrens smiled happily, stating that this was a most beautiful wedding.

"Kum nu," Olaf said leading them on to Jenny and Gustav.

"Du milde tid. Det har ar ett fint brollop," they complimented.

"Ja. Tack. Tack sa mycket," Jenny and Gustav responded. Everybody was in a happy mood.

Madam Persoens played the harpsichord, accompanying a string ensemble while the guest greeted the newlyweds and visited amongst themselves. Punch was served, along with a fine assortment of little sandwiches, salads and nuts. Jenny cut her beautifully decorated three tier wedding cake, making sure everyone would get a piece.

Of course, the menfolk had their special little table over in the corner. Cousin Rudolph brought a good supply of acquavit. "What is a good old fashioned Swedish wedding without acquavit?" he insisted. As he poured, the men laughed wholeheartedly, raising their glasses; "Skoal! Skoal!" They became happier and happier.

Later, the musicians struck up a number of waltzes. Jenny and Gustav glided gracefully to the center and dazzled all with their elegant dancing. The bride had taught the tall young bridegroom well. The guests applauded them generously.

After the Burbanks and the Blakelys had joined in the dance, Olaf finally garnered up enough courage to ask the gracious Matilda for a waltz. Smiling at each other, somewhat timidly, they took a few turns. Finally Olaf complimented, "You really put on a fine vedding for the kids. Thank you so much, Matilda. Such an affair they'll never forget for all of their living days."

"Thank you, Olaf," she smiled. They danced on. She looked up a time or two, as if wanting to speak, but Olaf thought she appeared embarrassed. The situation was awkward. Then she smiled again, saying, "I'm sorry Olaf, I was crazy and mixed up that time."

"Vell, Matilda, if I recollect, nobody had cut my legs off." Both laughed. The ice had been broken. "Matilda, I heard the tragic news of Mr. Vashburn's stroke. My condolences to you." After a few more turns Olaf added, "And I hear you have taken over the management of the mills -- magnificently, Mr. Burbank says."

"Thank you, Olaf. It's a challenge I eagerly accept," she smiled. Olaf held her out for a few wide twirls, relieved knowing the two would continue as dear friends.

Later, Olaf cornered the feisty little bridesmaid, Donna Jean, who with the newlyweds, talked to the musicians about playing something light and peppy. They agreed. The two couples, holding hands, began skipping ahead four skips, back two skips, and ahead again; starting a Swedish folk dance, lighting up the faces of all those from the old country. Before long, the Scandies all entered into the festive rollicking. The sophisticated guests were delighted, and soon tried the schottische themselves. Everybody had a most glorious time, it seemed to Olaf. The merrymaking went on and on, late into the night.

Finally, as the older brother rode to his little cabin toward morning, he smiled to himself, happy that brother Gustav had found such a wonderful mate with whom to share his life. Then he eventually became somber, anguishing for the woman he'd vowed to wait for years ago, so it was not unnatural for him to become envious of his little brother.

It was not too uncommon these days for the burly Swede to chat with his big partner up above, but he was getting a little bit fidgety about how slowly his prayers were being answered. So, this time, he spoke a little gruffly when looking up into the half star filled sky.

"Lord, I've certainly been patient, ya gotta admit that, but somevare along the line I recalled you indicating there vas valor in patience. But, maybe you've forgotten about my situation down here. Hey, Lord, Ya hear me?" Just at that moment there was a flash of lightning up ahead. Olaf was startled! "Ja, ja, all right Lord...all right...I'll just hang on here and show a little more patience."

❊ ❊ ❊ ❊ ❊

195

FIRST STAGE INTO THE VILDERNESS

A large gathering had already assembled in front of the new elegant five story Winslow House, where a variety of dignitaries waited to board the stage. It was the starting point for the first trip through dangerous Indian country, to terminate at new Fort Abercrombie two hundred miles west on the Red River.

"Whoa," Olaf shouted, pulling up with four perfectly matched sorrel horses, and smiled broadly. He stood in the front boot platform and tipped his wide brimmed hat. The crowd applauded the frontiersman who had distinguished himself as the most entertaining stage driver in the country.

John Blakely, company executive, approached as the Swede hopped down. "I'm delighted you consented to manage this trip-- and on such short notice. I want you to know how much the company appreciates your dedication. And, Swede, I got news for you, I plan to go along if you don't mind."

"Vunderful," Olaf grinned. "I vouldn't a turned down this trip for all the gold in the country." He glanced around at the dapper gentlemen from the East with their traveling bags in hand ready to go aboard. They cast an air of importance. But his lower jaw dropped in disbelief when his eyes focused on two ravishingly beautiful young women. "Vait a minute! I don't believe this! Vare did the vomen come from? Are they goin' along too?" He asked dumbfoundedly.

"Right. They're Scottish girls going to catch Anson Northrop's steamboat--the one we helped haul to Abercrombie. They're heading up to Hudson Bay, then by boat brigade through a maze of rivers to northwest Canada, a thousand miles away."

Olaf shook his head in amazement. "God, man, they got plenty a spunk in 'em to try that! I hope they make it."

"Oh, they will," Blakely assured. "Hudson Bay officials will see to that. The older one's going up to marry the Factor--he's the manager--at Fort Chipewyan on Lake Athabasca."

"And the younger one?" Olaf asked, noticing her teasing smile.

"Oh, she's just going along for the ride as a companion." Blakely winked, "She's unattached, Swede. Could be your big chance, hm?"

Nearing departure time, Olaf checked his pocket watch. There'd be no late starts. He had to meet the steamer in four days, and that'd be pushing it, he knew.

At that moment, three rambunctious characters stumbled out of the Winslow House, all decked out in hunting togs and carrying enough guns to launch a small war. The spokesman slurred his speech. "Oi am Sir Francis Sykes and these aw ma associates, Mista Shefful and Mista Petas," he babbled in a thick, soupy English accent. The three had obviously been celebrating the night at the hotel saloon and were unsteady in their walk.

Two young mounted troops had arrived from Fort Snelling, slated for duty at the new fort. They'd escort the stage as token military protection.

Burbank's attendants loaded and secured the luggage with skillful efficiency. The rear boot, the large leather covered compartment behind the coach, was packed with small personal cases. Large crates were tossed on top and lashed to the rack.

Olaf worried about the strain on his horses who'd be hard pressed, pulling nearly three thousand pounds on the grueling trek. He was always concerned for the faithful gentle beasts.

Checking his pocket watch, Olaf smiled and called out, "Folks, ve leave in two minutes. All aboard please. Must stick to schedule."

The Concord could haul more than eight people, but with the abundant luggage and freight carried, leg room would be limited, and tempers could be tested during the next four days.

The burly driver assisted his guests as they took the high step. "Enjoy the ride. Enjoy the ride," he repeated. Entering first, the young ladies smiled most cordially.

"Thank ye, driver. We ope fer a delightful trip, we do." One of the Scottish ladies acknowledged in her lilting speech.

Olaf nearly melted on the spot at such captivating smiles.

Glowing in self adulation, he forgot the gentlemen waiting to board behind him.

"Swede. Oh, Swede, would you help Mr. Marble and the others as well?" Blakely politely reminded, realizing the distracted coachman was in a slight fog from this 'touching' experience. His face became flushed as he assisted the others into the coach.

Olaf checked the hitch, then mounted the high seat with a tinge of dramatic flare, much like the captain of a ship, demonstrating the importance of being a coachman. Taking up the lines, he glanced around, making sure the spectators were clear, made a face as if to smile, enabling him to fire out his high-pitched whistle - the command for the horses to move out.

The spirited horses started strutting, eager to take off. With all the intrigue and excitement building, Olaf snapped the lines brusquely and struck his whip over the horses with a resounding crack; the crowd cheered as the huge Concord left on the dangerous trip toward Indian country.

Olaf smiled, putting the whip away, it being only for show. The road would be fast the first eighty miles to St. Cloud. He'd helped build that road and its bridges not too many years ago. At that time, Burbank's big boys had become impressed with his work and ability to manage men. His last major accomplishment was directing two hundred workers in completing the trail all the way to Fort Abercrombie. Now it would be tested.

The Swede was anxious to display the grand wilderness but was also mildly apprehensive, realizing his awesome responsibility in assuring the guests a safe journey. Rolling along, Olaf leaned back and lit his pipe; time for an enjoyable smoke, time to contemplate matters - some important, some trivial. He did a lot of that while driving. The travelers were having a good time laughing and chatting. But the English hunters were loud and raucous. If that were to continue the entire trip, it could become irritating to the other guests, Olaf worried.

The scenery was spectacular, trailing along the Mississippi River. The mantle of fresh green foliage on the trees and bushes, and the grand display of wild flowers along the rolling hills drew expressions of approval. "Look at that!" "Isn't that gorgeous?"

The patrons raved.

Olaf thought about the two Scottish ladies, so pretty, refined, and brave, pursuing such a dangerous venture, especially the young one who was unattached.

Eventually, the chattering subsided below. No more boisterous racket by Sir Francis Sykes and his cronies. As sated as they were, they probably rocked to sleep anyway, Olaf figured. The coach, a lumbering monster, pitched and rolled on its thoroughbraces, the large leather straps acting as a cushion reminding the Swede of his sailing days. Travel continued at a brusque pace as the stage passed the second ten-mile post. Olaf checked his watch. They were ahead of schedule. Another hour and a half would put them at the first Burbank station, where a quartet of fresh horses would be hitched - ready to go.

Suddenly, one of the Englishmen stuck his head out the window, calling up in a desperate voice, "Oh, drivah? Drivah?"

Olaf drew back on the lines. "Yes, sir?" He called down.

"Oh, drivah, we could stand a bloody rest stop, please." He sounded urgent, but being in a wide open meadow wasn't appropriate for such comfort stops -- at least not with ladies present.

"Sir, ve come to Villow Creek in about a mile. Vould that be satisfactory, sir?"

"That will satisfy, but please hurry along. Please," he repeated.

The considerate Swede had been worrying about protecting the dignity of the fair ladies in matters of personal comfort, so had planned stopping at Willow Creek anyway. Soon the wheels rumbled across one of the log bridges he'd constructed earlier and Olaf stopped the stage at a picturesque natural setting. He called out: "Ve're makin' good time. Vee'll make a stop for stretchiin." An appreciative cheer went up.

The English dudes sprang from the coach in haste, heading for the woods. Olaf dismounted to assist the others down the high steps; ladies first. Being most solicitous, he spoke softly and confidentially, "Ladies, there's a vunderful secluded spot down that path along the creek and through the villows. Like a 'Garden of Eden' it is. A spot virth seeing, for sure."

"Aye, thank ye," said the younger, sounding joyously relieved. "Yeer a fine yentleman to be sure," they laughed, scampering off.

A rest stop was taken at the pleasure of the passengers. Not so for stage drivers who had to attend the horses, and cater to rider's needs. So, grabbing a couple of pails, Olaf dashed to the stream. He unbuckled the bridle lines so the horses could lower their heads for a drink, have a small measure of oats and munch on the lush grass close at hand. Then, he opened a lunch box containing some juice and crumpets for the guests.

The fancy ladies, first to return from their hike, stood aside and watched the industrious driver hustling about, retrieving the lunch box.

Amused, the younger of the sisters spoke. "Ye ave to be a magician to do everthin. Let us help a wee bit, driver," she offered, pushing her sleeves above her elbows.

"Oh, thank ya. Ya are so kind, Mam," Olaf cracked his genuine smile.

"Nonsense! Ye ave so much to do," she insisted.

Olaf retrieved the juice jug, but the older sister practically grabbed it out of his hands.

"I'll pour the ade," she said, casting a mischievous eye. Olaf got all flustered as he heard her whispering to her little sister, "That is one big unk of a mon, I tell yee."

"Me name be Christina Sterling, driver, and me elder sister, Eleanora."

"Pleased to meet ya," he said shyly, "and thank ya for helping."

"Then, what is yeer name, driver? Ye truly ave a gentle manner."

"Oh, I'm sorry," he answered, realizing his oversight. "My name is Olaf Olsson, from Sveden." He grinned, "Most people call me Big Svede, or plain Svede, vich I like vell enough, I guess."

"All right, Swede. Me sister and I feel we are in good ands with thee. We air lookin forward to a delightful trip," the younger, Christina, added.

"Thank ya mam," Olaf blushed, leaving to fetch water for his horses.

The men, returning from their stroll, were pleasantly surprised finding a fine lunch ready. Soon Blakely sauntered over with the two dignitaries he'd attached himself to, each carrying a cup and munching a sandwich.

"Swede, these two gentlemen are quite taken with your professional manner, and would like to meet you. This is Mr. Manton Marble and Mr. Nathaniel Hathaway."

"I'm pleased to meet ya, Sirs," Olaf nodded respectfully.

"Swede Olsson, it is. Right?" The dapper one with the bowler hat questioned.

"That's right, sir."

"Well, Swede, I know more about you than you think. You see, I am a reporter. I understand you're driving this rig as kind of a lark, more or less, as a desire to savor the fruits of your labors, having engineered the trail." He chuckled. "I am right, am I not?"

Olaf grinned like a fox caught in a hen house. "Vell, I don't deny my love for driving in this great country, sir."

"Fine," Mr. Marble said. "And I'm on assignment to write a story for Harper's about the Indians, of which I've heard you have much knowledge, and I hope we'll have time for discussing these subjects."

"I'd be happy to oblige, sir. I hope vot you write is the truth. I have great respect for the Dakota and the Chippewa, Mr. Marble."

Mr. Hathaway stepped forward. "And I'm a naturalist, gathering knowledge of the fabulous flora and fauna of this vast region. Hearing that you've traveled about every mile of this wilderness, I'd appreciate any help you could give."

"Yes, Sir. I love this country. It's truly a sleeping beauty. I only hope that ven all the Europeans come, they'll respect it and its people." The bespectacled scientist nodded in agreement.

The gentlemen smiled, recognizing the Swede's strong commitment to the virgin wildernesses. Thanking him, they returned for another cup of juice.

Olaf heard Mr. Marble joking with his companions as he walked away. "The Big Swede would please me no end if he'd only arrange a small skirmish with the natives; a minute

altercation, mind you. Wouldn't that be fantastic to write about --
a first hand account. Not too serious though. I would still rather
keep my scalp, thank you," he joked.

Christina cheerfully brought a bit of lunch for Olaf. "Aye, we
put everythin away, big Swede. 'Ope we 'elped a wee bit," she
said.

"Aw, thank you. Don't know vot I'd done vithout you." He
smiled gratuitously. "I'll have mine up on the driver's seat now."

The party of travelers were getting comfortably acquainted.
With good roads to St. Cloud, the entire way would be a joy ride.
Olaf knew that next three days into the wilderness would test the
patience of those confined.

Reaching the horse terminal, the half-way mark, a quick
change was made, and the stage speeded along again. After a
while, hearing the folks singing below was encouraging to Olaf,
thinking it a fine way to pass time. Later, the crowding in the
compartment was wearing a little thin. Olaf had been hearing
some minor grumbling the last hour or so. The passengers'
excitement intensified though when the valley came into view
with all its splendor. On either side new, neat and orderly farms
graced the landscape, several still under construction. The settlers
were breaking ground.

But, the English dudes had started tippling again; acting
rambunctious, Olaf could tell. When sober, they were no problem.
It was the rum and brandy that triggered the horse play, much to
the chagrin of the others.

Olaf drove the stage directly to the Prairie House Hostel where
comfortable lodging and some of the finest German food in the
country awaited the passengers.

Burbanks had a contract with Hilda Shultz, the voluptuous
matron of the establishment. Oh, there were plenty of prudes
casting derogatory accusations about the goings on. Maybe it was
the flirtatious girls working for her that helped taint Hilda's
reputation some. Hilda herself was a lady when she wanted to be,
but could exchange profanity with the worst of the wagoners if
needed. Olaf hung out here a lot; it beat the devil out of the filthy
Hitching Post Saloon down the road apiece. He liked Hilda, who

had a heart of gold. He smirked, thinking how she once amputated Scarface Williams' little finger with a cleaver when he wouldn't keep his hands to himself.

Stella, Hilda's rosy cheeked young maid, showed the guests to their rooms. She was proper with the ladies and gentlemen, but giggled and blushed at the suggestive wry wit of the Englishmen. She learned well that catering to the whims of patrons resulted in gathering more silver through gratuities.

Olaf drove the horses and stagecoach toward the terminal, a mere stone's throw away. He was looking forward to greeting his little friend, Mousey Michaels, before turning in to the Prairie House for a needed rest.

Christina called, concerned Olaf was leaving for the night. "Swede? Oh, Swede, are yee leavin us? Won't we see our fine coachman agin tonight?"

Assuring he'd return after seeing an important business associate, he reminded Christina he had a room at the hostel, too. Having said that, the lass looked relieved. Olaf's heart was beginning to flutter a little with all the attention he was getting. He would hurry.

Though Olaf still had pleasant memories of Marianne, hopes of ever seeing her again were fading fast. If he didn't make a move pretty soon, he feared he might wind up out in the middle of the pond without a paddle.

He scanned the yards for Mousey, his old "pardner," as they had called each other on the trail. Jumping to the ground, Olaf gave Mousey a hearty hug. The little man idolized the big man who'd had faith in him from the beginning, and Olaf heaped praises on Mousey for his fine job in supervising the local horse and wagon facilities.

Being more than a little flustered by Christina's attention, Olaf did a quick step shuffle back to the hostel, drooling at the possibilities.

He always bunked in the small teamster's room just off the kitchen. Glancing through the open door, he saw the bubbly Hilda cooking up a storm. Olaf, oft times a prankster, sneaked up behind her. "Boo!" He barked, and pinched the jovial matron on her backside.

Almost dropping her pan of muffins, she turned to cuss out the guilty culprit, but seeing her lovable big Swede, she melted like thin ice on a hot skillet.

"Olaf, ya rascal! Ya scared the livin' piss out a me! Where in heaven's name have ya been, anyway? Haven't seen ya for ages." She laughed from down deep, and her massive bosoms danced in time with her deep ho-ho-ho.

He grinned, "Aw, I've been awful busy vith the company. But I got good news, Hilda. Today ve start our first stage run to Fort Abercrombie! It'll be good business for ya, tvice a veek soon," he boasted.

"Ya, and that must be some important crowd you got along. Heard they were some dignified gentlemen from Europe and the East. White table linens, wine, and everything they want."

"Gentlemen, Hilda? That's not all of it. There are two rather charming young ladies from Scotland along too." He winked mischievously.

"Women!" She exclaimed, giving him a solid punch on the chest. "Yah, ya rascal, and you goin' out on the prairie with women. I'm jealous!"

Olaf reared back and roared, "Naw! I'll vatch out," he laughed.

The inside walls were paper thin. When the company of travelers entered the big dining room, every word could be heard.

"Shush, we'll have to whisper now. I'll bring ya a little glass of wine on the company." She winked, and excused herself to go help Stella.

The group was in a most jovial mood.

Eventually the English dudes came to the wall, opposite where Olaf stood listening intently. It wasn't easy understanding their frumpy accents, but he could make out enough, especially when Sir Sykes was talking.

"Oi think awl tame thot little pussy cot, Christina. Awl waigah a hundred ponds that little lass'll be mine fore Aubercrombie." Peters and Sheffield laughed raucously.

"Ya big blowhard!" Olaf said under his breath. "Nobody's going to lay hands on any part of Christina's body, I'll see to that."

Then he heard the women ask, "Where is the big Swede? It would be nice if e'd join us."

In his wildest dreams Olaf never expected joining the dignitaries or he'd have put on his white shirt and a string tie. But, Hilda, proud of her pet trailsman, gave him a little nudge for a quick entrance.

The folks had dressed quite fancy - men with ascots and ladies in long dresses. Olaf was flattered when Christina sashayed over, begging he join the ladies, so he primped to the Englishmen, who looked a bit deflated.

Hilda served her fancy honey-glazed prairie chicken, wild rice, squash, and German creamed potatoes. Then she brought out the specialty of the house; sauerbraten and dumplings, and topped the meal off with desserts of wild plum pudding and apple strudel.

All gorged themselves at the fabulous supper.

Being the utmost authority on the western territory, Olaf found a most attentive audience; except for the imbibing hunters, who, even after being warned of the dangers of setting foot in the Hitching Post, the 'hell hole of the prairie' - were bent on finding out for themselves.

Olaf advised the travelers that the next three days would not be a joy ride, and suggested a good night's sleep. Though whites were rarely attacked, they traveled the boundary between the Chippewa and the Sioux; a place where the tribes had met in war regularly the past two hundred years, he reminded.

* * *

Olaf was awake well before dawn. While stretching and yawning, he detected a familiar aroma sifting through the walls. The sweet smell of fruit cooking activated his nose, and in the bat of an eyelash he leaped out of bed, slipped his trousers on, and made a barefoot bee-line for the kitchen for some of Hilda's coffee and goodies, and a chance to jabber with his favorite innkeeper.

He downed a generous stack of buttermilks, several cups of

coffee, and topped off his breakfast with freshly baked cherry strudel. It was always a delight bantering frivolously with Hilda.

The guests were heard coming down for breakfast. Olaf, anxious to move out, not wanting to fall behind schedule, was eager to check his hitch.

"Hilda, it's alvays a delight stopping at your place. Like home." Olaf stood, holding his arms out, inviting her to a playful embrace.

"Oh, you whopping Swede, I always hate to see you go. You could stay around here and be my boy, you know," she quipped, with a tinge of seriousness. "There's chores not getting done," she winked facetiously.

Olaf reared back, "That's the best offer I've had today, but ve've got to push on and get to Abercrombie in three days."

Suddenly, the usually joking matron displayed a worrisome look.

"Vot...vot's troubling now," he pressed.

"Olaf, that rotten Williams has been hangin' around town the past days. One of the wagoners overheard him say, when he was drunk, that he was going to get even and kill you."

"Vell, I've heard that talk before," Olaf acknowledged. "Thank ya for telling me. I'll be careful anyvay," he patted her shoulder and left.

Olaf hustled over to the yards to check out his hitch, and visit with his old sidekick, Mousey. The teamsters had the four fresh muscular black horses harnessed and ready to go. Not seeing Mousey, he went over to scratch the heads of each animal, and patted their backs while talking to them. Finally, seeing the diminutive Mousey approaching dressed fit to kill, as was his petite wife, Singing Bird, who carried the wee papoose on her back with two little stair steps hanging on, drew a roar of approval from Olaf. They'd come to give their devoted friend a royal send off. Next, the Sterling sisters anxiously came down the walkway, decked in riding britches and khaki shirts.

"Good mornin, Swede. We missed ye at breakfast," Christina greeted. The women, not seeing Mousey's family, came over to admire the horses.

"Aye, ye certainly ave the most beautiful steeds," Eleanora raved, "so well groomed and fit."

"Weel they travel swift as thee wind?" Christina asked.

"Ya, that they vill. Vun of Burbank's most prized matches," he said with pride, as the sisters stroked the animals admiringly.

"Oh, how darlin," Christina exclaimed, seeing Mousey Michaels with his Indian wife, her papoose and the two small children hanging on their mother's buckskin skirt.

"Precious," Eleanora echoed.

Olaf introduced his good friends to the Scottish ladies who'd probably never seen American Indians before. Signing Bird smiled brightly.

Blakely, Marble and Hathaway followed closely behind the women, all looking slightly apprehensive about the next leg of the journey. Blakely asked Olaf if he'd mind having a partner in the driver's seat. The Swede agreed for there were a lot of business matters to discuss.

Sykes, Sheffield and Peters shuffled their way down to the loading area in their usual self-assuming jocular form, howling over their night at the lowly Hitching Post Saloon. Their repulsive breaths scattered the others away to fresher air. Sykes, still half in the bag, reveled in telling of Mr. Peters' misfortune of having been taken in by a 'sweet little black-eyed Dalia' -- a virgin, so she avowed. When they'd returned to the hostel in the wee hours, Peters found his wallet had been heisted, but on returning to the "hellhole of the prairie" he found the little darling had already departed for St. Paul -- and at 3:00 a.m.! Peters hung his head, favoring a king-sized hangover.

Moving on, Olaf and Blakely rode on the high seat discussing the new trail Olaf had engineered, with the help of two hundred workers. They had removed rocks and trees, built bridges over creeks and rivers, and reinforced bogs and marshes by corduroying with side-by-side logs.

The early morning was uneventful and quiet in the coach. Most likely the Englishmen were sleeping off their doldrums from all night carousing. But, in the last hour the noisy threesome were back at it again. Even from the driver's seat, grumbling could be heard from the other guests, obviously disturbed by the tomfoolery. Olaf pulled the stage up to a small picturesque lake where he planned to stop, rest the horses, and allow the riders to limber up from the cramped confinement. Though the Burbank associates enjoyed their lofty business meeting, Blakely knew he'd better return to the coach and settle the boys down when they'd continue after the break.

The métis' encampment was on the shore of a charming place called Ferry Lake. Tempers were always quelled at such tranquil settings, Olaf knew, and the lunch Hilda sent along wouldn't hurt either. While Olaf tended his horses, Christina came over looking most troubled and revealed her fear and torment.

"Vot is it?" he begged. "Vot is wrong, for Heaven's sakes?"

"Oh, Swede, I'm upset with thee mischievous unters! They seem decent enough, but when they are drinkin, thee one with thee big proboscis casts unsolicited attention on me," she sniffled.

"Big vot?" Olaf questioned, never hearing that word before.

"Proboscis. 'Is nose." She snickered, realizing the humor of it all.

"Oh. Ya had me vurried," he chuckled shyly. "So vot does he do?"

"'E calls me a pussy cat." Tears rolled down her cheeks. "And...and...'e tries pettin me most indiscriminately."

"Vell, ve von't have any of that! Don't vurry. Try to enjoy your lunch now, and I'll figure out something." Now his gander was aroused.

Olaf cornered Blakely to discuss the crisis, and threatened to tangle horns with Sir Francis Sykes. Blakely cooled him down, not wanting adverse publicity, with the Harper's writer covering the trip. Olaf agreed he'd confront the perpetrator later, so there'd be no undesirable scene now. Blakely had a better idea. He'd overheard Christina say she'd relish a ride up on the driver's seat at least one time before reaching Abercrombie.

On their way again, Olaf grinned like a starved hog at the feed trough, with the charming Scottish lass next to him, laughing and giggling like a twelve year old -- though he knew she was a lady in every way. Removing her bonnet, she allowed her long red hair to blow freely.

"I rode in a carousel once. This is better. Ooh," she said, "it's fun swingin and rockin like this. Gives a ticklish feelin in me stomach."

Christina then raved about the beauty of the country: the rich green meadows, groves of cottonwood and oaks, enhanced by lakes in every direction. A huge bull elk with a massive wrack of antlers poked his head up from feeding off the bottom of a lake, it's mate and two calves flitted nearby.

"Oh, what a divine sight!" Christina exclaimed. "Most lovely."

Riding along, Christina, with a scintillating glow on her face, continued prodding the virile frontiersman, wanting to know all about him; about his romantic life. She admitted her coming to this country was to escape sadness, having lost her lover at sea. Olaf expressed sorrow for her, but he felt warm within himself at the interest she showed in him.

"Ay, those fine steeds are so powerful and graceful as they move." She brightened. "Swede, could I drive them, do ye think?"

"Oh, vell, I guess I don't see vare any harm could come, but I'll have to hold the lines, too, in case they rear up," he cautioned.

She nestled close to him. "This is so excitin! A chance to drive four 'orses. Nobody'd believe it! All right. I ave it now, me thinks."

The Swede's breathing was heavy, his hands behind hers, their bodies fixed together. After a bit, she seemed to wax dreamily too, for the horses left the trail causing a heavy jolt when one of the wheels bounced off a large rock. The horses shied! Olaf shouted, "Whoa," driving his elbow into her voluminous breast. "Oh, my!" he said, fearing he'd hurt her, and instinctively reached up to massage where he'd bumped her. Realizing the intimacy of his inadvertent patting, he became flushed and apologized.

"It's all right, dear Olaf," she assured, realizing his humiliation. "I'll drive a wee bit more, but hold firmly. I love to feel the strength in yeer strong arms."

The afternoon delighted the Swede, affectionately starved for so long.

Reaching the new Burbank stop over, Olaf was disappointed

finding the Wakefield caretakers gone from the newly constructed log house. They would use the shelter anyway. It had been a hot day and the travelers eyed the placid lake with envy. Hathaway, Marble, and Blakely soon shed their shirts and shoes for a refreshing sponge bath after the hot day of travel.

The two young cavalry boys, remaining out of sight the entire day, rode into the camp. They headed for the reed beds to do some fishing. Olaf secured his horses, then gathered wood for the outdoor fire. With the Wakefields gone, he'd be put to the task of fixing some dried beef stew and potatoes. Maybe the Sterling belles would lend a hand, he hoped.

But, the Englishmen had a better idea. The lake was dotted with hundreds of ducks toward the opposite side. "You'll see, big Swede, who the real hunters are in this crowd," they boasted, with their shot guns shouldered.

Eleanora came with her towel, inviting her little sister to accompany her for a private splash around the bend of the lake. Christina preferred waiting a while, intrigued with Olaf's every move, and wanting to help him. Marble and Hathaway prodded their guide for knowledge of the territory.

Eventually, Eleanora returned looking fresh and invigorated. "Oh, the water is so crystal clear. Heavenly!" she raved. Olaf noticed her whispering to Christina, and then both giggled giddily. Christina fetched her own towel and headed around the lake shore, as well, where Eleanora had been.

The hunters had been gone some time. Olaf, noticing his yellowish palms, stained from the leather driving lines, grabbed his strong lye soap, and moved back through the woods to a private spring fed pool he knew of, away from the lake about a hundred yards. It was cool and deep, he knew by the dark blue color. Besides, having dived down, he'd never touched the bottom.

Kneeling down, he doused his head. Ah, how refreshing, he thought. Then, suddenly a shocking form rose up from the water in front of him but ten feet away like a mystical mermaid surfacing from the watery depths! Quickly drying his eyes, he was startled finding non other than naked Christina before him, her torso breaking the water line.

She, too, was stunned! Neither said a word. Entranced, Olaf gazed at her natural beauty, and she, realizing her exposure was complete, didn't shy away, at first - just revealed herself innocently.

"Oh, Christina, I'm awful sorry," he blinked, steadying himself.

She lowered herself till the water reached her neck. "Ai, big Swede, don't blame yeerself. Oi was naive, oi was, plyin the water so daringly.

Drying his head with his towel, he turned, "I'll go now -- get supper."

"Big Swede," she called, hoping to ease the embarrassment.

He stopped in his tracks. "Yes, Christina."

"If it pleases yee, no man has ever seen me as yee ave."

Olaf paused for a moment, mustering up a shy grin.

"Big Swede," she called again.

"Yes Christina."

"I'm glad it was you rather than those English blokes."

Olaf grinned. "I am too. See ya back at the cabin, then." Her naked beauty had stirred his most sensual desires. He was baffled over how the women had found a path to his secret watering spa; but not unhappy though.

Personal anxieties were suddenly shaken by gunfire. With ducks flying overhead, Olaf quickly retrieved his own rifle and downed three fowl. The guests applauded Olaf's keen proficiency as a hunter. Before long, the two young army boys came back with happy smiles on their faces, having caught a beauty! An eight pound pike they wanted to share.

With darkness setting in, the *limey* trio returned looking dejected and humiliated with only one measly teal hanging from Mr. Peter's belt.

The dinner turned out to be a most festive one: wild duck, pike, roasted potatoes, heated biscuits, and a bottle of fine French wine sent along by Mr. Burbank. A songfest of familiar ballads by the campfire followed.

* * *

In the middle of the night, Olaf and his guests were awakened by the wildest violent prairie thunderstorms few had ever witnessed. The sky lit up and exploded, the wind blew with avengeance and the rain poured.

Olaf rose early, worried about his four overworked horses, now having the added burden of pulling the two ton rig through soggy turf. It was imperative Abercrombie be reached in two days to meet the steamboat.

Having given the urgent wake-up call, the Swede hustled out to get a pot of coffee heated, and set out leftovers of duck and fish. The young recruits had already saddled their ponies, ready to ride. They'd slept like a couple of puppies in a pile of hay in the horse shed, they said. With the sky, having cleared, the warming of the sun would improve the footing for the horses by noon, Olaf thought, but the stage must roll.

Water holes had to be avoided, so Olaf left the muddy Métis track, and drove over the sod for firmer footing. He dismounted often, walking ahead to check for standing water. Then the trail led through heavy woods - large oak, elm, and maple - for a time, and back again to grassy hills around the ever present lakes.

The passengers complained of aching backs and legs from lack of circulation, and tempers flared. Some objected to inconsiderations, like Mr. Marble's cigar smoking, or the constant perverse behavior of the jocular Englishmen's snoring, bickering and passing repulsive wind.

When Olaf reached a stretch of firm sandy ground the stage tracked better. This allowed for a relaxing smoke, a chance to rest his tired arms from pulling lines, and to think about exciting prospects of his blooming relationship with the high spirited Christina. My God, Olaf thought, how long can a man refrain from intimacy with one of the opposite sex, anyway.

A piercing zzzing! A clang of metal stunned Olaf. A bullet hole was torn out of the luggage rack a foot from his head. From where it entered he knew it came from the near north woods. Was it Scarface Williams out for revenge, as Hilda had warned? It's true Olaf had fired the detested Indian hater, known for raping and killing Indian squaws. But, he would avoid alarming the riders, hunch down to minimize himself as a target, and hurry the horses on.

The wooded hills ended. A mile or so of prairie lay ahead. Olaf stopped and walked into the high grass, checking. Blakely came out as well, and the two decided they'd cut time by crossing the meadow. The turf seemed firm enough at first, but the horses were stepping high, and leaning forward, releasing their great strength. Mud soon flew above the rig from the horses hoofs. Olaf urged them on. "C'mon, ponies! Move on! Hi! Hi! Keep a movin!" Soon, the large hoofs were slapping in standing water, but near the end of the lowland. "C'mon blackies, move on! Hi! Hi! Ya got only a hundred yards ta go!" he pleaded.

Though the tiring foursome struggled, the weighted hulk became helplessly sloughed; the rear right wheel sinking nearly to the axle. It was only a stone's throw to the bridge over the ravine; beyond were grass covered hills, but now they were a vulnerable target. Sinking to his knees, he struggled to the door of the tilting coach to unload his panicked patrons. Women were carried to dry ground first. The men, on their own, groaned as they sloshed through the muck; only Mr. Marble showing delight, as he anxiously sketched for his report.

With an eye peeled to the woods, Olaf quickly grabbed two posts--fortunately left by the bridge builders -- to brace the right side, keeping the hull from tipping completely over. Little time was wasted in removing heavy cases off the top rack, particularly one wooden crate, weighing over two hundred pounds, the Swede figured, destined for the fort. Olaf's clothes were muddy and soaked with sweat from the exhaustive battle; the men offered much advice, but little physical assistance.

All he heard from the onlookers frustrated him to no end.

"Oh, thee poor Swede," the women sympathized, repeatedly.

"Why don't you hook a chain to the wheel! Why don't you do this? Why don't you do that?" Suddenly everybody was an expert on freeing sloughed stages. Olaf's frustrations were escalating.

Exasperated, he shouted. "Vill ya all please shut up! Please!"

An hour of critical time had been wasted. The right lead horse had sunk so low his belly rested on the ground. Olaf bemoaned the possible tragedy of having to desert the magnificent animal with a mercy bullet before moving on with three remaining horses.

Suddenly, alarming shouts erupted from the marooned travelers. "Swede. for God's sake, hurry!" shouted one. "Indians!" several yelled.

The Englishmen scrambled back to the coach, retrieving their guns. Olaf grabbed his long glass for a close look, and seeing only five Indians, warned the men not to fire. They looked harmless, wearing the usual feathers and hair rings. Probably only hunters, he explained. But, he wondered if they might be the culprits who had fired at him.

With greater determination, Olaf pulled the king pin from the double tree, unhitched the two rear horses, and brought them to dry footing to the front. He hooked the tugs to a long log chain he'd attached to the wagon pole; the only way the mired horse and stage could be pulled out. With less weight to pull, the half buried horse flailed and rolled from side to side, miraculously coming free and the vehicle moved forward.

Again, a renewed alarm came from the anxious onlookers. "Swede, for God's sakes, ya better hurry. There's a whole bunch of them now!"

"Don't panic! Keep cool head!" Olaf commanded. Focusing his scope for a closer look, he didn't like what he saw. The Indians paid too much attention to the beleaguered stage. The passengers were terrified!

"Ve load immediately," he ordered. Everyone complied, feeling threatened by the intrusion, wanting to get the hell out of there.

The horses moved as quickly as their exhausted bodies allowed, and firmer footing was soon reached, allowing for a lumbering trot. All eyes kept scanning the woods for a reappearance of the Indians, until reaching a clearance a mile down. All breathed easier when none were seen.

With two hours lost at the swamp, it would be nearly impossible to reach the Alexander terminal. Olaf confided to Blakely that alternative camping would be found at Spring Hill, ten miles down.

The Swede's concern for the cavalry troops was laid to rest, seeing them gallop at full gate, as if a sense of urgency compelled them.

"We were worried about you, sir, but we've been out-flanked by red skins all day," the boys declared breathlessly.

"Settle down, fellas," Olaf smiled, calmly. "I'm sure they're freindlies. Only a hunting party, most likely."

Like a bunch of grackles, the riders shot questions at the boys.

"Quiet down! Quiet down!" Blakely insisted.

First one, and then the other boy gave information about how they'd avoided being seen, except one small party gave chase, they admitted. Their ponies were no match for the fast army horses, they boasted.

Olaf lowered his voice while talking to the boys at a distance from the stage. Describing a camp of Indians about eight miles away, the scouts reported spying on some forty hooting braves; all with painted bodies.

"Holy cow, boys, ve might be into something big. The vay you describe the large group, they could be Sioux. These others are Chippewa. The two tribes haven't had a prairie battle yet this year," Olaf informed them.

"Should we stay and help defend the travelers, Sir?"

"No. I think it's best you continue as a decoy, making a distracting appearance at times to show an army presence. And men, if serious trouble arises, best you head to Fort Abercrombie for help

"We'll keep an eagle eye out, sir," they assured, and trotted off.

Olaf climbed onto the stage as it moved ahead for several miles. The curious natives had apparently lost interest in the huge concord and had gone on their merry way. Nonetheless, the fearful coachbound adventurers displayed their frustration by pestering their trail boss: "Swede, can't the horses go any faster?"

Finally, coming to a clearance again, startling cries rang out: "There they are, the devils!" "Swede! Swede, do you see them?"

Olaf could see them, all right. The welcoming committee had grown to about two dozen, he reckoned, of which only about half rode horses. What the devil do they want, anyway? Is it the sleek stagecoach intriguing them? They just stay off in the distance and watch. Why? he wondered. He saluted them, showing friendship, but they wouldn't acknowledge him. Olaf hoped by ignoring them they'd lose interest and go away.

But, the feathered friends would not be cast off lightly, for they continued to flank the regal coach like a shadow along the ridge about a half mile to the north. Olaf and his patrons continued nervously. After ascending a long gradual hill, they reached the prairie oasis called Spring Hill, the night campgrounds. Olaf stopped, only to observe the natives replicating the stage's every move, they too, camped on the opposite hill and proceeded to build campfires.

"Looks like those reds are out to intimidate the hell out of us," Manton Marble suggested. "We'll be in for a long night, no doubt."

"Awm fraid these prairie sawvages'll wait'll we try to sleep, then swoop down and pounce on us like hungry wolves and devour us fer dinnah." Sir Sykes declared, making the others shudder at such provoking talk.

"Aye, 'eaven ferbid," Christina winced, coming to Olaf for protection.

Blakely, getting upset at the morbid attitudes interrupted, you folks have little confidence in your captain. I suggest you stop your fretting and listen to the Swede for some common sense, instead of this gloom talk."

"Yes. Yes, I'll second that," Hathaway nervously interjected.

Olaf had been watching the neighboring camp through his scope. Why they didn't come close enough to communicate was baffling to him. From time to time small groups rode off from the main camp and Olaf wondered if they were surrounding the stage, preventing escape. Sykes' English dudes timidly agreed to stand watch at the edge of the small clump of woods harboring them. The Sterling sisters fetched water from the spring, made coffee and set out dried beef, hard biscuits and dried fruit chips. All settled in for a woefully long tense night.

Olaf explained the red men were likely from the north woods, probably from Red Lake - the Pillager band they were called. Aptly named, it was more to worry about horses being stolen and plundering than a threat to their lives, so while the Englishmen guarded close by, Olaf roved back and forth to lend support and boost their morale.

The glow of the fires on the opposite hill silhouetted the half naked Indians and the eyes of the stage companions were fixed on them constantly.

Olaf, exhausted from freeing the sloughed stage, stopped and leaned on the back wheel of the coach. He hoped Christina and Eleanora were able to get some rest, too, but a soft nervous whisper came from within.

"Do ye think we might die here, Swede?" Christina fretted.

"No, Christina, ve're gonna be fine. Try to get some rest now."

"I'll try, but will pray a wee bit, though."

"Hm," Olaf acknowledged. Might not be the worst idea, he thought.

A gunshot broke the tense silence! It was close! The women and men gave cries of desperation. Men dove for cover under the stage, soon joined by Sykes and Peters, who'd deserted their posts. "Where are the devils?" "Are we under attack?" the folks yelled desperately.

Sheffield didn't show up! Olaf went out to check, finding the Englishman babbling incoherently about seeing several savages creeping up, so he shot: certain he had killed one of them. All Olaf found were a few bushes moving slightly in the breeze. Olaf became the lone sentry thereafter.

* * *

It was a long night. No one slept. Dawn breaking, Olaf made a small fire to heat water for tea. They would depart quickly, hopeful the natives, satisfying their curiosity, would not interfere. A sense of optimism prevailed when seeing a small group (about five) ride off to the northwest earlier - a good sign to the Swede.

The horses rehitched, the party entered the coach, and Olaf took up the lines in haste. All pretended being inattentive to Indian

217

presence, as instructed, but nerves were frayed watching the threatening Chippewa from askance. Hopes were denied as about twenty Indians paralleled the movement of the Stagecoach on a gradually closing course. It became apparent a confrontation was imminent as both groups would soon reach the river. Now, the bronze skinned braves were close enough so the detail of their painted faces, and wild hair styled around rings and feathers, had become intensely intimidating.

Two young braves quickly rode up, stopping about a hundred yards ahead of the besieged coach, waving their arms in a demanding manner. Olaf stopped immediately. Their Chief, and all others following, joined the two braves. The Chief gave Olaf the signal they would talk.

Knowing Indian hand signals well, Olaf gave the customary greetings. He then retrieved a pouch of his fine tobacco, and walked ahead to meet them. Being apprehensive, he still forced an agreeable smile. "Friend," he said. "Come in peace. Have gift." His words seemed to fall on deaf ears, but he'd hoped someone might understand English.

A tense silence followed while the Chief and young braves filled their long pipes, but their angry faces provided little consolation.

Sometimes that was all the natives wanted, a gesture of friendship. So, Olaf, being overly optimistic, said, "Ve go now. Thank you. Ve see you again sometime," and turned to leave.

The Chief, wearing a head piece of many warrior feathers, was not about to be cast off lightly, and grunted dissatisfaction. He had more to talk about. *"Wai abishkag nitagen anishinabekwe! Wai abishkag ka awiia wikan issan."*

Olaf was taken back. Through the Chief's hand signals, and a few recognizable words, he figured the Chief was angry at the white man and demanded satisfaction for something, but he couldn't understand what.

The young braves, intrigued by the stage - and no doubt, the white women passengers - gathered around the coach, leaving the Chief and Olaf alone to settle the Chief's complaint. The Swede watched from a distance.

Finally, after smoking a while, the Chief went through elaborate detail in trying to make Olaf understand. It seemed he accused a white of taking an Anishinabi squaw, abused her, and left her mutilated body grossly displayed. He demanded proof the culprit was not one of them.

Olaf tried speaking Dakota. "*Wai abishkag wikan issan,*" assuring that his white group were friends only passing through. Time dragged on.

At first, it appeared the twenty Chippewa crowded the big wagon out of curiosity, but Blakely, Marble and Hathaway and the sisters evacuated quickly when some of the braves entered and started plundering. Olaf was getting nervous, and wondered if the Chief purposely distracted him. The Swede worried about the women being pestered by those grotesque faces. He knew he'd have to have the Chief's help to stave off calamity.

Fifteen minutes passed; still the Chief procrastinated, filling his pipe for further peace talks. The altercation was taking on an ugly character. A few of the hostiles were already toting hunter's rifles. The Englishmen, demanding their guns back, were arguing loudly.

Olaf talked desperately, trying to convince the old warrior of his innocence. "Chief, I am Tall Like Oak; friend of your brothers, Chief Nug-aun-ub at Fond du Lac, friend of Chief Hole-in-the-Day at Mille Lacs. Friend!" Olaf looked at his watch; soon a half hour had elapsed.

All hell was breaking out at the coach. The men were arguing and the women pleading, "Please! Don't touch me!"

Horrible thoughts flashed through Olaf's mind about Scarface Williams, and the shot fired at him earlier. The Chief was adamant and convincing in his claim that one of his, a Chippewa girl, had been murdered.

The old warrior finally admitted hearing of a big man from the East who befriended the Red Man, and helped fight for their cause with the government. "Are you that big man?" the Chief asked.

Olaf wasn't about to deny anything. He was anxious to exert his efforts in quelling the braves before they destroyed the stage and harmed the women. "Ja! Ja! Ja! I am him." Further courtesies aside, he raced off to the scuffle in hopes of stopping it. But, when he got close, he saw a ghastly sight! Sykes and friends had gotten some of their guns back, but at a horribly dangerous cost. Not aware of the natives' love of and low tolerance for liquor, these men offered some canteens of rum for thier guns, and that not satisfying, the natives had ransacked the coach, and taken more. Now, they were already wild on fire water.

Suddenly, an ominous cloud of dust approached from the north, the frenzy ceasing momentarily as five Indians rode in, giving a cheer of victory. Olaf was surprised, recognizing a young brave, Tonkita, whom he had rescued from a flogging by white frontier bums two years ago. The young brave remembered Olaf, and gave a friendly hand signal.

One of Tonkita's comrades held up a tuft of black hair, satisfied the murderer of the young Indian woman had been killed, Olaf presumed. The main crowd chanted hoops of victory. Many, in their drunkenness, however, continued tearing through the luggage for more treasure.

Olaf made threatening moves to charge the thieves, but they were too eager to do battle. The Chief, trying to discourage his band, had lost all control.

A gang of greasy bodies crowded Christina and Eleanora. Feisty Eleanora's aggressors scattered having felt the business end of the sharpened darning needles she'd used for portection. But Christina's admirers grew in numbers, totally encircling her like a bunch of hungry wolves ready to devour its frightened prey. In desperation, she cried out. "No! No! God 'elp me! Swede! Swede! They are 'urting me!" Still another long extended plea, "Sweeeeeed!" she screamed.

Five drunken hostiles detained Olaf in a combative posture, holding their weapons in the ready position as if daring him to interfere with their party. The Chippewa, not large in stature, tried to provoke the huge *'wai abishkag'* by flailing their weapons, mockingly.

Most of the rum filled natives were feeling little pain, reveling in their prairie celebration, donning hats and white mans' apparel in childlike frivolity. Olaf was desperate, and connived a way to challenge them. Except for the Chief and Tonkita, the drunks were wild and belligerent.

"Swede, 'elp me!" Christina again cried desperately.

He could wait no longer! Impulsively, he reached out, grabbed a warrior from each side of him, and in one continuous motion, threw his full weight behind them, driving the other three guarding him, into a pile of mangled bodies. In their drunken stupor they lay dazed and confused, except for one who got up and charged, howling a deafening war cry, his knife in hand! Blood was running down Olaf's arm from the severe cut. The Indian made a second charge. This time, Olaf was gratified seeing Tonkita, the one he'd helped earlier, put his boot to the challenger, knocking him senseless.

Many of the drunken ones backed away in fear, as Olaf, filled with rage, dashed to the front boot of the stagecoach for his horse whip. What possessed him, he could never explain, but he had learned well the tactics of the Indian: frighten the enemy by painting the face, and instill further fear by screaming hellish sounds. The Chippewa were petrified!

Enraged, he cupped his hand along the bleeding cut, and with his own blood drew four finger marks on each cheek, and four more across his forehead. Most of the thieves stood shocked at the big Swede's antics as if in fear of an evil spirit's presence; all except those molesting Christina, still pleading for mercy and help. Swede's adrenalin was boiling with a strength far beyond his natural powers. After grasping his fifteen foot whip from the stage, he horsewhipped the enemy with deadly precision.

Poor Christina stood there, her clothing having been stripped off to the waist, humiliated and dazed. Olaf tore his own shirt off and draped it over her shoulders, shielding her from this disgraceful exposure.

Unnoticed, two ecstatic braves wielded guns from the top of the stage, having successfully broken the case destined for Abercrombie. Others rushed to claim the same contraband. But at that precise moment, fate proved to be on the side of the weary travelers. The two warriors, thrusting their trophies high in victory, were struck by a volley of arrows from out of nowhere, it seemed. The war hoops they chanted turned into a duet of death cries as the hapless warriors fell ten feet to the ground.

A deathly quiet followed, both Indian and traveler froze for what seemed to be an eternity. The full impact of the circumstance was fully realized by the drunken and bewildered Chippewa. There was no question about it when they shouted "Sioux!" Olaf, too, could tell, for he noticed the arrows coming their way were distinctively of Dakota design. Another battle was about to begin, such as had occured every summer for over two hundred years.

The Chippewa Chief, recognizing their vulnerability on the open meadow, immediately commanded a quick retreat of his floundering braves to the northern woods, a hundred yards away. Simultaneously, three howling Sioux warriors galloped in from the south on their fleet-footed ponies under cover of a rain of gunfire and arrows. The fearsome Sioux circled the stage coach one time, then a second time, stopping to display their horrendous skill with their scalping knives - their proof they had killed the two Chippewa.

The white travelers, never having seen such vicious hostility stood dazed and horrified. The aggressive Sioux, in warpaint and naked except for breech cloth made the blood run cold in the veins of those who witnessed the violent display.

The firing of guns and arrows increased from the two tribes, and once the stage was caught in the crossfire, Olaf shouted out desperate commands. They had to get out of there, fast! The age-old hatred between the tribes had boiled for centuries, and the arrows were striking like hailstones from a raging storm.

Peters, attempting to become a hero of some sorts, was firing at the retreating Chippewa, and took an arrow in the fleshy part of his hip. He gave a blood-curdling scream as though he were dying. Olaf pulled the broken shaft out and unceremoniously tossed the hapless Englishman headfirst on the stagecoach floor. The women and men alike, lay flat to avoid the danger of being struck through open windows.

Olaf quickly jumped on the steering pole between the two rear horses. Whacking the rears of the lead team, he stampeded them away from the gunfire, and the moniacal war hoops. Racing across the small bridge, the travelers miraculously had escaped one nightmarish calamity without loss of life to any in Olaf's company.

The Swede, looking up at the high bluff to the northwest, observed a warrior in full regalia atop his large spotted white horse. He recognized the tenacious leader of the Mdewakanton band as Shakopee, one of the most hostile Chiefs of the Sioux Nation. Olaf had always tried discouraging these Indian battles, but Indian warfare was an ageold tradition inspired by the natives' Great Spirit, and one hard to break.

He stopped the horses after a few miles; well out of danger. Eleanora had been calling up, ordering the people to rearrange themselves so she could treat the nasty arrow wound suffered by Peters. Eleanora had taken charge. All were amazed when that refined Scottish woman demanded all to evacuate the back seat needed for a medical cot. The battered coach would either have to stop, or some would have to ride on top, she ordered. The Englishman required immediate treatment lest he lose his leg from poison setting in. Olaf grinned at her spunk.

Of course, Christina was thrilled and wanted first chance to ride on the high seat, feeling safe with her hero. Blakely agreed to sit topside on the luggage. Everybody paused to listen to the gunfire and war hoops back at the Indian battleground, raging on.

Manton Marble excitedly wrote in his notebook of the fantastic battle to eventually appear in Harper's for the whole world to read "What a story!" he declared.

Eleanora had studied medicine at the University of Edinburgh, she explained, knowing those services would be valuable in the isolated northland to which she traveled. The men looked on in amazement at the surgical tools and medicines she had in that small black leather satchel she always carried with her.

The Indians hadn't gotten all the liquor. Sheffield and Sir Francis came up with some for medicinal purposes to ease their comrade's pain. The five men sat hard on Peters as Eleanora extracted wood fragments from the arrow shaft as he wailed in pain. She applied a disinfectant into the open wound; the patient gave out another excrutiating scream.

Eleanora, though shaking from the frightening ordeal, as were the others, was professional in every respect. As she dressed the wound, Peters' moaning finally ceased from a drug induced sleep.

After catching his breath, and a short respite, the big Swede reminded Blakely and the others he was determined to get the stage to Fort Abercrombie on time. Even though it seemed like a lifetime of ugly hell with the Indian fracas, he insisted they'd be at the Alexander Woods station by midday, in two hours. They'd be a few hours late reaching Abercrombie, but he'd guarantee they'd get to the new steamboat, Anson Northrop, before it headed North.

Two families lived at the scenic, but lonely, stage terminal at Alexander Woods. The attendants admitted they had been terribly disappointed when the expected entourage of dignitaries failed to show up the night before. The two women had put together some tasty bean and ham hock soup, which was still simmering. The famished tourists gorged themselves.

Again, the pair of young cavalrymen anxiously rode up. The youngsters were mighty hungry, and dug into the bean soup like starved bears. They were quiet and appeared shaken and red-eyed, and after eating their fill, the two quietly shuffled out to the horses. Olaf, recognizing their gloomy behavior, went out to cheer them, if he could. The others, ready to move on, followed.

The young men, sensing Olaf's concern, had already decided on sharing their experience, hoping to ease some of the pain they were harboring, they admitted.

"Well, sir," the one called Joe started, "we were making a sweep to the northwest," his voice cracked, "and such a sight I hope and pray I never come across again in my life, sir." By now, the other men and women gathered around.

"Vee understand," Olaf said. "Vould ya rather vait a bit?"

"Well, sir, we'd rather tell it and get it off our minds some."

"Well," the one called Bill began, "we were riding over a hill there, in a lone tree, a white man was hanging." He choked with emotion, and paused to regain his composure. "And they had cut off parts of him, and he was filled with dozens of arrows, and, and, they had scalped him." The boy swallowed hard, and tears stopped him from continuing.

Joe continued. "Well, sir," he looked up and addressed the tall

Swede, "we didn't know how to do it, but we have a short army shovel along and started digging a grave. The hawks were circling around and screaching and we didn't think that was the proper way to end things, so we buried him." He took his handkerchief out and blew his nose. "Bill said the Lord's Prayer over him."

"You are fine men to have done that," said Olaf. "Vas there anything else about the man you could tell me."

"No, I don't think so..." He paused in thought a moment, "except I noticed he had a large scar on the one cheek," Joe added.

Olaf breathed deeply, thinking that the Indian hater, the one called Scarface, would never be encountered again, for he had such a scar. The Swede kept that to himself.

Eleanora and Christina went over and patted the boys and gave them a compassionate hug. All seemed deeply moved by the boy's ordeal.

* * *

Anxious to move on, the strapping frontiersman promised his traveling troop they'd find the next twenty to thirty miles to be some of the most beautiful country in the world. Even though Christina put a claim on the spot next to her big idol, there would still be room for one or two to sit on top, behind the driver's seat, for a bird's eye view.

A different attitude persisted and a spirit of friendship began to bloom amongst the eight coach-bound guests. Everyone had been through the same terrifying experience and stress, and a sense of loyalty and camaraderie had evolved, even among Sir Sykes and his associates. The stage rode steadier over a series of magnificent hills, with Olaf delivering a running travelogue of the awe-inspiring wonderland.

"This beautifully scenic spot is called the 'Leaf Voods' or the 'Leaf Mountains,' and sometimes the 'Alexander Voods'. It is probably of interest to some to note that ve are on vot learned men call the continnental divide. I guess that didn't mean much until von scientist explained that two raindrops could fall but a few paces apart, one running to the vest and north to Hudson Bay, ending up as a piece of ice in the arctic. The other drop vould flow to the east and south down the great father of all rivers, into the Gulf of Mexico and on down to the tropics."

Christina was infatuated with her handsome Swede who had put his life on the line so heroically, keeping her from certain violent disgrace, and everything he said was lovely music to her ears. Nat Hathaway and Manton Marble, out to do serious research in the vast wilderness, found the host driver to be a walking book of knowledge, and helpful to their cause.

Whether sitting on top of the high stagecoach, or down inside, the view was spectacular. After every hill covered with groves of oak, ash and elm - a new display of dozens of shiny glistening lakes of every shape imaginable appeared like magic. The hills were partly enriched by lush green meadows leading down a natural path to each lake. The animals made their daily treks down for a cool drink, or to bathe on a warm day.

Though all could appreciate the aesthetic beauty of the fantasyland, none found it more inspiring and illuminating than Mr. Hathaway, the naturalist. He raved over having never seen anything like it, as he observed the great display of wild fowl and sea birds--hundreds of species--and a cloud of millions of passenger pigeons settling in the woods; the birds already extinct in the East, he revealed.

This land, mostly untouched by white man's guns, was filled with great numbers of water fowl on every glistening sheet of water. Swans glided gracefully and unmolested from one feeding spot to another. The great heron stood tall on its spindly legs, above the reed beds, and waited for a tasty fingerling to dine on or to take back to its young.

It seemed as though the hectic confrontation with the Indians was something that happened a long time ago, yet it had been only a number of hours since the arrows were flying indiscriminately around them.

Olaf had his sights set on settling down for the night at a spot he loved more than any other for its sheer beauty and enchantment. He was driving hard to get there before dark. Finally, his horses went up the trail to higher and higher ground, and then, over the summit, he saw the two large glimmering lakes appear. The late afternoon sun was beginning to set in the slightly hazy western sky, and a most spectacular sunset was doubly displayed as it reflected the orange and fiery red hues on the water. The many deep green wooded islands appeared as gems in the sky-blue water setting, as thousands of great white pelicans circled the clear sky in their graceful and orderly formations.

No one was disappointed, wanting to have a quiet relaxing night.

Christina had her own idea. Cornering her great idol, Swede, she suggested the two head up that tallest hill. Olaf had described this as Inspiration Point, and to share their last night together under the million twinkling stars and an inviting full moon while listening to the mysterious and mournful call of the wild loon. There was no question of Christina's adoration for Olaf, and he too, was heavy-hearted knowing the four-day relationship with the sensitive and refined Scottish lass was coming to a hasty conclusion.

They ascended the hill, arm in arm, happy and carefree, beneath a romantic sky harboring uncountable stars and a full moon, so bright it illuminated the adoring smiles on each other's faces.

She wore a dainty white dress instead of her khaki traveling togs, so Olaf carried a light blanket to sit on. For long periods the two sat quietly, gazing out over the placid wilderness. Christina leaned back, turned sideways and propped her head up on her arm, beaming in her ecstasy. He reached over, held her hand, and smiled admiringly.

Though the outer world around them was peaceful and serene, Olaf's thoughts were tormenting him, thinking of his wonderful relationship with his new found companion, and aching for love he'd been deprived of for so many years. She wanted to share with him, he was sure. Throw caution to the wind, and indulge in whatever passion presents itself.

"Olaf, I can't tell yee how aye really be right now, thee words never bein made to reveal me feelins completely."

"I know. I have become fond of you these four days," he

returned, leaning back and propping his head up to face her.

"Olaf," her eyes became filled with glistening tears reflecting from the moon light. "Olaf, aye owe me life to yee the way yee saved me form certain tragedy by thee Indians."

He reached over and held her tenderly to him. "Christina, ya don't have to feel indebted to me, but I felt so sorry for the humiliation you suffered. I vasn't about to let your life be scarred that vay." Then, hoping to lighten the mood some, he joked, "Vie, I vould've torn through a pack of vild cats, I vas so angry."

Christina giggled. "Oh, Olaf, yee are a delightful mon, aye say."

"Sure, I am," he laughed, making light of her flattery.

Leaning over, he kissed her softly on her lips, and held the embrace till their bodies began responding to each other. Another more rapturous kiss followed. And, still another.

Christina was breathless, "Aye, me dear Swede, I always oped to save meself for me life's mate, but if yee so want, I'll not deny yee, owin my life to ya."

Olaf's conscience was always sitting on his shoulder. He had an overpowering respect of the fine Scottish lass, and realizing the tremendous emotional stress she had been through, knew she was innocently vulnerable at this moment. He thought to himself; it would be unfair to deflower the radiant Christina now, he recalled his own vow to a dark-eyed beauty and would feel doubly to blame afterwards.

"Christina," he leaned up on his arm, smiling admiringly, "you are like a delicate flower vaiting to be admired by some fine gentleman in the North. There are many such gallant men in the Hudson Bay service. I've met them at Ft. Garry, myself, vell educated Englishmen vith vealth at their finger tips." He paused, "I'm only a frontiersman vith but a few years schooling." He kissed her lightly on the lips. "But I love you a vay I never knew before, and such a marvelous memory vill be ours for as long as ve live."

"Aye, Olaf. T'will follow me to the grave, it will," she languished.

The mutual adoration and respect for each other would not be compromised now and the endearing moments lingered, the two indulging in an endless embrace.

* * *

The stage sped over the great savanna cradling the headwaters for the Red River, whose snaky course flowed seven hundred miles north to Hudson Bay. Nate Hathaway marveled at the flatness of the land, once a huge lake, which left a rich loam to produce a lush vegetation as far as one could see.

Traveling north, most were anxious to see the new steamboat at Fort Abercrombie. Reaching there, the Englishmen haw-hawed, seeing the miserable few log buildings in the wilderness, called a fort. But, it was a joyful reception committee of troops and a few officer's wives who greeted the Stagecoach, first of a regular scheduled service.

Olaf grinned in accomplishment for staying on schedule.

James McKay, a Scotch-Indian métis, the rotund right hand man of 'Emperor' George Simpson, had also arrived with a party of twelve to escort the two Scot ladies. Jimichi, as McKay was called, had captained many cart trains over the years. He and Olaf had become good friends.

Adulation quickly reverted to despair, however, when the entourage learned the Anson Northrop had been abandoned by its owner, who'd high tailed it to St. Paul to collect a two thousand dollar bonus, having completed the first successful steamboat run to Ft. Garry, Canada.

Eleanora was devastated, desperate to reach her fiancee in Canada. After four years she was "passionately starved," she complained.

Finally, thanks to Baronet Sykes and Blakely, money was raised to convert a flatboat, made at the local lumber mill for hauling commerce north. The flatboats creeped downstream with the current at a speed of one mile per hour. In two days, barriers were built to ward off Indian attacks, awnings for the ladies, railings and a few other necessities were added. Olaf shook his head, pondering the monotonous month long trip facing them.

Jimichi had brought greetings from Marianne's Papa, Pierre LaMond, who was failing, and had said he prayed to see his treasured daughter once more. The Swede gave a sympathetic and resigned smile in acknowledgment.

Stirring strains of a robust male chorus abruptly filled the river valley, overshadowing the carpenter's pounding. Everyone in earshot rushed to the banks of the Red to greet the brigade of boats, as the colorful, flamboyant voyageurs pushed them along. Olaf grinned seeing his comrade, George Northrop in the lead boat; a man he admired as an astute wilderness guide, an avid reader of such classics as Homer and Milton, and fluent in speaking the Chippewa and Dakota language.

Olaf's exhausted brood soon joined in on a joyous prairie celebration instigated by the colorful voyageurs and the Canadians they brought, including a hefty matronly woman who escorted two giggly privileged girls from Ft. Garry, en-route to schooling at St. Louis. When evening set in, a bearded *Bois Brules* broke out with a rapid sawing of a fiddle, and the men of the North danced the popular Red River Jig with the twittering girls. Later, the stoic matron delighted the hand-clapping spectators, who overcoming modesty themselves, joined in on the jigging till wee hours.

Morning arriving, twenty-two passengers boarded the flatboat. Olaf called his fares aboard the stage: Blakely, the three Canadian women, two officer's wives, (out to boost their mate's morale) and two troops.

"Big Swede! Big Swede!" Christina ran over for a final good-bye.

"Christina," Olaf ran to meet her. "You'll be safe with Jimichi McKay and George Northrop. You're in excellent hands."

"But I'll miss thee. I've grown so fond of yee," she whimpered. "Don't ya ever dare fergit me, ya big lovable Swede." She sniffled.

"No. No, Christina. I never could forget you. That's a promise."

The two embraced rapturously -- in front of God and everybody- as the passengers of the barge and the stage gave one tumultuous cheer of approval to this endearing display.

SHE LOOKED LIKE MARIANNE

Olaf Olsson was no longer considered a country bumpkin with a thick Swedish brogue as when he first arrived in 1851. On the contrary, no one had done more than the strapping frontiersman in breaking trails and penetrating the vast wilderness. His feats of daring made him a legendary hero throughout the Northwest. He befriended the natives and advocated for them in their quest for retaining hunting grounds and the right to pursue their ageless culture. The government kept whittling away their territory as more and more immigrants flowed into the rich and beautiful land of forests, lakes and rolling farmland.

Though Olaf lamented the purge of the natives, he was excited to be part of the energetic building boom having taken place in his first ten years in America.

St. Paul was to lose some of its dominance and frontier importance to the new towns harboring the falls of St. Anthony, thus the new Mill City sprung forth. With the Dakota Indians relocated far to the Southwest along the Minnesota River Valley, thousands of immigrant farmers settled within the hundred miles of these population centers.

Every week, dozens of steamers unloaded flocks of tourists who rushed to the new northland gateway via this great thoroughfare, the Mississippi. Grand luxurious hotels mushroomed over night: the stately Cataract, the lavish Nicollet, and the palatial Winslow House, with its six floors of fancy rooms.

Tourists wanted to see everything: the St. Anthony Falls, the power of the erupting milling district, and the beautiful Minnehaha Falls (laughing waters), which inspired poets with its magnificence. They wanted to see, firsthand, the spectacular scenery; vast white pine forests to the north and thousands of lakes interspersed throughout the area. Their sightseeing included the enchanting Lake Minnetonka only a short coach ride from their hotels.

Not far away, the plains Dakota -- Sioux -- and the woods Chippewa continued their two hundred year war on the western prairie; except for a few eager hunters, folks dared not tread too aggressively.

Olaf, whose great physique was the envy of nearly every warm-blooded male, and the admiration of a good share of the fairer sex, occasionally enjoyed hanging around town. Being a basically modest fellow, he gloated plenty and felt good about having had such a big part in the country's progress. Always out at the break of dawn, he loved sauntering around the coffee room in the Winslow House where the Burbank Company's carriage office was located.

Three or four of the class steamers were due to hit town today. That excited him. He loved to hear people 'oooh' and 'aaaah' about his wonderful town. The classy "Milwaukee" and the "Ben Campbell," with its hundred luxury staterooms, were just two of the steam boats, he recalled, would be bringing up wealthy 'southern gentlemen' and their 'belles' today.

He'd already had one cup of coffee, and read a few of the daily papers. He grunted unfavorably at the editorials castigating Indians; smiled approvingly at those editors he agreed with; grinned at stories about Mrs. Higgenbottom and her Women's Temperance Union who was still trying to close the sporting establishments. Afterwards, he moved outside to greet the local folks who came by every day. Olaf loved to talk to everybody.

Being style conscious and striving to be neatly dressed, he took little extra pains combing his sandy colored hair, which he knew attracted the southerners and easterners. Primping real good today, he wore his round wide-brimmed hat, matching leather boots, his buckskin jacket, and rawhide string tie with a perfectly carved flint arrow holding the two ends together. Everybody admired this man who created a dramatic image of the true rawboned frontiersman. He stood about a head taller than anyone else on the street, smoking his long stemmed pipe with the authentic pipestone bowl Chief Little Crow had carved for him.

The local people were now hitting the street in good numbers.

"Good morning, Dr. Graham," he said, tipping his hat. "Good morning, Mrs. Englebritzen; it's a beautiful day." He loved tipping his big hat, and showing the million dollar grin he was blessed with. It was a joy being the self appointed welcoming committee, and he was determined to have everybody in a festive mood.

"Oh, Oh," he said to the folks gathering, "here come the coaches from the levee vith the tourists." A crowd of locals gathered every time the carriages approached, welcoming the guests to town. Excitement was at a high pitch as tourists streamed into the hotels with their luggage, anxious to check in as quickly as possible.

Even though Olaf didn't know the visitors, he tipped his hat to everybody. He was surprised to see the local priest, Father O'Toole, step down from one of the rigs with an entourage of nuns, and stop for morning breakfast. More than likely, they'd just arrived from St. Louis, as he'd notice, happened on occasions before.

"Aye, tis our ambassador of good will, it is. Meet the big Swede, Sisters; a most gallant and admired hero of this country." Father said.

"Good morning, Father, and Sisters," Olaf returned. "It is a lovely d..." His voice faltered as he stood in shock. There was a young one, not in long black robes and headdress the others wore, but with a light blue shortened robe, which clearly displayed her ankles. Her head was covered with a draped cloth of the same material and color of her dress. That's it! He thought. Those are the garments the novices wore when he saw them at St. Boniface, up in Ft. Garry, Canada.

That wasn't all that startled him. It was the pretty face of the young woman with the subdued smile making his heart pound within. Olaf watched as she ascended the three steps to the front door. He stared as the group entered, noticing the young one glance back before disappearing.

My God in Heaven! Could it be? She looked so much like Marianne. If she'd remove her head covering, then I'd know for sure, he thought to himself. It's been eight years since the buffalo hunt!

He followed them into the hallway; a wall separating it from the dining area. The big open double doors allowed him to peer in. He took another newspaper and stood back from the opening; hoping to conceal himself. When he peeked over the top of the paper, his timing had been bad; she was looking out towards him at the same time. He was exasperated. His paper noticeably shook. Knowing he had to get control of himself, he backed away. It had all been a bad idea. There was no way he could hide himself. By sheer size she would have recognized him.

"Damned fool! Now I daren't go back in," he mumbled. Frustrated, he stumbled to the stage office to catch his breath.

Amelia, the office clerk, noticed his ashen appearance. "My God, Olaf, are you all right? You look like death! White as a ghost!"

"Ja, ja. I think I just saw one," he mumbled.

"I'll get you a glass of water. Sit down. I'll be right back."

Olaf felt his heart pumping erratically, bringing on a foggy dizziness. Amelia rushed back with the water, which he gulped. She knew Olaf well enough to realize that what bothered him was more than physical pain. He was suffering a near nervous breakdown!

She begged, "Olaf, is there something I could do to help? Would you care to tell me what disturbs you?"

"Amy," he always called her Amy. "Thanks for the voter. It helped. Taking a deep breath, he started slowly. "Vell, I guess you know some of the misfortune in my romantic life," he mumbled. "I'm sure you've heard of the métis girl I met ten years ago." He caught his breath, starting again. "I had the most fantastic romantic encounter; it lasted only von night and von day. Then, I didn't see her again for two years." He began rattling on incoherently, lost in his memory, "I liked her father, and he like me. He vas a boatman -- voyageur, they called them. Ya see, her mother died ven she vas little, and Pierre LaMond vas his name, raised her as best he could. She vas becoming a young voman, and the church insisted they could provide the best care and schooling, and so on." Deep in thought for a time, he soon returned to the present again. "Amy, I didn't know vot happened to her for the two years the church shielded her, until she vas allowed to go on the métis buffalo hunt, for some religious reason, I think. She sent a messenger, telling me of the plan, and I hurried north and fortunately found her. And, though a priest vatched us like a hawk, ve ver able to have the most glorious time together; void of any physical contact, mind you; but ve pledged our total love and loyalty to each other forever." At times he rambled on as if Amelia wasn't even there. Finally stopping, he just stared into space.

"Olaf, can I maybe help some way? Perhaps I could go up and find out something. No one would suspect me," Amelia suggested.

"Vell, maybe that vould vork. Maybe I'm just imagining things. If I only knew vie she never answered the letters I wrote to the Nunnery in Montreal, I vould be relieved."

"I'm sure everything can be explained. I'll go," she said, and quickly disappeared up the stairs.

The terribly frustrated Swede sat in a stupor, trying to figure out why his whole life seemed to have fallen apart. He was convinced his was jinxed, and the beautiful future he had envisioned with Marianne had become a tormenting disappointment. He kept watching the doorway, hoping Amelia would have some good news, but he couldn't imagine what. He was at wit's end, and began pacing back and forth nervously.

Finally Amy returned full of excitement. "Swede! Oh, Swede! Do I have news for you! They registered the pretty one. You're so right; she is beautiful, I agree. I learned she'll be going with the others she revealed to the hotel clerk, and will spend the day at St. Mary's."

"Damn! I'd so hoped I'd have time to talk to her; to find out vot vent wrong! Vie she didn't answer my letters? That makes me feel like a fool, now." He really hadn't heard what Amelia was trying to tell.

"Olaf," Amy smiled reassuringly, her eyes full of excitement; "the young lady registered for the night in the hotel!" She emphasized each word of her revelation, hoping the possibilities might sink in. "Olaf, the signature read Novice M. LaMond, I'm sure."

"My God, it is her for sure. She is here!" He gasped.

"That is your old flame, Olaf?" She smiled in approval.

"Vot...vot happened then? Did you hear or see anything else I should know?" He pleaded.

"Oh yes, Olaf, this you'll certainly be interested in. The good Father was insisting Sister Therese, one of the nuns, stay with her, reminding that women in the church must always be in the company of a second when out in public."

"Ja. Ja. Ja?" Olaf urged her to continue telling more.

"Well, she did show some feisty spunk when reminding she was still <u>Novice</u> Marianne LaMond, and had not as of yet, taken the vows. She thanked the good Father, but said she'd be most secure by herself, which she would relish at this time, she insisted."

"My God. I can't believe my ears, Amy."

She was excited at the possibilities of the intrigue beginning to unfold; whispering slyly, "Furthermore, she arranged for the hotel to send a coach at half past six, after vespers, she said, to return her to the Winslow House for the evening."

"Oh, vell, I vill get to see her then," he brightened. He quieted as the idea was being contrived in his head. "I've got it! I know vot I'll do! There's no reason in the vorld I couldn't actually be the regular driver of that carriage, is there?" He laughed -- almost villainously.

Amy praised his brilliance. "What a fabulous idea you have, Olaf Olsson. And, I hope the best comes of this," she smiled.

During the day, Olaf walked about town like a stalking animal glancing down at St. Mary's Church where his mysterious Marianne was being harbored. He spied from the highest hill, and when no one was looking, he took his long glass and zeroed in on the garden where the Sisters strolled about. It was like he could reach out and touch her. She turned and looked up his way and he quickly dropped down behind the bushes, lest he be seen. He finally realized at that great distance, the naked eye would never be able to identify anyone. He felt guilty spying on her, just the same.

Time dragged on as he kept plotting the evening when he'd

have a chance to confront her, asking to explain her silence and absence for eight long agonizing years, which had been haunting him.

Still another grand idea came to mind. Going back to the hotel he cornered Rebecca, the head waitress. "Becky, I have to talk to you," he whispered, attempting to keep his plan highly secret. She looked more than slightly surprised, but led him into the small private dining room to the side.

"What's going on, Swede? You've got some mischief in your eyes."

"Becky, I have a strange reqvest. I know you're usually finished serving by seven, but I have an old friend staying at the hotel, and vell, she is close to becoming a nun, you understand."

"Oh, ya, I saw them this morning. The young one was lovely."

"That vas her. Now, it may not vork out, but I'd be beholden to you if ve could have this room privately: maybe a bottle of nice vine, and your house special, the honey glazed squab on a bed of vild rice."

"Swede, I'm not even going to wisecrack with ya. I see a serious and desperate look in your eye. And, my good friend Swede, I'll do all I can to make this a most special occasion. I promise."

"Thanks, Becky, you've alvays been most accommodating, and I'll see that you're vell compensated for your trouble, to be sure."

Still, another idea emerged, as he continued to conceive ways to impress the woman he loved so much. Reaching in his pocket, he took a five dollar gold piece and placed it in Rebecca's hand. "Oh, and I'd be so pleased if you'd see that a gorgeous bouquet of flowers, and...and an elegant bowl of fresh fruit grace my lady's boudoir before she returns."

"Oh, Swede Olsson, you are absolutely gallant! You even make my heart flutter," she winked approvingly.

Certain he'd left no stone unturned in his haste to please and flatter his once amorous object; he was doing it all to confirm the promise made eight years ago, that he'd love her forever.

Time dragged slowly; he wondered if he was only playing the part of the fool, again. At times the recurring thought of her not answering his letters dampened the thrill he was having. Trying to be positive and hoping to reconcile their love, tormented him.

The day was soon to end. He arranged for the regular driver to turn the reins over at the appropriate time, promising he would be paid anyway, which satisfied him, for sure. Olaf always kept his coachman's garb in the stage office, and when the time came, he slid into the white frilled shirt, the black trousers, a cutaway coat, gray ascot, and the velvet black top hat. He was pleased with what he saw in the mirror, as he slipped a white silk boutonniere in his lapel.

Mounting the coach, he nervously rode towards the church, hoping his disguise and devised scheme would work. Surely, no one would expect a junior executive of his caliber to be a common stage driver. He rode through town, looking away from people he knew, so not to be recognized. It would be dusk soon, and then he'd get by with his scheme, maybe.

Finally, pulling up in front of the Manse, he noticed the good Father O'Toole and the Sisters bid Marianne a farewell.

Olaf cringed. Why did they have to be so prompt? If they'd dallied a little longer it would have become darker. Still light, he bemoaned.

Father chuckled as soon as he noticed the tall driver, whom he recognized right off, as none other than his big friend, Swede Olsson. Olaf was mortified! Exasperated out of his skin, realizing his plot had gone awry, and that the Priest had blatantly called out his name. Worse, Marianne smirked, appearing amused over Olaf's embarrassment.

"Stay up there, big Swede. I'll assist yer fare into the coach." He helped Marianne into the small compartment.

"Thanks, father," Olaf acknowledged, properly humiliated.

"Novice Marianne, yee must remember ta greet Bishop Taché, and thee others, I beg of yee."

"I will, Father. I'll be sure to do that. Thank you for the glorious day, Sisters," she called out and waved.

Father O'Toole kept looking up, chuckling. "Me lad, bout the time I expect to see yee in the capitol as a senator, Swede, yee suddenly appear as an umble coach driver agin." He laughed heartily. "I thank yee fer takin a personal interest in these church arrangements; ye'r always so thoughtful that way, Swede."

Olaf was devastated, now that the Priest had recapitulated his miserable life so clearly in front of his evasive angel, his well-contrived scheme so dismally revealed. Now was the time to make his move. She was trapped like a weasel in a box. He recalled, a weasel is most dangerous when it is released. Maybe it would be the same with Marianne. That saintly smile. Oh, that saintly smile, he minced. How can she do that to me? I, who have written many lovely letters to her at the nunnery! Sometimes I have the feeling she's mocking me! His thoughts echoed in his head.

Olaf knew it would be near impossible hearing her soft voice with the wheels hitting the pebbles on the road. Oh, that lovely voice could turn him into a jelly fish he knew, so a way had to be contrived to get her undivided attention for a few moments. He stopped at a scenic point overlooking the river. It was quiet and serene. Goldfinches were twittering their last evening songs.

"Marianne?" He finally called down. No answer. "I know ya don't have to talk to me, but I've been so curious these years."

It was quiet for some time. Then she tittered smugly, Olaf thought. "Monsieur Olsson, you've been curious?" Another quiet pause. She added; "A lonely soul, isolated and forgotten in a northern Nunnery could also be curious, I suppose."

Olaf cringed at Marianne's uncompromising tone of voice. She sounded bitter, sarcastic, he thought. She calls me "Monsieur" now. What the Devil! What kind of an answer was that, anyway? Why does she ignore the sweet things I said about how much I loved her, and that I couldn't live without her? Of course, she knows I exaggerated that. The conversation not friendly, he hoped food might entice her.

"Marianne, I don't suppose a voman of the Church; though I don't think you've taken vows as yet, vould consent to dining vith an old confused admirer -- for old times sake, of course -- at the hotel dining room this evening?" Hearing her snicker, he bristled some.

"Oh, big old friend, fear the dining room will be closed by the time we return," she said, sounding unimpressed.

239

"No. No," he insisted! "I mean, yes, normally, but...but." He dropped his voice and revealed all. "I'm sorry, I arranged the evening, selfishly, for a most private dining room." Resigning himself, "I apologize. I presumed more than I should have, I just vanted to talk to you."

"Olaf Olsson, you arranged that?" she answered brightly, but still condescending. He held his breath hoping she'd accept.

"Oh, I have no bitterness. Hurt maybe" After another awkward pause, "I'm not above forgiving, old friend of years gone by. Yes. Yes. I am some hungry. We could reminisce about the wonderful buffalo hunt. It's nice of you," she said.

Talking to himself, again. *I don't understand how she could be upset with me. Not bitter, she says. What the heck, her voice is so lilting and heavenly now.* "Ve vill go ahead then. Is it all right I call you Marianne, or should it be Novice?" he asked.

"No," she snickered again, "please call me Marianne."

The Swede breathed deeply in relief. Excited, he tapped the horses -- pushing them along. Time was of essence now.

Pulling the coach up to the hotel, he hopped to the ground, opened her door quickly, and met the captivating angelic face. Reaching up to help her down, being overpowered by her smile, he inadvertently grasped her with both hands, lowering her by the waist. When he heard insulting groans by shocked near-by observers he realized his blunder. They saw a tiny delicate nun being manhandled rather crudely. "Oh!...Oh! Marie," he whispered, "please forgive me! I didn't mean to embarrass you."

"Oh, don't feel too bad," she whispered back, "may have shocked a few, but brought back lovely memories of happier days." She smiled. "Not called Marie since buffalo hunt," she smirked.

Olaf escorted her into the hotel, full of eager anticipation.

"Must take few minutes to freshen up in room," she said on leaving.

"Fine. I'll shed my driver's outfit, too. It's the room called 'Sky Blue Vaters', just past the main dining room. I'll be vaiting." After she left, he quickly darted to the stage office, shed his long dress coat and top hat, slipped back into his buckskin jacket, and traded his string tie for the cumbersome ascot. He hurried into the dining room to check it out.

Rebecca still waited to make sure the Swede approved.

"Oh, Becky, the table looks absolutely impressive, and the bouquet of flowers is very nice. Thank you."

"I waited around to see if there was anything else I could do. The other waitresses have gone, but we wheeled in the little warming table, and the plates are prepared under the tin canopies, you see. I have a bottle of nice French white wine in the ice bucket, there. And, Olaf, if you'd like me to stay, I would be happy to oblige."

"Becky, you've done vonderfully. I'll handle it now. Thanks."

It was less than five minutes since Becky departed, and a light tap sounded at the door, alerting the Swede his guest had arrived. He opened the door nervously, and the light of his life smiled radiantly as she entered.

"Oh, Olaf, flowers in room so elegant. Wish they last forever. Fruit bowl is nice, too. Thank you." She moved around the table admiring the lavish setting, and came back to him again. Taking his hand, she patted it and thanked him.

He thought, how different it was that first time we met on the prairie when she fell head over heels, and our responses were so free and natural. Now, only a pat on the hand. "I'll hold the chair for you," he said, while she seated herself. "Vould you like vine? Or can't you now?"

"Would love some. Course I can. Sisters make it at nunnery. You see, it used in church holy ritual." She was relaxing, he noticed.

Olaf served the food the hotel prepared. Marianne raved over the fine wine and exquisite dinner. Olaf smiled to himself. Becky hadn't missed a trick in embellishing the fine honey glazed squab with greens, scallions, pickles, cranberries, and a whole tray of delicate pastries.

As long as they kept indulging in small talk, the anxious Swede was mighty uncomfortable, for he wanted to get into conversation about them, and why she didn't bother answering his love letters. It was Marianne who got the ball rolling when she began

241

reminiscing.

"Was thinking, coming from St. Mary's in coach, how wonderfully thrilling our first meeting. I, injured badly, and you miraculously came on prairie. I look up, see immense man with kind face offering help. Fright only lasting a few seconds, for like fantasy I read once, you became kind noble prince." She chuckled softly. "I call you Prince Ole, remember?" Recalling the past, she smiled. Then, serious and contemplative, she said, "I was mere babe in woods, so it's said. Father always say I look more grown up at fifteen than most girls of twenty."

"Ya," Olaf agreed. "I thought you ver at least eighteen." There was another uncomfortable silence, then he continued. "It vas impossible to get you out of my mind, Marie," he confessed most seriously.

"Yes," she agreed. "Though world goes around, time stood still for me, too."

Olaf was bewildered. Why does she speak as though it's past? Done? Gone? he wondered. Oh, if I could love her, hold and kiss her again.

Abruptly, the conversation took a strange twist. She shocked him by asking, "You ever think we be together again after the hunt?" Showing sternness, "We made serious pledge, you know."

He stammered like he'd been hit on the head with a sledge hammer. "Vot? Vot ya say, Marie? I don't understand!"

"I was heart-broken you never answer my letters, but as time passed, my work and studies at convent absorbed me. I managed to rid myself of self pity, and relived wonderful moments in memories." She smiled at him- forgivingly, he thought, "And I still do," she confessed.

"My God, Marie! I never received a vord from you! Vot devilish thing could have happened? Vare did you send them, Marianne?"

"Post them where you told me; to Olaf Olsson, St. Anthony Falls, Minnesota Territory, United States." She fidgeted her glass nervously, as Olaf sat speechless from the shock. Marianne continued. "Felt bad when you not write me. Said you would at hasty parting, when Bishop Taché came for me after buffalo hunt," she scolded.

Olaf's heart nearly stopped from the sudden pain! "Marianne, please believe me, I have written many, many letters to you, and I mailed them to the Nunnery, the Order of the Gray Nuns, at Montreal, like you said. I've been agonizing these many years, trying to understand vie you didn't care for me." The Swede was becoming emotionally intense, "I couldn't think of anything else but that you'd probably left the Church," his voice faltering, "and as pretty as you are, I thought some other lucky fella got you."

They looked at each other in a state of bewilderment. Marianne rose, and her eyes widened. "Oh Olaf, my love!" her voice sounded tragic.

Olaf jumped up on his heels, and the two met at the side of the table and embraced rapturously. "Marie, I love you!" And they kissed and hugged insatiably, laughing and weeping, both together. Time was now needed to heal the agony of their loneliness, and to renew their love.

Eventually, Marianne, realizing what had gone wrong, tried to explain how she was forced into total isolation in that remote institution in northeastern Canada, and being a young naive novice from the wilderness, was intimidated into responding to the demands and teachings of her superiors. She shivered when describing her strict authoritative Mother Superior who had no qualms about punishing the young girls for questioning anything.

"I sorry, Olaf. She must have seized our letters."

"I'm sickened to hear of such treatment, Marie," Olaf groaned.

"Being taken from real world makes one think and act strange, dear Olaf. I so thankful be free and with you now."

"It's painful for me to imagine your horrible imprisonment, Marianne, I don't ever vant you to leave me again. Stay and ve can have a vunderful life together, and ve'll be happy. I promise."

"Oh, my love, I would adore that." Looking worried, she quickly avoided the subject, not wishing to reveal her painful secret yet. "The dinner was delicious! Olaf, my love, have only this night for now, and tomorrow morning must hasten to see poor ill father. Eight years we have to make up. Need you now more than my words can say. Come, love; save myself for you. My body cries out for you, Olaf." She kissed him passionately. "Allow a few minutes, my prince, then come to room by stairway on second floor," she whispered tenderly, and left.

The years of separation had not lessened her modesty, so when he tapped on the door, she opened it a slit, and then quickly slid under the covers as he entered.

Olaf grinned. He sat on the side of the bed, leaned over to kiss her, but could tell by her labored breathing, and her fidgeting with his shirt buttons, she wanted him disrobed...now! She had left the oil lamp on low to accommodate his undressing, and he noticed her eyeing his every move while removing his clothing. You sly fox, he thought, reveling over a man's modesty. You just wait my little tease; and he winked at her.

She giggled. "Leave lights on, Olaf. I love seeing your beautiful muscular body."

He turned the bed covers back, revealing her pulsating breasts, and lay next to her. Cupping her face in his large hand, he kissed her tenderly. She began stirring rhythmically, as he moved his hands down to her shoulder, and lower to her breasts, passionately caressing her, aware that it was not gentlemanly to overpower one's mate before her time.

"No! No! Olaf, I want you now." She pulled him over onto her. After many year's absence, they were finally home, and happy again.

It had been a most fantastic night for the two, having been deprived so many years. The threat of the Church was no longer intimidating, and she wanted, more than anything in the world, to spend the rest of her life with the big Swede, she said.

He felt rewarded, too, having waited for her as promised, and could honestly say he'd never pursued other women. Oh, there was that little episode with Matilda Washburn, who cried out for his help in overcoming her emotional crisis, but no man would consider that being unfaithful, he was sure. A man gets caught up in circumstances like that.

Morning was near. The fear of parting again haunted them.

"My dear Olaf, must be on stage at sun up! Cannot take time from going to see my Papa. I hope he waits for me," she sighed.

"Thank God Bishop Provincher helped by contacting the Cardinal, himself, or I fear I still be bowing to Mother Superior in most unyielding authoritarian way."

Olaf had his pocket watch hanging on the bed post. He lit a match to check it. "Thank the Lord, ve still have plenty time yet."

"Then, Olaf, hold me and love me till the last minute," she begged.

As the end of their sojourn neared, Olaf could feel Marianne's body trembling, and realized she was weeping.

"Marianne, vot is it that bothers you so now?" he pried.

"Oh, Olaf, time has come when I must reveal painful secret, and only hope you understand what I did was for you, as well. Didn't think it was fair to cast blame on you for anything, and when church offered to help me, felt I had no choice, so through much suffering, I gave in." Olaf could tell by her sobbing that she was in extreme pain.

"Marie, you're talking in riddles. You told me after the hunt, before they took you avay, that you vondered if I'd ever forgive you for something. Darling, I know you could never do any real harm."

"Oh, my dear Olaf, bear with me as I try to get through this! You see, I so planned coming down in springtime, like I promised after we first met, but lady luck looked the other way," she sobbed softly. She sniffled in her hanky, trying to get control of herself. "Oh, I knew I was with child by early winter. I cried and cried. Oh, not that I was to have your baby, but now," she whimpered, her eyes filled with tears, "I would not get to see you again," she confessed, trembling in his arms.

"My God! And you've kept it secret all these years!"

"Yes." She sobbed so the words wouldn't come anymore.

"Marie, please settle down. Tell me the rest; I must know! It vas the most fabulous night ven ve met." He jumped out of bed, turned up the lamp and came back. "Vare is the child? I must see him - or her. Vas it a boy or a girl, Marianne?" Olaf asked compassionately.

Seeing his elated reaction, she smiled through her tears, "My love, he is our son; and a fine young man he's becoming, too."

"Marie! Marie! I got to see him. Vare'll I find him? I'll go tomorrow," he said resolutely. "To think of it, I, Olaf Olsson, the big Swede! I have a son!" He could hardly contain himself. "Vare is he?" he pleaded.

"Oh, my dear Olaf, don't even know. He is near Montreal, for I get to see him about every six months. They bring him to me a few days." Her voice denoted sadness again, "And I do want him now with us, and Church has no legal right to keep him. I never signed anything." There was an uncomfortable silence. "That is why I have to return."

Olaf was silenced from shock by her disappointing news.

"I'll probably catch Simpson's flying brigade of boats back to Montreal, and am confident Bishop Taché see that my mission be satisfied."

"I don't understand how this kind of stuff goes on. The Church cannot kidnap babies! There must be some laws."

"Olaf, please, I had no way of caring for Peter Olaf. At St. Boniface I agreed to work with Church, and they agreed to raise him in the orphanage run by loving sisters." She sniffled. "You forgive me?"

"Peter Olaf?" he grinned. "That's a nice name. I like it."

"Ah," she sighed, "I was hoping you would. Anyway, the arrangements were good, and I got to mother him some. Olaf, it was after I went to Montreal that he was taken from me, and I had little to say about my life anymore." She reached over to check Olaf's watch. "My, the time is getting on, I must get dressed, my dear."

Olaf jumped up. "I'll pour some vater at the vashstand, and vile you're getting ready I'll run down and order some breakfast. Oatmeal or some meat, maybe? Or some fruit and pastry, love?"

"Oh, my prince, spoil me with so much. Fruit and pastry be fine - and a cup of tea, please. Dare not eat too much with long hard coach trip ahead." She grabbed him again for another smothering hug, "Oh, you! For some reason have intense appetite, *mon amour*."

They bantered as they had done ten years before, when meeting at the métis celebration near his cabin three miles north of St.

246

Anthony Falls.

Finishing breakfast, and while drinking her tea, Marianne hurriedly readied herself for travel. Putting on her head covering, she said, "Men will not be forward with me if look like nun."

There was time for one more kiss before hustling down to the stage.

The genteel Swede, man about town, acted casual and aloof when escorting Marianne to the stage, aware acquaintances might raise an eyebrow over the display of familiarity with the churchly traveler.

Marianne gave a subdued smile as Olaf assisted her to the coach, and bowed a thank you. Under her breath, she said, "Olaf, you were absolutely wonderful last night. I will hurry back, you can be certain of that."

Olaf grinned. "I vill be vaiting for such a thrilling encore. Have a safe trip, my love," he grinned and winked.

Watching as the stage faded off in the distance, and feeling sadness over such an abrupt parting, Olaf still felt exhilarated knowing his long awaited dream was about to be fulfilled.

It was a little unusual, however, that he inadvertently stood motionless for a long time watching the stage disappear down the trail. Finally, he looked around to see if anyone had noticed him. Sure enough, Mrs. Higgenbottom and a gathering of her revivalists were peeking around the corner, their heads bobbing in obvious gossip, and their fingers pointing.

Olaf quickly straightened himself, cleared his throat, began whistling innocently and hurriedly walked away, mumbling; "Vouldn't ya know it."

FOOD FOR THE DAKOTA

"Damn it, Governor, I'm getting tired of being your scapegoat!" Olaf pulled no punches in lambasting the government for mismanagement of Indian affairs, especially as it applied to the late payments and distribution of annuities for the hungry and destitute Dakota. Ramsey was taken aback at the ranting of the bitter frontiersman, whose labored breathing revealed his intense anger.

Pompous Governor Ramsey was overly condescending, unaware the Dakota situation had become explosive. He depended on the Swede to keep the Indians from retaliating against the government.

Exasperated, Olaf began pointedly, "Governor, just eleven years ago, the year I came to America, the Dakota ver forced from the 'big voods' country - their homeland since the beginning. For their millions of acres of fine voodland and lakes they ver promised payments for the next fifty years. Then, forced on the prairie, they now starve. Promises have been broken!" He pounded the desk. "Traders take their pay before it reaches Indian hands!" He got up, paced the floor, and his deep voice resounded, "My God, Sir, ve're two months late right now! Vare the hell is the food for those poor starving souls?" He pounded the desk again.

"Olaf, Olaf!" the Governor pleaded, "I understand your concerns and am equally disturbed, but I have better news, finally." He smirked - patronizingly, Olaf thought. "Yesterday, I received confirmation by telegraph, that Congress has passed funding legislation and authority to pay the Sioux in gold again. It is just a matter of weeks, now."

"Aw, Congress! Congress!" Olaf grumbled disgustedly.

"Well, Swede, you know what a crazy time we're in. The

North is not doing well. This damn Civil War now over a year old, and the South kicking hell out of the North makes these matters slow to materialize."

"Still, it's no excuse for starving the Indians!" Olaf stormed.

"No, but Swede, we spent a lot of money trying to teach the Sioux how to farm. They should be able to do something for themselves."

"Hell, they never lived as farmers! Do ya expect miracles?" Olaf countered. "Many have put on vite man's clothes, cut their hair, and have taken to the hoe and plow in desperation." Olaf moved toward the Governor. "How long vould you last, Governor Ramsey if you'd be forced to accept the Indian vays?" He paced again. "Damn it! You know last year vas a dry year. No rain, the ground parched. Then, grasshoppers came like a black cloud; in a few hours the land vas bare." He sat again, in frustration.

"I'm sorry, Olaf. We must keep the home fires going, nonetheless, and hope there's not an escalation of another war in our backyard."

Emphasizing the seriousness of the matter, Olaf continued. "I think I only need tell you Little Crow came all the vay from his village to varn that the young varriors are angry and ready for uprising at any moment."

"Little Crow? Came here?"

"Yes. They say, ven money comes, the thieving traders vill grab it." Olaf lowered his voice, speaking most directly, "I repeat, it is a tense situation! Agent Galbraith is unsympathetic and incompetent down there, and refuses to release their food from the varehouse."

Governor Ramsey was now shaken into a sense of urgency. "Swede, will you please go back to the Lower Agency with the news that it's only a mater of days, and the gold will be here."

"Vell, I vonder if they'll have much faith in me anymore, Governor."

Ramsey was outwardly nervous. "Swede, we really need your help - for the sake of the hundreds of unprotected women whose husbands are off fighting in the Civil War. Those brave heroes do not deserve a heinous fate such as having their women taken by unruly Redskins! My God!" he said disgustedly.

"I've heard of Indian maidens suffering such a fate at the hands of villainous vites in every Indian village I've visited," Olaf recanted.

"Well, I've heard that, but can one believe such claims?"

Olaf winced. "It's pretty damned easy telling a half breed, sir."

The governor was not above employing subtle bribery, and putting on an insipid smirk, he opened his desk drawer. "Oh yes, Olaf, I near forgot; here is a check! I sweetened the pot because of the urgency - for two hundred dollars." Olaf looked askance, thinking he'd not accept tainted money suspected of belonging to the Dakota anyway.

"It's a mere pittance for all the services you rendered as a loyal citizen."

Olaf looked at the money for a long time--thinking. "Will you go down there, Swede?" the governor pleaded, "and tell them their pay is on the way?"

"Yah, maybe I vill." Olaf suddenly had an idea and decided to pursue it.

"Thank you, Olaf. I'll be forever grateful."

The big frontiersman moved toward the door. Grasping the handle, he turned and delivered his exit remarks without showing emotion. "Oh yes, Governor, I understand you take fifteen percent of all federal Indian payments for administration. Is this part of it?"

Ramsey stood silent. News had circulated that the Federal government was investigating him for misappropriating funds.

"Little Crow said he thought you had deep pockets, like the traders." He opened the door and nodded. "Good day, Governor."

* * *

"Hello, Carrie, how in the vorld have you been?" Olaf greeted the petite and flirtatious pony-sized blonde waitress.

She laughed, "Oh, the Big Swede has risen! Where in the devil have you been? All kinds of rumors circulating about our mysterious world traveler."

"Vell," Olaf laughed, "just ramblin around the big country out there. Nice to be back to town, and the Nicollet House with lovely ladies like you, Carrie," he coyly toyed with a dangling ringlet by her ear.

"Ah, flatterer, you know how to make one blush, you joker."

"Seriously, my friend," he confided, "I have an unusual reqvest: I vould like vun of your private booths. 'Expecting someone for a important meeting, Carrie."

"Swede, I could write a book about the goings-on in those hide-a-ways," she winked.

He laughed. "Perhaps ve can contribute another chapter, then. Seriously, it is of utmost importance that ve are undisturbed. Besides, I'll tell you before hand it's," he looked aside, making sure no one could overhear, "Mrs. Vashburn. And ah, I'd like to have a carafe of fine vine at our disposal." He held his index finger to his thumb, showing how fine.

"Oo la la," Carrie rolled her eyes, tipping her head back in delight. "I will have her wine of choice, Olaf. It's Amontillado. Carry it just for her."

"Yes, yes, yes, Amontillado! I remember now."

Carrie lit the oil lamps, illuminating a walled mural of nude nymphs frolicking beneath a waterfall. Olaf smiled, waiting eagerly.

Finally, hearing the rapid tap, tap, tap of her heels on the marble floor, he knew immediately they were Matilda's. The red velvet drapes parted, revealing the tall, stately lady in a black tailored dress with white lace trim about the collar and at her cuffs; the epitome of entrepreneurial success. She threw herself at Olaf, who stood waiting with open arms.

"My big Swede, how are you?" She rose up on her toes giving

a tender kiss on his cheek. He responded with a congenial hug.

"Matilda! My goodness, do you ever look beautiful! It's a thrill for this frontier rascal to hold such a jewel."

"Ah, ah," she smiled; "but a charming rascal. The young eligible damsels are most flattering whenever your name comes up."

"Your compliments are overgenerous, Matilda," he grinned shyly.

"Where on earth have you been, Olaf? I haven't seen you for so long."

"Vell, I've been here and there; mostly vest and north - Dakota territory and Canada - vay up. My dear lady, such a vast interesting vorld it is in the northland. Untouched by human tampering, really."

"Tell me more about it, Olaf," she urged.

"Oh, it vould take hours. Hopefully, later, there'll be time for such a visit. I'd enjoy that."

"I'll look forward to it too," Matilda agreed. "Seems I detect a troubled look in those blue eyes, Olaf. Is anything wrong?"

"Oh, there are problems... but I'll get to that in a minute. First, I want to hear of your eventful life, Matilda."

"There's so much. The kids and Jenny, now the doting mother."

"I've only seen baby Trena a couple times. I promise to be a better brother-in-law from now on. I'll spend more time with her now that I'll be vorking closer to home. How's she doing?"

"Oh, she's strong-willed; the strength of a saint. She just returned from your cousins, Rudolph's and Marta's. Loves being with their children so much." Then, thoughtfully, she added; "it's so unfortunate - the times. Do you think it will ever end, Olaf; the Civil War?"

"Vell, I hope so, soon, but it'll take a miracle, I'm afraid."

At that moment, Carrie came through the fold of the bamboo curtain with a tray, holding a carafe of wine and two glasses.

"Oh, Olaf," smiled Matilda, "you're so thoughtful." Carrie served the two glasses and left, with a slightly teasing smile at Olaf. Catching the tantalizing bouquet, Matilda went into sheer ecstasy. "My Heavens, Olaf, that is my Amontillado. How delightful!"

The gloating frontiersman grinned, slightly embarrassed. "I thought a small glass or two vouldn't hurt. Remembered it from the time at your place." He held his glass up to her. "Here's to a vonderful, vonderful friendship." Olaf swallowed with difficulty, having inadvertently brought up that sensitive day a few years ago.

Realizing his discomfort, she renewed the childish interplay, "I'll drink to that." Clicking glasses they snickered like carefree youth.

"My, it's pleasant escaping bitter reality," he smiled warmly at Matilda. Thoughtfully, he changed his tone. "How are things going at the mill, Matilda? How are you surviving Mr. Vashburn's condition and all?"

"Oh, J.R. is no more than an empty shell now, but he seems most satisfied to sit out in the garden, watch the birds and look at the flowers and such." She twisted her wine glass between her fingers, and continued. "He doesn't know me, of course! He provided for me over twenty years, and I'll see that he's well cared for. He's absolutely no problem and has full-time nurses to keep him comfortable." She paused, momentarily, and smiled as if to indicate it was a moot time to change the subject. "I'm so worried for Jenny, though. It is sad, Gustav away at war. Olaf, do try to come over as often as you can. It's so comforting for her when you're close by."

"Matilda, I vish I could change places vith my little brother. I vould do it in a minute; but the Governor has made me hostage to the Indian situation and, I guess, right now I can do most good here."

There was another pause. She smiled. He returned the same. She fidgeted, leered up and down pensively, and then spoke softly.

"Olaf, you have forgiven em, haven't you, for that day at the mansion? That devilish tormenting time plaguing women at midlife?"

Olaf gave a sympathetic look, aware of her agony. "Matilda, vot ever the magic of the moment, I too, vas affected positively; and votever else, I am so glad to see how successful you're managing things - taking over the mill like you did. Everybody has such respect for you - I more than anyone."

Relieved, she winced nervously. "Well, I have my chicks all back in the coop, as you said." They then exchanged amusing glances.

"May I pour?" Olaf asked, noticing her empty glass.

"Olaf, I am so happy now. I have immersed myself into the business and it is growing rapidly." She paused thoughtfully. "Oh, I have a few casual friends in the East I enjoy seeing occasionally, but I'm not eager to make a permanent commitment. I just want to enjoy my life as it is, now. I do hope you'll come over often for Jenny's sake." She blinked sentimentally. "I feel I am part of your family now, having been her American mother for these wonderful years."

"Ja, I'll certainly do that. I love Jenny." He wanted Matilda to feel assured, so he looked directly at her and said in a serious tone, "And I really adore you, Mrs. Voshburn."

"Oh, how nice of you to say that, Olaf. It is wonderful to have such mutual respect between us." They smiled agreeably.

"Olaf, I wonder about you. It's probably none of my business, but there have been various and sundry rumors floating around through the years," she was prodding him coyly; "you do have a romantic relationship someplace in this world, don't you?" She winked facetiously.

The Swede looked uneasy, and laughed in embarrassment. "Ja, Matilda, I...I've been in love with a beautiful creature in that fabulous northland," he smiled reflectively: "and now, more than ever. Though lost for years, ve've found each other again, and my life has renewed meaning, finally."

"Um hm. I thought you displayed an unusually contented air about you. Is she pretty, Olaf?"

"Oh, yes, she's beautiful, and much like you," he smiled, "but she was young - as innocent as a baby ven ve met. It's been many years now." He quieted himself for a few seconds. "You're the first I've ever told this. She's a...she's a mixed-blood, Matilda," he confided.

At first, Matilda was shocked at the Swede's revelation. After an uncomfortable moment she said, "I never realized how narrow-minded I might be, Swede." She twisted her glass rather nervously. "Will you forgive me if I showed disapproval? I hope it all works out for you, dear Olaf." She took his hand as a comforting gesture.

"I hope so too. Ya know, Matilda, my dream vas to be a farmer in America. Now, vit her, our dream is soon to be realized."

"Olaf, I could talk for hours. It seems like we're a real family, especially having Jenny with me. I sense you have something serious on your mind, my dear Olaf."

"Ja." He nodded. "I nearly forgot. Our visit has been so pleasant."

"Is it the Indian problem? I read about it a lot."

"Ja, the Dakota are hungry and are threatening an uprising. If it happens there'll be a lot of bloodshed, my friend. They've been pushed to the edge. Matilda, I could use your help."

"Go on. Go on," she urged.

"Vell, the Governor just paid me two hundred dollars for services I supposedly rendered; 'seems like a bribe in a vay. Vot I'd like to do is buy milled flour, if you have some to sell me, to help sustain them 'til their annuity payments come in a veek or two."

"Olaf, you are an unusual man; and your eyes show so much anguish for them. I tell you what; your two hundred dollars will buy a full wagon load, and if it means that much to you, my friend, I would be happy to donate a load myself. Who knows," she smiled softly, "It might help me become more compassionate, and tolerant too."

"Oh, thank you, dear Matilda. I'll alvays be grateful to your kindness and friendship. Two loads of flour vill no doubt save some lives."

The Swede was pleased with his private meeting with Matilda Washburn: an enjoyable diversion from the pressures of the day, but now he had to hurry and make his urgent trip to the Dakota Reservation in an attempt to forestall a most threatening confrontation with the hungry, poverty-stricken natives.

A warm embrace was shared by the two friends, in parting.

SIOUX UPRISING OF 1862

• White Settlements
○ Indian village

MINNESOTA

DAKOTA TERRITORY

Mississippi River

ST. PAUL
KAPOSA
MENDOTA
MINNEAPOLIS
FORT SNELLING
HENDERSON
MANKATO
ST. PETER

Minnesota River

LOWER SIOUX AGENCY
FORT RIDGELY
NEW ULM
Cottonwood River

Birch Coulee

UPPER SIOUX AGENCY
HAZELWOOD MISSION
YELLOW MEDICINE MISSION

Redwood River

White Lodge

Yellow Medicine River

Lac qui Parle
Chippewa River

Minnesota River

DAKOTA RESERVATIONS

BROWNS VALLEY
Big Stone Lake

DAKOTA RALLY AT YELLOW MEDICINE

With a four-horse hitch and two heavily loaded wagons in tandem, the Swede sped southwest to the Dakota Reservation. The July heat slowed progress. Only strong horses were selected at each exchange station, replacing the tired and sweaty quartets completing each run. Olaf trailed his great riding horse, Dancer Girl, behind. She could move faster, cross rivers and cover rough terrain readily, if the need arose. Beside, he preferred riding the rangy gray mare over bouncing on the rough springless wagon seat any time. Fort Ridgely was nearly a hundred miles away, but Olaf cut off at Henderson, avoiding the river's bend at Mankato, saving fifteen miles.

It had been just ten years since the Dakota Reservation was set aside by treaty; a stretch twenty miles wide, bisected by the Minnesota river near New Ulm, and continuing west to Dakota Territory. Four years later, Congress reduced its size by half in another of its detestable treaties, confiscating the Indian area north of the river with the promise of increased annuities; the fertile farm land being coveted by the influx of zealous pioneers.

The Swede now-a-days spent endless hours daydreaming on his solitary journeys; thinking about his treasured métis and realizing the probability of soon being together with their son, Peter Olaf, on a farm of their own to the west. As a boy, his dream was to have a spacious place; he'd saved enough to start on a small acreage, if necessary. They would be happy enough, he knew. But, the pressures of the day, with nearly ten thousand Indians starving along the Minnesota, allowed little time for reflecting.

Approaching Fort Ridgely, sitting vulnerably on a bluff one hundred fifty feet above the valley floor, the Swede noticed the exposed buildings appeared deserted. Usually stopping to chat with his friend, Sarge Jones, he pulled in to satisfy his curiosity.

A young corporal popped out from the shady side of the barracks, saluting briskly. "Hello, Swede, Sir. Good to see ya." He seemed delighted that the popular frontiersman came to break the morning monotony.

"Hello, Corporal," Olaf returned a casual civilian salute. "Looks like a ghost town around here, or a holiday. Vare is Sergeant Jones and the rest of the troops, anyvay?"

"Oh, the Indians are getting restless, Swede, and have all gone over to the Upper Agency beggin fer food, I guess. Poor devils! The Agent won't release the food til the gold comes, they tell me."

"That so?" Olaf wondered if the spark about to set the prairie ablaze had already been ignited. Such confrontation could evoke the young Dakota malcontents to angry retaliation! He'd better hurry on to the Upper Agency! Might be needed now, he thought.

"What ya got on your wagons? Some beer, I hope," the young soldier joked, trying to get the Swede's attention.

Olaf's thoughts suppressed, "No, not this trip, my friend. I better get movin fast! Partner, vill ya git me some help unhitching my horses, and keep em in the stable till I get back? I make better time ridin my gray mare," he said anxiously. "I must hurry."

"Sure, Swede, I'll get some men on that detail right away. We'll wheel the loads under the shed, too. 'Take care of everything."

"Thanks, Corporal. You fellas have always been helpful. I'll make sure I bring a good treat of August Shell's beer from New Ulm next time; ya can bet on that."

Dancer Girl always seemed to sense urgency in the Swede's voice, his having to do little prodding for a fast trot the first hour or so. He was sure Dancer understood, always talking to her like she was human. "Ve've gotta move out now; you and I've got important business to take care of," he'd say. The lanky gray mare snorted and neighed, tossing her head up and down, in acknowledgment.

Olaf was tense. The Agent, government people, and the settlers had been smug and complacent, looking at the Dakota as aimless wanderers without the will to fight back. But he knew differently, having witnessed the ferocity in battle with their age old enemy, the Chippewa of the north woods. They'd only be pushed so far, he knew, but maybe - just maybe - he could calm them a little longer until the gold payments would arrive.

Having reached half-way, it was time to rest Dancer Girl, allowing her to feed on some prairie grass, and drink from the river. Ten minutes and she'd be ready to trot again, he knew.

Small Indian groups usually seen along the trail were noticeably absent today. Knowing the squaws often traveled with their Indian men, especially now they would be needed to plea for food, he guessed. Having gaunt and starving women along might induce sympathy.

Olaf doubted the recently appointed eastern bureaucrat, Galbraith, would be influenced easily though. He worried for fear the inevitable revolt might be triggered at this very time.

Pushing Dancer faster and finally nearing his destination, Olaf stopped to listen. He could hear them now! Drum beats and Indian wailing in the distance! Olaf always thought that nerve wracking high pitched wailing sounded like wolves dying in the claws of the hunters' steel traps.

Quickly galloping up a high hill he could see the Upper Agency less than a mile away, on the banks of the Yellow Medicine River. "My God!" Olaf exclaimed aloud, stopping Dancer in her tracks. The prairie surrounding the upper agency was a reddish brown, as if it had been scorched by a prairie fire. But, he soon realized it was a spectacular mass of natives coloring the landscape in numbers he'd never witnessed before. Remembering the thousand métis on the buffalo hunts, he guessed there to be five or six times that number; Indians as far as he could see.

He watched in astonishment. Then, riding down anxiously, the bands of Dakota recognized the Swede as he made an imposing approach on his gray horse. The beating of the big drums and the eerie chanting quieted for a while, but soon the whooping increased in intensity, as if the Dakota were paying tribute to their trusted friend, hopefully to help their cause. And they called his Indian name; "*Coda*, Tall Like Oak; and *Coda*, Big Oak."

Olaf was aghast seeing so many desperate Indians at one time;

some so gaunt their bones were outlined through sun-crusted skin. Being a hot day, meager clothing covered the skinny limbs, and many looked like ghosts who'd risen from the burial mounds, Olaf thought.

Passing close to the gathering of Mdewakantons, he saluted Chiefs Wabasha, Traveling Hail, Little Crow, Mankato, Big Eagle and the others as they held council among themselves. The stoic faced friends raised their hands, palm forward, in the usual salute. Olaf noticed Chief Shakopee, meaning Little Six, was not generous with his greeting; sub Chief Red Middle Voice and his gang of malcontents made insulting gestures with fists to show their anger. They came dressed to intimidate: head dresses, bodies painted, bearing guns and tomahawks.

The concerned Swede rode on in a large circle, not wanting to show partiality to any group. To the south and west of the agency buildings he recognized the Chiefs Red Iron, Akepa, Little Paul, and John Other Day, all residing near the Upper Agency. Even Standing Buffalo came from the edge of Dakota Territory, showing support for the tribe.

Riding back to the center, he passed the two companies of the Fifth Regiment commanded by Lieutenant Sheehan, who gave a strong military salute to his frontier friend. Olaf returned a strained smile, knowing Sheehan and his troops had no will for firing on the crowd.

The Swede kept riding among the Dakota wondering what he could do to ease the tensions of this potentially explosive situation. He was relieved finding none of the two thousand Winnebagos had left their reserve south of Mankato, nor that the Chippewa had left their woods' reservations in support of the demonstration, as Governor Ramsey had worried about. He knew most of the Dakota Chiefs were reasonable men and could control their bands. But, Chief Shakopee and Red Middle Voice continued to be a worry.

Bringing the news of Congress' approval to pay the Dakota might induce the egotistical Galbraith to open his huge stores early. On the other hand, the news might be enough to convince the hungry Indians to go home and wait. He must try, now.

Olaf glanced toward the large brick warehouse. Thomas Williamson, a missionary and medical doctor, and Stephen Riggs, both maintaining missions west of the Upper Agency, were obviously pleading with the Agent. This was a good sign; Galbraith talking with the two men who had dedicated their lives to the cause of the Dakota, including the composing of a Dakota Dictionary, the first written manual of their language. He hurried over to tell of the appropriation of gold.

The incessant wailing of the destitute demonstrators and the beating of the drums still echoed throughout the countryside; a constant reminder that if something goes wrong, this would become a tragic day in history. Olaf quickly dismounted and approached the trio. He presented his hand in greeting, first to Doctor Williamson, "It's good to see you, Doctor." Then to Missionary Riggs, "How are you, Reverend Riggs?" He had little love for the man many referred to as "the prairie prick," but he knew to shun him could only harm his cause, so he said, "Agent Galbraith, how are you?"

The agent, offensively chewing on a raw rutabaga, babbled, "Fine Swede. Now you're here, perhaps you can persuade these Sioux to mosey on back to their own villages." His bulbous cheeks and double chins rippled as his head shook uncontrollably, as if he were in the throws of a nervous disorder of some sorts. Either that, or the rum infested wind bag was shaking from over-indulgence, Olaf thought, the way he was weaving.

Incensed at the agent's despicable attitude, Olaf fired back; "You have a full varehouse. It belongs to them! Vie don't ya give em some, Thomas Galbraith?"

"My, you frontier boys sure don't understand how the bureaucracy works, do you?" He belched offensively. "We follow a procedure; they get the food when the cash payments come."

"Doesn't make a hell of a lot of sense, does it?" Olaf fired back. "People are hungry here, and the food, by treaty, belongs to them! Lincoln appointed you. Do you think he'd let people die of starvation if he could see this?"

"I'm only following procedures, Swede," he blubbered and belched again.

261

Olaf addressed the two clergymen, but spoke loudly enough for Galbraith to hear. "Gentlemen, I come with some slight encouragement; Governor Ramsey received an official telegraph message that congress finally appropriated the money for the Indian payments. Only problem, I'm afraid it'll take more than two veeks for the gold to arrive."

The Agent overheard. "There you are! Tell the heathen Sioux to go back where they came from and wait, like they're supposed to," he whined blatantly, then continued chewing on his raw rutabaga, and cackling at himself, convulsively. "I shouldn't eat these goddamned things; gives me gas." His jowls were pulsating in self amusement. "It's lucky it didn't come out the other end, anyway," he howled as he backed away and moved toward his living quarters at the end of the large brick warehouse.

Olaf continued conferring with Williamson and Riggs.

"This is a most regrettable reception," Williamson confessed.

"Our Wahpeton and Sisston people will not become violent, I'm certain. They only wish to demonstrate their need for food," Reverend Riggs added, "and their need for the annuity payments owed them."

"I believe that, too, gentlemen," Olaf agreed, "but I'm more vorried about some of the unruly Mdewakantons. I hope Little Crow can keep them in line."

The western Dakota were generally active in hunting on the prairie, and many had planted crops which looked good this year, Riggs and Doctor Williamson confided. Olaf told of bringing two loads of flour and would deliver one load to Pajutazee Mission tomorrow, he promised, for which the clergy men thanked and praised him.

The Council of western chiefs closed in; Akepa, Mazakutemani - Little Paul, John Other Day, Standing Buffalo, and the others. "*Token yung he,* Tall Like Oak," they greeting the white man they trusted.

John Other Day, whose wife was white, had returned with him from Washington when he was a treaty delegate in 1858. She had taught her husband some English, so he acted as translator to the others.

Olaf explained the action of congress in approving this year's payment, but cautioned they'd have to fend for themselves for at least two weeks, or more. Though being tense and somewhat bitter over the lateness of payments, they laughed when Olaf reminded them the great white Father often dragged his feet while carrying so much gold.

The Chiefs grunted appreciation when told of the load of flour to be delivered to Pagutazee Mission tomorrow, and pleasantly smoked pipes filled with the tobacco Olaf brought along.

"Tangyang nungwe, Koda, Tangyang nungwe, koda." Good bye, friend, the supportive Chiefs acknowledged and backed away to their bands.

Lieutenant Sheehan's Fifth Regiment stood in readiness in case the lid blew off, and the Dakota decided to break-in the warehouse. When seeing the Western chiefs withdraw, Sheehan gave the Swede a thumbs-up gesture, indicating the situation appeared reconcilable.

The Mdewakantons were closing in. The belligerence of Shakopee's and Red Middle Voices' war-like bands, yelping and drum beating, were downright threatening. Though Olaf sympathized with them in their grievances, he knew there was no turning back the clock. Too many whites now, so the white man's laws must be kept. He hoped Little Crow, Wabasha, Big Eagle, and Traveling Hail; all friendly Chiefs, could stop the violent demonstration before certain calamity set in.

Olaf mounted his horse for a more dominating presence.

"Tall Like Oak, friend of Taoyateduta, we come to demand food. Some claim will not wait any longer. What can Tall Oak do to help save us?"

"Taoyateduta, and all my Dakota friends, the Great Father sent his message; agrees to pay gold payments. Tall Like Oak asks Dakota to be patient. I am sad to see your hungry people, but Agent Galbraith says he cannot give food until gold comes."

Little Crow relayed Olaf's message in Dakota language so all could understand. The hostile braves interrupted with a howling defiance.

Red Middle Voices malcontents shouted threats: *"Dakota kte*

Ateyapi!" and *"Dakota tokang aya wayute!* Becoming more boisterous, raising their fists in anger, they threatened to kill the Indian Agent and began storming the warehouse to take their food.

Galbraith came out shouting at the military, who had raised their weapons in the ready position. "In the name of the United States Government, I order you to shoot these thieving heathens. Shoot them! Fire on the conniving savages!" But the soldiers held fast.

Red Middle Voices' Rice Creekers surrounded the terrified agent with scalping knives raised. Galbraith shouted for his very life, ordering Sheehan's Fifth Regiment into action. Though the Agent had no authority over the military, Olaf could see the anguish in Sheehan's face. Even the horses commenced rearing up in the fracas as the Indians scuffled violently under their noses.

"For God's sake, Taoyateduta, in the name of common sense, stop your people from acting like vild animals or blood vill flow like vater in the river below us," Olaf shouted.

Little Crow then signaled his braves to confront the perpetrators, and immediately angry battling flared between Dakota braves. Galbraith was screaming frantically, and Olaf thought the agent had been stabbed. Some of the Indians, too, were bleeding from knife wounds, but soon the violence ceased, and the attackers backed away grudgingly. Galbraith, dazed, staggered back to his quarters, walking like he had a watermelon between his legs, his pants dripping.

The skirmish ending, order was re-established. Olaf, being diplomatic, praised the Dakota for putting down their weapons. But resentment continued while horse dung pelted the arbiters who tried to resolve the riot, one of the mushy missiles hit Olaf directly in the face.

Little Crow orated powerfully. *"Nahong Taoyateduta,"* he demanded. "Tall Like Oak Dakota *wastedaca!"* Little Crow demanded they listen to reason and respect their friend of many years.

They listened reluctantly as Olaf told of being sorry the government had not treated them better, but warned that to defy would bring great numbers of white soldiers they could not resist.

"Taoyateduta, tell your chiefs Tall Like Oak has two vagon loads of flour vaiting at Fort Ridgely. I vill bring von load to Pajutazee Mission and von load to Lower Agency tomorrow. It is not much, but vill add to vot you grow yourselves, and from hunting and fishing."

Little Crow repeated Olaf's message. Still the grumbles continued.

Chief Wabasha stepped up on the log Little Crow had stood on. "Listen, my brothers, while I speak." Wabasha was the most revered elder statesman commanding respect from all of the Dakota nation. "I have cut my hair and taken white man's ways. They are good ways. You young bucks would be wise to take up the hoe and farm, and you too, will have food for your table. Wabasha is not saying Great Father in Washington should not pay for Dakota lands we sold him. I will trust good friend, Tall Like Olaf, that Great Father will pay as he has agreed. White brothers have war now. We should wait some. Go back to our own villages and have faith in our government."

The Mdewakantons talked amongst themselves after seeing the Sissitton and Wahpetons gradually disassemble, and few by few, began moving away toward their own villages to the west.

Olaf breathed easier, seeing the gradual exodus. He spoke directly to Little Crow. "Taoyateduta, tell your people I vill hope to see them all come for some of my small gift of fine milled flour tomorrow." He gave the usual friendly salute to both the Dakota and to the soldiers who had exercised restraint by not firing their guns. He then moved back up the hill where he first witnessed the awesome sight of five thousand Dakota gathered together. He paused to wonder how long the young hostiles could be kept from the inevitable war he felt certain to come.

265

OLAF TRANSPORTS GOLD

It was 2:00 A.M. as Olaf drove the Concord stage up the steep hill and through the gate at Ft. Snelling on September 18, 1862. The four evenly matched strawberry roans made an impressive appearance in the bright moonlight. Seventy-two thousand dollars in gold was to be delivered to the Dakota; weapons and ammunition were loaded under a veil of secrecy. A paymaster, Mr. Wycoff, and four young riflemen boarded the rugged coach.

"Move out! Hiya! Hiya!" Olaf shouted, and the four horses trotted away. The Swede glanced back, making sure Dancer Girl trailed comfortably.

The roads to the southwest were in good condition. The government had financed the improvements on the major trail to Fort Ridgely, which was becoming a heavily traveled route for European farmers as well. Lately, pioneers streamed in. Olaf, recollecting the past, was amazed at the transformation in such a short period of time, with Henderson, Le Sueur, Mankato and New Ulm growing in population; providing the required needs and services to the industrious farmers. They were plowing the sod faster than a runaway prairie fire, it seemed. Always something new to see from the high seat of the coach, he thought.

Olaf lit his pipe and contemplated the situation. He grinned, recalling Ramsey begging him to take the Concord for transporting the gold, thinking it to be the safest conveyance as few would suspect his hauling anything but human cargo. The governor wasn't such a damned cantankerous old coot as usual, he thought. On the other hand, the rascal never could be totally trusted, having pulled so many devious political tricks.

An advance rider had been sent ahead to inform each exchange station to have the strongest and fastest horses harnessed and ready to go so the record-breaking trip could be realized. Olaf insisted the gold would be at Ridgely by 2:00 P.M., allowing both the Upper and Lower agencies to be notified for disbursement on Tuesday morning. The Indians had waited long enough, he contended. It was now three months late.

Being a pleasantly warm day, the wide river valley looked serene and peaceful as the stage turned west over the prairie. Olaf was feeling more relaxed nearing the half way mark. What a relief to have the situation under control again, and the Dakota could continue their normal ways with plenty of food to sustain them, he thought.

The Swede smiled, hearing the young troops in the coach laughing and acting up. Good to hear youngsters horsing around that way.

Drawing on his pipe, Olaf had flashes of Marianne pop into his mind, and thoughts of seeing his own son for the first time. He laughed out loud at that too. The amazing luck of having a son, and not knowing about it; all because his dear métis thought he would have blamed her, so she kept it secret all these years. He chuckled, and shook his head at such a ridiculous thing. His daydreaming was soon interrupted. He'd forgotten about the responsibility of carrying all that gold. He'd better remain alert.

Maybe it was the ominous cloud coming into view on the southern horizon shaking him back to reality. Dust or smoke, he couldn't tell. Grabbing his long glass for a closer look, he could make out several horses and wagons heading directly toward them. Abruptly there was concern for the valuable freight he was hauling. Realizing the sizable train was a military unit, Olaf instructed his guards to hold off. They'd already had their rifles aimed out their windows. When the thirty or more horses and wagons closed in, Olaf relaxed, recognizing Company C of the Fifth Minnesota Regiment.

Lt. Sheehan howled at meeting the strapping stage driver on the open road, inasmuch as it had been only a few weeks since the Yellow Medicine episode.

"Where ya headin' with such a fancy rig, partner?" Sheehan shouted.

Olaf stood on the platform, which he did ofttimes when meeting people on the trail, and to stretch his legs. "Howdy, Lieutenant Sheehan. Ve're headin' on down to Ft. Ripley vith a load of treats for our friends. Ya know vot I mean," Olaf winked after they had stopped.

"Well, it's a small world. We just came from there," he joked. "I'm glad those presents came," the Lieutenant chuckled, knowing what Olaf alluded to. "Guess they won't need us down there for awhile, so we're headin' up north to Ft. Ripley for a stint, to watch the Chippewa."

"It's purdy country up there in the pines, my friend. See ya later. Ve gotta mosey along; deadline to meet, Lieutenant Sheehan."

"Ya. We do too. See ya later, big fella."

The fifty, or so, enlisted men all piped up, "Good luck Swede, have a good trip." Everybody got a kick out of the witty frontiersman having heard of some of his heroics, many times blown out of proportion, much to the chagrin of the modest tall Swede.

"You boys keep your pants up, now. Votch the cockleburs," Olaf jibed, giving a robust horse laugh, as they parted company.

He again leaned back, lit his pipe, and let his mind meander some. He smiled about the young soldiers; only young boys like him when he left Sweden a dozen years ago, he recalled -- full of pee and vinegar.

After traveling about a half hour, the tiring horses were replaced by another fresh foursome at the last changing station, and the stage rolled on at its fast pace. Olaf was satisfied with making good time. About an hour passed when a lone rider came flying over the hilly terrain from the south like the devil was after him. Olaf first thought any lone horseman traveling that fast had to be trying to escape someone, or something. It wasn't all that unusual finding a young army deserter hightailing it away from his unit these days, lonesome for his loved ones, or just bored with military life. A young soldier soon pulled up along side the stage; both he and his horse winded.

"Sir, did you see Lieutenant Sheehan and Company C pass this way?" he shouted nervously.

"Ja, they're probably ten -- fifteen miles ahead. Vot's wrong, anyway, soldier?"

The boy was slightly incoherent, and his speech was raspy. "Oh my God, man! You've never seen anything like it!" He ranted with difficulty, trying to catch his breath. "Sir, all hell's broke loose, and I've got to get Company C back to Ridgely fast," the army private yelled.

"Vot's going on, young fella?" Olaf pressed, sensing the urgency.

"The Indians! They're killing all the whites at the Lower Agency! Major Marsh took most of his troops to try to stop the killing. There are just a few soldiers left at the Fort. Refugees filling it fast! Sir, got to keep going now! Got to catch Company C fast!" He galloped away.

"Boy, stop at the Burbank horse barns two miles up for a fresh horse. Tell 'em Swede Olsson said so," Olaf shouted after him.

"Thanks, Swede, I will. So long!" The boy sped off.

Suddenly the peaceful day had turned into one of despair and tragedy. Olaf's fears of being late with the gold had proved prophetic. Now his only concern was for the mass of unprotected humanity throughout the whole river valley, stretching for a hundred miles, east to west, both Native Americans and European pioneers.

Wycoff, the paymaster, begged to turn back. The young guards, sensing excitement, wanted to get into the action. Olaf would satisfy the boy's wishes, for if what the messenger said was true, and with over half of Fort Ridgely's compliment of men heading north, there'd be a drastic need for every available rifleman should the Fort be required to protect innocent refugees.

Olaf raced his horses at a fast trot, and when reaching the five-mile marker without confronting hostility, he breathed easier. The Lower agency was thirteen miles west of Ridgely, and he was certain the attackers would be obsessed with plundering, and celebrating victory over the hated traders. Or, a worse threat, the possibility the Fort had already been overtaken and forces, quietly playing possum, could be awaiting unsuspecting arrivals. He stopped the horses to listen for any strange distant noises. There was nothing at first, except one of the horses pissing. Then, a strange sound caught his attention, like the faint cry of a wounded animal back of a small knoll.

He called down, "Men, hear anything unusual?"

"Ya, think I do, Swede. About ten o'clock," the man pointed.

"Ve'll take a qvick look, but vill have to make a dash for it if it's an ambush of any kind. Should it be Dakota, they are experts at imitating all natural sounds," Olaf warned.

Heading to the backside of a small mound for a better look, Olaf called out, "There! Over there!" A wagon and team of horses stood tangled amongst some bushes. There were no people in sight. He drove closer, cautiously avoiding unexpected danger. All were on the alert.

The sounds became alarmingly discernible, definitely the crying of a small child. The farm horses acted nervous, one's head turned clear back. They'd been spooked plenty, Olaf knew.

"Jeff and I'll go take a look, Swede," the tall boy called Stretch offered. The young eager guards jumped out and jogged the fifty yards to investigate. The child stopped crying from the obvious distraction.

"Be careful," Olaf cautioned. "Untangle that horse's line that's caught on the veel so he can straighten his head. Go easy to settle them down."

"Oh, my God!" one yelled, as he looked in the wagon box. The other returned a few steps, and said, "He's deader than Hell, Sir! The man looks like he was shot, and blood covers the bottom of the box! Oh, Heaven forbid such a fate." The one called Jeff shouted back. "There's a woman, too. She's alive, but looks dazed and don't talk, Swede."

Olaf's bird's eye view of the surroundings assured it being safe to drive closer. He could see clearly from above the chilling sight the young men had described. The child looked to be about two or three years old; her tiny white calico dress was covered with blood stains from the man's body, he lying 'spread eagle' and face up across the bottom. The distraught woman, her hair in wild disarray, sat in the corner in obvious shock, staring into space. She was covered with little bloody hand prints, the same appearing on the little girl's face from her wiping tears, no doubt. The woman, mumbling a hymn, was totally oblivious of the men present, "God be with us" -- her voice fading out to indistinguishable words.

"Fellas, ve can't stay here too long! Those doing this might cut off our drive to the Fort," Olaf warned. He paused, and studied the two youngsters, Jeff and Stretch.

"Are you brave enough to drive that vagon to the fort, fellas?"

They didn't hesitate one second. "We ain't goin ta leave em here, sir." "I'll drive," one said. "I'll tend the child best I can," said the other. Again, the little girl did not appear frightened by the strangers.

"Fine," Olaf acknowledged, "They sure sent fine men along."

Plenty of reason to be concerned now. Olaf was certain the one who killed the man in that wagon showed little mercy. Hopefully, they'd be ahead of any organized attack, and could get to Fort Ridgely unmolested. Olaf hung back, waiting for the wagon; the farm horses seemed worn from their wild run-a-way.

Over the next hill, Ft. Ridgely came into view, sitting vulnerably naked on that high bluff. No bastions or barricades, just a series of scattered buildings. A stone two-story barracks stood at the north end of the ninety-foot wide parade ground. On the east and west sides were two-story frame barracks and officers' quarters. The single-level commissary, and the Commandants' and Surgeons' quarters completed the rectangle around the parade area. Other buildings were scattered beyond, including a row of small log houses on the north, next to St. Peter Road, housing a hospital and residences for the non-commissioned officers. The stables were located across the New Ulm road to the south.

Closing in, hoards of people could be seen milling about the exposed parade grounds, but at closer range, they proved to be mostly women and children; few men to be seen anywhere. A quick glance to the west told the rest of the story. Smoke clouds dotted the distant horizon. Farms burning everywhere!

Olaf pulled the coach into the north end, near the hospital, where people were scurrying about frantically. Dr. Muller was attending a wounded man. He advised Olaf to take the dead man to the vacant cabin with the others. Noticing that the woman and child were in extreme shock, he suggested taking them to Mrs. Muller, his assistant.

Olaf stopped the stage at headquarters. A young anemic looking officer came inquiring of the unexpected arrival, but was relieved seeing the five riflemen, he admitted.

"Who's the commanding officer here, Sir?" Olaf asked.

"I am Lieutenant Gere, temporary commander. Captain Marsh took forty seven men this morning to quell the uprising at the Lower Agency. God, we've got two hundred refugees here now, and more coming!" he added.

Mr. Wycoff, the agent's clerk, agreed to have the barrels of gold hidden for the time being.

"Sir," Olaf steadied the young officer by his arm, thinking he was about to faint. "You all right?":

"No, Sir," the young officer admitted. "I have a miserable headache and fever. Came down with measles yesterday." He then instructed Sergeant Jones to take over and shuffled back to his barracks.

"Swede. Ya picked a Hell of a time to come calling."

"Right, Jonesy. Looks bad, don't it?"

"Not good. All this grieving by the women and children, and screaming by the wounded! Had to be awful damned gory out there, Swede," the rugged, red-faced sergeant lamented. "Ya know what the hell we got, Swede, to defend this bastion? I'll tell ya.

272

Twenty men!" He mopped his sweaty brow. "I got some cannon, four of em, and I had sense enough to train a couple of men to handle em. May not save us, but it's gonna help."

"All right, Sarge." Olaf removed his hat, and scratched his head. "I've got my horse trailin' along; planned riding to the Upper Agency. Vithout a doubt, she's the fastest animal around this country and could run avay from the whole tribe. I think I could do more good out there, keeping an eye on vot they're up to, along vith vorning farmers to hightail it out of the country."

"Ya. It'd be mighty big help, Swede. But be careful!" He shook his head, showing sympathy. "God! I know ya must feel awful, bein' so friendly to so many of the good Indians, and what you've done for em and all. They're gonna suffer with the rotten ones, ya know."

"I know," he agreed. "I'd protect innocent Indian vomen and children vith the same determination. The vites have slaughtered a lot more of them in the past."

"Gotta run, now. Watch yer ass, Olaf," Sarge warned.

The Swede was anxious to move out of the fort, but decided to make the rounds of the refugees, gathering information on what had transpired since the first shots. Most were too distraught to make much sense.

Mr. Dickson and his family were about to go shopping in New Ulm when the shooting started at daybreak, Dickson revealed. He told how the traders and their clerks were shot in cold blood, including Andrew Myrick, the most hated, who jumped out his upstairs window only to be mowed down before reaching the woods. Dickson scampered away immediately, he admitted.

Reverend Hinman gave the most pertinent information, however. "Some of the 'cut hairs', the Christian farmers, came to my house late last night, after the council meeting at Little Crow's. They said all the chiefs were there -- every one -- even the dastardly Rice Creekers, with Red Middle Voice. My parishioners looked most fearful, Swede."

"But, vie? Vie now?" Olaf asked dumbfoundedly.

"They told of murdering some unfortunate farmers over a few chicken eggs. It happened up at Akton, in Kandiyohi county, they said."

They were the same hoodlums who roughed up Olaf near the Lower Agency a few months ago, and he was certain they would eventually cause trouble.

"I don't understand, Reverend Hinman, vie vas the council held at the house of Little Crow? He vas replaced as leader by Traveling Hail."

"The Council reinstated him last night, Swede. He tried to refuse, but the young braves called him coward. Nobody calls Little Crow 'coward.'"

"No. No one calls Little Crow 'coward,'" Olaf repeated, resignedly.

The clergyman was most bewildered as he continued. "The hostiles in control, the Council agreed to kill all whites and cut hairs, alike, before this is all over." He smiled feebly, "Only yesterday, Little Crow attended my Episcopal services, and I took special note of the fact he shook hands with everybody before he left," Hinman said.

"Before this is all over, and before he dies, I vill find a vay to see Little Crow. Thank you for telling me about that, Reverend Hinman." He nodded and slowly walked away.

Olaf was fit to be tied. Seeing death and destruction, he must try to save farmers out on the prairie now. At once, he hustled his coach back of the north barracks, unhitched the foursome and secured them in the stables.

Dancer Girl was ready to go. Riding west, the whole scene played through Olaf's mind as the refugees had described it. They told about Dr. and Mrs. Humphrey, and their two children; Phil Prescott, the old fur trapper, whose wife was Chief Shakopee's Mother - in - law; and Charlie Martell, ferry operator, who helped many across the river to safety - all lay dead back on the lower Agency road. These people had dedicated their lives to the cause of the Dakota. It didn't make sense to him; but war never

274

did make sense, he thought.

Buildings were burning everywhere! The Dakota were serious about taking their land back, as it was, the way their Great Spirit designed it. The white man's monuments and fences offended them, and all the farm buildings marred the landscape. The compassionate Swede was feeling mighty low, and had mixed emotions over the unfolding tragedy. He was sympathetic for the German farmers, who were devastated, having found their dreams being realized over long hours of sweat and toil, only to see their farms destroyed in a few horrendous moments.

There'd be no turning back, Olaf knew. As soon as the hostiles take their revenge out on the Lower Agency, they'd set out to kill all intruders west of the Mississippi. So, he rode hard and shouted loudly: "Farmers! Farmers! Run for your lives! Leave everything! Save your lives, first!" He had a strong voice, and it seemed today, the spirit moved him. His baritone voice boomed over the hills. Several families sped away in desperation, hearing his warning, but he was mighty short with those he had to argue with. Too many thought the Indians were weak, lethargic beggars, with little gumption to do battle; but Olaf knew of their ferocity as warriors seasoned in war against their ancient enemy, the Chippewa of the North Woods.

He came upon a poor wretched young mother with three little children crawling frantically through the high grass next to a ravine. Her clothing torn, and with an injured leg, she wept pitifully.

"I'll get help. Your husband. Vot of him?" Olaf asked.

"Ve come from Chermany. I run farm. He at var." she sobbed. Olaf hailed another wagon racing by, who gave them a ride to the Fort.

Darkness setting in, Olaf returned; tired, but satisfied he'd done as much as he could. About fifty more refugees had made it to the poorly-defended fortification. Every available person pitched in, building barricades, digging trenches; some stacking hay, cordwood, or anything else they could get their hands on. It was a miracle the Indians contented themselves with plundering, and celebrating the first days' successes. Because of this, Fort Ridgely was spared with less than thirty men defending.

At nightfall, Olaf volunteered to be a picket, and remained close to the ravine on the south side of the compound; if the Dakota were to attack, it would more than likely be at this point, under cover of the bush and high grass along its sides.

About 9:00 P.M., Olaf heard a rustling in the grass. He leveled his rifle, fearing the worst, and alerted the men with him.

"Hold your fire! Hold your fire!" a desperate voice called out. "We are men from Company B, Fifth Minnesota Regiment, Sergeant John Bishop in charge. Don't shoot for Christ sake!" he shouted again.

A dozen emaciated troops straggled out of the brush. Five wounded -- three severely. Shortly behind, eight more straggled to safety.

"Sergeant, what of Captain Marsh and the others?" Olaf asked.

"Ambushed at the ferry, Swede.. It was hell!" he gasped. "Captain Marsh drowned crossing the river. We're all that's left of the fifty."

Sergeant Jones brought a detail of men and assisted the weary and exhausted survivors to the hospital for treatment and some food. The embattled men of Company C, plus those remaining at the fort, and the stage guards, now numbered forty four effectives; not exactly a viable force, but double from when Olaf first arrived; it was much better

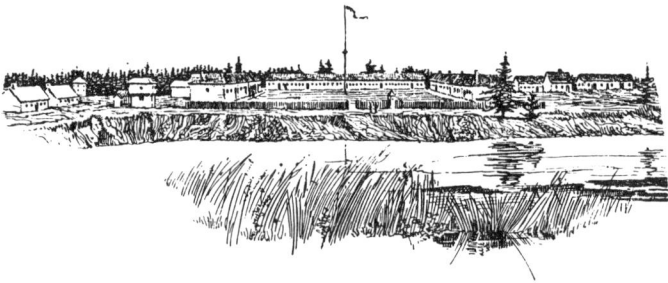

FORT RIDGELY.

276

HOSTILES THREATEN FORT

No one slept. An incessant mournful dirge consumed the night. The suffering of the wounded and grieving, praying, and hymn singing set a somber background. Many anxious women desperately dug trenches and built barricades from farm wagons, hay, cordwood - anything to shield them from the enemy.

Olaf, feeling pity for the anxious refugees, dug as hard and as fast as his tiring muscles could stand it. He tried consoling those who lost their husbands and boys, killed by the rampaging hostiles.

Leaving to scout at the crack of dawn, Olaf saw the people gaping toward the horizon in fear of catching sight of the violent red man who'd returned to his savage ways. A brilliant sun was rising. It could have been serene, except for memories of yesterday's tragedies.

Riding onto the prairie, and not seeing the Dakota at first, Olaf hoped the council of chiefs had contained Red Middle Voices' belligerent braves before all out war would be declared. He thought of the terrible massacre of pioneers at Spirit Lake, Iowa, just five years before, by Inkpaduta, a Wahpekute, and twenty of his renegades. They had been cast out by the council of Dakota Chiefs. Olaf had traveled along with Chiefs John Other Day and Little Crow, and saw Indian justice applied when several of Inkpaduta's murderers had been overtaken on the Dakota, and killed. Maybe this uprising could be stopped now like that had been, Olaf hoped.

Unfortunately this was not to be. Having traveled out ten miles, he spotted a substantial war party snaking throughout the woods on the north side of the river. They were heading east all right - directly for Fort Ridgely. Olaf made sure of not being detected, having cautiously come up over a small rise behind a clump of bushes. Watching a while through his scope, he estimated the size of the force, and then backed down and headed quickly back to the fort.

Not wishing to terrorize the civilians, he slowed Dancer from a fast gallop to a brisk trot on entering the compound. He waved at the people and smiled while dismounting, hoping to avoid panic a little longer. He then entered Headquarters. Lieutenant Gere, Sergeant Jones, and Dr. and Mrs. Muller were coordinating their efforts.

"You have precious little time to organize the troops, and get the frightened civilians in their crowded quarters, my friends," he warned.

"The Dakota are on the vay and near as I can guess, there are about two hundred. They look most grizzly the vay they've painted their bodies!"

"My God!" Gere exclaimed. "How much time do we have, Swede?"

"At the outside only a half hour, Lieutenant."

"I'd so hoped Sheehan and his company would have come," Gere agonized.

"I'll expedite getting the cannons positioned and manned, Sir," Sergeant Jones belted out, and dashed out the door.

Though no alarm was immediately sounded, Dr. Muller hurried over to his hospital, and Mrs. Muller went to the block building and rushed the terrorized refugees within.

Olaf crawled atop the mound covering the munitions' supplies. There he scanned the horizon and waited of the advancing Dakota.

At 9:00 A.M. the feared attack appeared imminent on the northwest prairie in plain view of the fort. The military sentry, making the sighting about the same time, shouted "Indians! Indians on the western prairie!" Immediately the refugees panicked, trying to get a glimpse of the ferocious enemy wearing only breach clouts and awesome headdresses of eagle feathers representing scalps taken in previous combat. The grotesquely painted faces and bodies were most terrifying. Olaf scrutinized the gathering, out of musket range but visible through his telescope, and could see a great assortment of horses and wagons, taken from farmers only yesterday, most likely. No doubt feeling confident with their bellies full, and coffers loaded with plunder from the trader's stores, they knew they could kill whites like sheep.

If only Sheehan's forces would appear from the north, then maybe, it would be a halfway fair fight, Olaf thought. He wondered, how many more were hiding back of the hills. A thousand? Two thousand?

The natives' indecisiveness was bewildering. They were holding council in plain view of the fort. Focusing his scope, Olaf could see Little Crow on his spotted horse in the middle of the circle, sawing the air with his arms, presumably making a persuasive point. Next, three braves took the center; and they, replaced by Mankato on his large black horse, each making a statement. Again, angry braves came forwards.

Abruptly, an eerie howl of war whoops split the air! A decision had been made! The terrorized civilians, never having heard such ear-piercing 'demoniac yells', as people called them, scrambled like frightened chickens, crushing inside the rock building; obviously resigned for the worst! Forty soldiers against two hundred. "God have mercy," people shouted.

Olaf, holding firmly to Dancer, observed a most mind-boggling turn of events. The chiefs, and a dozen loyal braves turned, and withdrew to the west from whence they came. The young braves, meanwhile, yelping like coyotes, headed across the river to the south side and moved east toward the town of New Ulm. Miraculously, Fort Ridgely had been spared!

Eventually the fort, near defenseless, quieted down. Gradually, the bewildered refugees tensely came out on the parade grounds searching for an answer to the miraculous escape from what appeared to be certain death.

Olaf's work was just beginning. He quickly moved out to trail the disorganized warriors. While they traveled the south side of the river, he would take the north, but remain up on the prairie, out of sight.

The young upstart braves, defying their chiefs, evidently thought New Ulm would be an easy conquest, knowing its young men had nearly all left to fight the Civil War, Olaf figured. Each could have his choice of a fair-haired German lass to take away to the Dakota hunting grounds.

Racing Dancer along again, he headed for the high hill he'd remembered, from where a wide panoramic view of the river basin could be seen to the south. Keeping alert to the possibility of roving Dakota watching his movement, the Swede was most relieved not finding them.

As he paused to watch, the snake-like line of Indians could be seen stealthily moving along toward New Ulm. A sudden sense of urgency came over the Swede. He must hurry along to warn the folks in that picturesque German town of the impending attack! Though he thought other fleeing refugees to the east must have alerted them, he had to make sure. He prodded Dancer, knowing every minute counted now.

The war party moved at jogging speed. Indians attack from concealment; surprising the enemy from behind trees or heavy bush, so those on horseback traveled only as fast as the foot warriors. He passed them by, moving Dancer along at a fast pace.

Olaf worried when seeing a body of horsemen come into view a few miles ahead! Could it be another band of Indians approaching? Through his scope he was relieved to find a detail of volunteers coming from the direction of St. Peter and heading toward New Ulm. Anxiously giving Dancer another bump with his heels, he closed quickly to find the twenty or so horsemen were captained by his old friend Sheriff Boardman from St. Peter.

"Swede, I could tell it was you a mile away!" Boardman called excitedly. Meet you in the damnedest places!"

"Sheriff, good to see ya, my friend, but I'm afraid ve have to forget the pleasantries this time. Ya see, if ya go like Hell, you can get into New Ulm just before the fireworks."

"What do ya mean, Swede?"

"There's over a hundred vild hostile Dakota about to close in on the town! Just passed them a few miles back, heading down the south side of the river! You can get there ahead of them, if you move fast!"

"A hundred and fifty, you think?"

"About. They got no chiefs with them. An unruly bunch!"

"Holy shit, man, I meet you in the God damnedest places, Swede. Hear it's a blood bath back at the Lower Agency from the little news we get."

"Ya, I've seen all I vant for avile. Get to New Ulm fast, Sheriff."

"Yer comin along with us, aren't ya, Swede?"

"I'd sure like to, friend, but I'll spot things from a vays off. As

280

unpredictable as they are, they might turn back to Ridgely. They'll need me more there. Only forty men defending two, three hundred survivors.

Boardman turned back to his unit. "C'mon men let's get goin and show them Indians we old farts ain't gonna be pushed around. We gotta protect the women with all their men off to the war," Boardman reminded. They galloped off to the South.

Olaf eased off some, knowing reinforcements were on the way; he rode up another dominating bluff, northeast of town. He'd have a bird's eye view of the goings on from less than a mile away. Reaching the top, he quickly brought the target closer through his glass. He smiled. Then yelled out loud, "Thank God."

The worry of New Ulm not being ready was all for naught, as the citizens had made the center business district into a veritable fortress. One block of street openings between brick and stone buildings had been barricaded as if the town had spent a month on the project. The enterprising Germans had risen to the task, and Olaf wondered if the hostile war party might even back off. He hoped they would.

It was further enlightening when seeing Boardman's volunteers fording the river into the town. "Whew, they made it just in time!" he sighed.

The Swede loved the place, recalling the good times he'd had when driving the stage on that run for a time. 'Could almost taste a huge foamy glass of dark German beer from the Shell brewery, which sat back on the hill a ways. He worried for the many friends he had in that delightful place, including some charming frauleins he'd danced the polka with.

The pleasant interlude with his past abruptly ended! The naked warriors had arrived on the top of the southeast bluff, two hundred feet above New Ulm, though still a mile away. Following the trees they descended as cunningly as wildcats in their pursuit. Though the center of town looked secure, there were hundreds of homes and out buildings spread throughout the residential area. No doubt the invaders would use those to conceal themselves from citizens' gunfire, and for certain there will be some burning, Olaf figured.

He was more nervous as the Indians crawled ever closer. They'd descended to the second of the three wide steps to the valley floor. Why haven't they seen them? He wondered. Taking

281

his scope for another look into the town's fortification, he was surprised to find the folks meandering around as if it were a holiday or something.

Several braves had reached the outer neighborhoods, and were weaving in and out between the ghostly vacated buildings. The undisciplined young braves, without leadership of chiefs, abruptly commenced shooting from the distance! Some of the shots hit their mark!

Olaf watched as the wounded were quickly whisked away, and he thought he saw a young child carried from the street. Now the citizen volunteers quickly took up positions behind the walls and returned fire, and the crackling of rifle shots filled the air. The daring young warriors made a dash for closer empty buildings. The citizens responded with heavy fire, indiscriminately, Olaf thought, wondering if they had cartridges to waste.

Suddenly the howling braves, at least twenty of them, tried storming the wall at the west end of the business district. Olaf was now getting nervous, as the volunteer riflemen seemed to be shooting blanks, hitting not one of the attacker. The redskins were stymied at the rear of one of the brick buildings, and kept firing as they withdrew to empty buildings - some burning now. Olaf breathed easier.

Though the over anxious braves retreated, they had been no less undisciplined than a detail of anxious citizens aspiring to becoming instant heroes, charging after them throughout the open area.

"Damn," Olaf raved. "Vie the Hell don't you stay vere it's safe?"

One of the advanced guard soon dropped. His comrades realizing the folly of their action, quickly carried the lifeless body back to safety.

Both sides contented themselves by shooting from long range for the next hour, from where little damage could be done.

Olaf's earlier concerns the warriors might be intimidated by the fortification of New Ulm and return to attack the more vulnerable Fort Ridgely were laid to rest, so he chose to watch a while longer.

The hostiles had retreated further back, having made another logistical error. The closer buildings, now burning, no longer could shield them, so they satisfied themselves by ransacking and looting the vacated homes.

The first attack on New Ulm had been completely thwarted. Thank God they had time to fortify themselves, Olaf thought.

Luck was playing into the defenders' hands in another way. The skies were darkening in the west. A thunder storm threatening, the Dakota warriors withdrew further up into the woods. The skirmish had obviously been called off. The town would have time to build defenses for a future assault, which could be by a much greater number of Indians after the antagonists would force their friendly brothers to join them in the battle.

Feeling relieved, he scanned the valley for one final time. Something caught his eye to the west of town. He took a closer look. "Vait a minute! My God! Oh, my God!": he muttered, His mouth dropped open in startling disbelief seeing a tragedy about to unfold; a train of five horse drawn wagons heading east along the Cottonwood River and within a few minutes of penetrating the woods infested by Indians. The wagons filled with men, unsuspecting of danger, no doubt. "Oh, My God!" he repeated, now recalling the town of New Ulm had set this day for a patriotic rally with emphasis on recruiting youthful farmers for the Civil War.

"You're heading right into the pit of Hell!" he shouted. "Hi! Hi! Go back! Go back!" It was only a desperate impulsive reaction; no way could they hear him. His mouth parched; his voice faltered, gasping for breath to relieve his pounding chest as he watched the slaughter! Men falling dead from the wagons! One horse falling tripped another, and the wagon flew end over end sending three more to a fateful plunge. Only one of the five wagons racing through the fiery gauntlet miraculously made it to safety.

"God help them," Olaf mumbled. He didn't know how many, but would only be able to report what he saw from the opposite hills; a whole lot of folks were killed in the ambush of the small wagon train returning from the west along the Cottonwood River, as the clouds rolled in over the normally peaceful town of New Ulm that Tuesday, August 19, 1862.

There were streaks of lightning across the heavens with numerous fingers striking the ground, and a powerful crash of thunder. Olaf pulled his animal skin capote over him and nudged

283

Dancer. "C'mon girl, let's move back to the fort."

Rain poured out of the heavens. Olaf hardly noticed, his mind too cluttered with ugly thoughts of what had happened -- and what was to come. He agonized over the hundreds of farmer pioneers viciously murdered by the young hostiles, and was confounded by Little Crow's decision to lead the attack. "Vie Taoyataduta? Vie vould ya do such a crazy thing," he scolded. "I know you're a proud varrior, but vun time you could a laughed at em ven they called you coward. Aw!" he shook his head in disgust.

All the way back he grieved for the hundreds of friendlies, many converted Christians, now forced to shed their farmer clothes and wear breach clouts or die at the hands of hostile brothers, or unjustly by the government troops, surely to come.

One thing he was certain of, a long devastating struggle had just begun. the proud Dakota nation would be dealt with most indiscriminately. After all, good or bad, they were all thought of as "just" Indians.

284

TWO DAY SIEGE

Olaf had been challenged and nearly shot by a nervous sentry when returning from New Ulm the previous night. Escaping that, he'd put Dancer Girl in a stall on the south stables. Totally exhausted from his sojourn, and though his raincoat and hat had kept his top dry, his legs were soaked.

No one had to tell him the defenses had been bolstered; the stables full except for a single stall. He was certain his friend, Sergeant Jones, saved one space for his horse, as several other animals were staked outside.

Worn out, he eyed a pile of prairie hay; most inviting. He quickly brushed down his prized mare, and told two young troops standing guard he'd prefer they not announce his return just yet. Then, retrieving dry pants and socks from the stage near by, and dousing his face at the spring below the hill, he returned to the hay pile and stretched his six-four frame for a bit of shut-eye.

"Swede? Swede? You all right?" A voice interrupted his sleep.

Olaf rose up on his elbow with a start. Recognizing Jonesy, he shook his head and squinted, "Ja...ja...ja, I'm fine, Sarge."

"I didn't tell anybody you were here, Swede. Everybody's asking for ya, but I figured they could hold their horses till you rested up."

"Ja? Thanks, Jonesy. Lord, I didn't think I could sleep, but I vent out like a light, fer cryin out loud. Dreamed I vas back on my ship."

"Well, I checked on ya a couple times." He chuckled to himself,

"Vell, vot's so damned funny, Sarge?"

"Listen, ya big Swede, don't tell anybody you don't snore? It sounded like the horses all blowin off steam the same time."

"Vell, ya knew I vas alive then, anyvay," Olaf snickered.

The two friends talked intensely about the uprising. Olaf related what had happened at New Ulm, and how well the citizens were prepared to ward off the young Dakota, and that more and more reinforcements were coming to protect the town. He also described the ferocity of the attackers on the wagon train, ambushed, coming out of the Cottonwood River.

Sergeant Jones explained having improved defenses at the fort, with Lieutenant Sheehan returning with fifty-one men of Company C, and another fifty or so from Company B, and Renvilles' Rangers were brought by Agent Galbraith. Olaf winced at the name, but was relieved for the support of the volunteers. Two hundred effectives; a lot better than twenty.

"Jonesy." Olaf was deep in thought about what was to come. "Jonesy, two hundred is a lot better, but I vas thinkin, vee'd be as helpless as rabbits to a pack a volves if five thousand attacked, like that bunch at Upper Agency several veeks ago."

"Yah. We'd be wiped out for damn sure," Jones agreed.

"Vell, I know vun thing," Olaf stretched his arms, "The Dakota have never battled cannon fire before, but they've vatched ven ya trained a company of artillery here last fall."

"Ya, I'm still with ya, Swede."

"They're terrified of those 'rotten balls,' they call em, that explode in a thousand pieces. Better have those cannon ready, I think."

"Yah, it's lucky I've found a few experienced men to handle em. I'll be ready," Jones said. "Well, partner, daylight's not far off; better get set for reveille."

"Ja, see ya later. I'm hungry as a bear; goin over to the commissary to see if there's any coffee and hard tack, maybe."

Civilians and soldiers were still working together in hauling hay and grain sacks for barricades; others digging trenches in the twilight.

"Seen the Swede? Has anybody seen that big Swede around?"

Olaf recognized the whiny voice as that of the detestable Galbraith. He slid around the backside of the commissary to get

286

his coffee before an expected boring confrontation with a man he partly blamed for the uprising.

Volunteer women kept the coffee hot and made lunch throughout the night. Takin a mug of coffee, and surprised to find freshly made potato pancakes with hot syrup, he sat at the dimly lamp-lit long table to feed his famished appetite. Much to think about, he relished the private time.

Olaf was surprised when he saw Mrs. Muller come for coffee; he wondered if she ever slept. Having eyed Olaf, she hurried down for a short visit.

Olaf, always a respectful gentleman, stood. "Mrs. Muller, how nice to see you--even at this God forsaken hour." he smiled.

"Hello, Mr. Olsson, glad to see you're back," she smiled warmly. "But, do sit and enjoy your breakfast. I have to go right away, anyway."

"Vell, I hear people heepin praise on your efforts in caring for the sick and vounded. You're a Godsend, Mrs. Muller."

"Oh, hogwash," Eliza Muller smiled, "just doing what I'm here to do. Besides the women help so much. Real troopers!" She then asked thoughtfully, "But, I wanted to hear of my New Ulm friends. Are they safe?"

"Yes," he smiled reassuringly. "They ver ready. Only a few causalities, I think, Mrs. Muller."

"Oh, thank God, for that comforting news! Olaf, we all feel much more secure with you here. God be with you, my friend."

Olaf smiled to himself as Mrs. Muller hurried off to treat the wounded, and then he went back for a second cup of coffee. With the dawn nearly breaking, it was time to scout the prairie again. He could give advanced warning to the defenders, should the Dakota decide today will be the day they try taking back their land. There would be time to confer with the pompous Indian agent later, he decided.

Olaf hurried over to the stables. With the first signs of light showing in the east, he was anxious to know if the Dakota warring numbers had grown.

Reaching the stables, Olaf was disturbed to find Galbraith

waiting. He'd undoubtedly figured he'd more likely find the Swede close to his horse.

"I've been looking for you, big important one," Galbraith blurted insultingly. "Why are you avoiding me anyway, horseman?"

Olaf ignored the devious greeting. "You'll have to talk fast vile I saddle my horse, Sir. I've got vork to do." He went about readying Dancer, but noticed the agent's lower lip twitching quite violently, and his eyes showed fear and worry, Olaf thought.

"My family! My family!" Galbraith blubbered; near sobbing. "They're trapped at the Upper Agency - if still alive! Oh, those damn Sioux savages! We must kill them all! Kill them, I say."

Olaf could see immediately, the agent was even more mentally disturbed than when seeing him last at Yellow Medicine with the five thousand.

"Aw, settle down, Galbraith. Those vestern Dakota vill more than likely protect em," Olaf answered rather coolly. "But, I spose you might be having second thoughts about not feedin em ven they ver starvin. Vot about that, stingy man?"

Galbraith's self pity turned into a revengeful charge. "Olsson, I wonder about you! I should report you to Washington, that's what!"

"Vot ya inferrin, Galbraith?" Olaf demanding an explanation.

"Maybe the great Indian lover plays into Sioux hands dishonorably; helping them against the government!" He said accusingly, in a quick change of behavior.

Olaf grabbed him by the collar, and angered, lifted him so his feet left the ground. "Don't you ever accuse me of being a traitor to my country, you miserable pussyfoot Easterner!" Olaf quickly regained his self composure and lowered him to the ground, realizing the pathetic man was far from being rational. Olaf then lectured him. "Get this straight, Galbraith; there are a lot of honorable Indians-most of them-but, regardless how opposed they might be to the uprising, they cannot admit it, or the hostiles vill kill the good ones in cold blood, by law of their council. It is a thin line the Indian valks now. Noble and honorable natives vill die."

His horse saddled, Olaf looked down at the pathetic and mixed-up excuse for an Indian agent, and tried to console him somewhat. "I am concerned about your family, Galbraith. There are many good Indians at the Upper Agency. They may have helped." Olaf rode off in darkness.

It was an eerie uneasiness riding over the prairie within view of the river and the destroyed pioneer farms. Only burnt rubble from farm buildings created a ghostly sight to the once placid pastoral setting. On more than one occasion, the heavy-hearted Swede interrupted his search of Indian presence to cover the dead and properly mark the site so a more dignified burial could be held later.

Five hundred folks at Fort Ridgely were depending on him for advanced warning of attack, so he hurried west to a few miles north of what used to be the Lower Indian Agency. It was quiet. He scanned the river area with his telescope, which seemed void of any life whatsoever. Riding closer to the river, he abruptly, and intuitively felt a strange threatening presence, but wasn't sure why. Suddenly, feeling blood rushing to his head, he knew danger surrounded him.

Realizing the bushes had shifted in relationship to the trees shading them, he knew he had inadvertently moved too close to the woods. A blood curdling chorus of war cries; "Yi! yi! yi! yi! yi!" pierced the air! Olaf froze momentarily. He was surprised the Dakota turned on one who'd defended them through the years. Ten or more, screaming red-skinned, fiercely painted warriors peeled away from the brush and charged from not more than fifty yards away. the big gray mare reared up and catapulted out of the area like a shot!

A rain of arrows and gunfire whizzed by, deathly close, and a sudden thrust and a neighing cry by Dancer Girl alarmed Olaf. She had been hit! He patted her rump to settle her down as she galloped away at blazing speed, but withdrawing his bloody hand revealed where she'd been wounded. The Swede galloped to higher ground; the braves left behind. When reaching a safe distance, he found she had about a six-inch crease on her left rump. It wasn't too serious, considering the number of projectiles barely missing which could have cast a fatal blow to either of them, Olaf knew.

"You gonna be all right, Dancer Girl." Olaf spoke assuringly. She sputtered, bobbing her head, as if to affirm she was fine, and Olaf understood. "Ve'll stay up here on high ground and votch how many vill be coming, girl. Then, ven ve get back to the fort I'll put some horse salve on yer vound. It'll heal up real fast. Don't vurry."

From a high point on the prairie, the trail of approaching Indians was evident. Large clusters would totally disappear in heavy growth of hazel and willow bush, but the movement was steady to the east. It was evident Chief Little Crow had organized a viable force. Olaf estimated a number to be at least four hundred foot fighters leading the way, and mounted braves tracking farther down, concealed in the river bottom.

Satisfied having observed the numbers on the attack, Olaf turned Dancer and raced back to the fort. He had valuable information for the defenders and they'd have only about an hour to get ready for the obvious onslaught.

The worried Swede tried acting undaunted riding into Fort Ridgely, but a few of the young recruits saw the wound on Dancer, and the word spread fast through the camp of an ensuing attack.

Commander Sheehan, Lieutenant Gere, Sergeant Jones, and the few other non-commissioned officers met in the warehouse to consult with Olaf.

"You have precious little time, men. Four hundred varriors are now vithin striking range of the Fort!"

"How much time, Swede?" Young Lieutenant Sheehan fired back.

"An hour, at most. All your armed troops and Sergeant Jones and his cannon details should man their stations for a major attack, Sir. I vant to alarm you to the fact they look ferocious, they yell ferocious, and they fight ferocious, Sir!"

"Yeh, I'm not a seasoned soldier, myself. Scared as Hell!" the young officer admitted. "Thank God for some old troopers like

Sergeant Jones and MacGrew. Men, get your units in position immediately." The entire fort was taking on a frenzied air.

"Swede, you've been closer to these redskins more than anybody I know. We've got our mountain howitzers and the six pound cannons positioned directly at them, toward the prairie. What do ya think?" The Lieutenant asked.

"Vell, I'm not a military strategist, as you know, but the Indian is a master at surprise attacks, and usually does the opposite von expects. If I ver you, Sir; no insult intended, I vould guess a couple cannons, one in each east corner, aimed at the closest point of the northeast ravine, and one down the south ravine vould be your best bet. They'll probably hit us with two, three hundred screaming varriors at the outbreak, and you could catch them in a crossfire."

"Sir, I agree with Swede," Sergeant Jones echoed. "I could reassign Whipple and McGrew back to the east side, if you want."

"Then, expedite, men. It's beginning to feel extremely quiet and close, like the stillness before a violent storm strikes." Beads of sweat covered the young commander's forehead.

"What about small arms? I better shift more firepower in support of the Cannons, then," the Lieutenant rattled nervously.

Jones poked his head in the door. "Will ya give me a hand, old pal, on wheeling the howitzer across the square?"

"Ya bet, Sarge," Olaf agreed, tearing after him.

The Swede was feeling the same tenseness the Commander had expressed. After getting the big guns in place, Olaf took it upon himself to move amongst the troops, joking some to relax them, and lending encouragement to the young inexperienced soldiers. It helped. They idolized the Swede as a man of bravery and heroics.

Olaf casually impersonated the Indian warrior, war cry and all. They'd soon hear the blood curdling yells. They should know, he thought. The fellows grinned as Olaf's antics had a supporting effect on them.

"When was the last time you had Sioux after you, Swede?" one of the young recruits questioned.

"Vell, I tell ya, men. Most are my good friends, but only about

291

two hours ago I had ten renegades after me, and it vas a mighty close call." He gave a reassuring smile. "Keep alert, now."

The waiting game was soon to end. The deathly silence was intimidating and nerve-wracking.

Suddenly, shrieking war cries echoed across the bluff with deafening intensity! Wave after wave of grossly painted warriors closed to take over the fringe buildings to the northeast. Two soldiers were hit as they returned fire from their lines at the center of the parade grounds. At a hundred yards the artillery was fired; the howitzers struck at the strength of the throng approaching, and the converging blasts, and musket fire from two hundred supporting troops, had an astounding effect, scattering the attackers away from the buildings and back to the ravine. Lieutenant Sheehan, realizing the error of exposing troops, ordered his men to take cover and fire at will, in support of the cannons.

The Swede, forced to deny his loyalty to some of his friendly Dakota, assisted his comrade, Sergeant Jones, on the south and west. After all, there were two hundred and fifty terrified civilians crowded into the stone building, and it was of top priority to defend them, he thought.

As the first rush failed, the Lower Sioux warriors, frightened by the 'rotten balls' of the cannon, withdrew in disarray. They contented themselves to fire from the woods for about five hours after that.

Commander Sheehan was relieved his unit sustained only two dead and six wounded, and registered disbelief in the enemy's seemingly uninspired attack. Olaf agreed to being surprised, as well, but reiterated their frightful shock in confronting cannon balls that exploded, sending a rain of debris in all directions. The Dakota had never experienced such devastating weaponry before, he explained.

Olaf complimented Sergeant John Jones and the three other artillerymen, who really saved the day then, as if it were commander Sheehan's idea to move the cannon to the east, he commended him on the brilliant move. Sheehan gloated, agreeing he thought so too, and would appreciate such a fine compliment be repeated for his superiors.

* * *

It rained that night after the first attack. It rained and rained through most of the next day. It was a God given blessing, allowing the fort to replenish the water supply from the spring far down the bluff. Barricades and trenches were bolstered, while they waited the next expected charge.

The fort had a meager supply of munitions, musket shot nearly being depleted. Mrs. Muller's volunteers ingeniously produced cartridges from open spherical case shot, to be ready for another possible Dakota attack. Meanwhile, the confined civilians were frightened and irritable.

Olaf relished the uninterrupted respite, as well. Dancer Girl had stiffened from the wound on her right hip, and needed time to heal. She was only taken out on the prairie for exercising jaunts. Olaf thought how the farmers would have praised the soaking rain, except they weren't around anymore to benefit from such a blessing.

By mid afternoon the skies cleared. The Swede found a good observation point in the loft of the stone barracks from which he scanned the open prairie for any signs. It gave pause to wonder if others reflected, as he did, how Indians had felt having been confined these many years.

He stewed over Little Crow's unfortunate decision to lead the Dakota against the government, and guessed the Chief was building his forces for a major show down. No doubt he was recruiting from the western Sisseton and Wahpeton bands, even though Olaf knew the chiefs were much opposed to the uprising. With three of Little Crow's six wives being daughters of a Wahpeton Chief, he would no doubt find some interest there, as well. The Swede continued to worry and empathize for the future of the Indian. At the same time he felt pity for the immigrant farmers who had sought a life of comfort and happiness. It all seemed so futile and disheartening.

"Hey, Swede, see anything yet?" Sergeant Jones called as he came up the ladder to the loft.

"Naw. Not yet. Just votchning the prairie dogs going about their daily routine gathering food, tending their young. Their life seems so sensible compared to ours." Olaf handed over his long glass. "Vanna take a look? They're straight northwest about a quarter of a mile."

"Ya, they're sure fun to watch, all right," Jones chuckled, scanning the landscape. "Boy, that rain sure brought out a lot of wild flowers. Never seen so many yellow ones out there before."

"That so?" Olaf said, casualty taking back the scope for another look.

"Think the Sioux'll come today, big fella?"

"Maybe not. It's getting pretty late in the day." Olaf kept looking out to the west while they visited.

"'Could sure stand a cool beer, only we ain't got none left."

Olaf glanced up in the sky as a threatening hawk circled, bent on diving for a morsel for itself, or its young. "There's alvays some threat in life," Olaf remarked, watching the prairie dogs dashing for the protection of their sub-terranian caverns.

"That's right, Swede," Jones answered, sustaining the small talk.

But Olaf's attention was fixed on the rolling prairie about three quarters of a mile away. He noticed something startling! "You say there are more flowers than ya ever noticed before? Oh, my God!" Olaf blurted.

"What? What's rattling you, Swede?"

He handed the glass over. "Take a qvick look! The flowers move! The Dakota vear them!"

"Holy shit, man! There's a mess of em!" Jones darted for the ladder. "I better move the cannon back to this side, and fast!"

"No! No! They'll be needed vare they are. Those boys in the field are for distracting. The main forces vill come from the ravines, I'm sure."

Jones flew down the ladder! "I'm gonna double charge the

294

howitzers."

Olaf figured they'd have, at most, five minutes to get the defenses ready, so hustled down to help where he could. The cannon detail were stoking their cannons in less than a minute, Olaf could see, but riflemen were not in position, so he dashed into headquarters with the alert. "Commander Sheehan, they're sitting on your front door step with flowers in their bonnets!"

"What do you mean, Swede?" Sheehan jumped up.

"The Dakota! They've come cunningly concealed under flowers. You only have a few minutes at the most, Sir."

"Bugler, sound call to arms, and fast!" Sheehan shouted. The boy hurried out and blew his horn impetuously, slurring every note! Soldiers came running, half dressed, some of them, knowing how sudden the Indian could descend from the shadows of the woods.

Abruptly, muskets thundered from both sides of the fort, shot striking the buildings like a hail storm. Simultaneously, the sky was aglow with streaking, flaming arrows from the southwest ravine, targeting all of the building roofs. Insidious, ear piercing Indians yelping grew in increasing intensity as the gruesomely painted warriors closed in from three sides.

Finally, at the last moment, Jone's big guns roared, striking at the heart of the invading force with perfect precision. The exploding 'rotten balls,' as they were called, scattering the Indians for shelter in the stables and other outer buildings.

Olaf watched mounted Indians come into view along the ravine, including Little Crow on his spotted horse. The chief was waving his arms. directing the attack. By his side was Chief Mankato.

Gunfire was intense from both sides. Olaf held his breath, wondering if the desperate Dakota force would penetrate the lines, knowing how gory it could become if hand-to-hand combat be realized. The Indian was most viscous in such combat, as the Swede had witnessed between the Dakota and Chippewa. Inexperienced soldiers would be like lambs to wolves, he knew.

Only a few minutes later Olaf was shocked to see Little Crow fall from his horse! Mankato helped him remount. Humped over and wounded, the Chief moved off to the west toward his village. Mankato now led.

The blazing arrows struck directly on most of the buildings, but the roofs were wet from the rains. Civilians bravely doused the flames and Olaf, seeing women struggling, grabbed two buckets in one hand, climbed a high ladder and extinguished a blaze of the main barracks himself.

The first charge being unsuccessful, the braves took refuge in the stables and sutler's house and continued firing at close range. Many of them had hatchets and knives, no doubt intended for the vicious hand-to-hand combat. Brilliant action by Sergeant Jones and his limited artillery was saving the day again, for well placed cannon fire, doubly charged with canister shot, blasted the buildings - setting them on fire, and the Dakota were forced to retreat in disorder. Ineffective shooting from long range continued for hours, till darkness set in again. Then the warriors withdrew to the west, no doubt to prepare for another battle.

Olaf was sure that six hundred - or more- Dakotas had joined in the attack, but he recognized many friendly Indians who'd been forced to wear breach clouts, and were not there of their own free will.

The wounded Little Crow must be getting demoralized from his losses, Olaf thought. The native style of warring had become inferior and their weapons were not match to the powerful rifles the troops employed now-a-days.

Many of the refugees were singing praises to God for deliverance from a fearsome slaughter this day, and the civilians thanked the soldiers for their valiant fight at what appeared to be overwhelming odds in favor of the Dakota.

Olaf sat in on the debriefing of the officers and civilians' leaders. Dr. Muller reported three of the military had been killed, and twelve were wounded. A round of hand clapping followed - not for the dead and wounded - but for the amazingly small number of victims in such a fierce battle.

"How many Indians were killed do you think, Olaf?" Sheehan

asked.

"It's hard to tell, Lieutenant. They alvays take their dead vith them. As vulnerable as they made tnemselves, I'd guess a hundred." Olaf paused a moment. "But I think ve should commend Sergeant Jones and his cannon units, headed by Sergeant McGrew and refugees Whipple, who I understand vas a hero at the Mexican var a number of years ago. They should have a special medal of valor, for had it not been for them, maybe none of us vould be here talking. They ver the ones that stood behind their big gun, unprotected, vith arrows and gunfire all around them. They ver the real heroes this day, Sir." He looked at the commander, but spoke to all.

Recognizing the truth in Olaf's speech, the group was unanimous in its praise for the three heroes.

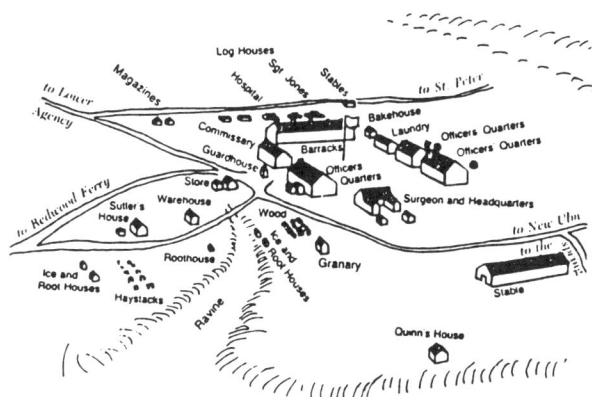

SURPRISE CALL ON LITTLE CROW

Five hundred military and civilians waited anxiously at Fort Ridgely. Stark quietness kept everybody on edge, fearing another frightful invasion by the grotesque, howling natives, bent on reclaiming the land they had nurtured for untold centuries.

Olaf saw no hostiles along the river this morning, so he angled back to inform the commander. The defenders were most relieved getting the temporary reprieve, which would allow time for reorganizing defenses. The Swede was not convinced the Dakota were giving up and rode on to the southwest. His hunch proved true. Finding a massive army of warriors moving toward New Ulm, he proceeded farther south of the river. He assumed the chiefs were now leading with so many on the move. Had Little Crow recovered from Thursday's wounds? He wondered.

This was the largest force he'd ever seen in war paint at one time. Hurrying to his observation point, he wanted to see if Little Crow had assumed command of his Dakota. With the throng snaking through the trees along the river, it was reasonable to guess a few had been left behind. If the Chief was absent today, it'd be a good time to visit him, he thought.

Remaining far to the north, out of sight to the thousand warriors, Olaf was surprised to spot a small splinter group in front of him. The Indians had set a huge swamp afire, directly in line between Fort Ridgely and New Ulm. Knowing well enough the cunningness of Indian strategy, Olaf assumed it was only a ploy to distract New Ulm defenders, giving the impression Ft. Ridgely had been taken and that the smoke was from the burning fort.

Olaf played possum well behind the firebugs. They, having completed their mission, crossed the river and joined the main body. Shortly thereafter, a hundred New Ulm defenders crossed to the north of the river, having fallen for the ruse. Contingents of warriors quickly cut off the detail, who retreated north toward St.

Peter, reducing New Ulm's defensive forces. "You sly foxes," Olaf smirked, recognizing the native craftiness.

Another hour passed. The motley Dakota lined themselves along the top ridge of the bluff overlooking the beleaguered town of New Ulm from a mile and a half away. There was no attempt to conceal themselves this time, wanting instead to flaunt their massive numbers most intimidatingly. Scanning with his telescope, Olaf could easily see Chief Mankato was in command, and it was surprising seeing the honorable peace maker, Chief Wabasha, riding his great white horse next to him. Wabasha had no gaul for war, but he was bound by the Council like hundreds of others, or be threatened to die at the hands of his hostile brothers.

Fort Ridgely had information that the targeted town had been reinforced with one hundred and twenty-five frontier guards from St. Peter and La Seuer: Charles Flandrau, the most prominent area citizen, commanding the total forces. Another hundred citizen guards came from Mankato, and units from other communities brought the defending force to about three hundred and fifty; that is, before the detail retreated north only an hour before. He'd also learned Dr. Asa Daniels of St. Peter and Dr. William Mayo of Le Seuer had arrived to render medical aid, so the town was well prepared.

The huge curved line, a human rainbow of colors, gradually moved to a mile from town. Like giant pincers, the ends closed around, giving the impression the aggressors would soon encircle the community stockade for their final assault. Olaf was frustrated. He felt responsible to report what was happening to the Fort, maybe a hundred troops from the Fifth Regiment could counter-attack the Dakota and save New Ulm. On the other hand, we don't need another ambush like a few days ago at the Lower Agency, Olaf decided. He knew those inexperienced recruits were no match for the crafty Indian, who'd fought like animals from the bush against their ancient enemy. There wouldn't be time, anyway, so he'd just watch some.

Wave after wave of redskins charged on a dead run, midst screaming of war hoops, gunfire roaring. Olaf wondered if the sounds might be heard back at the fort. Arrows streaking through the sky looked like a giant comet through his telescope. Flandrau's advanced units took up positions in buildings outside the barricades, and met the invaders with close range fire. Being inexperienced, they panicked and withdrew behind the fortificaiton while under the fierce attack.

Olaf watched anxiously. The Dakota, daring and determined, advanced, overtaking many of the buildings. Several structures were set afire, especially along the river where the smoke blew over the center of town. For a time it looked like the whole town was burning. Smoke completely covered the barricaded business district.

It was nerve-wracking to Olaf, wondering if a total and complete massacre of the once glamorous German community would become a reality. After several hours, it was comforting to hear heavy gunfire continue. Gradually, as the smoke began to clear, a wide charred buffer zone resulted. Over a hundred buildings had been destroyed in a blazing inferno, and the Dakota were forced to withdraw to the wooded steps of the bluff.

Again, the battle had become a stalemate, Olaf was sure, as both sides contented themselves with firing at long range. With Chief Mankato and the thousand warriors occupied, and Little Crow absent, it seemed more and more inviting for Olaf to go call on the Chief. Speeding along at a fast gate with quick footed Dancer Girl, he figured the trip would take about four hours. He'd arrive at the Lower Sioux Agency near dark, a good time to avoid being discovered by the young malcontents bent on killing every white in sight.

Riding along, thoughts of better years came to mind, when fishing with the Chief and his son, Wowinape, were gratifying times and everyone seemed to get along. The young boy was about six or seven then, and theirs was a most admirable father-son relationship. Of course, a lot of water flowed down the Mississippi, past Kaposia, across the river from Fort Snelling, in the nine years since the Dakota were forced out of their great hunting and fishing region, and moved to the prairie. Olaf learned most of his knowledge of Dakota ways from his Kaposia friends, particularly their love and respect for nature, and their survival from hunting and fishing.

Already bypassing Fort Ridgely, he angled southwest where he could ford the river. With his great mare's long legs, he'd hardly get wet, whereas the small Indian ponies often found it necessary to swim part of the way.

The sun had just set, and as he crossed over to the woods, dusk was closing in fast. He carefully proceeded to the west to check the destruction of the agency. Only six days before, the Indians killed all the white traders and their clerks in a savage attack without warning. Nearing the ferry landing, he detected a repulsive odor. Pausing momentarily, he forced himself to go forward to a point where the air became highly putrid. He found the source, and most foreboding it was. He held his handkerchief to his nose, and Dancer Girl pranced nervously. The bodies of Marsh's soldiers lay scattered over the north side of the river in gory display. He rode back to that side for a closer look, and reaching it, wondered why he was so damned inquisitive, inflicting so much agony on himself. The skin on his head tightened and he sweated heavily at the horrible decomposing remains. Further down the road a ways, Doctor and Mrs. Humphrey lie, their two children next to them. He shuddered, thinking he had a son about the boy's age, whom he had not yet seen, and realized how tragic the situation was. The distraught Swede shook himself, suffering from the massiveness of human loss before him.

It was deathly quiet up the hill where the agency had stood. Added to the odor of death, was that of burnt wood. Reverend Hinman and the others had described the torching by the infuriated Sioux. It was a ghostly sight. Here Olaf remembered, on a normal day, one found a constant hustling of activity, but now most of the wooden structures had been burned to the ground. The stores of Forbs, Roberts, Myricks, all lay in a heap of charred rubble. By each store the mutilated bodies of the traders and their clerks were sprawled about with a variety of hardware penetrating their bodies. Andrew Myrick was there too, the most hated of all. He once refused the Indians' credit, and told them if they were so damned hungry they could go eat grass. His mouth was jammed full of grass.

The disgruntled Swede had misgivings about proceeding. Surely the Dakota would turn on him, too. Why would they treat him like an honored guest, when they destroyed their own doctor, women, and children? Besides being curious, the big Swede had a streak of stubbornness running through his veins, so he cautiously moved ahead to Little Crow's community.

It was more than the small sleepy village of two weeks ago, overnight it grew to a camp of great size. Tepees and lodges covered the ground in a tight network around the home of the Chief. The women were preparing food--probably taken from farmers--who planned to honor their victorious braves. It made Olaf's mouth water. He was hungry, having had only a piece of beef jerky for the day, and had hoped Little Crow might offer some sustenance to quell his hunger pangs.

Olaf had to hide his horse. He thought of Traveling Hail's village, only a few miles away, and so he high tailed it over there. Traveling Hail, too, had been conscripted against his will, and was away fighting the war, the two older Christian braves said. The men helped hide Dancer.

"I see you've all shed your farming pantaloons," Olaf commented. They used hand signals which Olaf understood, relating to the fact that all Christian farmers were made to wear breech clouts, or hostiles would kill them like they'd kill whites. They gave him a big Indian blanket to toss over his shoulders, and pull over his head, if necessary, they suggested. Thanking them, he hurried back to Little Crow's village on the dead run, and entered the maze of tepees. Hunching down to disguise his large size, he soon realized his blunder; the women whispering, one after another; "*Wasicung! Wasicung!*" Glancing to the ground, he quickly realized his size thirteen clodhoppers were a dead give away. Reaching the shadows, he closely hugged the darkened side of Little Crow's house, and tip-toed along like a stalking tomcat.

Heated discussions were going on in the temporary lodge next to his big house, which Olaf assumed to be the Dakota Council center. Finding the front door standing slightly ajar, he quietly slipped inside; unnoticed, he hoped. Women were laughing and jabbering upstairs, enabling a move farther in where he could remain hidden and catch his breath a moment.

The Swede became startled when a small voice tittered slightly close to him. It came from the near shadows behind the fireplace.

"Tall Like Oakee," the sweet voice said. Nawki stepped into a beam of light from the fire, and smiled brightly. He was shocked as she folded back the edge of the blanket she wore, exposing her shapely bronze breasts. My god, Olaf thought, not now you sweet innocent cherub, so devastatingly denied. Then, his eyes fell on her little jeweled broach, which she really wanted to show; the one he gave her the night he felt sorry for her when trying to entice him to coddle her. The Chief had always rejected her for his more doting, desirable fat wives.

Olaf had given the brooch as a token of friendship; Nawke took it as the Swede's unyielding commitment of love. Like most Dakota, she could not speak English, and Olaf's limited knowledge of the Dakota was not much better, but he could make do.

"*Tukten unga Taoyateduta?*" Olaf asked where the Chief was.

"*Hi ecudunga,*" she said, assuring he'd be back soon. She moved coyly to him. "*Miya wastidaca,*" she swooned.

Olaf grinned, partially in embarrassment for what she said. "Tall Like Oak, *Aiokepe, Nawki,*" admitting he liked her, too.

She was delighted having revealed her love for the big white man, but Olaf really liked her and felt sorry the way Little Crow treated her, her only sin was being thin. He certainly would have argued the point, for he thought her small shapely body beautiful.

The men spoke heatedly outside the door. The meeting had ended. Little Nawki, fearing her ungrateful husband, stole away quickly.

The Chief stomped in, not in the happiest of moods, it seemed. Catching sight of Olaf, he growled threateningly, "Where Tall Like an Oak come from?" Olaf didn't answer immediately, but tried a feeble smile, in hopes of relaxing the troubled Chief. Reaching in his pocket, he retrieved some of his fine tobacco. Little Crow relaxed and shook his head in what seemed to be confounded disbelief.

He lowered his voice, and said in a pleading way, "Why you come?" There was no doubt the Chief was extremely embarrassed.

Olaf filled the bowl of the Chief's favorite long stemmed brown stone pipe, lit it, and returned it to him. The Chief inhaled deeply, giving a gratifying sigh.

"I know Tall Like Oak questions why I turned against my white brothers so quick, but even I don't know all reasons for my actions. It happened. That is all I can say."

He took another puff from the pipe. "Ah, you have good smoke, friend; beats corn tassel and bark." The Chief had mellowed again, and his pent up anger against all whites seemed to moderate some.

"I only come to tell my old friend who taught me much about Dakota vays, and even gave me a family name, how sorry I am to see our old friendship has to come to an end," Olaf conveyed.

The Chief was preoccupied, and quickly diverted his train of thought. Always a most congenial host, he worried for fear he wasn't doing enough to honor his old friend properly. "Tall Like Oak, forgive me, Taoyataduta not offer food. We have plenty on hand now as you probably guessed."

Olaf was ravenous. "Vell, to be honest with you, I have a gnawing in my gut from not eating since early morning."

"Nawki! Nawki!" the Chief called. She came obediently. "Bring cabbage and beef stew for guest," he demanded.

Acknowledging the order, Olaf noticed her wide eyes blink a pleasant response toward him as she left. The two now commenced visiting about the old times back at the big river at Kaposia, and for a while avoided talk of the conflict, as if there wasn't such a thing as war going on.

Nawki brought a large bowl of cabbage and beef stew, and before he'd had enough, devoured two more bowls of it, delighting Nawki, he knew. The Chief rose, as if some sudden business needed attention. "Excuse me, friend. Have small matters to attend." He brightened, noticeably, "Have someone want you to meet. Nawki," he called. He sent her on an errand, but Olaf could not understand what he said.

Soon, the youngest wife returned with one of the hostages. Olaf was shocked seeing Mrs. Joseph Brown escorted to the house.

"Swede!" she exclaimed, "I'm happy to see our good family friend."

"Now, you two visit good. I come back soon," Little Crow said, and went out in the village.

"You look vell, Susan Brown. I can't tell you how relieved I am to see that. Your family? And Joseph? Are they vell, too?"

"We only have a few minutes. Yes, Swede, I have all my family here, except Joseph, who was away to St. Paul on business when the sky fell in. You are not a prisoner, I pray?" She whispered.

"No. No. I came of my own free vill. I vas at Fort Ridgely vith the gold payments the day Lower Agency vas destroyed. I came to see the horror vith my own eyes." His voice trailed off showing his anguish. "But I thought all the vites and mixed bloods vould all be dead."

"Not at all, my friend, though I'd like to be back with my own people at the Upper Agency, I can only say Taoyateduta has been most protective and considerate."

They spoke hurriedly, expecting the Chief to return soon. Joseph Brown was the Indian Agent for several years before Galbraith. Brown knew the ways of the Dakota and could speak their language fluently. Having married a Dakota, he always had a close relationship with the tribe.

Mrs. Brown passed on a wealth of information, much to Olaf's relief. She told of the capturing of George Spencer, Mrs. and Dr. Wakefield, Amos Higgins, Nancy Faribault, and dozens of other whites and mixed bloods being held at the Chief's camp, and were being protected by friends of Taoyateduta. She admitted that being a western Sissiton didn't hurt her chances, for it was the hope of the Chief, the western leaders would join him in his war. She assured that would never happen, as Chiefs Little Paul, John Other Day, Akepa, and others were Christian farmers, and would not join the war. Speaking quickly and quietly, she also told of Chief Little Paul's and Chief Other Day's heroic actions in leading almost one hundred whites and mixed bloods away form the Upper Agency and guiding them to the north and east to freedom. Agent Galbraith's family was among the groups, she revealed.

"Oh, glory be, Mrs. Brown," Olaf exclaimed, "my faith and trust in all my good Dakota friends has been partly restored. I vill relay all this information to your husband, relatives and friends." They continued whispering as excited voices approached form outside.

"We pray the Governor and Commanders will hurry. These

wild young savages are undisciplined, and the Chief has little control," she told.

Little Crow came back inside. "I hope you had a pleasant visit, two of my good friends."

"Thank you, Chief, our visit was most delightful. Good bye Olaf," she smiled and left.

The Dakota leader looked tired and somewhat despondent. After all, things didn't go well for the tribe. He explained how Red Middle Voice, and Shakopee and their crowd of young renegade braves awakened him late in the evening on August seventeenth and demanded a Council meeting. They related the story of the families murdered at Akton, way north on the prairie. There was no way to back down now. The hostiles had gained the upper hand.

Little Crow told how angered he'd become. The Lower Agency had recently replaced him by Traveling Hail as Speaker and that infuriated him, he admitted. Then, they came to beg he lead the assault against all whites and drive them back east of the Mississippi. There was anger in his voice as he spoke. The Chief, an excellent orator, continued as if mesmerized.

"I told them they were like little children who did not know what they were doing. I told them they were full of the white man's whiskey, and they were like dogs in the hot moon, when they run and snap at their own shadows. I told them we were like little herds of buffalo left scattered, and that the great herd that covered the prairie were no more. I told them the white men were like locust, when they fly the sky is like a snowstorm. I told them they may kill one, two, ten, as many as there are leaves in the forest yonder. I told them they could count their fingers all day long, and white men would come with guns in their hands faster than they could count."

Suddenly, there was a ruckus outside. Olaf heard what sounded like angry men shouting threats and insults. The Chief went out quickly. Olaf listened at the crack of the door, and could hear the men accusing his host of harboring a *Wasicung*, and they said they'd come to kill him. After a while, the irate braves cooled down and left the area. The Chief came back in the house looking more than slightly concerned.

306

"Tall Like Oak, we have little time to get you out of here. They will be back with their unruly chiefs!" Little Crow went to the staircase, and shouted upstairs. *"Tawicu,* come quick! Make Tall Like Oak Indian!"

They came, and though Olaf resisted, they stripped his clothes off and wrapped the embarrassed Swede's crotch with a breech cloth. Then they rubbed charcoal on his hair, fitted a head band, and quickly painted his face and body with vermilion.

The Chief mentioned the untimeliness of his visit, but insisted he was pleased they had a chance to talk some.

Olaf asked one more time, "Taoyataduta, my friend of old, is there any vay you vould consider pursuing a peace agreement vith the Government? I vould do everything in my power to speak for you, in defense."

"No. Have gone too far. Will not hang from a rope as the white enemy scoff," he declared. "Will die like true brave Dakota. In meantime, family and others will leave here tomorrow. Move up river, then, will leave great hunting grounds to live on Dakota prairie as long as last buffalo give us life," he said. He reached up and entwined his arms in the Swede's. "You, best *wasicung* friend, Tall Like Oak." He said with wetted eyes.

"Good bye, my friend," Olaf smiled sadly, then dashed out the door and ran east through the trees.

The woods were full of the arrogant devils! A few came, and he'd hide behind a tree. Then, moving on a bit farther, another group were met coming back from the New Ulm battle. He slid back of another tree. There the world seemed to cave in! He had no idea what caused the blow, but the ground met him and he sprawled out like a fallen log. Another blow, and still then another, and he tried pleading for mercy, but had no voice to cry out. Lights were flickering through his brain, like a thousand fireflies circling for a way out, and he could not think at all.

It was impossible to guess how long he'd been tormented, the blood dripped down his face, and his stomach felt as though it had been slit open. Gradually the blackness faded in and out, and he moaned and struggled to clear his mind. Finally, the vertical lines took on the shape of individual trees around him. Then, a deluge of water splashed his face. One breathtaking spray after another, like gusts of wind whipping the rain at regular intervals with each, his ability to reason improved. He finally could feel he was tied to a tree by a tight rope, and wondered why in God's name they hadn't dashed his brains out.

Another splash hit his face. He saw something move, and feared it being another revengeful redskin deriving pleasure from tormenting him. Looking down at his reddened body, he remembered Little Crow's wives dressing him like an Indian, his body naked except for the breech cloth. Thank God they left them, he thought.

He commenced cackling like a man who had lost his total senses and wondered if he would ever get his full measure of sanity back. If only the ropes could be loosened, he could run free as a deer. He struggled, but with no success.

The specter returned one more time. "Whish", another spray of refreshing water. This time, gasping in relief, he realized he was being saved. It was Nawki who'd followed and now would help him to freedom, he was sure.

But, Nawki was not too eager to untie her great man, and she snickered and caressed his chest, which billowed larger than usual, with his arms tied behind the tree. She giggled her luxury of having what she wanted; he having little to say about it.

"Please, Nawki. Please untie me!" He begged.

Olaf's head was still quite groggy, but he realized he had a problem on his hands, especially as she fingered along the edge of his breech, and he felt he was about ready to go out of his mind in frustration.

"*Miya wastidaca,* Tall Like Oakee," she pleaded and tried climbing her tall oak tree.

Maybe, in more normal times, the big Swede could have come up with enough Indian words to have made sense, but in his acute anguish, this wasn't the time.

"*Hi wau.*" she begged on.

Well, he knew what she was saying this time. She wanted him! Besides she kept petting him like a puppy dog, and even though the thought entered his mind, she should have been rewarded a little bit. It was all understandable.

Voices could be heard in the distance. The braves were

308

returning to show off their prize catch, more than likely, Olaf thought. He pleaded with Nawki. This time she recognized the urgency, and after indulging in a couple pleasure pats, she had the rope off in a bat of an eyelash. She twittered most giddily, as the big pseudo-Indian streaked toward Traveling Hail's place to his horse that would take him away from the nightmarish encounter. Few if anybody would ever believe his latest brush with death.

✻   ✻   ✻   ✻   ✻

THE ST. PAUL TOWN PUMP.

A REVARDING BREAK

"Get up, ponies! Get up!" Olaf snapped the lines, moving the four strawberry roans along. It was just ten days ago he hauled the gold payments for the Dakota, but he had arrived too late as the starving Indians had already begun their uprising. Returning, the stage was filled with wounded defenders from the battle.

Physically and emotionally drained, Olaf's mind was cluttered with thoughts of the bloody rebellion by the ruthless young braves. Scores of anxious European immigrants, seeking freedom and a new life, had been murdered; the lucky ones escaping the inferno with only their lives. It was just a relatively small number of hostiles instigating the rampage, but every honorable Indian would suffer further revenge and indignation in retaliation, Olaf feared. He wanted to put the tragedy behind him, yet visions of death replayed through his mind. The Dakota temporarily ruled the land again. In time, the government would send great numbers of troops, he knew.

Contemplating more enlightened matters, Olaf hoped another sweet letter form Marianne might be waiting for him in town. Maybe she's found our son, Peter Olaf, in Montreal, and we can all finally come together on a fine piece of land and enjoy life's more fruitful blessings. Oh, how peaceful and beautiful it would finally be, Olaf thought, with delusions of grandeur replacing the ugly reality of war during the past ten days.

"Come on, ponies! Move along!" he urged anxiously.

* * *

It was past midnight when the stage rolled into Fort Snelling Hospital. Having had assistance in unloading the wounded, he wasted little time in getting the rig back to the Burbank yards. Worn out, he soon collapsed on a cot in the teamster's room instead of riding out to his remote cabin.

He awoke early, as usual. Anxious to find his friend and boss, John Burbank, he quickly doused himself with water and freshened up a bit. If he hurried, he could still get to the Cateract Hotel where Burbank always had breakfast. They'd eaten there together many times before through the years.

Arriving early, Olaf glanced in the door, and sighting his distinguished boss, smiled at the anticipation of a warm greeting. Mr. Burbank was looking a little older, he thought, but Olaf admired his dignified look; slightly graying hair and neatly trimmed mustache. He was downing one of many cups of coffee he'd consume in a day, being totally addicted to the stuff he called sheep-dip.

Olaf entered, donning his big broad smile. Glancing up from the paper he was reading, Burbank burst out, "Oh, my God! Man, it's good to see you!" He stood, grasping Olaf's hand in a boisterous shake, followed by a bear hug. "Whenever a crisis comes up in this world, Son, you always seem to get in the middle of it."

"I'm glad to see you, too, Mr. Burbank. It's sure a different vorld out there than ven I left over a veek ago, isn't it?"

"Lord, I was worried sick. A man only gets what the papers want to print, so now I can get it straight from the 'horse's mouth,'" he joked, delighted to have his fair-haired young associate back home.

"Right, Sir," Olaf grinned.

"How about the gold? Did ya get it to them in time?"

"No, Sir. The lid flew off the morning I got to Fort Ridgely, so ve stashed it." Olaf stroked his forehead showing disappointment.

"Well, sit, my friend. Let's chat a while. God, Swede, I know how rough it must be on you, having worked so damned hard to help the Dakota. Tell me the whole thing, will ya, my boy?" The boss always showed a deep concern for what Olaf went through, and treated him as a son through the years. Olaf didn't get a chance to open his mouth before Burbank noticed his gaunt appearance. "You've lost weight! Twenty pounds, I bet! Hardly more than skin, bone and eye balls left of ya," he quipped.

"Naw, not that much, I'm sure," Olaf laughed at Burbank's

humorous remark.

This public display the men were putting on drew giggles and he-haws from the two dozen patrons, but most knew Olaf anyway, so he enjoyed it.

"Oh, Missy!" Burbank called the waitress across the room. "Bring my big friend a cup a coffee, and a tall stack of buttermilks." He held his hand a foot above the table to show how high. "Put a bunch a eggs on top, too. God, the man is hungry!" The other guests snickered again.

"Right, Mr. Burbank," she acknowledged. "Nice seeing you back, Swede," she added, coming over to the table.

"Thanks, Missy. 'Blessing seeing your happy face again." He patted the hand she'd placed on the table in front of him.

The two men settled in on Olaf's lengthy and vivid account of the tragic ordeal, from meeting the death laden runaway wagon, to his tearing through the country, warning farmers to abandon their farmsteads for safety, the battles he witnessed, the daring visit to Little Crow's village, and observing the death and destruction at the Lower Agency that occurred the first day he'd arrived with the gold.

Missy came with Olaf's breakfast, set it down, and without saying a word, stood listening for a moment. Shaking her head at the detailed re-enactment of events, she moved away quietly repeating, "My! My!"

Burbank, totally engrossed in the breathtaking account, interrupted only by saying "Ya, ya," and "Uh huh," not wanting to interrupt the Swede's description of battles and his dangerous involvement in scouting.

"My God, Olaf, I'm glad you got back in one piece!"

"Ya, vell..." He smiled to break the mood. "So goes the vorld, John. Today the sun shines, tomorrow maybe it storms again, maybe."

"Well, we'll have to pick up the pieces. Rebuild. There's no service out of here, south or west." He shoved back his chair some, satisfied he had the facts. "Swede, I could listen to you for hours, but I know you have business and personal matters to attend to."

"That's for sure, Mr. Burbank."

"Oh! For cat's sakes! I forgot. It came yesterday." He took a letter form his pocket, and handed it to Olaf.

He grabbed at it eagerly. "Excuse me sir. It looks short. Can I just browse through?" He tore it open and began reading.

Burbank laughed. "Of course. Important matters first."

Olaf had been a private man through the years, in fact, some had joked about his being downright sly and illusive at times. It was pretty common knowledge he had a rather mysterious relationship with a lady of churchly connections in Canada, but people only got little bits and pieces about that situation. Burbank picked up his paper and pretended reading, courteously allowing some privacy, but Olaf noticed his boss kept peering over the top of the page, observing his reactions.

A smirk expanded to an ear to ear smile. "Thank God!" he said in a horsy whisper.

"What say? What say?" J. C. responded, as if he were deeply engrossed in his reading.

Olaf babbled unihibitedly, "Finally! Finally, she's coming back! She's coming home! And vith my son!" He nearly choked with emotion.

"Your son?" Burbank repeated in disbelief.

The Swede, in his ecstasy, poured out his whole romantic story: the fantastic meeting eleven years ago at the pasture cabin when Peter Olaf was conceived, the sentimental romantic love on the buffalo hunt, and the spectacular accidental meeting a year ago when they reunited at the Winslow Hotel after eight years of being separated. He related how his Marianne had literally been a hostage of an authoritative and conniving Mother Superior in a Montreal nunnery, who had intercepted and confiscated their letters for years.

Burbank chuckled dumbfoundedly. "Olaf, we had an inkling of such a bazaar romance, but I never dreamed, in all my life, you had a son! And, you never told me," he said, sounding hurt.

"I hope I haven't offended you sir, but you see, I didn't know it till last year myself. She thought I vould have felt trapped, so kept it from me all these years, John. You understand how vomen can be."

Burbank was moved by the revelation, knowing how the big

fellow had suffered over his sad romantic struggle throughout time. Admiring his resourceful assistant, as he had, his eyes were noticeably glossy from the emotional outpouring.

"Mr. Burbank, I've alvays admired you from the first day I started vorking. I have dreamed about my own place vith my Marianne at my side, and now our son, too," Olaf confessed.

"Well, damn it," He shuffled uneasily in his chair, "I never had a son of my own, and you've always kind a filled that void, Olaf." He took his handkerchief and blew his nose, attempting to conceal his compassion. He stiffened. "Swede, you remember George Simpson, the 'Emperor' of all Canada, practically, for Hudson Bay?"

"Oh, Lord, yes! I'll never forget his grand entrance to Fort Garry vith his flying brigades, the cannons roaring from the tower; Sir George, standing in the lead boat vearing his vite capote and the fifer piping a vild cadence for his colorful Algonquin Indians. They vere masters of all in propelling those flying brigades through death defying raging rapids throughout Canada, as Simpson ruled his Hudson Bay Empire."

"I know. One would have to see it to believe the drama." He paused, emphasizing his purpose. Then he said pointedly, "Olaf, Simpson and I had several parcels of land together; eight hundred acres where we built the town of Georgetown at the head of navigation on the Red, and another beautiful spread like it farther north, near Canada. Anyway, when George died two years ago, the northern property became mine exclusively."

Olaf looked baffled, but said, "Ja, I understand, Mr. Burbank."

"Well, my boy, you've contributed so much to the company. I want you to know the northern property is yours. It's a big spread, Olaf."

"Vot!" Olaf's mouth dropped open.

"We'll work out the details later." Showing more emotion than intended, he stood, "Well, I have to go, so I hope you'll accept my offer as a partial payment for all you've done to help build the Burbank Company."

"Mine? Mr. Burbank, this is far more than I ever dreamed of."

"Now, don't say anymore. We'll talk about it later." He stood, ready to leave the table, not wanting to show his soft hearted disposition by the unmanly shedding of tears. Then, inhaling deeply, he straightened himself. "Oh yes, Swede, the Governor told me he had another important mission for you. Be awful careful when you return to the conflict, my boy." He left quickly, his eyes blinking noticeably.

Olaf sat stunned! His lower jaw quivered at the realization that his dream was unfolding so unbelievably; his head spun with plans for his new farm. He wondered how he could stand the anxiety of waiting to reveal the wonderful news to Marianne and son, Peter Olaf.

* * *

Olaf relished the break in the action. Besides, he knew there'd be a hiatus pending while Colonel Sibley recruited and trained two thousand men to conquer the hostile Dakota.

Olaf wanted to spend some time with Jenny and baby Trena at the mansion. Jenny'd received a long letter from Gustav, but it'd been written six weeks before. Even so, it was still comforting to read his words about how he loved and missed being with his family and the serenity of their farm near West Lake.

Jenny was still grieving for their friends at West Lake. Two years earlier, she and Gustav had traveled to their farmstead with several other anxious Swedes: the Anders P. Brobergs, Daniel Brobergs, and Andreas Lundborg families, and a few others. Jenny and Gustav's farm was reached first. The whole group stopped a day and helped the kids put up a temporary shelter, Gustav would travel the two miles to West Lake and pay off a day to each of the families who'd helped. That was the pioneers' way.

Olaf was shocked when reading the news clipping of the fourteen Scandinavians murdered at West Lake on August twentieth by the Indians. It put a sorrowful pain in his heart for those families, and the one surviving girl, who escaped to tell of the slaughter. Jenny had been stunned, of course, but admitted having no more tears to shed. Still, she showed impenetrable faith in believing her Gustav would come back to her.

"Come to Uncle Olaf, Trena," he reached down to pick up the happy baby. Swaying with her, he added. "She's sure adorable,

315

dear Jenny."

"Oh, I hope your Marianne comes soon, Olaf. I worry about you, ya know. Life hasn't treated you all that kindly, I think."

Olaf chuckled while handing Trena back. "Vell, then. I got the good news! She wrote. She found our son! What do you think of that?"

"No! Oh, glory be!" Jenny screamed.

"My dear sister-in-law, I'm so happy I could almost bust! She'll come in the spring when the rivers flow again."

"Oh, thank the Lord! You've waited so long, Olaf."

"And guess vot? Good things come in bunches. My boss gave me some land up on the Red River, ver ve both vant to go and make a good life."

"Oh, all our prayers are coming true! There's only one left to be answered, Olaf. Then we'll all be happy again."

* * *

Olaf conferred with Governor Ramsey daily on the progress of the uprising. A steady flow of couriers brought urgent requests for more federal help from all sectors of the front. The poorly trained and equipped volunteers were holding out valiantly, but Ramsey's requests for trained troops, horses, Springfield rifles, and usable ammunition was ignored by Washington. Ramsey paced the floor nervously.

"Damn it! Olaf, the War Department ignores my every request."

"Vell, vot vun reads in the paper, seems they've got their hands full all right. They're killing our young men by the thousands." Olaf reflected. "Vot's the status of New Ulm? Still holding out?"

"Hell, they had no more ammunition. The two thousand evacuated that burned out place, and marched east to Mankato -- some farther north. Flandreau torched the forty remaining frame buildings -- that made two hundred, including those the Sioux burned. That beautiful town of nine hundred? Nothing but a wasteland now. The barricaded center of town stands as a ghostly reminder of what it once was," the Governor bemoaned.

"Governor Ramsey, I'm going to head out to Yellow Medicine

in a few days. I think Little Crow is sitting there vaiting for Sibley. There'll be some fireworks before they go to the dried up vestern prairie, for sure."

"Colonel Sibley's army of two thousand is slowly building at Fort Ridgely. We were damned lucky, if you ask me, the Chippewa stopped kicking up their heels after we got Chief Hole-In-The-Day cornered. With Fort Abercrombie in Dakota Territory threatened by the Sissitons and Wahpetons, there's not one acre of land west of the Mississippi that's safe! What a catastrophe, Swede. The goddamn ammunition wouldn't fit any of the foreign guns! Jeeesus, Swede!"

Olaf began chuckling. He'd never seen Ramsey throw a tantrum this bad before. He couldn't turn it off either. He just kept laughing.

"Well, goddamn it! When our weak-sistered Indian Agents flip their lids and blow their brains out, like Chippewa Agent Walker did, there's something damn rotten in Denmark, if ya ask me." Seeing Olaf convulse at his antics, Ramsey started laughing, too. Both were releasing nervous tension.

The two men had had many disagreements in the past years, but there was need for a cooperative effort if this Indian uprising was to be resolved and both men recognized that need. Governor Ramsey begged Olaf to return to the western front, seek out peaceful chiefs, and relay his promise of rewards to those who helped bring the struggle to a sensible conclusion. Olaf felt it was his duty to help save lives, and worried as much about Dakota fighting Dakota, as well as the several hundred white and mixed blood hostages, whose lives were seriously in danger. He agreed to go back and do what he could.

BIRCH COULEE AMBUSH

Olaf, as usual, was contemplating the world's problems as he rode Dancer Girl back to the battlefield. What's going to happen to the natives now? He wondered. Will the friendly chiefs dare oppose Little Crow openly and bring this war to a sensible end? Will there be enough forgiving in the hearts of the white man to allow those Christian Dakota a chance to return to their farms? They were just beginning to make inroads in adapting to the white man's ways, and it would be a shame if the efforts were wasted.

No...guess not, he answered himself. The land's too rich. It'll be devoured by the eager European immigrants, as it had been when the government had taken half of the reservation by treaty, promising payments for many years. They'll push them on to some worthless land where they'll starve, he predicted. Gold payments will be forgotten about...like now.

Then he thought of a more hopeful matter, the return of Marianne. He was plenty excited. The second letter he'd received before leaving on this assignment put the kibosh on an early arrival. She could not bring Peter Olaf until he'd completed his term of indenture, which was to expire at the end of the year. Now, it'd be spring before the rivers opened for steamboat travel. He worried. She was naive to the harsh realities of the world, having been cloistered in a religious environment most of her life. The demands of her confinement to absolute prayer had been lifted, she wrote, and she was thrilled about being allowed to work with orphaned children under the new arrangement. Then, he laughed out loud, thinking how Burbank's gift of land spurred excitement beyond his wildest imagination.

* * *

"Holy horse feathers!" Olaf blurted, seeing Fort Ridgely

coming into view. It sure looked different from when he'd left here a week before. Colonel Sibley, the once prominent fur trader, was finally accumulating his army, and cavalry presence was evident by the four hundred horses pasturing on the high ground. Approaching closer, he could see several hundred army tents had been set up outside the parade area. These were the thousand fresh recruits making up the Sixth Regiment, Olaf figured.

"Hut two! Hut two!" The platoon leaders called out in brisk cadence, training the newcomers to army discipline. "Straighten those lines, you clodhoppers! Pull in those bellies! Get those shoulders back!"

The recruits looked as green as grass, Olaf thought. Sibley wasn't about to move until he had his two thousand troops, including the Civil War veterans he was promised, giving unquestionable advantage against the enemy.

"Hey Swede! Oh, Swede!" A husky voice called from the first cabin closest to the St. Peter road as Olaf approached. It was Sergeant Jones calling. "Come in here and shoot the crap a minute, ya ol' reprobate."

Olaf guffawed back, "Vell, it takes vun to know vun."

Jonesy had finished his duties for the day and had retrieved a jug of cool beer stashed down in the river. He'd never reveal the secret of how he came by his supply, but he'd always had refreshments around. Old sarges were a privileged lot; independent as hogs in a mud hole.

Having worked his way up through the ranks, Jones was more than a little bit miffed at the "instant wonders" throwing their weight around. Why, he complained, Ramsey's made colonels and majors out of jackasses.

Olaf admitted he'd turned down a commission himself, but got plenty hot under the collar on learning the miserable Galbraith had been commissioned a Major and assigned to the Sixth Regiment, now at Ridgely.

Having swapped tales of their escapades on the western front, the two adventurers parted company. Olaf agreed to return to Jonesy's cabin and spare bunk for the night, glad to accept such courtesy in the crowded camp.

Now on official business for the Governor, he thought it urgent he report to headquarters. The tensions of the week before had pretty much been laid to rest, with the lifting of the siege and removing nearly three hundred refugees from the ten day incarceration. Off duty trainees were playing ball and pitching horseshoes, after the strenuous day of basic training. Several men greeted the big frontiersman as he sauntered by on horseback for he exemplified the epitome of courage and bravery to them.

"Oh, Swede! Oh, big Swede!" A voice called out from the direction of Headquarters. It was Commander Sibley, himself. He was with Major Brown and Captain Anderson, whom Olaf respected as a fine horseman who was now in charge of the cavalry.

"Colonel Sibley, Major Brown, Captain Anderson." Olaf appropriately addressed his comrades, and shook their hands. They, who had worn hats of a different profession only weeks before, greeted Olaf congenially.

"I got word you were coming, Swede. Our runners are beating a path back and forth to the Governor, daily. Why don't you join us for dinner in our Officer's quarters? Frankly, the food's a hell of a lot better than what you'd get with the non-coms," Sibley boasted.

"Vell, thank you, but I think first I better tell Major Brown the good news of my visit vith his good vife, Susan, a veek ago."

"Susan! Awe, you're kidding me, man! You really saw her?" Brown gasped.

"That I did, and it was at Little Crow's house vare she vas being treated most respectfully, Joseph."

"My God! Oh, my God!" Brown nearly collapsed from the startling news. Captain Anderson steadied him. Brown sobbed, "I thought she might be dead. Can we talk inside, privately?"

"Sure, Joseph," Olaf agreed, and they went into headquarters.

Olaf found ex-agent Brown immensely overjoyed knowing his wife and all of his children were still alive and protected by Little Crow. Mrs. Brown had further confided to Olaf that nearly two hundred whites and mixed blood hostages were getting respectable treatment at Little Crow's camp. Brown agreed that his faith in the

Chief had been somewhat restored, and that what his wife had revealed about the large number of whites and mixed bloods in captivity would demand extreme caution to assure their safety.

Olaf's dinner meeting with the officers was companionable, except for his having to look at the insipid an unbearable Major Galbraith whose face had a negative effect on his appetite.

Colonel Sibley told Olaf of the arrangement to send out troops with a burial party on the next day, August 31. Major Brown would be in charge of the operation, taking Company A of the Sixth Regiment under Captain Hiram Grant, and fifty mounted guards under Captain Anderson, twenty teamsters and wagons, as well as a fatigue detail of soldiers and citizens who wanted to look for the bodies of relatives. No one had seen the area fifteen miles to the west since Olaf had visited Little Crow a week before. They depended on the Swede to pin-point on a map where he had seen at least fifty bodies on that gruesome mission.

Though Olaf would have offered to accompany the detail of one hundred seventy men, Sibley begged that he stay to assist him in formulating plans for the major push west. Both Olaf and Sibley warned the men not to bivouac too close to the cover of the river or creeks in range of marauding hostiles.

* * *

Five o'clock and reveille was called. The thousand young recruits hustled over to the mess hall for breakfast and soon would be out to the drill field for calisthenics and vigorous marching.

The burial party had been gone two of the four days planned for the horrendous task of identifying and burying severely decomposed bodies. Returning citizens from the first day reported that only about twenty had been properly buried. The second day, the detail was to cross to the south side of the river where the largest number of dead would be found near the Red Wood Ferry and the burned out Lower Agency. Olaf was relieved to know the scores of dead folks were getting a decent burial, for the dreadful scene had been playing over and over in his mind.

Colonel Sibley was tediously thorough in his planning for the eventual march on the main force of Dakota. He depended on Olaf's knowledge of the terrain, every knoll and ravine was charted. Though Sibley could speak the natives' tongue and knew their signs from being Agent of the American Fur Company the past twenty years, he had little knowledge of their warring tactics. Olaf wasn't convinced the Colonel had much compassion for the primitive lifestyle of these native Americans, having taken advantage of them by giving miserable pay for the valuable furs they'd gathered through the years. Sibley called them Sioux, the demeaning name of "Snake," or "Snake like," given them by their age old enemy, the Chippewa. They preferred Dakota, meaning, "friend."

* * *

Olaf was eager to move west and seek out friendly chiefs, and relate the Governor's promise that those helping end the war would not be punished, but instead, be rewarded. These smoke filled sessions with Sibley, Colonel McPhail, and junior officers were not overly illuminating for the Swede. He'd rather be out breathing the smell of clean prairie grass while riding his faithful dappled gray mare.

So, this morning Olaf took Dancer Girl out for an early limbering up, and rode west about five miles just at the break of dawn. Promptly, a strange crackling caught his ear, so he stopped to listen. "Oh my God!" he gasped. The crackling was gunfire! Heavy gunfire! Olaf knew this was no small encounter, the shooting as heavy as at Fort Ridgely only a week before. It came from the direction Brown's troops had camped.

He raced back to the fort where all appeared quiet. They had not heard anything. "Colonel Sibley! Colonel Sibley!" He shouted as he approached the Officers' quarters. Sibley and a half dozen of his comrades stumbled out in their long-johns. Reveille hadn't been for them.

"What, Swede? What the hell is it?" Sibley countered.

"Gunfire comes from where your troops were bivouacked last night, I think. Sounds like a major attack, Sir."

"Oh, shit! McPhail, on the double! Soldier, find the goddamn bugler! Expedite call to arms immediately!" he ordered a recruit guarding outside.

Activity became intense at Fort Ridgely that morning. McPhail took two hundred forty men, companies B, D, and E of the Sixth Infantry, fifty mounted rangers, and a unit of artillery, and rushed the foot soldiers the fifteen miles.

Sibley was dumbfounded. "What the hell happened, Swede?"

"Don't know, sir. Except one messenger said they camped too close to trees, making them vulnerable as hell. They were warned against that."

It went from bad to worse. Hearing some of his cannon booming late that afternoon, Sibley figured his forces were in control again. Just intermittent shooting continued, as the Dakota had done previously.

But, such a presumption proved premature, for as the afternoon sun lowered, a lone rider came racing in with ugly news from the battlefield.

"It looks bad, sir! It looks bad!"

Olaf recognized his friend from the Yellow Medicine debacle when five thousand Indians came for food two months before. It was Lt. Sheehan, then the junior commanding officer of Ridgely, after Marsh was killed.

"What the devilish bad news you bring now, Lieutenant?" Sibley stormed.

"Sir, we were closing in on the main coulee, and suddenly, we were surrounded by Indians. Colonel McPhail sent me back for reinforcements."

Sibley quickly readied his entire remaining force; eight companies from the Sixth and Seventh regiments.

"C'mon Swede, ya better come along and see what the hell's going on."

Olaf moved out with Sibley, two hundred fifty mounted men, seven hundred infantrymen, and units of artillery, arriving at McPhail's bivouac about midnight. The exhausted foot soldiers, having done double time, were allowed to rest until dawn, after which they got the urgent order to "move out." The area of brush cover was shelled with artillery fire as they advanced. Finally at 11:00 a.m. on September 3, the beleaguered camp of Major Brown was reached. The Dakota had left.

"So damned unnecessary!" Olaf mumbled under his breath, slowly riding around the circle of a hundred horse carcasses, and wrecked wagons to which they had been tied. Glancing within the circle, a hundred yards across, he saw how the desperate men had scratched out rifle pits with tin plates and bayonets. Dead men lay where they had fallen, and dozens of badly wounded cried for water and attention, having been deprived of it for nearly two days.

The stench was as bad as the one he'd experienced at the Redwood Ferry a week before. Young recruits became nauseous and gagged, covering their noses while trying to clear the area. Many with weak stomachs lost their breakfast, as young farm boys had their first taste of war.

Olaf soon realized that, had it not been for the barricade of a hundred horse carcasses, the unit would most certainly have been annihilated. As it was, Colonel Brown, Captain Grant, and Major Galbraith--the glory seeker--all lay injured. Thirteen were dead, but that number would surely grow from the forty-seven seriously wounded troops, plus those with less serious injuries.

Cavalry horses replaced the slaughtered wagon teams and were hitched to the badly shot up rigs for transporting the wounded. The dejected forces spread out for miles on returning to Ridgely.

Olaf wondered if the inexperienced volunteer officers had learned a lesson; that it would be pure folly to pursue the Indian with less than a large well-trained army. Now Washington might take notice that this was no little backyard squabble out here on the western prairie, he was thinking, and they best send some men back to tend the home fires. Sibley's army returned to the fort on the morning of September 4. They had been soundly threshed by a relatively small number of Indians. The government forces hobbled back in humiliation, licking their wounds.

OLAF ENCOURAGES SISSITON

Colonel Sibley, expecting to be promoted to General, was showing signs of depression after the sound threshing he took from a few hundred Dakota warriors at Birch Coulee. Many of the rifles he had available were foreign made, and often times the ammunition supplied didn't fit. After the slaughtering of a hundred horses at the coulee, and another few hundred volunteer cavalrymen returning home to finish harvest, Sibley was left with only twenty-seven mounted troops; hardly enough to challenge the Dakota's overwhelming numbers of mounted warriors.

Governor Ramsey's appeals for help from the war department were turned down repeatedly, but token support was given when the Twenty-fifth Wisconsin Regiment and the Twenty-seventh Iowa Infantry were sent to help. The war was regional, and it needed federal and regional support, Ramsey declared.

Olaf had waited long enough, he decided, and was anxious to move out to contact western Dakota Territory chiefs opposed to the war and eager to cooperate with the Government. He wanted to give them the much needed assurances Governor Ramsey had promised. Checking in at Headquarters, Olaf had a final conference with Sibley.

"Well, Swede, I was so damned pissed off at Washington, I was about to chuck this whole damn thing! People calling me chicken-hearted and coward! Finally, we've raised enough hell, though, so we're getting some action, and we'll be proceeding in a week."

"That's so?" Olaf chuckled, humored by Sibley's flamboyance.

"Yah, ya damn right! Thought you'd like to know before leaving that the War Department is assigning Major General John Pope out here. Of course he lost the second battle at Bull Run-but previously he had a good record."

"Vell, no vun's perfect," Olaf mused as Sibley expounded.

"Finally, we'll be getting fifty thousand cartridges and clothing for our young recruits, who've been about as effective as a bunch of boys on a weekend campout."

Olaf couldn't help but grin at the prairie commander's ranting over the government's inattention to the Dakota War.

"Besides, we're promised two hundred seventy infantrymen of the Third Regiment to be assigned from the Civil War. That'll give us some experienced punch!" Sibley boasted.

"Vell, it'll be good to get this over vith, Colonel," Olaf reassumed a serious attitude. "I'll pass that good news on to the vestern chiefs who'll velcome your arrival. Uh...how soon should I say you'll be there? Three, four days?"

"Oh, Hell, what do ya expect? Miracles? Better think more about two weeks, Swede." He too, squirmed at his own pessimistic projection.

"Vell, then I'll be off," Olaf started to leave. "Good luck, Sir."

"Oh, one more thing, Swede, something you should know. I just got word that Fort Abercrombie, in Dakota Territory, has come under siege the last few days. Something to keep in mind as you're riding that western prairie. They'll be comin' and goin' all around ya."

"Thanks, Sir. I appreciate that information." Olaf saluted and left.

* * *

Olaf skirted the ten-mile wide Dakota reserve on the north side, but carefully closed in to scout the Upper Sioux Agency at Yellow Medicine. All looked peaceful and serene along the rolling hills as recent rains had turned the prairie a lush green. The fragrance of wild roses greeted him at the edge of the woods, and except for the worry of lingering hostility, it could have been a tranquil moment.

Stealthily and cautiously, Olaf went only close enough to level his scope for a scan of the area. His fears were soon substantiated. What was once the Upper Agency had been reduced to ashes. His heart pumped with difficulty as he anguished over the desolation and fear that many had died there, as well. Two distinctive camps of tepees had been set up to the west; one obviously comprised of Wahpeton Indians, the other Olaf made out to be the temporary headquarters of Little Crow's Mdewakantons. No doubt, Olaf thought, the peace-prone Wahpetons were being pressured by the demands of the Soldier's Lodge, which now, even overruled Little Crow.

Feeling a renewed urgency to talk with the chiefs farther west, Olaf quickly rode on across the rolling plain. He kept recalling the turbulent life of Little Crow. The Lac qui Parle region he approached was the Chief's playground in earlier times, where he'd romanced and married three Wahpeton women. Later he returned to the Mississippi headwaters to take back command of the Mdewakantons. Control was not his until he killed his half-brother who had laid claim as band Chief in Little Crow's absence.

* * *

Having traveled two days, Olaf reached grand Big Stone Lake, headwaters of the Minnesota River. It had been a fur trading center for a century. An ominous sign loomed ahead. Olaf breathed laboriously. Ravenous vultures circled the site where the trading post had stood. The distressed Swede cringed at seeing the desolation of the usually active trading center on the eastern point of the lake. The hostiles had not spared this friendly fur trading camp even though it was well within the region dominated by Wahpeton - Sissitons. It was clear, war had become widespread.

Taking a few more hours to reach Standing Buffalo's village, Olaf rode the high bluff ridge to prevent interference of renegades on the war path. He was always charmed by the wide expanse of water and the high stony bluffs cradling it. Remembering that the area had always been a hunting and fishing haven for the local Dakota bands, the Swede felt sorrowful, but had little time to contemplate the situation with threatening war parties around him. Once, he saw about twenty-five horsemen riding north toward Fort Abercrombie, straight up the Red River about sixty miles. He remembered Sibley's report that Fort Abercrombie, too, was under siege.

Finally, having traveled several hours along Big Stone lake, another large body of water came into view. To the northeast stretched Lake Traverse, the opposite direction from Big Stone Lake. Lake Traverse was the headwaters of the River Rouge (Red River) which flowed north into Canada and drained into Hudson Bay. Olaf was always intrigued by the subtle rise of land where the water ran in opposite directions.

Olaf envied the life of the Sissiton Dakota, who planted their crops of corn and squash in the spring; then went on the buffalo hunt. They returned to harvest in the fall; stored their surplus foods, and traveled to their winter home in the Devils Lake region, an oasis on the prairie - a few hundred miles north. What a delightful carefree life, Olaf pondered.

Standing Buffalo's village was nearly deserted. Just a few skin lodges remained standing, the homes of elderly and those squaws with children, too young for the hunt, were left behind. Olaf was disappointed that Standing Buffalo was with his hunters, but he'd wait to see him.

The Swede's attention was drawn to an ancient Sissiton chief atop a high knoll at the edge of the village who was obviously communicating with his Great Spirit. Moving closer, Olaf saw the old fellow in colorful regalia: parched skins, quills, animal teeth and feathers, symbols of his accomplishments. Below the mound, out of the Indian's sight, Olaf paused to listen, not wishing to disturb his spiritual experience. "Aiee ah-ha-ha-hoi-o-o-haia. Aiee ah-ha-ha-hoi-o-o-haia," the old chief chanted. Olaf was moved by the Indian's reverence to his Great Spirit. He'd always found it hard to think of Indians as savages.

Seeing smoke rise from the center of the village, Olaf moved on. He found an audience, two old bucks and several young squaws - some with papooses. Olaf remembered the comical old one-eared brave. His other ear had been cut off in a vicious encounter with an unfortunate Chippewa who had lost more than an ear, so the Sissiton bragged.

Olaf shared some of his store-bought tobacco and smoked with the men while they told him that Standing Buffalo was off to the

Sheyenne River on the prairie with his hunters. They knew of the Mdewakanton uprising and did not approve of their actions, they said. Nor would Standing Buffalo tolerate such behavior, for he liked the white man and would help put Little Crow's wild savages down, they asserted.

The young squaws kept looking at Olaf and giggled among themselves. He enjoyed teasing the young women, and enjoyed being teased himself. Maybe it was his size, Olaf figured, but he didn't mind being the brunt of their joking if he could encourage them to share some of their stew, or soup - whatever it was they were cooking. He'd been riding all day and only had a little hard-tack and jerky. He salivated from the food smells.

With a smirk of anticipation on his face, Olaf took his old mouth harp that usually won him favors from those he entertained, and started playing Yankee Doodle and a few other patriotic rousers. Sure enough, soon he was the center of attention. The young Sissiton women laughed and hung on him as if he was a celebrity from a wild west show. Olaf ate plenty, and could've had other considerations no doubt, as they doted over him.

Watching with guarded curiosity as night closed in, he saw the infatuated women fixing a soft bed for him by the fire. More alarmingly, they giggled while making another bed next to his. They were up to some kind of tomfoolery causing him some consternation.

"No. No. No, ladies! Tall Like Oak sleep alone," he said.

Well, several of those giggling Sissiton women gathered around like a bunch of cackling chickens, all trying to make a point.

All Olaf could do was object. "No. No. I sleep alone," he repeated.

It became obvious the women were determined. It took a great deal of effort for Olaf to understand what they wanted, but he finally got the drift that there was a beautiful eligible Sissiton widow who was in a long lasting mourning. Her brave had fallen in battle six months ago. The good women hoped Olaf, being alone, would be interested in the beauty of royal Indian blood, a descendant of the families of Akepa and Tiwakan. This impressed

Olaf, having known those families. He lit his pipe and commenced puffing nervously while gazing at the alluringly handsome woman the squaws arranged for him. The instigators went to their own tents to most likely be entertained from their escapade.

As beautiful as the woman was, how would Olaf ever make her understand he was already spoken for, waiting for his own love to return? She had a most intoxicating smile, Olaf thought. Not wanting to insult or harm her in any way, he wondered how he could possibly explain.

She pouted, looking hurt. "No like Winona?" She said, "Hm?"

Olaf's pipe nearly dropped out of his mouth when she spoke. "My God! You speak English!" He contemplated the situation. "I thought you looked somevot different -- lighter skin, and some foreign."

She smiled. "Father, Dakota -- and Canadian too. Mother, same." She thought to herself a moment. "You, Tall Like Oak? Hear some praise of big man from East."

Blushing at the flattery, he said, "Awe." Realizing he'd been rude in rejecting the women's good intentions, he apologized. "You are pretty, and I'm sorry I vas so bull-headed, not vonting to talk to you."

"Hm," she acknowledged with a sigh. "English not good. Good when small at trade post. 'Member some. Speak Sissiton now."

Olaf enjoyed conversing with the charming woman. Though she spoke broken English he had little difficulty understanding her.

She told him about her marriage to a Sissiton brave, and her sadness that he had died in battle with the age-old enemy, the Chippewa, about six months before. Though she said she'd relish a fine man like Olaf, she admitted to having other aspirations, as well.

Olaf smiled, thinking how coyly he was being let 'off the hook'.

She agreed the old ways of the Indian were gone and that the white man, though often bad to her people, brought Christian missionaries, like Dr. Williamson, who taught her to become literate in the Dakota language.

As she talked, Olaf was becoming entranced with beautiful Winona. "I'm glad and feel honored to meet you, Vinona, Daughter of Tivakan -- known to me as Gabriel Renville, trader and farmer. Your mother, Vinona Crawford, had genuinely fine qualities; highly respected," Olaf praised.

They talked for hours. Each telling of their interesting and diverse lives. Winona was entranced by Olaf's description of his mystical foreign homeland, and finally realizing his dreams of coming to her great land.

There were periods of simply regarding one another when nothing was said. Time was spent when Olaf thought only of her intoxicating beauty, and wondered if he could restrain himself, and not succumb to her alluring charm. The Indian war had suddenly become of trivial importance. His pesky conscience seemed to have fallen asleep, not telling him to abide by his pledge of faithfulness to Marianne -- now a world apart. Olaf indulged in Winona's demanding smile. He wondered if, she too, was thinking of the compulsive desires of her body. She was craving the same erotic needs, he was sure. Reason finally overcoming sensual desires, Olaf forced himself to converse with Winona. She impressed him with her bright and keen intellect.

After hours of obvious infatuation with each other, a warm feeling had grown between them. The magnetism of the attraction drew them so close at times, Olaf could feel her hot breath on his neck. Yet neither spoke much, as they purely enjoyed the indulgence of their passion.

Finally, Winona trembled noticeably. "Ooo, such chills not have -- long time, Tall Like Oak." Winona admitted her uncontrollable shivering.

Realizing the passion of the moment, and obviously not wanting to tempt fate any further, Winona stood. "Not fair to tease Tall Lake Oak-or Winona. Go to own bed and dream now." She smiled. "Make head spin, Tall Like Oak."

Olaf rose and smiled shyly. "Vinona, vun varm tender hug vould help us both, I think." They embraced-more tenderly than if sister and brother.

"Thank you, big friend. From that, ached all night," Winona drooled.

The spectators were heard giggling, again. Exotic Winona smiled.

"Thank you, beautiful Vinona, I vish you a vonderful life." He watched as the stately Winona walked gracefully to her lodge.

Well, Olaf had a little trouble falling asleep again. He wondered why it was so darned easy to get himself all wound up like that, and felt guilty having such distracted thoughts. "Vell hell, I'm only human. It's just that things don't alvays vork out so a fellow can prove it," he mumbled. Then he chuckled to himself to punctuate the end of those thoughts.

Soon, Olaf's mind turned to the purpose of his western jaunt. Tomorrow he would ride down to Scarlet Plume's village on the Dakota side of Big Stone Lake. Maybe he wasn't out hunting at this time, he hoped. Olaf knew Scarlet Plume was opposed to the uprising, so he would be a good one to confront Little Crow before he plunged the whole Dakota Nation into war. Then he would take a few days to visit Wanata and Sweet Corn's villages west of Lake Traverse. He also considered the possibility of riding out to find the hunters on the Sheyenne River country. Olaf finally drifted off to sleep with a whole range of problems weighing heavily on his mind.

* * *

Chiefs Wanata, Sweet Corn and Scarlet Plume were eager to stop the uprising. They wanted peace and continuation of friendly relations with the white government in their Dakota Territory. After all, their lifestyle on the fringes of the western plains was not threatened by the whites who considered it a wasteland anyway.

So Olaf conferred with these chiefs and found them willing to travel to Little Crow and register opposition to the war in progress. The three chiefs agreed that the powerful and influential Standing Buffalo, off hunting on the prairie, should be asked to join them in a show of strength.

* * *

Now Olaf was on his way northwest to reach the big bend of the Sheyenne River where it changes course to the South, joining the Red River. Winona, who'd been on many hunting trips with her brave before he was killed, had drawn a map where Olaf could find Standing Buffalo's hunting party. Hurrying on his mission, Olaf still found time to contemplate matters while riding his ever faithful Dancer Girl. He smiled, noting the lush growth of grass this year. Last year it would have been different during the devastating drought.

The Sheyenne, not being a deep river, enabled Olaf to cross several times in cutting off meandering bends. He became excited seeing a hunting party over a rise to the north, so galloped Dancer toward the group of about thirty Indians. He soon learned they were not Standing Buffalo's hunters at all, but a confrontational band of Yanktonais from farther west. Becoming concerned, Olaf quickly gave the threatening challengers a friendly hand greeting. Then the lead Indian returned a sign indicating they would hear him out.

"*Wasichu sni tang yang hi Dakota,*" the leader spoke firmly.

Understanding he was not welcome on their land, Olaf had to come up with some convincing explanation that his presence was not a threat to the Yanktonai's cherished hunting grounds, so he said, "*Koda, vastedaka,*" Dakota words explaining that he was friendly. "*Koda etang hang Vamdenica.*" He was glad he remembered Standing Buffalo's Dakota name which, he noticed, relaxed the tightly formed circle around him.

Immediately, the Yanktonais, who were friendly with Standing Buffalo's people, became agreeable and informed Olaf he was only a few hours from where the Sissitons were busy processing their meat. The prairie Indians quizzed Olaf about the trouble to the east, having heard the Taoyateduta had gone on the warpath with the *wasicung*, and they didn't think it was a good idea. Olaf said he agreed with them. Then, thanking them, he hurried on to find Standing Buffalo.

The Sissiton hunters were where the Yanktonais had said they'd be.

"Coda, Vamdenica," Olaf greeted Standing Buffalo by his Indian name.

"Wasu Wasdedaka Tall Like Oak," Standing Buffalo called out as Olaf rode in hastily on his big gray mare. *"Niye ewastdedang nina sungktanka,"* he said, complimenting Olaf on his beautiful horse.

Olaf thanked him, admitting he loved her, too.

Standing Buffalo was saddened to hear that the Mdewakantons had dug themselves in so deeply, and became adamant when thinking of the possibility that the war might spread into Dakota Territory.

The campfires were already glowing as night darkened the sky. Olaf stayed in the Sissiton camp and enjoyed the dinner of fine fresh buffalo meat, prairie turnips and berries the women had gathered along the Sheyenne River. The two men smoked their pipes long into the night and discussed the consequences of the war and the ultimate threat to the peace and tranquillity of the great Dakota prairie. The Sissiton Chief had heard of Little Crow's skirmishes, but he didn't know the seriousness of the war until Olaf told him of vicious battles and the murdering of hundreds of pioneer farmers.

The next day the hunting party hastily returned to their village. Standing Buffalo was anxious to go see his old friend, Taoyateduta, and persuade him to stop the fighting in the name of all that was sacred to the Dakota Nation.

PRISONERS OF VAR

Sibley, known as 'the tortoise', waited two weeks before making his western march. Olaf had time to counsel with all the western Sisseton chiefs who, after his urging, jointly confronted Little Crow and refused to support the uprising. They warned that if he were to continue, the white government would descend upon the whole Dakota Nation mercilessly.

The Wahpeton chiefs who didn't support the war were coerced into shedding their farmer's clothes lest they be shot by their Mdewakanton cousins, who were under constant surveillance by the hostiles. Nonetheless, Chiefs Akepa, John Other Day, Little Paul, Red Iron, and mixed blood leaders like Gabriel Renville, were flexing their muscles as the peace party, as they called themselves, grew in numbers. They sent messengers to Sibley informing him that they would be welcoming him. All Mdewakantons were required to abide by the dictates of the council, and were forced to shed white man's clothes and wear the breach clout.

Olaf kept encouraging the opposing chiefs, but was getting frustrated at the indecisiveness of Sibley. Evading the hostiles, he returned with letters from many Indian leaders pledging cooperation with the government. Sibley was elated to hear of the tribal dissension when Olaf returned to Fort Ridgely. Finally, the army was ready to move on the offensive.

Olaf sped ahead to the Yellow Medicine peace camp with the news that two thousand troops were closing in on the hostiles. He entered the friendly camp from the south and concealed Dancer Girl in a natural corral of bull rushes and willow bush, avoiding the enemy camp. Little Crow's forces were already terrorizing the friendlies with the threat of death, so Olaf laid low, so as not to add fuel to their antagonism.

This night the enemy were shouting vulgar threats from their camp, less than a half mile away. Olaf noted the friendly camp had grown by several tepees and their peaceful leaders dared construct a large shelter – Soldier's Lodge – of their own to challenge the hostile's authority.

"Tiwakan," Olaf called. "What goes on, Tiwakan? You dare challenge Taoyateduta?" The whites knew the mixed blood leader as Gabriel Renville, but Olaf, out of respect, always addressed the Dakota by their Indian name.

"The hostile Soldiers' Lodge make threats of murder on all whites and mixed blood hostages in their peace camp," Tiwakan declared.

"We have retrieved some of their prisoners and will save all or die as honorable men," said Little Paul, "to show loyalty to Great Father."

"You good men, take heart, for as ve speak, Commander Sibley comes with two thousand troops. Mend all your fences qvickly," Olaf advised.

In moments the Swede looked around, observing women and old men hurriedly setting up simple barriers before their tents, in anticipation of invasion by the savages. Women were digging holes in the ground within their shelters – to hide their children, Olaf figured. Oh, how desperately the honorable Dakota struggled for their own freedom.

Though the friendly chiefs were happy to have Olaf's support, they were concerned that if Cut Nose captured him, there'd be a 'short haircut'. "Mad Indian, Cut Nose, threatens to take Tall Like Oak's scalp. He knows you support peace camp which makes him a madder dog than even before."

"Thanks for reminding me, Tiwakan. I'll stay out of his vay," Olaf assured him.

The renegades suddenly grew more frightening and violent.

Little Paul shouted. "Get weapons ready! They may try to take the whites and mixed bloods we shelter! Be ready to protect our own, my brothers!"

Chief Akepa pointed protectively to Olaf, "In there! In there!" Olaf entered a lodge, knowing the on-coming charge of howling Indians – three hundred strong – would be angered finding him present.

Watching through the tent's opening, Olaf saw that the hostiles were painted for war. They rode their horses around the peace camp, threatening to strike at any moment. Then, they stopped. Olaf didn't know why, but he heard the strong deep and resonant voice easily identifiable to him as that of his old friend, Little Crow himself.

"This is great time! Coward Tortoise, Sibley, dares come to Dakota ground. White soldiers fight like women! We will devour them as hungry wolves feast on sheep!" Deafening howls cheered the Chief. Quieting again, Little Crow continued. "Now, hear Taoyateduta. The Solder's Lodge has ruled that every man in camp go at once to Yellow Medicine and meet the enemy. Hear Taoyateduta loud and clear. Anyone, I said <u>anyone</u>, who brings the scalp of Sibley, or Brown, or Forbs, or Myrick – or the American flag – will receive all the wampum beads in the camp, and honored by all the people as the hero and chief warrior of the tribe." Again, the three hundred mounted warriors screamed an ear-piercing chant, making Olaf's flesh quiver.

And then they rode away. Olaf was surprised at how much he understood of Little Crow's decree, but he had known the Chief for several years, and they had talked much.

Looking around in the darkened tent, Olaf was surprised to find a woman resuming the digging of a hole she had started earlier.

"Vie are you digging a large hole in the ground?" Olaf asked.

She smiled and shook her head indicating she didn't understand him. Olaf noticed two young children, and his mouth popped open when he saw a young girl – about twelve. "My Lord! You're a vite girl, aren't you?"

"Yes, Sir," she said meekly.

"Vot are you doing here? Vare's your mother, young lady?"

"Snana protect me, Mister. Saved me from bad men." She was nearly crying recalling her tragic experience. "Many times this good Christian Indian hides me with her own children – in a hole below where she sits."

Olaf gave a gracious smile to the Indian woman named Snana. She folded her hands together in a prayerful pose. Olaf knew,

337

then, she was Christian.

"Vot of your family?" Olaf asked compassionately.

She sobbed softly. "All killed by the bad Indians the first day."

"Bless ya, my girl." Olaf patted her arm. "And you too, Snana," he smiled tenderly. "This horrible nightmare vill soon be over."

Fear and a calculated plot were being contrived by the peace party. Olaf was surprised when the Chiefs and their braves painted their faces and took up their weapons, obeying Little Crow's order to march to Yellow Medicine. Gabriel Renville and Little Paul explained that tonight was the moment of a final decision. Though the men were all leaving, he was told they would be back – in an hour, or longer – but they would be back to help build breast works and trenches, and protect their families behind earthly barricades. Tomorrow they would boldly defy Taoyateduta, they said.

As night wore on, a number of warring riders rode swiftly around the camp shouting hi-y-yi-yi in an attempt to frighten the friendlies who responded to the order that all must go meet Sibley's army. Olaf watched as the camp became deserted except for old men, women and children. They all continued digging holes in the ground.

Thinking he could scout the hostiles and gather valuable information for Colonel Sibley, Olaf hurried Dancer Girl along the south of the river, away from trees and brush where the enemy could be hiding. He planned to head east, past Yellow Medicine, and hoped to contact Sibley's forces from the rear. Later on, he carefully dismounted and entered the woods in hopes of reaching the government camp on foot.

Gaudily painted warriors streaked by. My God, they're thick as fleas on a mangy dog, Olaf thought. Soon, realizing his plan to reach the army would be unattainable, he began to withdraw, but near the outer edge of the woods there was a shot at deathly close range! Olaf hugged a tree and broke out in a cold sweat. He scanned the deep shadows of the woods wondering who would be using him for a target.

Then he vaguely detected Indians racing back and forth as if

338

one were in pursuit of the other. Another shot rang out! Olaf held his breath, it being all too close for comfort. Then it became deathly quiet.

Suddenly, he heard the snapping of twigs close by. Pure instinct guided his actions as he drew his handgun from the holster and held it in readiness. In a flash, a shadowed form burst out from the bushes, and stood with a rifle aimed directly at Olaf, at close range. Olaf aimed his weapon at the darkened form, but something kept him from pulling the trigger. The thought flashed through his mind that he had never killed a man. The mysterious other did not fire.

Finally, Olaf asked dumbfoundedly, "Vie do you not shoot?"

"Tall man, I think I know you from before. I am Otakle. Live at Wabasha's village," he said in a husky whisper.

"Vot the Devil! You speak English!"

The Indian chuckled some, "Better English when with trader father at Mendota ten years ago."

"Vot?" Olaf still didn't recognize the man.

"You knew me by Joseph Godfrey, son of trader Joseph Godfrey. You remember mother...Negro...only one."

"Ja, Joseph, I vaguely remember that, and I know your family vas vell respected, but," Olaf chuckled, "you ver vun hell of a vorker ven ve ver building trails back then." They both laughed at the strange twist of events bringing them together after all the years.

The two men were speaking under their breath, both tense from the chase.

"Vie you run, Joseph Otakle? You are vun of them?"

"No. No, big Swede. Hostiles try to kill me. I will shoot no white man. I now return to join peace camp."

"Ven? Ven do you expect the hostiles to turn on the friendlies?"

"Win or lose at Wood Lake in the morning, Little Crow will show much anger finding peace camp grow bigger than his own, many ahead, and many follow. Finally, we be strong to tell Taoyateduta-no more."

"Vot of Little Paul - Mazakutemani - Tiwakan and the others?"

Olaf inquired, a concern in his voice.

"They be back soon - long before cock crows. We will be brave."

"Good to see you, friend of long ago at Mendota." Olaf reached out with a handshake, "I vill be nosing around Yellow Medicine for avile. If I can't get over to the troops, I'll probably do more good on the business end of a shovel, helping you fellows. Get back safely, now."

Otakle scurried away on the trot.

Olaf peered from the bush to see many forms darting through the woods, but couldn't identify anyone, nor tell which were good and which were bad, for all had painted bodies. One observation was noteworthy to Olaf; there were a greater number of Indians moving to the West, a good sign. It would be foolish to try to reach the government troops now, Olaf thought, with the woods infested with so many warriors. He wished he could have relayed Godfrey's warning that the hostiles planned ambushing government troops early tomorrow morning on the Yellow Medicine road.

After an hour or two, the only sound to break the nocturnal quiet was the occasional hoot of an owl. A hazy moon waned above the woods giving an eerie, dismal setting for the expected tragic battle, Olaf thought. At any rate, he could see little sense in waiting, so decided to go back and help in the peace camp. He walked the considerable distance to Dancer Girl. She displayed nervousness at first, but after recognizing Olaf she bobbed her head and sputtered, showing approval of her master's return. The mare was allowed to set her own trotting pace while her master agonized over the ensuing conflict, destined to come.

Olaf was pleasantly shocked seeing the peace camp when he returned. He climbed down from Dancer Girl to notice that the number of lodges kept increasing. Some of Little Crow's braves had become traitors and mutinied, even before the final battle with Sibley's army. There were at least two hundred people diligently digging trenches around the camp.

As he approached, the braves frantically working to build their earthly fortress, Olaf saw the desperation in their faces. With the battle at Yellow Medicine yet to begin, all feared the expected wrath of the hostiles. Olaf walked about greeting the many hostages he knew, now being protected. Again, he saw Susan Brown, her entire family whom he had visited at Little Crow's house during the final battle of New Ulm, and many others: Mrs. Amos Huggins, Nancy and David Faribault, Mrs. Wakefield, and George Spencer - one of the few men protected from the murderers that fateful day of uprising. Oh, what cheerful smiles were on the raggedly clad prisoners, nearly three hundred, whites and mixed bloods, all captive for six weeks - most fearing being massacred by the renegades.

Olaf felt pain in his heart for those women who had been viciously beaten and raped, and tried to show them his compassion. He spoke with as many of the hostages as he could, then took a shovel to help dig. Although the hostiles were mostly Mdewakantons, Olaf was gladdened to know that Chiefs Taopi and Wabasha advocated peace and had taken the leadership to join the Wahpetons and Sissiton in opposition to the war. Olaf praised the men, his Lower Dakota friends, for their courage.

* * *

An amazing number of braves had returned from the battlefield throughout the night. Now, in the heat of tension no one slept. They kept digging relentlessly.

The camp was too far from the battleground to hear rifle fire, but all tensely watched as the autumn sun finally rose in full glory. Then, signs of the battle became evident as booms resounded down the river valley from fifteen miles away. Sibley's cannons had been activated. Anxiety mounted as a few, and then more of the peace party took up weapons in preparation of the anticipated confrontation. Everyone worried, wondering if Little Crow had been successful in his contrived ambush.

Two anxious hours passed, and then, the first of Little Crow's braves limped back, looking downcast. Several Mdewakantons hurried to the hostile camp, gathered their property and rushed over to join the peace forces. A feeling of optimism reflected off the faces of those who'd waited for this chance. There was no question that the friendly Indians now outnumbered the war party. However, Olaf knew that several of the converts were warriors with 'not clean hands,' and they would surely be punished.

Many antagonistic instigators shunned the peace camp, those most loyal to their Chief. Instead, they shouted insults and made vulgar death-threat gestures. As time dragged on, more and more of Little Crow's braves came back, dejected and humiliated in defeat. They said, "Because of moles dug in holes, their great Chief, Taoyateduta, had been thoroughly disgraced."

Little Crow rode his black and white pinto in a defeated posture as if to shy away from those he'd promised victory and glory. No more. The once revered Chief moved by, and surveyed the deteriorated state of his forces - many having already absconded to the protection of those who, all along, dared defy his military action.

Eyes were glued on the famous Chief as he rode back and forth between his and the larger friendlies' camp. Olaf felt the pain of defeat on Little Crow's expressionless face, and the anger and resentment within the once great leader over the total loss of his authority. Yet, he slowly paced his horse and glared at his loyal followers for a while, and then, at the great camp of deserters. No one from either side moved, in anticipation of some dramatic demonstration by the once great and bombastic Dakota Chief.

Olaf felt sickened for this man he knew had many good qualities. Taoyateduta had represented his people in Washington. Like his father and grandfather before him, he had tried to adapt to the white man's ways, but hadn't complied fast enough for many. He and his son, Wowinapi, had fished with Olaf many times, and the two large men found great delight in playing trickster with each other. These were things clouding Olaf's mind in Little Crow's humiliation before his Dakota legions.

Suddenly, Taoyateduta the warrior emerged once again. He

straightened in his saddle and assumed a powerful posture, then raised his hand in defiance. "I am ashamed to call myself a Dakota!" He thundered. "Nine hundred chosen warriors whipped by cowardly whites! Better run away and scatter out over the plains like buffalo and wolves!" He raved on, "Ho, the whites had big guns, better guns, and outnumbered us, five to one. That is no reason we should not have beaten them! We are brave men while they are weaklings!" He practically screamed the next line. "I cannot account for the disgraceful defeat!" He rode over closer toward the opposition camp and completed his tirade. "It is the work of traitors in our midst!" Then, he left. His warriors kept shouting insults and threats that they would kill all whites and mixed bloods by nightfall. The enemy warning aside, a feeling of confidence and superiority of strength dominated the attitudes of the friendly camp. They remained ready.

More Indians trickled in from the prairie. A group of murderers came by with a white women and two young girls they had captured. Tiwakan and his braves overtook them and saved the three destined to a barbaric life on the plains. Though the militants threatened violence, none took place.

* * *

As evening fell, curiosity ate at Olaf's heart, and little action took place except the saving of three more white prisoners. The Swede had the cunning of a wild cat, and wanted to know what was going on with Little Crow's maligned warriors. He rode to check it out. He ascended a small hill to observe Little Crow's camp, but didn't realize that in the moonlit night he presented a perfect silhouette for an enemy bullet. A clammy fog hugged the ground at the river bottom obscuring any clear vision of encampment. Olaf wondered if perhaps the camp had moved already.

"Taoyateduta? Oh, Taoyateduta, are you there?" Olaf shouted.

No answer or sounds of any kind came from across the river.

So he called again. "Taoyateduta? It is Tall Like Oak."

Olaf didn't know what to expect. Certainly the Chief wasn't going to be in a humorous mood, but maybe he would listen to someone who really felt pain in his heart for all that ended so tragically for the Chief.

A deep resonant voice spoke from close behind him. "In bright moonlight big man invite bullet."

Olaf whirled around. There was Little Crow, but he carried no gun.

"Why come, Tall Oak? To rub Taoyateduta's nose in the dung of defeat?"

Olaf was taken back at such a sardonic retort. Finally, he responded. "No, friend of years past, I come to tell Taoyateduta one vite man honors a man of good qvalities, and vants to speak to that."

"Ah, ha," Little Crow laughed, "I will be the one blamed for this war."

"I know better, Chief of all Dakotas. It vas Red Middle Voice and his vild men caused the murders and took vite vomen, not Taoyateduta. I know. I vill tell that for as long as I live."

"Well, there is no place here for the Dakota, now. All will be blown away like cottonwood fuzz in the wind."

"For that I am truly sorry, Taoyateduta, you ver not treated fairly. Some day, my friend, people vill realize how you fought for justice for your people, and you vill be honored as a great leader in time to come."

"Ah, ha," Little Crow laughed again, "I wonder. You have been good friend since lived where the rivers meet. Those were good times."

"Remember then, Taoyateduta, I am vun vite man who vill miss you." Both sat quietly in thought. "Chief, vot vill you do? Vare vill you go?"

"We are ready, our tents folded. We go to Dakota, far north, at Devil's Lake where we have traveled before. Some go to Canada. Some, west to big mountains for a breath of freedom from those who'd take that, in time. At least, for short while, there'll be clean fresh prairie air that harbors no ills to the Dakota."

"Taoyateduta, I vanted only to say good-bye, and vish you peace. Thank you for answering my call."

"I am one who thank you, Tall Like Oak. By coming, you have brightened Taoyateduta's heart. See my arms reach out to touch my friend, whose white brothers call 'Big Swede'." Olaf responded by grasping Little Crow's arms. Fixing their eyes on each other, both blinked in sadness before parting.

Olaf sat quietly. Finally, in the distance a deep resonant voice softly chanted, "Ooo-ah-ha-ai-ha-hi-o-wa... Ooo-ah-ha-ai-ha-hi-o-wa." Soon other voices joined in, then there were many, Ooo-ah-ha-ai-ha-haaaaa...." Olaf listened as the melancholy and sad voices faded in the distance.

* * *

For all basic considerations, the Sioux War was over. Little Crow and his legions: Shakopee, Medicine Bottle, Red Middle Voice, and the rest of his loyal warriors had evacuated their camp, taking their families to the upper Dakota prairie for the winter. Sibley did not have enough mounted men to pursue the party of two hundred, so their escape had gone unhindered.

Olaf waited to celebrate the grand entry of Colonel Sibley's forces a few days later: bayonets glistening in the bright sunny day, colors flying, drums beating, and fifes playing. The soldiers dressed in parade uniforms made an awesome display to the tattered and grubby three hundred whites and mixed blood prisoners. Most thought they would certainly die, but now cheered jubilantly. The friendly Indians were equally wild in demonstrating their happiness at being freed from the violence of their rebellious brothers. They waved flags and decorated their horses. Olaf noticed some of the young soldiers weeping in sympathy for the many women and children who went through the horrible seven week ordeal.

* * *

Days later a huge train of wagons was formed as the insensitive Major Galbraith took two thousand Indians back to the Upper Agency. Olaf felt angered and depressed seeing the Dakota men being corralled like savages. Revenge and resentment of all Indians was in the eyes of the conquerors who now saw them all as criminals. Reaching the Upper Agency, the burned out rock warehouse was used for screening and dividing the captives. Men were pulled aside, allowing women and children to return to their camps.

Galbraith sneered, "Finally, you get your gold payment! First, you must put your tomahawks, guns, and scalping knives in the barrels provided." The ecstatic Indian braves were willing to do that, of course.

Olaf, standing in the shadows, seethed, not believing what he saw. Then, the deceitful Major marched them into another area where they were chained-two together, an iron ring on the left leg of one, the other end to the right ankle of another. Terror and bitterness were in their faces.

Olaf was exasperated! "Thomas Galbraith, I've never seen a snake crawl any lower! You are a miserable disgrace to humanity! May God have mercy!"

"Oh c'mon, Swede, you're too soft on these heathens. I think the end justifies the means," Galbraith babbled pompously.

"Some of these brave men risked their own necks to save your vife and children from the Upper Agency and then took your family to safety." Olaf could feel the blood rushing to his head as he raged. "Damn you! You are a detestable coward!" His voice strained, he added, "Don't ever cross my path out of uniform, coward dog, or I'll beat the livin' daylights out of ya! That's a promise!" He'd seen more than he wanted, so Olaf angrily stormed out.

* * *

Olaf's frustrations didn't end with the humiliating chaining of all Dakota, including the honorable ones. The demeaning treatment against them was to continue. Immediately, a military commission was set up to try the Dakota who participated in the uprising. It didn't take long for the obvious mood of the commission to be established. If any Indian happened to be at the battlegrounds, armed or not, and he could not speak English nor defend himself, the death penalty rang out loud and frequent.

The first Dakota to be sentences to hang was Otakle, whom Olaf knew as a friendly supporter. Hundreds more would be condemned to hang.

Totally disenchanted with the mock court, the irate Swede left the unjustifiable travesty of justice, convinced the Indian was doomed to total banishment from the land that belonged to them and their forefathers for untold centuries. There was nothing more he, as a frontiersman, could do. He was needed back home to rebuild the Burbank horse and wagon business. So, riding off with Dancer Girl, he departed from a tragic period in the settling of the beautiful northwest country. He forced himself to think of positive things. He needed Marianne more than ever to bring a little sanity and happiness back into his life.

MUSIC SOOTHES

Olaf had become somewhat sophisticated through the years, due to Mr Burbank's exposing him to various cultural events. Olaf looked forward to attending the prestigious concert, so he could suppress tragic memories of the last few months. He thought it would be good for his lonely sister-in-law, Jenny, grieving Gustav's absence, as well as for her gracious sponsor, Matilda Washburn

The frontiersman sat entranced at the lyrical beauty emanating from the Swedish soprano, protégé of the world famous Jenny Lind. Gustav's Jenny had met the 'Swedish Nightingale' in Sweden, and had been inspired by her. The audience sat spellbound by the strains of the chamber orchestra and the brilliant voice. Olaf thought it was divine, like a spring day when nature resounds with the song of thrushes and larks.

Jenny, thrilled at being present at the performance, leaned over and whispered, "Isn't music wonderful for soothing our worldly troubles?"

"Oh, ja," Olaf whispered back, "makes me feel like all giddy-up. Gives a man goose bumps all over." She giggled. Others chuckled at her inadvertent outburst. He was pleased Jenny had momentarily overcome her loneliness from missing Gustav, off fighting the Civil War.

Matilda, a most respected entrepreneur, leaned over from his right and patted his arm, giving a gratuitous smile to show her appreciation for his escorting them to the concert.

"I feel honored to be in the presence of two such adorable ladies," he whispered to each.

It seemed everyone was there--the Burbanks, Sig Moens and John Blakelys, company associates; Governor Ramsey, the

Pillsburys, the Mendenhalls, all trying to find some diversion from the troubles of the day.

Seven encores were granted to the enchanted audience.

Olaf was downright proud escorting the two charming ladies in their stylish long formal gowns nodding greetings to the patrons, as they stepped into the fancy company coach he'd taken for the occasion.

Of course, Mrs. Higgenbottom was there with her prudish 'busybodies'. She gave a playful, but intimidating, shake of her finger. Olaf smirked - sheepishly - recalling that's what she'd done a few years ago when spotting him leaving the mansion late one afternoon.

Olaf declined a nightcap of Irish coffee at the mansion stating that he'd better get a good night's rest for the big meeting at Burbank's tomorrow.

* * *

The meeting of the Burbank executives had been going on all day.

"Men," J. C. expounded, "those German farmers and the New Ulm citizens are desperate to get on with reconstruction. Those several hundred buildings burned in town will be rebuilt within a year, I'm sure of that. Our business is flourishing as a result, but we're going to give a substantial discount in transportation costs so we can get our economy revitalized."

"How many rigs we got on the Southwest road now, Swede?" Associate Blakely asked.

"Ve're pulling a little better than forty right now, but I believe, by next veek, ve can up that by tventy more. I'll relocate another hundred horses to the changing stations - that is - if the mills can get the pine boards out," Olaf reported.

"It's amazing how Washburn Mill's expanded since Matilda took the reins, but hundreds of thousands of board-feet will be needed now that the Dakota are gone." Olaf shuffled in his chair, reminded of the tragedy. It was noticeably quiet for a spell.

"Swede, are you doing all right? Maybe we should take a short break. You know, men, we don't have to solve all the world's problems in one day," Burbank suggested.

"Nah. Nah, not for my sake, J. C. It's better to keep busy and there's no time to feel bad about anything. I'm doing fine, Sir," Olaf assured.

"Well, we'll soon wrap this session up. Sig, how you comin' with rebuilding the burned out stations?"

"Oh, they're not finished by a long shot, but they're functional."

"That's fine. Well, fellas I sometimes don't recognize excellence in achievement like I should, and I apologize for that. Damn it, you've all done one hell of a job these last weeks." J. C. smiled broadly, "God! What a team we put together in this fine enterprise!"

At that moment, Bizby, the messenger boy rushed in, breathless, and handed Mr. Burbank a note. A startled expression struck Burbank's face as he paused to read it. Noticeably disturbed, he quickly announced, "Gentlemen, that about does it for today. Thanks again."

Everyone seemed to sense the seriousness and began filing out. Olaf followed and hoped his kind boss would be spared any serious tragedy.

"Oh, Olaf, would you wait up a minute, please," Burbank called.

"Yes, sir." Olaf returned to offer any help he could.

J. C. approached the big fellow somberly, putting a hand on his shoulder. "Olaf, I have sad news! Matilda sent this note saying they got word about your brother, Gustav. He's been seriously wounded in battle."

Olaf walked to the window and peered out at a now blurry landscape, not saying a word. Finally, swallowing with difficulty, he murmured, "Lord, how I've agonized over this possibility." He turned, hoping to hear more positive news. "Did they say how seriously, Mr. Burbank?"

"The note just says - seriously, Swede."

"Oh, God," Olaf exclaimed, "Poor Jenny - and little Trena!" His voice cracking. "I must get over to the mansion right avay. I must remind Jenny, Gustav is a survivor. We Olssons all are!" he vowed optimistically.

"Olaf?" Burbank called.

Olaf paused, and turned. "Ja?"

"We'll all say a prayer for him, you know."

He gave an appreciative smile. "Thanks."

* * *

Driving the seven painful miles to the mansion, his thoughts flashed back to Sweden to when they were boys. Gustav had always idolized his big brother. When herding sheep on the hillside, Olaf kept telling of pursuing dreams, one being America. My, how Gustav's eyes would widen when Olaf described the great American prairie he'd read about. A land just waiting for people like them to go, breaking away from the grips of poverty.

And, then the family! Gustav hasn't heard of Papa's dying, even. How devastating when Mama hears of this, especially if it should snuff out Gustav's youthful and promising life, Olaf agonized .

He would have to wait, of course. Oh, how unpredictable life can be, he thought. I wish I could have gone with him, maybe I could have made a difference. But they said I was needed here to help resolve the Indian problems. What good did I do? Nothing! He lamented. Then his thoughts becoming positive again, "Oh, he'll be fine. He'll be fine," he mumbled.

Stiffening, he walked into the mansion unannounced. Matilda, standing in the alcove, smiled sympathetically and nodded toward the verandah. Jenny, obviously drained of tears, sat stunned in the high-backed wicker rocker, a dampened handkerchief crushed in her hand. She'd not seen him approach. He knelt down, putting his arm around her shoulder in a sensitive show of compassion, and she wept again.

Finally, after an endless silence, she sighed deeply, saying,

"Thank you for coming, Olaf." She smiled through her doleful eyes, continuing, "I have been saying powerful prayers for my beloved Gustav, praying God will bring him home to me."

"Oh, Jenny, I'm so sorry!" After a few moments he began, "I vish I had gone vith him. I alvays tried to look after him, ya know." She smiled compassionately and patted his great weathered hand in a mutual gesture of comforting to Olaf's pain.

"I feel I should have gone instead of him, just the same."

"No, Olaf. Don't blame yourself," she said resolutely. "Gustav mimicked you in every way - he worshipped you - and I pray he will come back and we'll be able to enjoy our beautiful family in this great country together."

The delicate 'Dresden doll' image he had of Jenny quickly faded, and he gave a surprised but confident smile at her strength. "You're a fabulous sister-in-law, Jenny," he said admiringly.

The hours passed. Matilda brought baby Trena out, placing her in Jenny's arms. She rocked and fed her baby most lovingly. They would be together many times in the coming weeks, Olaf promised, and though an uncertain future faced them, Jenny displayed an unyielding faith, showing a steadfast sense of courage.

✳   ✳   ✳   ✳   ✳

352

OLAF VISITS THE IMPRISONED

The downcast Swede lost his appetite, just picked at his breakfast, which he usually devoured with avengeance. He was missing his 'treasure' in the far north, resigned to the fact she couldn't come until the following spring. That, and the thought of his friendly Dakota down at Fort Snelling, fenced in like sheep ready for slaughter, pained him. Gustav off to the Civil War was a worry too.

He was having one dastardly time trying to get into the spirit of Christmas. There was little peace on earth, and not a whole lot of good will shown amongst men around the country this year. Olaf was wondering if he was simply in a bad mood. Others were at least trying to get into the spirit of the season. He would try, he decided.

He glanced out the window and gazed at the tundra, how last night's light snow brightened the landscape. Then he watched the black-garbed street corner carolers, led by none other than his old friend, Mrs. Higgenbottom and her blushing daughter, Nettie, who beat the dishpan like she was getting some real physical pleasure from it. As Nettie glanced in and saw Olaf watching her, she beat it harder. Well, they were singing a bunch of the old favorites. That was nice, he thought.

The aroma of pine from the bough decorations permeated the Nicollet coffee shop, and Tena the waitress, was humming along to the strains of the street carolers. Still, it was tough getting into the season spirit, and overcoming his melancholy.

Surprisingly, Matilda Washburn, came through the archway of the Coffee Shop. Immediately spotting Olaf, she made a beeline for his table.

"Good morning, Olaf, and Merry Christmas," she beamed.

"Ja, the same to you," he said with a weak smile and less exuberance.

"Hm. Olaf, I detect a rather gloomy Swede, I fear. Serious?"

"Naw, Matilda, just down in the doldrums a little," he moaned.

"Well, may I join you a minute?"

"Oh, sure. I'm sorry. Excuse my bad manners. Please do." She seated herself as he continued to make excuses for his strange behavior. "Naw, I'm not doing vell in accepting the ugly treatment the Dakota are getting. Hain't fair, Matilda."

"I heard they were attacked marching up here. How bad was it, Olaf?"

"The settlers became the savages! The Christian friendlies who risked their lives protecting vites for seven veeks ver bound and marched - a four mile column - all the vay to Ft. Snelling. Little George Crooks, six years old, lived, but his mangled body vill never heal right. His fourteen year old brother vas clubbed to death, vhile bound. I saw a baby torn from his mother, bashed to the ground. It died soon after. They call us civilized people?" Olaf shook his head, and then apologized for his gruesome account. "Awe, I'm sorry, Matilda."

"Oh, my big distressed friend. people can be so vindictive and revengeful, can't they?"

Olaf recanted. "No reason to put you through this. I'm sorry."

"No, we should all know what the real situation is. The newspapers don't print such truth. My dear friend, I really want to talk more about this, but I'll soon have to be at the mill," she apologized. Contemplating for a few seconds, she cheerfully tried to change the subject. "Olaf, you will join Jenny and Trena and me for Christmas Eve, I hope?"

Olaf softened noticeably. "Oh, sure, Matilda. You know I vould vant to be vith you all."

"That's great! Oh, yes, Jenny got another letter from Gustav! Guess what? He's feeling better! Says, by the grace of God, he hopes to be healed enough to be home by March or April. Isn't that wonderful?"

"Ah, that is vonderful news! Thank God! Jenny sure had a lot of faith in his recovering, didn't she?"

"Yes, that she did." A reflective pause followed. "Swede," she hesitated again, more than likely arranging her thoughts for her next consideration. "Swede, the new flour mills are going great

354

guns!'"

"I know. J. C. and I've discussed your phenomenal growth since you took over the reins after Mr. Vashburn's stroke. You deserve every bit of the credit. Since you've gone into grinding grain into flour, the expansion of your enterprise has become most obvious."

"Oh, no, Swede. I'm not soliciting praise. I've just been lucky, that's all. Thank you for the compliment, though," she smiled. "I've been mulling things over. You know, you've done amazingly well managing the large organization for Mr. Burbank, and well, he admits the role of the horse and wagon will diminish when the railroad comes through. So, to get to the point - I need someone with your talents and ability to help in the mill's expansion, Olaf."

He was absorbing every word flowing out of Matilda's mouth, and his self esteem was nearing the explosion point from her praises.

"Confidentially, I know of no one who'd qualify for the position better than you. You have proved yourself a leader of men, and have shown a keen aptitude for organization. Mr. Burbank has praised you for that many times in our conversations. Rest assured, Olaf, there are no personal considerations intended in this offer. When one recognizes such management capabilities, it is only natural for a company, such as this, to seek the best person to do the job."

"Matilda, thank you for those kind compliments. I am speechless."

"Olaf, the property on the bluff goes with the job. You and Marianne and your son would have everything any man could ever want."

"Matilda Vashburn, you flatter the hell out of this country boy! For sure, you've brightened my spirits." He stopped to light his pipe always feeling more secure exhaling those little puffs. "My dear lady, you humble me beyond vords. Please try to understand, Marianne is a mixed blood, I told you. In the concentration camp at Fort Snelling there are many mixed bloods being persecuted unjustly because they have some Dakota blood in their veins. I don't vant to embarrass my precious mate. Matilda, ve ver both raised in poverty and have dreamed of our own big piece of land vere ve could breathe unbigoted and unprejudiced air, and raise our family in a fresh, clean vorld. Matilda, my good employer, Mr. Burbank, has made it all possible by giving me a large tract of land north in Red River country, as you know, and that's vare I vant to be now."

"Swede, I guess I understand. Though I didn't see her, those who did, raved about her French appearance, and her incomparable beauty, of course." She glanced up at the wall clock. "Oh, oh. I really must get on to the mill," She stood, smiled warmly. "Well, I tried anyway. Olaf, the offer is a standing one, should you ever change your mind."

"Thank you, Matilda. You've brightened my day. I should really count my blessings - Gustav recovering, and all." He stood, smiling.

"Bye now. See you at Christmas Eve, then." She hustled out, leaving the frontiersman in a much happier mood.

* * *

Feeling inspired after Matilda's chat, Olaf rode Dancer down to the smoke shop for a good supply of his favorite southern grown pipe tobacco. Dozens of imprisoned Dakota men would be waiting for their regular treat of a good smoke and his warm encouraging handshake. So, with snow on the ground, Olaf bought a little extra to fill their pouches, as the north wind was now cutting cold. What would it be like when the temperature reached twenty-thirty below, with raging blizzards lashing at their breezy shelters, he wondered. How many would survive the sickness and cold?

Reaching the encampment, he descended the hill to the river bottom. A blanket of white smoke hung close to the ground, and the tips of the tepees looked like spires of pine poking through. Nearly two thousand Dakota, mostly women and children, struggled for life in that fenced hell-hole.

The guards were pleasant enough. In fact, they were much more sympathetic to the prisoners than Ramsey, Galbraith, and all the beaurocrats together, bowing to the demands of their constituency that all Indians be banished from the state forever.

"Morning, Big Swede. They've been coming out to the gate looking for ya," the young gatekeeper said, as he saluted.

"Fine, Martin. How's everything going?" Olaf returned the salute.

"Well, Swede, if I had my druthers, I'd rather be off to the Civil War. At least, one could feel pride and patriotic helping a sensible cause. Seein' people treated this way makes me sick in the guts. 'Don't sleep good at night." He continued, "Young ones are dying like flies from the measles epidemic. Father Ravoux brings boxes so they can have a decent burial. Nine died yesterday. I try to be friendly to them, Sir."

"Downright tragic! It's decent ya give them encouragement, Martin. You've got a good heart, my boy." He rode in.

Smoke drifted out of the open vents. Only few blanket-robed Indians meandered about the prison yard, most content, undoubtedly to keep as warm as they could within their own shelter.

Olaf stopped by one shelter where he heard mournful cries within. Only a few minutes before, the woman's young five-year old died of measles, he was told. He wondered if that might have been her last surviving family member, or hopefully, she had others to keep her from total devastation and loneliness.

Finally a few of the men came out in the cold. "Tall Like an Oak, *Koda, Koda,*" they called in greeting. Hearing his name, many came.

"*Token young he, Tiwakan,*" Olaf greeted the mixed blood, known as Gabriel Renville to the whites. He was followed by his young son, Victor. His father-in-law was Joseph Brown, the Indian agent for many years, and he and his brothers and cousins, like so many here, were Christian farmers who protected hundreds of white and mixed blood captives during the uprising.

Joseph La Framboise, also of a French father and Dakota mother, came along sporting his big bushy mustache. He had alerted the traders at Yellow Medicine early August 18, so they could escape. Then, he helped organize the Western Wahpetons and Sissitons against the hostiles.

Olaf greeted them all in his limited Dakota vocabulary. Thomas Roberson, a mixed blood, whose father was a Scotsman, could speak English fluently, and helped in interpreting the information Olaf had.

They all responded. "Good! Good!" when Olaf announced President Lincoln had reversed the death penalty for three hundred Dakota, the Military Commission had sentenced to hang at Mankato. Olaf named off as many as he could recall: *Wakanhinapi,* known to whites as Charles Crawford; *Wamdetonka,* Big Eagle, *Wakandayamani,* Lightning Blanket, and many others who were spared the hangman by the benevolent Lincoln.

Olaf shook hands with all those he knew as friends. He then went to his saddle bag and brought out an unusually large amount of *Cangde,* for they'd all brought their leather pouches along, certain the Swede would not let them down. "*Cangde! Cangde!*" they smiled in appreciation. "*Waste cangde*, Tall Like Oak."

He reminded his good friends he'd be back in a couple of days then waved good-bye. As the benevolent Swede was leaving, Missionary Williamson met him at the gate, and exchanged warm greetings.

"Swede," the Reverend spoke, "You are a kind and noble servant to your fellowmen." He chuckled, "Sometimes I think you have a more profound effect on their well-being than the four of us administering to their spiritual needs put together."

"Thank you, Reverend, but I'm not trying to vie for your jobs, ya know," he joked. John Williamson chuckled at the good humor.

Olaf gave Dancer Girl a little nudge with his heels. "Come on babe girl, let's move on up the hill, now." He blinked, having moist eyes.

A NIGHT OF GOOD CHEER

It was decided at the outset when Olaf arrived at the mansion, that this would be a night of joy and good cheer just for the four of them. Forget the heartaches and pains of the times, the grieving could continue tomorrow. Tonight, only happiness.

Olaf had arrived all dressed up in a new white pleated shirt adorned by the loudest bright red suspenders the ladies had ever seen. From the start Jenny giggled at her colorful brother-in-law.

"Where in heaven's name did you find those, Olaf?" she asked.

"Awe, I thought they looked kinda festive. 'Picked 'em up for a good price at Izak Rosenbloom's haberdashery this afternoon."

Matilda came out with a tray of Christmas grog to initiate the happy occasion. Jenny took about a thimble full, and later swore it tickled her funny bone, and made her feel like floating in air.

The wealthy Matilda really fussed, roast goose and all the trimmings. Olaf gorged himself. Finally, pushing his chair away from the table, he groaned, "I'm stuffed! Absolutely stuffed! Matilda, your roast goose, raisin dressing, and everything vas best I've ever eaten! If I eat another bite though, I think I'll pop."

"Oh, no, Olaf. You must have some of my creamy plum pudding," Matilda pleaded.

"She made it just for you, Olaf," Jenny added.

"Vell, then, if I must, I'll have to make a little room." He stretched his arms up, and raised his chest, as if that would help settle his stuffed stomach. Suddenly, he looked startled as one of his suspenders snapped loose and slapped the table, whack!

Jenny went into convulsions, "Olaf popped," she yelled.

Matilda got caught up in the silliness. Laughing so hard, she had to excuse herself to the kitchen. The jovial snickering continued until she returned with the dessert. It was Christmas

Eve, and things were moving along fine, not a sad or painful subject dented the festive chatter at dinner. The gracious hostess insisted she clear the table, refusing any assistance from the others offering help. She wanted the kids to have a good time, she said.

A little foreign sound came from down the hall. Jenny excused herself to investigate the suspected cause. Appearing with baby Trena, who'd become hungry and begged for nourishment, doting mother successfully satisfied her hunger pangs. Of course, Olaf wanted to hold and rock the darling cooing babe for a while. It wasn't long till the little tyke was off to another stint in dreamland, so Jenny tucked her back in bed.

"Are you ready to open the gifts, my dears?" Matilda asked. Receiving unanimous agreement, she suggest they move into the drawing room where a warm crackling fire awaited them.

Just like little kids, Olaf and Jenny started shaking their packages, trying to guess what goodies awaited them. "Oh, this is such a grand festive evening we're having," Matilda said, accentuating the pledge that only happy thoughts be shared. "Olaf, you do the honors and distribute the gifts," she suggested.

"Ho! Ho! Ho!" He bellowed, playing Santa Claus. "Here is vun for you, Matilda; and here is yours, my dear sister-in-law."

"And here is yours from me," Jenny beamed.

"Olaf, being that we always open our Washburn gifts on Christmas morning, and you'll have two to open tonight. I suggest opening mine first."

Hastily tearing the wrappings, Olaf was elated finding an impressive leather business case from Matilda. "Look at this! Vow! Now I can throw away that old ratty thing I've been using all along. My, vill the boys down at the office take notice ven I flash this at 'em." On further investigation, he found a secret compartment containing a full flask of brandy. He cackled wildly, "This just might see me through a treacherous vinter trip, I tell ya." The women giggled at that.

Jenny begged off till last, wanting to savor the anticipation of her surprise package. Matilda would open hers from Olaf next.

The women raved about his artistically wrapped gifts.

"Awe, heck! You know I'm all thumbs. Frankly, Myrtle, down at Max Vinter's Emporium did the fancy," he admitted.

"What a gorgeous brooch! Why, it's just beautiful, Olaf!" Matilda gasped. "And the stone is a huge amethyst, my birthstone! How did you know that, you big generous, lovable Swede?"

"A little bird told me." He winked at Jenny.

"Olaf, open mine next," Jenny begged. "I hope you like it."

He took his time, loosening one end of the ribbon, took a sip of his coffee, and prolonged the excitement. Chuckling at the grinning Matilda and the simpering Jenny, he finally retrieved the present from the package.

"Oh, my goodness!" Holding up the long woolen scarf, admiring the workmanship in the natty garment, he gave a gracious smile. "I've alvays vanted a varm muffler like this, Jenny. It's beautiful!"

"She's spent long happy hours knitting it, Olaf. She really adores her brother-in-law, you know."

He leaned over and gave Jenny a hearty hug in appreciation.

Jenny beamed with excitement, about to open her gift from Olaf. "It's a little bigger than a shoe box, she admitted, and it's pretty heavy." She placed it on the table to remove the object from the box.

"Here, I'll help you," Olaf came to her rescue. He lifted it out of the box and set it on the serving table in front of her.

"Oh, my! Oh, my!" she exclaimed. "Is it what I think it is?" She was almost becoming hysterical. "It is, isn't it? My Lord, it's a music box!"

Olaf could only grin at her elation as she touched the finely varnished wooden case, and studied the intricate interior through the top glass. The round cone was covered by hundreds of tiny pins. Then she read from the card attached inside, 'Selections from Brahms.'

He chuckled at her excitement. "Here, dear Jenny, I'll vind it and play some." It started playing.

"Brahms' Lullaby!" she drooled. "Oh, such heavenly music! Sounds just like a harpsichord, doesn't it?"

The three sat admiring their gifts, listening to the music box, and visited joyously for some time.

"I have a few things to do in the kitchen," the gracious hostess said overruling any assistance from her two eager guests. "Jenny, I think it'd be lovely if you'd play the new pieces you've learned on the piano. You've become accomplished, my dear."

"Oh, I would be delighted! Come along, Olaf, I can play a new piece by Frederic Chopin, a French-Polish composer, I believe. It's called 'Nocturne' - Opus nine - Number two. Oh, he writes such beautiful music."

He took her arm, escorting her back to the music room.

"Oh, Olaf, I'm so thankful for your kind visits these last months. Sometimes I look down the roadway, hoping to see you coming up with your buggy, or on Dancer Girl, as you do sometimes."

"My dear Jenny, I relish our time together, too."

They came to the archway; she stopped suddenly, tittering a bit. Olaf glanced down at her mischievous face, and noticed her playful eyes glancing up, and then to him, and back up again.

Finally catching on, "Ah ha, Matilda's festive decorations. Vouldn't you know it! Mistletoe!"

Jenny leered playfully - and enviously - so Olaf reached over and drew her to him and kissed her tenderly. Caught up in the magic of the moment, the embrace had obviously become more sensual than either intended. Olaf was certain of that, having felt Jenny's small body begin to tremble. It seemed as though neither wished to break the spell, lest reason take over and end the overwhelming sensation.

Olaf restrained himself, sensing Jenny's innocent vulnerability. "I vould love to hear you play for us now, my dear."

"I will try, Olaf, but I'm weak beyond words." Her face was hot and flushed and she fanned herself with her hand in frustration.

It was an uneasy moment for both, Jenny trying to manage her shaking hands as she sat down at the large square grand piano. Olaf wanted to say something, but was temporarily tongue-tied.

"This is a lovely song; I'll do my best," she said breathlessly.

Beginning to play, she struggled at first, but soon her head began swaying in tempo to the melodic theme. Confidence returning, a tiny smile came across her face. She looked up at Olaf, who nodded in appreciation for her lilting music, and she spoke as if the chords inspired her thoughts.

"It's strange, Olaf, you being so considerate, endearing, and supportive," then she'd play a few more bars, and continue, "at times I almost think you are Gustav, you look and act so much alike."

Not wishing to disrupt her enchanting music, he spoke quietly, "I know, Jenny. I absolutely adore you, and find my time vith you most gratifying."

After a long pause in the conversation, she continued pouring out her feelings. "Olaf, I am a God-fearing person. I was raised that way. A few minutes ago my body did not respond to my mind." Olaf smiled in agreement. "I have to confess, brother-in-law, I have given thought to what would happen if my husband would not return from the war, and I hoped then, you'd love me. Isn't that sinful?"

Olaf chuckled softly. "Ya know, my dear, I have had the same thoughts ven I'm lonely and it seems impossible I'll ever be united vith my distant love. Sweet Jenny, don't lament over yielding to such a minor amorous distraction. Your heart vouldn't let you stray too far, nor vould I ever betray the trust my brother has in me. It's the times, so frustrating."

She played on for several minutes, but softened her music, and smiled. "Those were nice things you said." Playing on some, and with a glint in her eye, she added coyishly, "I doubt, Olaf, if I'll ever forget the feeling of that kiss just now."

"Nor vill I," Olaf nodded in agreement.

Matilda was standing at the door, he noticed from the corner of his eye. How long she'd been there was uncertain, but by her quizzical smirk, he assumed she'd overheard some of the conversation. She, too, eyeing the green sprig with the little yellow flowers and the pearl like berries, demanded some attention. So, he slowly moved behind the piano chair and responded cordially with a good firm hug and a robust kiss. Matilda rolled her eyes back in silly jest and pretended fainting. Then, both walked slowly around the piano and became attentive to the performance. The music was reaching a crescendo, and the tempo slowed as the piece ended. The two applauded her work.

"Jenny, you sure get a lot of beautiful sound out of this big block of vood you're sittin' at. I've alvays loved your playing, but that vas the best ever."

"I agree," Matilda echoed. "Someday, when you get into your fine permanent home, that's going to be your instrument, my child."

Jenny went into a mild frenzy at the thought of having such a magnificent piano for her future home, and on a little urging, she played a portion of Brahma Intermezzo. The musical interlude contributed an ecstatic fineness to the evening.

"Let's go back to the drawing room and sit by the warm fire for a while longer," Matilda urged, "and I'll bring something festive, as we enjoy our blessed Christmas."

"Sounds delightful" Olaf agreed, "but I vill have to leave in time, for I'll have a long vay to travel tomorrow."

"Olaf, it's a pity having to work Christmas Day," Matilda said, as she moved away toward the kitchen door and waited for his answer.

"Oh, I have to, uh" - He caught himself, remembering nothing sad or negative would be brought up this evening. "Oh yes, I vill bring Christmas greetings to several folks who have few friends at all, tomorrow."

Matilda then went into the kitchen. Jenny and Olaf sat looking at the fire, both smiling over an obviously delightful evening. Then the gracious hostess returned with a tray of tiny stemmed cordial glasses containing a festive liqueur. "Here, let's have a little Benedictine with the coffee and cream I added. It'll warm the cockles of your heart, for sure."

"Will it make my nose tingle again?" Jenny quipped, jokingly.

"No, of course not. It'll just make you feel mellow and warm inside," Matilda said grinning.

"The evening has already made me feel warm" she reflected with a coy grin toward Olaf.

Jenny smiled at the melodic strains from the music box. There were kind thoughts exchanged in the sharing of Matilda's wonderful dinner, and everyone seemed to get just the perfect gift this year.

"Now, I must really move on, my dear ladies. It is rather late." Olaf rose to leave.

"Well, if you must, I'll get your coat and hat," Matilda offered.

"Jenny, as chilly as it is tonight, your Christmas present is going to be put to immediate use. I think I'll vear it." He winked at her.

"Please do." Jenny urged. "And our thoughts will be with you on Christmas Day, my brother-in-law."

"And mine with you both at the mansion," he concurred, then kissed and warmly hugged both Jenny and Matilda as he left.

As Olaf rode away in his sleigh, his new warm muffler wrapped about his neck, he smiled on one of the most enjoyable and heart-warming Christmas Eve's of his life.

❋   ❋   ❋   ❋   ❋

AN ACT OF SHAME

On this bone chilling morning, Olaf was riding south on his sturdy gray mare. He wore his wide brimmed hat, sheepskin coat with the high fleece lined collar, and his new scarf wrapped around his face and neck allowing only a thin slit to peer through. Jenny couldn't have given a more appreciated gift, he thought.

His mind was charged with thoughts of the enchanting night just passed. Why can't life be filled with such pleasantries all the time, void of such conflict now tearing the country apart? He wondered.

It was an all day ride, only a few stops at company stations so Dancer could rest and feed some. She was still strong, but being twelve years old, he wouldn't push her too hard on this frigid Christmas day.

The long grueling ride ended after sunset, as he approached the town of Mankato. A primitive atmosphere prevailed; the saloons filled with revelers, and the overflow gathered in the square in gangs of angry, vengeful characters. There was little peace on earth, and these men were demonstrating no good will.

"Death to the Sioux!" They shouted, while waiting the grand affair.

Thirty-eight condemned Sioux would be hung in the morning at 10 a.m. in the town square, and throngs of spiteful whites had descended on Mankato. The Military Commission had sentenced three hundred additional Sioux to hang. They were frightened like caged wild animals. Imprisoned near the scaffolds, they feared the worst. Though President Lincoln had granted a reprieve, they had not been told, so they asked for their friend, Tall Like Oak, to come and hear their pleas for mercy.

Olaf's statuesque presence on his great horse quieted the noisy crowd. He circled the square illuminated by numerous bonfires, which had been hastily set by unruly gangs. He rode to the newly built structure, elevated high off the ground, and observed the pillars which supported a framework of beams around the edge of the platform. Thirty-eight nooses swung in the cold wind, creating a sinister, chilling setting.

"Hello, Swede. How goes it, Swede?" some gave distant greetings. Olaf didn't answer, thinking his greeters were there only for the thrill of seeing men hang. He rode to the hotel a block up the street.

Cold and tired, he sat in the corner and downed a bowl of ham and bean soup. There was nothing to say to anybody now. The only reason he came was to fulfill the promise made to Chief Big Eagle, and the three hundred imprisoned Dakota fearing the angry crowd would kill them, too. Major Brown and a few officers from the Seventh Regiment came into the lunchroom. Noticing Olaf, Brown shuffled over to say hello.

"Swede, my friend, I wondered if you were coming down. The Sioux were asking for you. May I sit a minute?" he asked.

"Sure, Major. I just rode in less than a half hour ago."

"Now that I'm representing the government in this mess, I must admit I'm rather torn between sympathizing with the defeated, who I'd worked with as agent for so many years, or reveling in making the country an exclusive place for my white European brothers." He scratched his head in contemplation. "Damn it! I wish there'd been some common ground for settling the war, but Little Crow dug himself in too deep."

"I know," Olaf returned, not eager to debate what transpired. He was baffled the ex-Indian agent had suddenly switched his allegiances.

"Swede, the citizens are adamant in seeing justice served."

"I understand, Major." Olaf still avoided getting involved.

"Well, I'm going to try to get some sleep, if I can, sooo," he stood as if to go. "Oh yes, Olaf, Susan and the children were treated well while in Little Crow's confinement. She spoke of your visit and the reassuring conversation she had with you. I appreciate that."

"Thank you, Major, it vas a most amiable meeting."

As Brown walked away, Olaf wondered what might happen to Mrs. Brown, a half blood Dakota, and the part Indian offspring. Would they be banished, too? Not likely, he figured.

* * *

The Swede slept little, too much noise and hell raising through the night. He was up before sunrise and made his way down to the huge log jail to offer what little condolences he could. The thirty-eight condemned were in a separate stall within the jail. He hadn't planned on seeing them, but through the cracks of the boards, Father Ravoux and colleagues could be seen administering to the Christian converts. Many of the doomed, in strict Dakota tradition were painting their faces, and had already begun singing their death cry. "Hi-yi-yi-yi, Hi-yi-yi-yi," they chanted. Others sat stoically silent, much more becoming to a Dakota brave, ready to meet his Great Spirit with dignity.

Though outside was cold and airy, the jail was dark and dank. Olaf could hear many of the inmates coughing from colds, and possibly pneumonia.

"Which of these Indians would you like to talk to, Swede?" One of the soldier guards asked, having recognized Olaf from previous visits.

Olaf smiled and said, "All of them! I'll see Vamdetanka, first. You know him as Big Eagle. He asked that I come see all three hundred."

Proud Big Eagle shuffled toward Olaf. *"Hangska Utuka! Koda, Koda!"* Soon other voices were heard, *"Hangska Utuka? Hangska utuka?"* Many called Olaf in Dakota, but others called him Big Oak or Tall Oak in English. Their chains clanged as they gathered around their white friend. Everyone greeted, *"Koda, Hangska Utuka."*

Olaf passed his tobacco. In minutes the air was thick and smoky. The three hundred were uneasy. *"Unkiyepi Ta? Unkiyepi Ta?"* We die! We die! They feared, hearing the wild commotion from the street.

The Swede assured them they would not be harmed; that a reprieve had been granted them by their great benevolent President Lincoln. They had been told that before, but didn't believe those who had lied to them time after time, they said. Olaf promised he'd work to get their prison sentences reduced, and eventually, pardons from the government. He praised them for being honorable Dakota who helped save whites, and opposed the war from the start. Eventually the terrifying fear in their sickly eyes disappeared and they thanked Olaf for his efforts to their cause.

Olaf agreed, there should be severe punishment for murderers and rapists, many soon to climb the eight steps to the scaffold, including the vile Cut Nose, who was the head of the soldier's lodge; the real perpetrators of the war. He was saddened, though, for a few caught up in the confusion of the trials like Rdainyanka, Chief Wabasha's son-in-law, who would not steal or hurt any man. He did not deserve to die with the likes of the vicious White Dog, Red Leaf, or murderous Cut Nose.

With time drawing near, Olaf dejectedly went out to the town square where the fourteen hundred troops assigned to keep order were taking their positions. Rows and rows of armed soldiers were aligned, shoulder to shoulder, in a perfect rectangle thirty feet from the scaffold. Behind them, at twenty feet, another double row. Then a line of horses, side by side, held their riders in rigid parade form.

The crowd of raucous citizens gathered behind, and farther back, people leaned out of windows and sat on roofs for a better view. Checking his pocket watch, he noted, at exactly ten o'clock, the condemned were marched to the scaffold between rows of soldiers. All was precisely on schedule.

The chains had been removed, but cords were tied about their arms as they were led, like dogs on a rope, to view their last glimpse of light and inhale their final breath of air. The "Hi-yi-yi-yi," Dakota death song came in earnest now, and the eerie cry made Olaf's flesh cringe from chills.

The crowd's excitement reached a near deafening roar as the thirty-eight mounted the steps and were placed under their respective nooses, but then the on-lookers quieted, as the deathly wailing intensified. The attendants reached up and secured the nooses. The hoods were lowered over their heads--against frenzied objections. The wailing reached deafening intensity, overshadowing the crowd's cheering. A role of the drums sounded once, twice, and three times. The rope holding the platform was cut-thirty eight flailing warriors were soon to lose their last battle.

A wild cheer followed! Then, all became noticeably quiet, as if the mass of humanity felt the guilt of this blasphemous act. Some crossed themselves; a few of the women fainted, and one vomited near where Olaf stood. Still, a few brazen characters shouted insults to the deaf ears. Gradually and slowly the streets cleared as attendants began removing the dead bodies and placing them on wagons.

Olaf stood in a confounded stupor for a long time, but aware of being conspicuously distressed, he decided to shuffle away. He had company business to transact at the Burbank station the rest of the day, but his mind was clouded from the deathly horror, and little was to be accomplished. Later, Olaf watched as horse drawn scoops excavated a trench near the river where the thirty-eight bodies were disposed and barely covered with a foot of earth.

When evening arrived, his mind still reeling, he decided to take a long walk about town to contemplate this dismal day. For some unbeknownst reason, he found himself heading down through the trees to where the new grave was. He was shocked to see several men and horses and a wagon there. He moved closer within the shadows and listened.

"This one is Cut Nose, Dr. Mayo -- the one you're to have. The bearded one is Baptiste Campbell, part Scott. Dr. Jennings is to have him. And this one goes to Dr. Meecham," the voice directed.

"Fine. Fine. Then load them in the wagon and haul them to my place in La Sueur for now. Gentlemen, my sons will learn osteology from this cadaver, Cut Nose. He is worth more to humanity now than when he was alive, no doubt." The men laughed over the remark.

"Thank you, Dr. Mayo, for notifying us of the opportunity to get real human bodies. A man shies away from buying specimens from grave diggers: might get that of a respectable person, you know."

Olaf backed away dejectedly, agonizing over the plight of the Indian, and reflecting on his twelve years in America. He couldn't remember one promise the government had kept. Not one treaty had been honored. He only remembered friendly Native Americans chased from their hunting grounds to a barren prairie, where they starved and died like flies. Now, those remaining were fenced in like cattle, their numbers diminishing like the buffalo on the plains. His heart filled with anguish, and his eyes welled up with tears, he headed back home with Dancer Girl, his most faithful friend.

BROR GUSTAV HOBBLES HOME

Office work wasn't one of Swede's most appealing tasks, but there were schedules having to be posted and a large organization was dependent on it. He worked out of the Burbank Stage Office in the Winslow House Hotel these days. The horse and wagon business was booming again.

Having just returned from St. Paul and a meeting with J. C., he asked Amy, the office clerk, for an updated report on Concord arrivals through the morning.

"Swede, the first coach from New Ulm was on time, but the Stillwater Stage was only fifteen minutes late. Not bad for this kind of weather, I guess."

"Not bad? I think it's terrific!" Pulling on his watch fob he added, "Should be one in from the southeast pretty soon."

Amy strolled over to the window for a look. "Here comes a stage from Prairie du Chien now, I think," she called back.

"Oh, good," Swede acknowledged. "They made good time in this devilish frigid veather." Olaf sauntered over for a look. "Holy cow! Those ponies are hot, putting out a cloud of steam. Erik must've really been pushin' 'em. He better get 'em down to the stable right avay so they don't come down vith pneumonia."

"Oh, I'm sure he will, Swede. Erik's a good one."

"Ja," Olaf smiled, "those guys are something. Damned reliable."

Noticing the rig was loaded with passengers, and a lot of baggage--the boots and the top rack full--he threw his heavy mackinaw on. "Think I'll go out and give 'em a hand," he said, hurrying out.

Not only being generous in helping his drivers, he relished in extending greetings to all. "Velcome to God's country," he'd say, always the self appointed public relations' crier for the Chamber of Commerce. He loved putting people in a good mood.

Amy had a hot mug of coffee ready for the driver, as usual. Erik's nose was as red and shiny as an apple and he laughed jovially through his handlebars, accepting the warming treat.

"Pretty cold riding, Erik?" Amy asked, expecting a usual wisecrack.

"Cold! I guess so." It was time for the old driver to spring one of his jokes, undoubtedly one he'd told before. "I saw a couple jack rabbits playin' tag out there on the frozen tundra, and -- it was so cold, one had to push the other to get 'em started."

"Oh, you old rascal, Erik," Amy giggled and blushed.

But, Erik Severson's joking mood changed suddenly. "Olaf, I've got important news for ya. Didn't want to spring it on ya till we got everybody unloaded."

"Vot is it? Vot is it, man?" Olaf recognized his seriousness.

"Gustav, your brother, will be coming in real soon. A whole load of the poor devils are coming home from the battlefield, and it isn't pretty, my friend."

"How soon? How soon?" Olaf laughed nervously. "Thank God! How did he look? Tell me man!" He begged, anxiously.

"I only saw he had both legs and arms, about the only one, but he's well wrapped up. He hobbles with a crutch, though. The mud-wagon was waiting for another rig from the south, but the driver said they'd be heading up within the hour if it didn't show-one way or the other."

"My God!" Olaf raved, "Vot vonderful news! He'll be fine!" He pulled out his watch. "Oh, I'll never have time to run for Jenny! Erik, have the boys send a rig vith good tight panels. Vill ya?"

"Sure. I'll run right over to the barn and do that."

Amy tried settling her boss down, but he paced nervously and kept looking out the window for sight of the mercy wagon. Olaf ran to the window to check out every horse drawn rig passing by in hopes it would be the military coach. Time dragged on. He made several trips outside, stomping a path in the snow to the

373

corner in hopes of seeing the coach. Finally, his surveillance seemed to pay off. The closed mud-wagon pulled up. Olaf dashed out like a flash in anxious anticipation. A medical aide hopped out first, to expedite a quick unloading.

"Mister," he called to Olaf. "We need some help to get these men inside! Their bodies are cold from lack of circulation."

"Yes sir. There'll be plenty of help, don't vorry," Olaf assured.

The anxious Swede was about to call for help, but it was not necessary. Folks came running frantically from all points, once they could see wounded soldiers had returned from the war. Everybody had sons, brothers, or fathers in the Civil War, and many came in dire hopes of greeting their loved ones. The first out was Emil Raftavold from St. Anthony Falls. He had lost an arm. The second man Olaf didn't know, but he had no feet, just stubs. Two men carried him into the warm hotel.

Olaf desperately looked in the wagon with the leather side panels, it was dark as pitch. Other maimed soldiers were helped out, and Swede's heart pounded with tense expectation. Finally, a tall gaunt man leaned out of the opening, a leg and an arm heavily bound. The medical attendant helped him out and to the ground, handing over a hickory crutch for support.

"Gustav! My God, how glad I am to see you, bror," Olaf shouted.

"Hello, bror." He answered, his eyes watering, as Olaf's were. He looked around. "Jenny? Where's Jenny? And baby Trena?"

"Gustav, I just heard of your coming, and had no time to fetch Jenny. I have sent for a closed rig, and I'll take you home. Come in and warm up some." Olaf helped support his brother's frail body. Amy brought coffee.

Gustav was very stiff from the confining travel so was content to stand and shuffle about, getting the kinks out. Then, Olaf, putting his arms around Gustav, consoled him, and raved about his beautiful baby.

Words did not come easy, driving to the mansion, both were caught up in the tension of the moment. Olaf finally spoke reassuringly.

"Jenny's fine, Gus. She had so much faith and fortitude. Alvays displayed the strength of a saint." Gustav nodded and smiled. "You look kinda peaked though. It must have been tough, bror."

Gustav remained silent for a spell. Then, measuring his words, said, "It was Hell! The best part was when I was out of my head. Didn't know anything."

"How long ver you like that? Vare did it happen, Gus?"

"Oh, they said about two weeks. At Bull Run - second battle." He paused for a few moments, and then, reliving the tragedy, "It was just before I got hit was the worst. We lay all night, more dead than alive, all around. Moaning and crying was terrible," he sobbed.

"Ja, sure. Better not talk about it now. Think of Jenny, Gus."

"Oh, don't worry, I'll never tell her the bad part, it's just that I worry about Jenny putting up with less than a whole man," he gasped.

Big brother looked shocked. Was there more wrong than he knew? "Gustav, you've got your arms, and legs. Is there more you're not telling me, Gus? Vot do ya mean, not a whole man?"

Gustav grunted, giving a restraining chuckle. "Oh, Olaf, don't make me laugh. It hurts too much." He held his side. "No, I got all my vital parts, if that's what ya mean. Now I know I'm home again. I forgot how to laugh, I think. 'Feels good," He sniffled and laughed at the same time.

Olaf grinned. "Vell, ya had me vorried there for a minute."

"I've always admired you, bror. I don't look any worse than you did after the shipwreck, so I'll be all right, soon."

"Ah, Jenny's going to be so happy. She'll get you vell in no time."

He smiled pensively, "I hope so." Then he shifted as if to ease some pain. After a bit, he asked. "Olaf, how are the folks?"

Olaf wanted to avoid any more heartache, but he couldn't lie. "Vell Gus, sorry to have to tell you, but Papa died last fall." It quieted. He noticed a few tears flow down Gustav's cheek. "Ve didn't vant to write it. Vie make it vorse, ya know." Gustav nodded his head affirmatively. "He died peacefully in his sleep,

375

Mama said. Gus, Papa wrote more'n once, how proud he vas, especially of his youngest *poijka*. I think you ver alvays his favorite."

"Awe, that was only cuz I was the littlest, ya know."

Again, quiet time for contemplation.

"There's the mansion ahead, Gus! Excited?"

Gustav smiled broadly. "Like I'm 'bout to go out of my mind! 'Feel a little uneasy about intruding on Mrs. Washburn, though."

"Nonsense! Matilda vants you to stay until you're vell. Vith Mr. Vashburn gone, she needs the company, too." Olaf knew it would be an emotional homecoming, and the family would need the initial time together. "Bror, after I help you in, I'll not hang around - you two'll need time for yourselves. I'll come back tomorrow and ve'll rehash some of our old times together. Vot do you say?"

"Thanks, big bror. You've always been my example. I want you to know I thought about you very much. It gave me courage."

Jenny waved out the window, more than likely thinking it was probably Olaf paying another kind, friendly visit. When the buggy stopped, as Olaf walked around to open the side door, Jenny flew out without a coat of any kind, screaming, "Gustav! Gustav! Oh, thank God, my prayers have finally been answered." They held each other and wept quietly.

It was a touching scene. As Olaf watched, they entwined in a most tender, rapturous hug. Assisting his brother into the mansion, Olaf gave a quick, brief, welcome home, promising to return tomorrow when Gustav'd had a chance to rest some. It was clear, observing their expressive faces, the reunited longed to be alone.

* * *

After leaving the mansion the previous day, a completely exhausted Olaf avoided the routine of his office, opting to seek out a quiet place for thought and reflection on the past eventful months. For some strange reason, the wheels on his rig took him to the Old Wooded Horse Saloon where he sat, casually sipping a foamy beer. Gustav's return was thrilling, but now, Jenny wouldn't even need his help filling time. Olaf was envious and lonely. He could only wait for Marianne, now the days would drag like years.

Driving back to see Gustav, he recalled his pleasure in talking with old Jake Honneker about the first exciting years with those gala nights: girlee shows, wrestling matches, oyster feeds, and the like. It was probably a silly diversion but the Swede needed to clear his mind of all the tragedy cluttering his life. He and Jake laughed, remembering how he won the strong man event, even after overcoming the adversity of his unscrupulous opponent.

Jenny answered the door displaying her animated joy.

"Oh come in, dear Olaf, your brother is feeling much better today, having rested in our big comfortable bed. He slept like a baby most of the night," she chattered excitedly.

"That's good news, Jenny. I vas sure you'd pamper him vith sveet loving care - the best medicine there is," he grinned.

She led him into the sitting room where Gustav was half reclining on the imported French couch he remembered well. Stopping in the archway, he stood to observe, unnoticed. There, the returned war hero lounged under a white chenille cover, his head and shoulders propped up on several soft pillows. Like royalty! Olaf mused to himself. He winked at Jenny, who snickered a bit.

"Gustav. You have company," she announced brightly.

He looked over, amazingly transformed in appearance. Jenny must have spent the whole time catering to her special man, Olaf figured, for his hair and beard had been trimmed immaculately, and looking like an altogether different person from the decrepit raggedy war veteran stumbling out of the stage yesterday.

"Come in. Come in, my bror," he beckoned in his normal resonant voice, contrary to the hollow speech of the previous day. Jenny pushed a soft chair next to the bed so the two could be close, and then excused herself to fetch some coffee and pastries she'd been baking for her heroic soldier.

Olaf put his hand out and clasped Gustav's right hand, his other being supported by a clean fresh sling. The two just sat and looked at each other, communicating by smiles and chuckling.

"Vell, how ya feeling this morning, Gus?"

"Oh, much, much better. But, I'd be a damned liar to say there's no pain, I tell ya." He grimaced as he altered his position.

"I remember vell enough. Pain is something you'll have to live vith for a year, I expect, thinking back on my own, years ago."

"Ja, I used to feel so sorry for ya back then. Now maybe I'll get a little sympathy back, I suppose," Gustav said jokingly. "Dr. Thompson was here this morning. I'd have been so embarrassed if my dear Jenny hadn't bathed me good. I stunk like a cow barn, but when she got through, I smelled like Mrs. Washburn's flower garden."

The two bantered and laughed.

"Here, Olaf, take a look at my wound." He threw the cover off revealing his thin mangled leg. "I don't need to wear that awful tight binding anymore. Much of that was done so I could withstand the trip, anyway."

"Oof! That is a bad one." Olaf studied it closely. "My, that shot took an awful lot of your flesh, too, didn't it? It's lucky you didn't bleed to death, my bror." His eyes moistened.

Jenny brought some warm muffins and coffee, fetched baby Trena for doting father to fuss over for a while, till sleep would take over. She pulled up a chair, and they visited like in old times.

Gustav raved on about getting back to the farm he'd left by going to war, felt it was his patriotic duty to go. But now, he promised, as soon as he got well, he was anxious to get on with their beautiful lake country farm out at New London.

Olaf could see the desperation in Jenny's face, and he was sure she hadn't told of the West Lake Massacre in which their friends, the Peter and Andrew Broberg, and Anders Lundbergs--thirteen of them--all shot and tomahawked by the hostile Indians only six months ago. The kids had traveled with them, in caravan, only a few years before to establish their Lake County farm out at New London.

Jenny's hands were shaking from the anguish she was suffering. "You boys have got much man talk to discuss. Would you like me to play the piano some, while you visit?"

"Oh, yes, please do, Jenny. I'd like that," Gustav said.

It was time for little brother to know all about Olaf's intriguing romantic life, and the impending reunion of the fairy-tale love affair. He omitted nothing, even to having a son. The battle-scarred soldier lay spellbound as Olaf unfolded his fantastic tale.

"Oh, God, Olaf, I can't believe what I'm hearing, man," Gustav exclaimed. He reached over and patted his big brother's arm. "I'm so happy for you." He grinned. "Now we both can get serious about our families."

Olaf took a deep breath, paused and shuffled uncomfortably.

"Well, what is it that you're afraid to tell me, Olaf?"

"Gus ... ah ... she's a mixed blood, bror. She's part Indian."

Gustav stared into space, numbed. "Is the world coming to an end?" He snickered mockingly, as if big brother was 'pulling his leg,' as he oftentimes had done, "I s'pose the other part is she's half Norwegian. Mama would really jump out of her skin." He guffawed at Olaf's silly joke.

But Olaf wasn't joking. "She's very beautiful, you'll see, like Jenny in some vays. You'll get to love her," he said seriously.

Gustav finally settled down, regaining his composure. Jenny, already knowing of the romance, joined them in anxious anticipation of meeting Marianne. Finally, the shock reverted to happy support for Olaf.

"Well, Olaf, I wouldn't expect you to do anything commonplace, I guess," Gustav admitted about his adventurous brother.

"Gus, she's the 'cat's meow!'" Big brother laughed boisterously. "You certainly couldn't expect me to be a 'lone wolf' forever." Olaf stood on a chair and gave a pretty good imitation of the nocturnal timber wolf, to the delight of his ecstatic brother and sister-in-law.

379

BURYING THE HATCHET VITH RAMSEY

Tomorrow would be doomsday. The Dakota, stripped of their pride, were to be banished from the land that their ancestors had inhabited for untold centuries.

The Swede was surprised to learn that Governor Ramsey had sent word, requesting a meeting at the Capitol. Relations had been strained between the popular frontiersman and the ofttimes impetuous politician over Indian policy, but the strong-willed Olaf was not one to hold a grudge. He decided he would go as a courtesy. After all, the two had mingled socially through the years with mutual friends and business associates, and he thought it was time to 'bury the hatchet'. Olaf chuckled at the irony of his thoughts.

Ramsey smiled solicitously, "Mr. Olsson, it's so good to see you." He offered his hand.

"Hello, Governor. I prefer 'Svede', if ya don't mind."

"Of course. I hear you're moving on soon, and I merely wanted to show my gratitude, Swede, for all you've contributed in shaping this country. No man has done more, I'll vouch for that."

"I enjoyed my small part, your Honor."

"Yes, I know." He thoughtfully continued. "I realize we've had our differences and misunderstandings, but I'm really pleased you obliged by accepting my invitation. Lord knows, I've had misgivings about the Indian situation, feeling some remorse for banishing them from the country, and all, but undo pressure applied by the settlers and the United States Government helped influence that decision, of course."

Olaf listened. There was a time he would have stormed back with harsh charges of the Government's blatant thievery and broken promises forced on the natives in the time since he first arrived thirteen years before.

"Olaf, as you know, we've altered our policy so that all Indians will not be punished. We released many of your friends, thirty of them, including the Renvilles from Fort Snelling. I guess at least a hundred more have been absolved of hostilities in the Southwest, I'm pleased to report."

"Vell then, I'm relieved some of the honorable Dakota and mixed bloods have been exonerated -- long past due," Olaf agreed.

"Olaf, you are a man of immense energy and talent, and I have always admired you for that, but I've wondered why you championed the Indian cause so diligently. Most people wouldn't give a damn for the fate of others, but it's been an obsession with you. Why?"

Olaf contemplated the question for a few moments, smiled, and returned a question of his own. "Governor, have you ever left the table still hungry after eating the only meal of the day?"

"Well, of course not," he snickered, at what he obviously considered a flippant question, thinking the Swede to be only joking.

Olaf never talked much about his personal life before America, but he now believed it wouldn't be a bad idea to enlighten the Governor concerning the lot of the poor and oppressed. So, with a reflective smile, he continued, "Governor, by sheer fate, I vas born in Sveden to a family of indentured farmers. For generations they ver locked into such dismal poverty that I shudder to recall the ugliness of it all. My father, and his father before him, and back as far as records show, the Olsson family eked out a mere existence on a few acres of the most God-forsaken rocky ground imaginable. All the people in that district ver the same."

Governor Ramsey leaned forward attentively, not wanting to miss any of the Swede's revealing story.

"Ven I vas ten years old, I vas sent to vork as a farm hand for a tyrant farmer three miles avay - it might as vell have been a thousand, for vun could not leave the place but vun veek out of a year. My father vas paid earnest money for the seven-year contract. There vas no escape from the drudgery of vork, nor from the blows to my head by my brutal master, blaming me when the horse, fighting flies, stamped down a plant of corn. The laws ver written that landlords ver justified to punish at their vill."

Olaf hardly noticed the secretary bring in coffee for the two. He finally smiled a thank you to the young lady and continued, "Ven I vas twelve I ran back home vare my mother applied balm to my velted back, and they vorried, knowing the Sheriff vould be calling soon, for escaping such bondage assured imprisonment on bread and vater."

He paused, and took a sip of coffee. "I escaped the district, and to avoid being caught, hiked at night toward the coast, forty miles avay. My uncle assisted getting me assigned to a life at sea, for which he received a portion of my four years' pay, but promised to hold the money for me. My ship vent down ven I vas seventeen, and I think everybody knows about that part of my life. So, taking my little brother, and vith some money my father saved and that of my uncle's promise, ve managed the unbelievable feat of vorking our vay to America."

"God, man, that's an amazing story. And, more baffling is the congenial and non-bitter demeanor you convey. You know, you've inspired and made me more tolerant of life, Olaf. Maybe it doesn't show, but it's the God's truth. You have that rare gift of influencing others, ya know."

"I didn't intend to run off at the mouth that vay," Olaf said, embarrassed for his rambling. "It's just that I've felt so damn much pity for the two thousand prisoners -- vomen and children mostly -- about to be crowded on the exile steamers in the morning like cattle, sent to the Dakota vasteland vare they'll die from starvation."

"They tell me it's good farm land where they're going, Swede."

"No. I vas there ven I spoke with the Yanktons who still survive on hunting and fishing, but they're not penned up like the four thousand Mdewakontans and the friendly Vinnebagos vill be, taken from the rich farm land the vite man vonted."

"Damn! I'm disturbed to hear this, but the decision was made be the Federal Government. I had no say in the matter."

"My heart aches for them. Someday, maybe ve'll all feel the shame."

Both men, deep in thought, contemplated in reflective silence.

Finally, Ramsey broke the quiet. "Swede, General Pope is now in charge of the Indian situation. He's planning a sweep through Dakota with several regiments to apprehend the Lower Agency escapees, and round up three, four thousand Upper Agency wanderers so there'll be no future forays to threaten returning settlers. They'll be leaving soon, but I suppose you knew that."

"Ja, I've known." He gave a disapproving grunt, continuing, "Governor, they'll send three thousand troops, who on returning, vill claim decisive victories to boost their egos, but in my mind, I see the action as stupid folly. I've hunted buffalo on Dakota territory, and can vow for its flat and barren rolling hills. Many, including the few hundred hostiles, have scattered like chaff in the vind to their cousins at Devils Lake, in Dakota Territory; to Canada, and the Black Hills beyond the prairie. The Dakota Indians vill know of their presence before troops reach vithin a hundred miles of their encampments."

"So, you're not optimistic the army will be successful?"

"Not in the least, Sir."

"Olaf, you know better than anybody. How many Sioux are out there?"

"Oh, I don't know. Including the Lakota Sioux in the far vest, I expect maybe fifteen, tventy thousand. Vite man's diseases have reduced their numbers substantially. There are many sad stories. A smallpox epidemic some thirty years ago, nearly viped out the whole Mandan tribe, ya know. Only three dozen survived out of two thousand. I saw their domed earth lodges still standing, a ghostly reminder, overlooking their once productive farm land."

"Olaf, you've been most helpful." Continuing to engage Olaf's mind, "What do you foresee, now the buffalo are disappearing?"

Giving a sarcastic grunt, "Vait for the railroad, Sir, and that land vill be confiscated the same as here. Buffalo vill be gone. Hunter vill slaughter them like we read they've done in the southern railroad building."

"That's progress, isn't it?" He paused. "Think the Indians will ever give up the battle. They've been soundly defeated here, Swede?"

Olaf was getting exasperated. "Hardly, Governor, for as ve make treaties only ven ve vant more of their land, there vill be more bloodshed and vor. There are Sioux Chiefs on the vest edge of the prairie who have promised to defend their land to the death; Chiefs Sitting Bull and Crazy Horse vill be heard from, mark my vords."

It was obvious the Governor's negative attitude about the Indian would not be altered -- for now at least. Olaf was anxious to visit the Dakota prisoners one more time before they were to be extricated. He thanked the Governor for his time and stood, ready to leave.

"Oh, Swede, I've heard rumors of your giving up the trail."

"That's right, Mr. Ramsey, dreamed about farming since I vas a boy in Sveden. The place I'm going is hundreds of miles northvest of here, Sir."

"There's no doubt you'll do well, but how the devil will J.C. get along without his right hand? He absolutely idolizes you, Swede. Told me that many times." Walking to the door, Governor Ramsey patted Swede's back, a "buddy-buddy" move as he tried delving into Olaf's private life. "Olaf, I've heard the damned rumors for years about a romantic involvement, but even Burbank won't tell me, and I'm sure he knows."

Olaf laughed. It only reinforced respect for his boss.

"Well, Swede, aren't you going to tell me who she is? You aren't going to be a farmer as a bachelor, are you?" He kept trying to penetrate Olaf's shell.

Pondering the situation, Olaf decided it was time to reveal all. "Governor Ramsey, I'm proud to tell that my life's mate vill soon be joining me. It's been a most agonizing time these dozen years realizing it vas only my vorrying about vot other people'd say that kept me from being forthright."

Ramsey stood with his mouth agape, wondering what was next.

384

Olaf, standing tall and confident, continued. "She's a beautiful voman, I must say. She speaks many languages vell, and has served in a distinguished vay, her Roman Catholic Church in Canada. Ve've loved each other for those tvelve years."

"My God, Swede, that's astonishing. Why haven't we known?"

"My lady's a mixed blood from old Pembina County," he smiled proudly. "She's a real American, with some French thrown in." There was a pause in the conversation, as the Governor recovered from the shock.

"Thank you for your time, Governor Ramsey. I really must go now, and bid farewell to my future relatives," Olaf chuckled, referring to the departing Dakota. It felt good to have revealed the truth of his romance to the Governor who remained speechless.

Ramsey, gathering his wits, expounded, "Why would we expect anything different from our heroic frontiersman. Of course, you'd have to marry a Native American." He looked off in space, visualizing some historical significance. "Olaf Olsson, brave and daring frontiersman, revered by pioneers everywhere, adventurer and leader of men." He turned back to Olaf and confided, "You will assure your place in history, big Swede, with the noblest of men; the brave and daring hero of the northwest, ingredients from which legends are created. A legend that will live in the hearts of the pioneers, and will be retold for generations to come. Oh, how happy I am that you've revealed your secret, Swede."

"No, Governor Ramsey, there vas no such motive in our relationship. Ve've had a basic and natural love through the years. Now ve vish to be alone to enjoy our lives simply, in the great open vilderness. That's all."

"I do hope you'll come back to see us often. Good luck. We'll miss you, Olaf Olsson." He extended his hand in friendship.

"Vith the railroad coming soon, Burbank promises I'll be shipping grain to the Voshburn mills in a few years. The iron horse is taking over my vork now, and I expect to visit my friends back here often, then. Good day, Governor."

In spite of their differences, the two men parted affably, as friends.

SHIPPED LIKE CATTLE

Olaf was dejected riding up the hill away from the miserable Fort Snelling prison where the corralled Dakota were being herded on the steamer Davenport. Like so many cattle shipped to market, nearly a thousand were crowded on the two hundred by thirty foot packet.

Though most of the Indians survived the winter's cold in frosty tepees, and with inadequate clothing, their numbers had decreased profoundly. Three hundred died, most were elderly. A measles epidemic, the first to attack the tribe, claimed scores of children, up to ten a day.

Due to the benevolence of Father Ravoux, small boxes serving as coffins were placed in a large trench. The priest promised the mothers and the few fathers present, who'd become hymn-singing Christians, that the dead would receive a more appropriate burial come summer

Few able-bodied men were included among the two thousand natives at Fort Snelling. Several hundred Mdewakantons, the most hostile band, had escaped to Dakota Territory, beyond General Sibley's reach. More than three hundred warriors, reprieved by President Lincoln, remained imprisoned at Mankato, after the thirty-eight had been hanged in the gruesome spectacle the day after Christmas. Many died in the cold confines at Mankato through the winter, while waiting to be moved to a prison in Davenport, Iowa, where they'd serve their reduced sentences.

Olaf's mind clouded, recalling the tragedy. Thank God, he thought, the Government had finally restored a sense of hope and dignity to thirty honorable Dakota leaders by releasing them. They would serve as scouts in the service of Sibley, their wives allowed to leave as well. Maybe the time will come when most will be exonerated, Olaf hoped. Riding on a ways, he decided to stop at the top of the hill to watch the tragic exodus unfold and wave good-bye to his many good friends.

Olaf had arrived early in the morning to pay his last respects. He saw mothers and children in agony, wondering if they'd ever see their husbands and fathers again. The distressed souls had no idea where they were going, though Olaf tried to explain they were being re-established on the Dakota hunting grounds, which eased the minds of some. He tried showing compassion and conveyed a sense of hope their families would one day be reunited. Many felt relieved hearing that.

It was the insulting and demeaning manner in which they were being exiled that pained him most. The grueling trip down the Mississippi to St. Louis; shuffled to another river packet for the stressful trip up the shallow meandering Missouri river to Dakota, a thousand miles of crowded, unsanitary conditions and, with meager food rations from which many would never survive, Olaf feared.

Stopping at the top of the bluff, he kept watching for the three-deck steamboat to make its appearance from around the Minnesota River's southwestern bend. He would wait and watch it turn down the Mississippi.

His years in America flashing before him, thoughts of the early Dakota generosity came to mind. The Indian hunters had saved the first farmer immigrants, many times, by supplying venison and rice, when their food supplies ran out. It happened to some of his countrymen at Chisago Lake, he recalled, his heart hurting. Oh, how this life has changed for many, in this much sought-after land of the free and the plenty, he lamented.

Olaf recalled his friendship with Taoyateduta. The two fished and hunted together quite often that very first year, along with Wowinapi, whom Olaf became fond of. The Swedish immigrant was charmed by the simplistic lifestyle of the natives who revered nature; not claiming ownership of land, but sharing unselfishly with their fellow man the abundant fruits herein.

It would be a while for the steamboat to come along, no doubt, so thoughts of those early years were most pleasant to recall. Olaf chuckled when thinking about Little Crow's climbing up the back of his stagecoach and tickling him with a feather. He then begged Olaf to help the Dakota retain their fishing and hunting rights, which whites wanted to take away.

Once the Mdewakanton band of Dakota were moved to the isolation of their prairie reservation, hunger and deprivation had steadily worsened.

It was a thrill for Olaf, as he blazed trails and helped organize settlements along the river, to stay with the Chief in his fine government-built house. The house was an inducement (or bribe) given to leaders like Little Crow, so they'd sign more land away for promises of future payments.

Coming back to reality, Olaf wondered why it took so long for the boat to come, it being nearly loaded when he left. It was tormenting for the compassionate Swede, who'd tried to make life better for the Dakota, but now was feeling blame for his failure.

Those great Indian women. My God, for unsung heroines, he smiled. They deserve to be praised and honored for their brave deeds. So many helped protect white and mixed blood sympathizers at great risk to their own lives. Thank God for Snana, wife of Good Thunder (now himself a loyal scout) for she bravely protected little Mary Schwandt, whose entire family was murdered by the hostiles near New Ulm. Snana dressed her as an Indian in disguise and then dug a hole in her tepee by hand, hiding Mary with her two children, vowing to defend them with her life, until Sibley saved them at Camp Release. What a great heroic story to be retold.

It was a comfort knowing that Reverend Hinman, his friend from the Lower Agency, would accompany them on the extended voyage, vowing to stay with them. He and the other missionaries, the Ponds and the Williamsons, taught the Dakota to be literate, and encouraged farming, which many pursued until losing their land. He revered these men of dedication.

Olaf glanced down-river; still no sight of the fateful conveyance.

Again, the past would not be turned away. Olaf finally relived the time he stole into Little Crow's house in the final days of the war, when the Chief was recovering from wounds. He admitted how foolish he was to have been coerced into leading the trouble-makers of Shakopee's and Red Middle Voice's bands, when they called him coward. It was as if Olaf was there again, hearing the Chief's arguments.

"I told them they were like little children who didn't know what they were doing. I told them they were like dogs in the hot moon when they run and snap at their own shadows. I told them we were like little herds of buffalo left scattered ..." Little Crow gave all the reasons why the Indians couldn't win.

Then Olaf recalled the ruckus outside Little Crow's house, how the hostiles called, "We will kill your white friend, Taoyataduta!"

And how he begged Little Crow to yield. "Friend of many years, you have honorably protected many whites and mixed bloods here. I have seen them with my own eyes. I would do everything in my power to speak for you. Is there no chance for an agreement?"

But, he had gone too far, Little Crow said and would not hang from a rope to be scoffed at. He would die like a true Dakota brave.

Olaf sat for a moment in a daze, then shook his head as if returning from a dream. "Taoyataduta, where did you go?" He looked all around as if to make sure the Chief was gone. "My God, I must get hold of myself. I svear my mind is playing me tricks. How can a man dream like that? It's something I'd never tell anyvun or they'd think this Svede had lost his mind, for sure," Olaf mumbled.

Still the prisoner boat was not coming. But surprisingly, a bright white steamer appeared from the east, around the bend of the Mississippi. A thin stream of white smoke trailed lazily in its wake. The paddlewheeler glided gracefully toward St. Paul like hundreds of others the past years, bringing tourists from the East. Only a few came now since the Civil War.

Olaf's cluttered mind was momentarily distracted by the occasion with the happy prospects of Marianne's return on such a friendly boat when she'd finally arrive from Montreal. Mr. Burbank had made arrangements with Hudson Bay officials to see that nothing would interfere this time. Through his scope he could see colorfully dressed tourists. Olaf smiled, recalling the memories of the time he and Gustav came to the area. The steam paddlewheeler churned on to the levee a few miles ahead.

Finally, a mile back, the awaited river craft came lumbering along, its stack belching puffs of black smoke, forcing it out of the Minnesota River into the "father of all rivers." The cruel mission was underway.

Sitting motionless, the dejected Swede looked sadly through blurry eyes. As the prison boat came closer he searched for people he knew, but crowded together in their burlap-type blankets, the mass of humanity looked like a load of freight, like sacks of grain or flour stacked together.

Olaf waved from three-hundred yards, and the Dakota, recognizing him, saluted, arms raised high in a unanimous show of appreciation.

This was an immensely sorrowful moment, for Olaf realized the weary departing were saying their final farewell to Kaposia on the banks close by. In this Dakota village most of the exiles were born and lived in happiness, as did the generations of long ago. The Dakota cherished the place, often alluding to the fact that the rich holy land had been nourished by the bones of their forefathers since the beginning of time. It had been ten years since the government moved them from this place to the reservation in the Southwest territory, and, ironically, they were brought back home for a final view of the land of their childhood before being banished forever. As the Davenport passed by, Olaf grieved for the Dakota.

But realizing the departing would soon reach St. Paul on their dismal journey, he decided to ride on. Leaving now, he could reach the levee and be in a position to call out some words of encouragement, and wave for a last time. Maybe a friendly wave and calling "God be with you" would be consoling, he thought, so he encouraged Dancer Girl along.

Reaching town, Olaf was shocked when his attention was drawn to the large crowd at the levee. Oh, he knew the rabble rousers were celebrating the occasion, the beer halls already overflowing this morning with hoards of characters descending on St. Paul to cheer the "savages" on their way; final vindictive insults, shouting them along. The agitators were gathered on the hill above the levee. The scene was quickly becoming wild and disorderly. "Kill the savages," and "Death to the half breeds," he heard them chant.

Riding closer, he could see the distressed pleasure boat visitors running for their very lives from the crazed, unruly drunken mob, some into business establishments, others just scurried frantically up the streets in obvious terror. What a horrible welcoming for visiting strangers to witness. What a black eye for his town, he thought.

Abruptly, the hoodlums stormed the dock with fists raised in intimidating gestures at the frightened, already panic-stricken, frail women and children on their floating island of exposure, at such close range. Olaf rode up behind the crowd, now numbering in the hundreds.

A crazed exhibitionist stood on a box, wearing a shabby top hat and tails, ranting and raving some biblical quotations.

Olaf listened for a moment to the tall man, resembling Abe Lincoln to the extent of his black beard and profound jaw. His makeup was grotesque and fake. Olaf presumed the warped malcontent to be a cast-off from some failed traveling show, flaunting his words as a pompous orator, and sawing the air with his hands, wildly.

"Cast these imbeciles, these heathens, far out of Canaan - my disciples. Hear me out for I am Abraham, and God has sent me to rule this land." Raucous howls blocked his words, for a while, but he only shouted louder. "This is the Armageddon as prophesied. Cast the evil forces out of this land! Banish them forever!"

Though the flamboyant character was riling the crowd, people soon turned on the fool, mocking and pushing him in ridicule, until he scampered for this life, to the amusement of the infidels.

Olaf grimaced at the hypocrisy, but his attention was quickly drawn to the Davenport again. The pilot had cut its engine and it drifted slowly toward the levee!

"My God!" Olaf gasped! "It vasn't scheduled to stop here." Glancing down from his vantage point atop Dancer, he could now see crates and sacks stacked next to the water on the levee. "Oh, my God! Vot an untimely moment to take on supplies vith this unruly mob!" he mumbled.

Eyeing the boat intently, Olaf saw the prisoners bunched together, away from the levee side, trying to withdraw farther inboard like frightened sheep flocking together from attacking predators. There was no place for the women and children on the outer fringes to hide.

Watching closely, Reverend Hinnman, wearing his white collar, stepped forward of his flock, bible in hand, making a visible pleading for peace and respect. The violent, foul-mouthed devils only mocked and ridiculed him. The forty soldiers of Company G of the tenth Minnesota, sent along to keep order, took up positions on the near main deck and, for a time, it looked as though further tragedy might be avoided.

Olaf tensely studied the faces in the mob, but saw only a few he recognized. The West was full of outcasts, crooks, and hoodlums, passing through, bent on flaunting their violent ways. He was sure most of them fit that devious category.

The military presence only quieted the crowd momentarily. Soon, the yelling of insults and vulgarities reached a deafening roar, as deadly rocks pierced the air from a distance. "Kill the savages," some shouted. "Revenge," others yelled, and, "Get those dirty half-breeds." Rocks soon filled the air like a pelting hailstorm, and all hell had broken out.

Olaf sat stunned for a time. Reverend Hinman had been hit on the side of his face and was bleeding badly. Several women and children lay on the deck, some wrenching in pain; with others, there was no movement at all. Farther down, three guards helped a fallen comrade. The soldier fixed bayonets, taking positions on the levee. Rocks still rained from the mob as they grudgingly backed away from drawn bayonets. Sheriff Sam Sullivan, mounted on his horse, approached from the far side, swinging his baton with authority, and making direct contact on some of the perpetrators Olaf observed.

Seeing that his assistance was sorely needed, he quickly employed the same tactics unleashed in his daring confrontation with the Chippewa on the first stage trip to Fort Abercrombie. He grabbed his sixteen-foot whip from its holder, unraveled it, and commenced cracking it over their heads, while Dancer Girl bolted into the crazed, angry mass of humanity. Those resisting were dealt a piercing sting to their bodies, the whip striking its mark, resulting in painful screams by the recipients. Stones threatened Olaf's high exposure, one knocking his hat off. Then, his tousled blond hair flew wildly as he aided the Sheriff in scattering the retreating cowards, running for cover and disappearing.

The immediate danger quelled, Olaf moved back to the Davenport and found the supplies had been quickly loaded. The pilot was already building a head of steam as the beleaguered river packet quickly moved away from the levee, continuing its downstream course.

Olaf followed along, making sure no further reoccurrence took place, and escorted the steamboat several miles along the bank. At a large bend in the river, several miles down, he stopped and waved to the departing Indians. They waved back in a show of gratefulness for his efforts.

"God bless you, my good friends, " he called after them.

"*Tangyang nungwe, koda. Tangway nungwe, koda.*" Good-bye, friend, they called back in unison, a sorrowful dirge fading off in the distance.

Emotionally limp and exhausted, the world around him seemed empty and unforgiving. Dancer Girl was allowed to set her own pace back to town, there being nothing of consequence hurrying them on.

MARIANNE VANISHES

It was early evening when Olaf returned to the Burbank office. He was certain J.C. understood his not working the entire day, but it had been many hours since the violence at the levee. There might be important notes left for him by the boss, or by Betsy. He thought he'd better check.

A strange, eerie silence had fallen over the town, now that darkness had set in, arousing Swede's curiosity. The demonstrators were conspicuous by their absence, and it was hard to realize such violence had taken place only six hours before. Still, he felt something strange was going on.

Turning the corner, he was shocked to see the Burbank offices were lighted. Burbank's carriage and horses were still out front.

Hastily he hurried in to see if anything was seriously wrong. Betsy was busying herself around her desk and acted like everything was hunky-dory, which was strange in itself, for she rarely stayed late.

"Hello, Swede," she smiled, looking somewhat sympathetic, he thought.

"Hello, Betsy," he returned a courteous, but strained smile.

Burbank, hearing Olaf come in, rushed out of his office, a desperate expression on his face. "Olaf, you doing all right?" he asked in a concerned voice, putting his arm around the big fellow's broad shoulders.

Olaf was a little bewildered. "Ja. Ja. It's all over now. Life must go on. I'll vork harder for the company and put all this behind."

Burbank fidgeted nervously. "Betsy, please bring us coffee. Come into my office, Olaf, my boy." He spoke in a compassionate, fatherly way. They sat down at the desk.

Olaf looked around, thinking the attention overly condescending. Surely he was strong enough to handle adversity, he thought. No one has to baby this weather-hardened Swede, he told himself.

Betsy brought the coffee, but showing tenseness, left quickly.

"Olaf, my son, I have something important to talk to you about." Olaf observed Burbank shaking like a leaf. "Olaf, I've never known a stronger willed man in my life." Sipping his coffee, he spilled some in his saucer.

Olaf leaned forward. Confused and curious, he waited.

"Boy, I have all the Burbank field staff, and many others already helping solve our crisis, so I beg you to reason out things sensibly before jumping off the proverbial cliff at this latest development."

"John Burbank, I'm sure tough enough to handle anything now."

"All right, Olaf," he looked his devoted field manager straight on, and patted his muscular arm resting on the desk and spoke. "Olaf, I'm not dead certain, but ... but I believe your Marianne arrived on that tourist boat just before the street violence took place."

"Vot!" Olaf jumped up. "Ver is she then?" He raced to the door. "I've got to see her right avay!"

"Olaf. Olaf, wait a minute," he begged. "Listen to me! She's here, but I don't know exactly where." Burbank intercepted him at the door.

"Vot do you mean?" he shot back.

"My boy, listen to me carefully. A Captain Peters of the excursion boat had come across a package, a large one, addressed to Olaf Olsson in care of the J.C. Burbank Company. It had been carried on by its owner, but, in the clamor, she left without it," Peters said.

"Vell, ver did she go?" he shouted. "I'll have to go qvick and find her." He pulled away, nearly panic-stricken.

"Olaf, listen to me now!" Burbank raised his voice to get Olaf settled down. "The boat captain, and others, reported that when the mob shouted 'kill the savages,' and 'kill the half breeds,' people ran in fear. There were those who said they saw a young woman wearing a hooded garment, with a young boy, run to the north, out of town, they thought.

"Olaf, please wait and hear me out." He spoke quickly, trying to detain the near crazed Swede. "Man, I have sent word to all our stations, and drivers, too, that they be on the lookout for the lady and the boy."

"Oh, My God, I feel limp as a jellyfish." Olaf stumbled back to Burbank's office and collapsed in the chair. "Vie does everything rotten have to happen to me, I vonder."

"Olaf, the package is in the meeting room. Why don't you open it? It's addressed to you."

"Ja. Ja. That I can do." He hurried in to investigate. It became quiet in there, at first. Then, Burbank and Betsy exchanged curious glances when hearing the big fellow react excitedly over the contents. "Mr. Burbank! Betsy, you too. Come in here and see vot it is!"

Olaf sat in absolute shock with a whole display of portraits and paintings spread on the huge oak table. At least a dozen of them. One was a perfect likeness of himself. Another, a most gorgeous woman with a handsome reddish-brown haired lad, bearing a strong resemblance to the excited Swede, himself. Others were men, some in boats, voyageurs, like her father, Pierre LaMond. He remembered clearly, how she spoke of her paintings, done at the nunnery.

"My God!" Olaf grieved. "I must go find her." He was further realizing the treasure he didn't want to lose.

Mr. Burbank explained he had sent notices to all the stage stations in all directions, that they be on the lookout for the woman and the boy. The Governor, too, had heard of the tragedy and reported the state militia had been alerted. He was sure they'd finally find the panic-stricken pair and send word as soon as possible.

"Olaf, Governor Ramsey even wants to help you, Son. He says he owes you much and hopes this is a way he can repay you."

Olaf showed an appreciative smile and tried controlling his anxieties. "I vill go look some, too. I don't understand. If I could only talk to her," he said feebly.

"I won't be able to sleep, either, my boy," Burbank confided. "Come back here, Olaf. I'll wait here for any report from the field."

"Good God, John Burbank, I don't know how I can thank you enough," he said before hurrying away.

It was totally dark. Bewildered and desperate, Olaf would not rest but would search the countryside until he found his precious métis.

REUNITED

It was near noon and an air of tenseness prevailed in the Burbank organization. J.C. paced the floor of the St. Paul office, waiting for some clue to shed light on the mysterious disappearance of Olaf's missing treasure.

Sig Moen, Blakely and the other executives showed up at daylight when the office opened, hoping for a positive report, but no one had a vague idea where the woman and the young boy accompanying her had disappeared.

Could it be that some of the violent riffraff at yesterday's riot had actually followed the desperate couple out of town and viciously murdered them in their hateful revenge, some asked? Had she in her frightful plight escaped under cover of the woods and traveled northward toward her homeland for safety with her people? Could she have found a refuge in the local area, others wondered?

No one was more heavy-hearted than Mr. Burbank himself, for he and Olaf had been trusted allies in all matters, and he'd treated the strapping Swede as a family member. Business associates and friends sent messages of support and concern from all over the community. Amelia, the hotel stage office clerk, who raved over the beauty of Olaf's adorable lady, having seen her when registering at the hotel two years before, sent her prayers. Matilda Washburn conveyed a most sensitive letter of assurance. And co-workers sent supportive thoughts, and told how they were actually helping in the search. Everyone was rallying to the Swede's cause.

Olaf had left a note at the office in the morning saying sleep had evaded him, so he went out early to search the woods along the northern trail.

Sheriff Sam Sullivan bolted through the door. "Any luck,

J.C.?"

"Not a word, Sheriff."

"Goddamn it! She couldn't have just faded into thin air! It's the damnedest thing. Just yesterday Swede helped bust up that rotten bunch of bastards! God, what a show he put on with that whip of his. Well, I'll keep workin, too. See ya later." He hurried out.

"Thanks, Sam, we appreciate it," Burbank called. He watched at the window as the Sheriff mounted his horse and headed north, as Olaf had done.

It was nearly noon when the St. Mary's black coach pulled up. Burbank watched as a quick moving Father O'Toole departed the coach and rushed in.

"Good day, Father. I detect an urgency in your manner. How can I help you Reverend?" Burbank asked.

"How kin ya help me, ya ask?" He looked around the place. "Well, is Swede Olsson here?" He was noticeably excited.

"No Father, he is out searching for his missing fiancee."

"Aye, so I heard, J.C. Me Lord, I wish I had know about his dilemma hours ago," he said, breathlessly. "I merely came out to do me some errands, I did, and lo and behold, I've never seen such a disenchanted place in all me life. When I found out the reason, I came here lickety-split."

Burbank perked up. "Tell me, Father, do you have that information?" He nudged the Holy Father, "Please come into my office and tell me all."

"Yea, yea. That I do," he said, seating himself.

Betsy called out excitedly, "Oh, Mr. Burbank, Olaf is here! He just rode up."

"Thank goodness!" Burbank replied. "Send him right in."

Betsy hurried into the door to tell Olaf that Father O'Toole had come to see him. Olaf's face became ashen, hearing the Father had come, and he hurried into Burbank's office.

"Is it bad news ya bring? A clergyman alvays comes ven something bad happens," Olaf asked resignedly.

"No, no, no." The Father stood and patted Olaf's shoulder. "I bring ye good news, me lad. I have talked with Marianne LaMond."

"Thank God," Olaf gasped. He sat down chuckling nervously in relief of the emotional stress. "She is not dead then?" he sighed.

"I'm sorry, Olaf, for if I'd known of yer involvement with the lovely lady, I could ave relieved your mind in the wee hours of the mornin'."

Burbank explained. "Olaf, Father just arrived moments before you, so I heard for the first time of your good news, myself. I'm glad this is coming to a happy conclusion, son."

"I must go to her now, then!" Olaf stood to leave.

The priest intercepted him. "Lad, ye'll be able ta ride to her today, but I would caution, thee young lady has been under considerable stress havin been frightened almost to death by yesterday's incident."

"Lord, we searched high and low for her. Ven? Ven did she come to you, Father O'Toole?" Olaf questioned.

"'Twas about eleven last night, she pounded at the door. The boy with her told that two drunken men grabbed 'em; one held the boy while the other threw his mother to the ground, and she cryin' fer mercy - poor soul."

"Oh, my God," Olaf groaned, "Did she get hurt bad?" He was imagining the worst.

"Aye, that young man, Peter Olaf, I think he is called, managed to wield a knife he carried for protection. He lashed at the one holding him and cut 'em badly, he said. Then he bravely charged the one who was about to harm his mother. Both, cut severely, ran away much for the worst, young Peter had nervously related. What a brave, heroic boy, that one!"

"Oh, my God. Poor Marianne and Peter," Olaf murmured "I must go to them now," he said in a determined show of passion.

"Please, Olaf, hear me out! For her sake - and for yer son's sake - and for yer sake."

Olaf was visibly shaken, and felt as though he was nearing a nervous breakdown himself. He was frustrated, trying to make some sense out of the chaos that had befallen him.

"Swede, they had tried escapin' to the north mind ya, but became disoriented in the woods and returned to St. Paul. As a last resort, they sought sanctuary at the church."

"Oh, my poor Marie. She has gone through so much. Father, I vill hurry to her." He stood, anxious to go. "Ver is she?" he demanded.

"I'll explain in a hurry, but please hear me out, Swede," Father begged.

"Oh, the agony of it all." Olaf was exasperated. "I'm sorry for my childish behavior, but my nerves are on edge."

"Lad, ye'll be able to go to her now, but I think ye'd like to know the rest. I'll hurry." The weary Swede sat up to hear more adverse details, not expecting good news, anymore.

"Listen, now. Yesterday morning I served Mass to several devout métis before they hastily departed with their small cart train - less than twenty, I think. I talked to the Captains, Marcel DesLauriers and Jean Baptiste after services."

"Marcel and Jean Baptiste?" Olaf looked surprised.

"Yes. I know ye knew them for they asked to greet ya."

Olaf's urgency to leave restrained some. "My God! Excuse me, Father, but I haven't seen them for some time. I spent a month hunting buffalo vith them on the Dakota prairie many years ago."

"Well, anyway, they were concerned, for bein' such a small group, they did not have many weapons for protection. That's why they always traveled in large number years past, guaranteein' safety against the Sioux."

The impassioned Swede smiled anxiously, anticipating the rest. "She is vith them, then?"

"Yea, lad, ye'll be able to ride to them before dark."

"Oh, vot a veight has been lifted off my heart," he sighed.

"Olaf, the Frenchmen were worried havin' received threats on their lives by the hostile crowd of yesterday, so they moved out, plannin' to stay on the meadow encampment north of St. Anthony

Falls last night. When I told this to the desperate pair later, they begged to have me coach take them, which I arranged immediately."

"That means they vill probably reach the creek camp by tonight, only traveling about fourteen miles a day vith the slow oxen," Olaf mumbled.

Father O'Toole chuckled to himself. "Ye know, lad, this old clergyman is not the smartest person when it comes to worldly matters. I blush at me naiveté in recallin' your drivin' the company stage to return her to the hotel a few years ago. I never dreamed such a bizarre scheme was unfoldin' under me nose, like that." He chuckled. Mr. Burbank joined in, and it became a chorus of humorous relief. Olaf laughed, too, in embarrassment.

"Mr. Burbank, I think I'll ride Dancer Girl over to the barns at the falls and take the carriage and the speedy bays, in hopes she vill return vith me," Olaf said anxiously. Suddenly looking worrisome, "God, I hope she'll trust I can protect her from any harm and she'll come back vith me, so ve can move on vith our dream, to our own land in Red River country."

Father O'Toole and Burbank shook his hand, wishing him a successful journey.

Olaf, showing a relieved smile, moved confidently to the door.

"Bless you, my good friend," Betsy called after.

"And thank you, Betsy, for all your help in these trying times."

Before Olaf could ride away, the good Catholic priest ran out with some last minute concerns. He reminded him that the unusual and saintly woman Olaf pursued, had been under strictly controlled, cloistered confinement. It would take some time for her to adjust to the natural world. He urged patience and understanding.

"Olaf, though the two of you have obviously shared mortal love - havin seen the boy clearly establishes that - I beg you respect her soul until the proper spiritual blessings are bestowed on your reunion. It will be a far more rewardin life for the both of ya, I promise."

"Don't vorry, Father, I'll treat her vith the utmost respect and love. Ve'll enjoy the good life, having vorked so hard for that. So long, Father." He rode off quickly.

* * *

"Gettyup, Bessie and Bell," he urged the fleet-footed ponies along, racing north past his cabin and the valley of his romantic fantasy eleven years before. He relived the exotic night; meeting the pretty métis virgin; the captivating love following; and the sincere vow they made, not to rest 'til brought together forever. The carriage sped along smoothly on the rock-free road. He was anxious, hoping Marianne's terrifying fright and stress would soon be forgotten.

Olaf approached the creek, where in years past, upwards of two hundred oxen and carts filled the campground. Now he worried, not seeing a single cart or campfire. He stepped out of his carriage and listened; only the sound of crickets and frogs could be heard. Then, finally, he heard a lowing of oxen, so he headed through the woods toward the sound.

"Halt, Monsieur!" A gruff male voice ordered from the nearby trees.

"Vot? Vot?" Olaf was startled. He wondered if it might be one of the hoodlums of yesterday's levee violence, at first.

Then the man gave an amused chuckle, and spoke. "Monsieur, you are very tall." He laughed louder, much to Olaf's dismay, but he recalled the mystery voice as that of a métis, he was sure. Making certain, he said, "I think I detect a miserable old Frenchman from the buffalo hunt. Marcel, it is you!"

"Yes, it is Marcel," he laughed heartily, coming to the open, and the two old friends exchanged a warm hug.

"Friend, I'm happy I caught up to you. But, Marianne?"

"Ya. Monsieur, she's here. I expected you, big Swede." He scratched his beard. "I hope her nerves have settled down."

"Is it bad, Marcel?" Olaf asked with concern.

"She was quite shaken when the church wagon brought her to us. She's resting easier now, in the tent closest to the campfire. There," he pointed. "Be patient, my friend, 'till her head clears from the devil's intrusion."

"Who is that sleeping next to the cart, then, Marcel?"

The kindly, chubby Marcel chuckled. "Who is that, you ask? Why," he laughed again, "big Swede Olaf Olsson, that is your son!" He kept chuckling at the humor he saw in the strange set of circumstances.

Olaf rushed over to meet his slumbering son. Kneeling down, he wanted to touch him, but withdrew his shaking hand, nervously. Noticing his tousled hair, he smiled, finding some Swedish in that reddish-brown color. His eyes blurred from the thrill of finally seeing his own son. Lord, he thought, how he'd like to hug him right now. Life had treated the youngster unfairly, too, Olaf knew, and his heart went out to him.

"Handsome boy," Marcel whispered. "Now then, I must see that the camp is secure, friend. I'll be back later." Marcel left.

With cautious anticipation, Olaf moved slowly to Marianne's tent. Gently he raised the flap. The light from the fire faintly illuminated her face near the entry. From the terror she suffered, sleep was no doubt the best medicine, Olaf thought, so he entered as quietly as he could. There he saw her facial wounds, and he half sobbed in sympathy. Oh, how desperately he wanted to reach over and touch her, but restraining himself, he was contented just to languish for her the while.

At times, her breathing became labored, breathy gasps indicating her sleep was far from peaceful, and he felt sorry for her. Maybe if he'd hold her, she'd sense he was there comforting her. He tapped her shoulder. She moaned softly.

"Marianne," he whispered. She stirred some. "Marianne, I love you."

Her face appeared to become more relaxed, it seemed, and he kept talking in a soothing voice, hoping to bring to mind thoughts of a more romantic and serene time between them.

She smiled slightly. Surely, she knows I'm here, he thought to himself.

"Marianne?" Again, softly, "Marianne?"

Her eyelids flickered a time or two, and finally parted as she awakened. Her first words were indiscernible. "Ah ... I ... ave .. no," She stopped. Her forehead and eyes displayed tiny frown lines. Then, as she regained her senses, she stared, and whispered softly, "Is it true? Are you really my Prince Olaf, or is this just another cruel dream plaguing me?"

"Marianne, love, this is Olaf, and I'm here to velcome you back to our beautiful vorld together. You, and our son, Peter Olaf."

"Oh, hold me Olaf. Hold me." She clasped her arms around him, and whispered, "Oh, how I've prayed for this to happen."

"I know. I know," he repeated, half rocking her.

Showing spells of fear and pain, again, she was reliving her frightful escape. "Only yesterday, people going to kill me for what I am, and ... can't change that! Then, could only be a burden to you, Olaf. I so confused." She was near weeping again.

"Shhh ... shhh," Olaf repeated tenderly, trying to quiet her. "Ve don't have to change anything my sveet. Ve've alvays loved each other so naturally, free of hate and jealousy. No one can deny us for vot ve have hoped for these many years."

Marianne was fully alert, shaken from her close brush with death, but clear headed. Olaf leaned over and kissed her again.

"Mmm. Oh, Lord, how I've yearned for such kisses through desperate years," she confessed.

Hoping to cheer her, and relieve her mind of ugly thoughts, Olaf said anxiously, "Marianne, I have a question to ask." He grinned mischievously. "Did you pray at the Nunnery for our dream land in Red River?"

"Oh, yes, did I ever," she returned his smile. "Though I never told Mother Superior about that." She laughed, just like she used to. "I hope the Lord wasn't angry with me, wishing for such personal gain and luxury," she added, giving a smirk.

"My Marianne, miracles do happen around you!" Olaf was excited now, believing their reunion was more than purely luck. "Love, do you remember how, at first, the church thought your visions ver inspired by God?"

"Yes, I know. I always told you I sure they were easily explained." Her cloud of confusion lifting, Marianne was feeling better, and playfully stroked Olaf's hair.

"I remember your telling of your faith in miracles ven ve first met near my cabin vare you camped," he reminded her.

"Oh, yes, I remember," she smiled, recalling the moment.

"Marianne, I have the most astonishing news to tell you." He assumed a serious attitude. "Your friend, George Simpson - the Emperor - and my most grateful boss, Mr. Burbank, had this land up north - only a day's ride from your métis village, mind you. Vell, ven the great Hudson Bay leader died two years ago, a large tract of land reverted to my employer. He alvays liked me, dear Marie, and I respected him, too."

"I understand, Olaf, but why important to us now?"

"Marie, it is our place now!" he said emphatically. "Mr. Burbank gave it to us as a revard for vork I've done for him," he said.

Marianne had a bewildered look, as he related the amazing news. "You mean we can have sheep and cattle and horses?"

"Ja. Ja. Ve can ride on our land all day if ve vant, Marie."

"Oh, my great Prince Olaf, what different world is with you at my side." Marianne's eyes were full of hope again. An impassioned kiss followed, but it was not the sensual kiss of the past. It was an outpouring of devoted love binding them together. A reverent experience.

"Marianne, vill you come vith me now, and bring our son so I can get to know him and love him as a father should? My dear, ve vill go to my cabin ... Oh ... I promised Father O'Toole I vould honor and respect you by restraining my desires until our union is blessed properly by a holy man. I think you'd vant that, vouldn't you?"

"Olaf, how thoughtful of you. You have breathed new life in my veins, my love."

A shuffling of feet was heard coming from the tent opening. Marianne, nerves frayed, gave a frightful start. Olaf grabbed a leg of the intruder but, surprisingly, a spontaneous giggling young lad broke the night's silence.

"Monsieur, Papa, got me like fish on hook, mon?"

Marianne gave a restrained laugh, her mind freed from yesterday's violence. "Oh, it's a jackrabbit with awful big ears, I think." She'd realized Peter Olaf had heard their conversation.

"I'll catch that jackrabbit, my love," Olaf reached out, playfully grabbing his leg again. Crawling out, he continued holding on to the little culprit whose eyes were as big as a night owl's leering into the smiling face of the tall frontiersman, his Papa.

The youngster was exuberant, finally speaking in awe. "Mama Marie told you were big man. *Mon Dieu*! How big you are!" he giggled again.

Olaf chuckled, kneeling down to be on eye level. "Let me get a good look at you. Holy Cow, boy! You're handsome - like your father," he joked. He was flabbergasted at the keen resemblance to himself.

Marianne was elated that father and son had finally met, but reminded Peter Olaf it was not polite listening to private conversations. "What did you hear, son?" she asked.

The happy boy looked at both parents adoringly. "I heard my Papa say kind things, like you told me. When tell of dream come true - big farm like Scotty Selkirk's - Peter Olaf want to yell for joy," he laughed.

Olaf was amused at the boy's youthful spunk.

"Will Peter Olaf have horse to ride, Papa Olaf? Or should it be Monsieur Papa?" he rambled exuberantly.

Olaf couldn't stop chuckling, he was so taken with his son's vigor.

Marcel, hearing the commotion, hurried back. "Is there any

trouble, my good friends?"

"No, none at all, Marcel. Ve're just getting acquainted at a rare family get-together," Olaf joked.

"Marianne, you all right now?" Marcel asked, concerned for her frightful escape from the angry mob.

"Thank you, Marcel, think so. Trust Olaf with my life, now." Putting her arms around him, she was showing her complete trust. "Will do all in heart to please and honor husband."

"Then ve vill go," Olaf said decisively. Playfully, he teased, "Peter Olaf, my son, you drive. Ve old folks vill ride in the back seat."

The youngster folded over in spasms of snickering. "No, Monsieur, don't know how. Watch you. Learn fast, then drive," he said with determination.

The whole party of métis had been awakened by the joyous reunion, and now had gathered around to cheerfully say good-bye. The three rode off to Olaf's little cabin to begin the long-awaited life they'd dreamed of for so many lonely years.

CHAPEL OF THE PINES

It was a fabulous coming together for Olaf and Marianne who'd been denied their dream for many sad years. And now they'd have their son, too; a thrilling close to the adventure of their never-ending hopes and prayers.

Marianne didn't blame the church for her detainment; only the strange circumstances allowing a few of the aged, slightly addled and disoriented retirees to tragically keep her from her mortal lover these many years. Steeped in religious doctrine, Marianne would forgive those responsible, and relished the thought of having their reunion blessed by the church. That was going to happen today, this afternoon.

The little cabin in the woods was taking on a quaint and festive appearance. Early in the morning, Olaf, Marianne and Peter Olaf eagerly gathered arms full of plum blossom branches, making large arrangements for the entry to the little cabin. Olaf cut long branches from the willows, from which he made an archway for framing his beautiful bride in the ceremony. He laced gorgeous wild trilliums and more plum blossoms, forming a spectacular arbor.

Marianne, raving over the abundance of spring flowers, eagerly picked bouquets of pale yellow and red columbines, wild daisies and violets in the woods, and added brilliant yellow and gold marigolds from the marshes: lovely bouquets for the tables and for the bride.

"Is like a Garden of Eden," Marianne exclaimed, admiring their handiwork.

"Ja," Olaf agreed. "Like our new home vill be up in Red River." Soon, Olaf noticed Marianne taking on a despondent and worried mood. "Marie, vot is wrong? Did I say something that offends you in any vay?"

"Oh, no, Olaf. Don't think you could do anything to offend me."

He put his hand on her shoulder, as she sat in contemplation on a tree stump. "Vot is it then?"

"I am concerned. I am Indian," she said, dejectedly.

"Vot?" Olaf reacted in surprise at her feelings of inferiority.

"I am an Indian. Will people accept me?" She looked sad. "Will my dear lover be shunned because of my blood?" she agonized.

He took hold of her arms, gently lifting her up to him. "My dear, it hurts me to hear you say that as much as you feel that hurt vithin. Listen, my love, I told you in the métis camp that ve've alvays loved each other. No one can deny vot ve have hoped for these many years."

Her eyes were a bit moist, looking adoringly up at him.

"Furthermore, Marie, you are also half French. The mob at the levee would have killed if they vere convinced you ver Indian." Olaf tried easing her mind on their wedding day, relaxing tensions. "Marianne, our son is vun quarter Indian, vun quarter French and vun half Svede. I vill always be justly proud that my son is part American Indian. For this I'm certain." He kissed her tenderly.

"But, Olaf, you were not there. The anger was vicious."

"I know. Marianne, I'm not making excuses, but a lot of German folks ver killed in the uprising. People are spiteful. It'll get better."

"Oh," she smiled, "why should I doubt my prince will protect me?"

"That's my girl," kissing her again. "Now then, Peter and I must get the outside cleaned up like you have the inside shiny and clean."

"I'll try to stay out of your way, but maybe I'll come and visit if it doesn't bother your work," she added.

"Do that," Olaf agreed, leaving to find Peter Olaf. He went around the barn.

411

"Whoa, Bessie! Whoa, Bessie!" Peter pleaded, trying to get the little bay mare settled down. The boy was a stranger, and his mannerisms and quick actions made the spirited pony nervous.

Bessie, one of a matched team standing thirteen and a half hands, was quick and speedy, and a good size for smaller riders. Olaf had left her saddled so young Peter could practice handling her. Olaf watched from behind the horse shed, amused at his young son's eager but somewhat awkward actions. He could tell Peter had a lot of gumption, and in due time, he'd learn just fine. Figuring he needed a little more coaching before starting work, Olaf crawled back through the fence.

"What do I do wrong, Papa? He don't act like he should."

Olaf chuckled, patting the boy on the shoulder. "Peter, yer doin' just fine. Don't vorry, it'll come soon."

"Don't know. Peter scares her. Don't think she likes me. Maybe not be helpful partner big Papa Olaf needs," he said dejectedly.

"Ah, nonsense, pal. Here, I'll show ya somethin'." He took the bridle lines from the boy. "First, ya have to talk to 'em so they understand, like this here, 'Nice Bessie. Settle down now'. Go nice and easy. 'That's a girl. Ve're all going to get along just fine, Bessie'." Olaf patted her on the shoulder a few times until she calmed down.

"Son, be real careful not to pull too hard on the lines. She might get a sore mouth from the bit. See this bit in her mouth, Peter?" He showed how pulling too hard might make her mouth tender.

"Mon dieu, not like piece of iron pulling in my mouth all day. Does that hurt her, big Papa?"

"Naw, not if she's handled right. The bit don't hurt a bit."

Peter repeated the play on words, and giggled at the humor in that.

Olaf laughed, too. "Well, partner, yer goin' ta be fun to have around, I can see that right now." Getting serious again; "Son, just keep talkin' low and easy to the horses and I guarantee they'll know vot you're talkin' about." He demonstrated again. "Now, Bessie. Ve're gonna help this young fella back up for another short ride. That's all right, Babe girl." It was amazing how Olaf relaxed his horses with easy talking. "Vot do ya say, Bessie, that fine vith you?"

Peter's eyes nearly popped out when Bessie whinnied, raising and lowering her head as if to agree.

Olaf helped him back up on the saddle. Though looking a bit nervous, Bessie allowed the young rider on her back. They walked around the yard a few times. Olaf assured his tenderfoot he'd soon be riding wherever he wanted to go.

"But now, Peter, ve've got a lot to do before the vedding; folks vill be comin' soon. 'Gotta repair the vooden rails so the heifer doesn't come over to mess things up for everybody. 'Gotta cut down the long grass and rake it to keep the mosquitoes avay, too. Let's go do it, huh?"

One thing for sure, the young eleven-year old knew how to work. The young man had been subjected to brutal bosses in the fisheries where he did common slave labor, like Olaf remembered when he was a boy, often flogged unjustly.

Olaf was amused as the young fellow dug in. "Peter, ya dig postholes faster'n most men," he praised.

Soon, a most delightfully happy one flew out of her cabin singing "tra-la-la-la, tra-la-la"; twirling like a fairy in the green grass on her bare feet, and swinging her arms and legs as if she were about to fly like a bird. Olaf beamed, having finally come together with the light of his life. Nothing else in the world mattered anymore.

"*Mon nuptial* dance for you, *mon amour*. Did you like it?" She threw herself in Olaf's waiting arms. "Oh, love you, big Ole." She used to call him Ole some of those first times together.

Olaf laughed, "Look, sweetheart, I got dirt all over you from my vork jacket; even on your pretty cheek." He tried rubbing it off.

"I don't care, dear Olaf! It is clean dirt! Can't wait 'till I work my own garden, and burrow myself in it," she laughed. She nodded toward Peter Olaf, who sat grinning like a barn cat with eyes as big as saucers.

"How is our son doing, Olaf? Will he be a good partner?"

"Oh, yes, ve're going to get along just like buddies."

She was full of happiness in her new life, Olaf could tell, and for a moment he knew she was filled with sentimental thought, a tear nearly coming into her eyes.

"Oh, no," she caught herself, "I not going to cry on my wedding day! This going to be most joyous day of my life, Olaf. I hope it's that for all of us."

"Mine, too," Olaf agreed.

They reached over, drawing Peter Olaf to them.

"Mine, too," the boy echoed.

Realizing the time was flitting by, with only a few hours until the guests arrived, the boys hustled to finish their work. Marianne already had the cabin shiny clean, and now needed to relax a while before fussing on herself, wanting to be most presentable for Olaf's family and friends.

"Olaf, was most kind of Jenny to offer use of her own wedding dress. Never could make one in such short time, but, want you to know I, Marie, am fine seamstress. Will prove that soon, I know."

The boys kept working as she chatted on.

"Sure love that sister-in-law of yours. My, she's sweet and lovely. And your brother, poor fellow, will he ever be all right? Ya know what I mean, will he walk straight without cane, you suppose?"

"Oh, sure, he's no vorse than I vas about the same time after the shipwreck, with my crushed leg. Ve Olssons are tough. He'll be as good as a three-year old bull, I'm sure," Olaf boasted about his family grit.

"You must get much respect from people. Never knew church could bend rules like that. Imagine, Father O'Toole and the other churchmen -- forgot his name -- coming all this way to give blessed ceremony."

"Pastor Tollickson, our family's Lutheran parson. Nice man," Olaf added.

"Hmm," she acknowledged. "Marianne still some nervous about meeting other friends and family; the rich milling lady, Mrs. Washburn; your boss, Mr. Burbank; your cousins, and the others. I hope they like me." The prospective bride was wound up like the old wall clock.

"My darling, don't vorry vun bit, Gustav and Jenny have raved ya up plenty already, I betcha. My, how Jenny adores you!"

"Well, I better go, and not distract you men. You're a big help, I see, Peter."

"Thanks, Mama, good working with big Papa," he laughed.

"Oh, happy day!" Marianne reeled, spinning away on her continued maiden dance. Olaf and Peter laughed at the exuberance she displayed, skipping around the shed toward the horses.

About five minutes passed since she disappeared. Then, suddenly, like a shot out of a cannon, the little bay horse streaked from behind the shed. The pastoral silence was shattered with Marianne's wild shouting, "Hi ya, hi ya, hi ya," as she rode down the trail.

"*Mon dieu*, Papa!" Peter shouted. "Mama go fast! Is she all right, you think?"

Olaf reared back, laughing from the pit of his stomach, for he recalled the race on the buffalo hunt, when Marianne beat him resoundingly before a thousand métis hunters, cheering them on.

"Peter, don't vorry. Your mother is an excellent horsevoman! You ver too little to remember, I suppose. She's just free now, and knows it and feels it, and she's letting off pent-up energy from years of frustration. Let her fly, son," Olaf howled happily.

She made a couple of right turns, masterfully handling her steed, as she had done as a young girl. She trotted Bessie back to where the men stood, jumped off like she had done a thousand times before at her métis village up at Red River. Peter Olaf cheered. Marianne and Olaf held each other for several moments, laughing all the while, knowing this was just the beginning of the wonderful life awaiting them.

But, Olaf was getting mighty concerned, there still being much to do before the guests arrived. He and Peter Olaf hurriedly arranged the table and benches, and cut the longer grass near where the people would be sitting.

Finally, finished, Olaf checked the yard making sure no stone was left unturned, and was pleased with the beauty of the place. It is a nice day for the outdoors affair, he thought. Maybe he'd better get himself washed and dressed, there being little time now.

"How ya doin', my love?" Olaf called into the foliage-covered outdoor bathing area he'd made, hearing his lovey singing to herself.

"I'm through bathing now. Just to dry myself. You boys better hurry and clean up, too. My, what a fine thing this bath is. Will you make one for our new place?" she called out.

"Sure, I vill. Just need a tub up high for the sun to varm the vater, a piece of hose, a tin can vith holes punched in. Nothing to it." Olaf was standing close, only the grape vines shielded her beautiful body he remembered so well. Smiling to himself out of sheer lust, he hoped she'd come to the open side.

"Where is Peter? Is he there?" she asked.

"He's back in the horse pen with Bessie, again," he chuckled.

Wow! Olaf's wish had been granted! Marianne obliged, revealing her soft tanned body, and her shiny, wavy black hair; only a small towel shielding her modesty. "Olaf, I can hardly wait for you," she said teasingly and with an inviting smile.

"Ja, vell, I'm ready to jump out of my stall, too." He was tongue tied for a spell, grinning. "I love ya so much, my dear."

Marianne leaned forward and kissed her man most tenderly. Realizing the powerful temptation, she quickly patted his cheek, and hopped back behind the vines. "Now, dear love, cannot see me until I come out to wedding music dear Jenny plays on her lap harp." She quickly dried herself, slipped on her kimono, and skipped most giddily into the cabin.

* * *

"Here comes the first vagon everybody," Olaf shouted.

Jenny and Gustav arrived early with baby Trena. They were just as excited as at their own wedding, Jenny said. "Remember Christmas, when we dreamed about this day, Olaf?" she smiled and hurried in to help the happy but nervous bride-to-be. Having met only yesterday, the two young women hit it off like doting sisters.

Olaf helped Gustav down from his rig and handed him his cane. The boys had agreed to wear their gray dress coats and dark pants, not perfectly matched, but close. They looked quite dapper, the tall tow heads. Before the ceremony, they would slip on black ascot ties and stick a white flower in their lapel, they agreed.

"Well, Peter Olaf," Gustav said, "how'd ya like farm life so far?"

"It good, Uncle Gustav. It been dream for me, too. Not quite got hang of riding horses, yet. Papa help, he says."

The brothers checked out the yard and livestock. There was a raft of planning to do. Olaf was determined his family would head north on Monday, and brother Gustav, not ready to do active farming yet, decided to take Jenny and baby Trena along and trail Olaf's livestock up later. They'd leave about a week after Olaf's departure.

An old storage shack stood on his new place, used years earlier for the fur industry, but shelters and fences would have to be made for the animals Gustav would bring, Olaf had explained.

"It's a Godsend your offering to help me build our cabin, Gus. It's sure kind and brotherly of ya," Olaf granted.

"Aw, we want to see some of the wilderness, too, before tying ourselves down on our place at West Lake. Only thing, brother, you've been like a father to me these years, and this is a way I can repay you a small bit." The brothers would miss each other, of that they were certain.

Olaf watched as another carriage approached from a half mile down. Heads popped out from all sides, meaning only one thing; cousins Rudolph, Marta and the three children had made it down from Center City. He was pleased, for the cousins had put the boys up those first months they arrived, and found their first jobs, including Olaf's at Burbank's.

"Hey, everybody," Olaf shouted frantically, "here comes Rudy. Now the fun vill start," Olaf promised.

"*Gud dag*, Olaf and Gustav," Rudy called happily. "*Gud dag*, boys," Marta greeted from a hundred yards.

The boys returned the Swedish greetings. Jenny stuck her head out the door to yell hello, too, hearing all the commotion. "Marta, Marta, come right in with us ladies, we could use your expert help," she called.

"*Horsum jorda, Kusin*," Rudolph grinned, looking around for Olaf's young son, whom he'd never seen, and just learned about.

"*Oh, fine, tack*, Rudy. Here, I vant ya ta meet my pride and joy. This is Peter Olaf." Rudy, always ready for a little fun, shook Peter's hand.

"Don't stay away so long next time. We're good people."

"*Monsieur*, I glad meet you," he giggled.

Marta came running with Amy Lou, her oldest daughter, to meet young Peter, and being the same age, they eyed each other coyly.

"*Mademoiselle*, come, I show you horses," he coaxed. She smiled timidly, but followed after, impressed by being "*Mademoiselle*."

Olaf checked his big pocket watch. It was getting mighty close to his great moment. Having joked about his ability to keep cool under pressure, it was obvious the big Swede's nerves were being tested.

"Hey, Bror, settle down," Gustav joked. "Yer nervous as an old cat about to have kittens. I can't forget how ya razzed me before my wedding, Olaf now the shoe's on the other foot."

"Ja, and yer gonna wear out those new shoes, pacing like that," Rudolph kidded. The boys were having fun with the big pussycat.

"Holy cow," Olaf bellowed, "there's a whole train of 'em coming, boys. Hey, you girls in the house, better get set, here they come, the whole damn bunch at once." Olaf began tearing around like he had a bee in his pants

The one-seated doctor buggy pulled up. The two black-coated clergymen, both wearing high, white collars, presented a statuesque appearance. Few would have believed the Protestant preacher and the Catholic priest would be out joy riding on a sunny day like this.

"Olaf, me lad. By gory, 'tis like a natural cathedral in the pines, it is," Father O'Toole raved.

"Well, Father, I have on occasion, chastised the big Swede for not attending services at times. I can see, it is probably more enlightening communing with God here than sitting through some of my less-inspiring sermons." Olaf snickered in embarrassment, the others chuckled.

Matilda Washburn's white carriage wheeled up to the stone walkway. Olaf hastened to assist her to the ground.

"Matilda, my dear friend, I'm so glad you could honor us with your presence." Olaf greeted her with a kiss on the cheek.

"Ah, I wouldn't miss this great moment in your life, Olaf." She scanned the landscape. "Oh, my, what a fabulous setting you've had up here all these years! Your flowers are gorgeous, and the air is filled with such sweet fragrances. How absolutely lovely, my dear Olaf."

"Thank you, Matilda, but I think the best part is still to come."

"I'm anxious to meet her, after Jenny's raving over her. I have a few things for this grand occasion; maybe someone can show Oscar, my new valet, where to unload these boxes."

Olaf's buckboard was parked back from the table, and already wedding gifts were being placed on it. Knowing Matilda, as he did, no doubt she'd overdone her generosity. She insisted doing all the food preparation for the affair, having considered Olaf part of her family, since Gustav and her Jenny were married. She had the means to do nice things for people, and relished in doing them.

419

Jenny came, begging Matilda to come meet the bride.

The Burbanks, the Blakelys and the Moens all strolled up together, having parked their rigs along the roadway. Mr. Burbank gave Olaf a hearty hug, but was feeling a little down in the mouth about to lose his good friend and favorite associate who was planning to head north. The other men and their wives responded equally graciously.

Not paying much attention to the time, the Olsson boys were shocked to see Jenny and the others come out to take their places for the ceremony.

"Olaf, where are the ascots you said we'd be wearing?" Gustav asked eagerly.

Rudy's wife, Marta, came out all flustery. "Jenny says our little Genevieve is supposed to be flower girl, and little Robert is to be ring bearer. We haven't seen the ring yet."

"Holy cow, Marta, I forgot. Tell Jenny to look behind my tobacco box in the cupboard. I hid it, vanting to surprise my dear bride."

"Olaf, you shock me," Marta tittered. "Talk about being skittish on your wedding day," she kidded. Olaf smirked wryly.

The boys dashed behind the cabin where Olaf had stashed the ties, quickly fixed them and plucked a couple white flowers off the arbor. Acting nonchalant, brought on some obvious snickers by the guests. Everybody was ready for the wedding to commence.

Matilda came out first; cousin Rudy escorted her to a prominent place in the front row. Marta and Peter Olaf were seated next. Jenny came with her lap harp, smiling gloriously at the prestigious gathering, perched on a stool next to the arbor, while the clergymen assumed their position opposite Jenny.

The joy of anticipation was shown in the smiling faces and the excited whispering of the guests. Then, all quieted down.

Jenny paused, smiled at the people, and strummed her golden strings with a dramatic flare. After a melodious introduction, she began playing the new popular Wedding March, by Lohengrin, same as was played for her and Gustav three years before.

Olaf, trying to look confident, stepped out, taking his place next to Jenny; opposite the Reverends. He attempted a strained smile, but his lower lip was twitching erratically, and his knocking knees seemed to keep time with the music. All those nice people out in front were smiling with him, but he wondered to himself, maybe they were really laughing at him, thinking he was only making a big spectacle out of himself.

Marta had dolled her youngsters up fancy like. Genevieve, eight, with a large, white ribbon in her hair, carried a lovely bouquet, and Robert, five, a little black coat and knickers, hair neatly combed to the side, held the little box like it was full of jellybeans,

What an inspirational setting for such an occasion. Birds twittered brightly, triggered by Jenny's beautiful music. The folks sat spellbound in anticipation of the final moment, when most will have seen, for the first time, the mysterious revelation of the big Swede's affections through these many years.

Finally, the grand entrance was at hand. And grand it was, as the lovely, dazzling Marianne stepped out of the cabin, and gracefully moved forward through the arbor Olaf had made for her entrance. She stepped, paused, and tip-toed her way in a state of sheer ecstasy.

Olaf watched the expression of the guests and knew immediately by the approving smiles and whispers, his bride was coming through the arbor. Olaf wasn't nervous anymore. Her radiant smile to the guests revealed more than simple beauty; here was a woman of dignity, strength and confidence.

The white, satiny dress, covered by a sheer sky-blue veil, and the delicate tiara of wild violets and daisies enhanced her natural beauty.

Olaf was so entranced, he didn't hear a thing that either Father O'Toole or Pastor Tollickson said in their sermonettes. He snapped out of his daze only after Gustav elbowed him, reminding it was time to put the ring on his bride's finger. "Good Lord, I'm a lucky man," he said out loud.

The clergymen joined in unison, "We pronounce you husband and wife."

Remembering brother Gustav's wedding kiss, Olaf wasn't to be outdone. He literally smothered his blushing bride with spontaneous kisses, to the delight of the prestigious guests, who chuckled aloud. "Tum, tum-ta-dum, tum, tum-ta-dum," Jenny stroked on her lap harp punctuating the conclusion.

A delightful reception followed, and talented Jenny again played the music so that everybody could dance the new popular waltzes introduced to the area the last few years. The newlyweds had been practicing the dance as Olaf hummed the melodies -- best he could -- and the bride did well.

The guests were generous in extending best wishes to this rare jewel who'd become the spouse of their beloved friend and frontiersman. The charm and keen intellect displayed by Marianne was inspiring to all, for few realized the extensive demeanor she had acquired through churchly training.

The gay festivities continued for hours. Olaf's family and friends were spellbound, learning of Marianne's and Olaf's unfortunate separation for so many years, and now happily celebrated their glorious moment.

Though Marianne was modest and shy about her paintings, Olaf was proud, and begged she display them in the cabin, to which Marianne had finally yielded. The guests, when observing, marveled over her artistic accomplishments, asking her to explain about the boatmen on the rivers, and the hunters on the plain, She described well the ways of her people.

Olaf grinned with pride as he and the men indulged in the Swedish tradition of "skoaling" the aquavit that Rudy brought. Then, as they got happier, the menfolk offered Olaf the usual instructions on how a gentleman should conduct himself on the first night of his marriage. "Skoal! Skoal!" they laughed.

It was a quaint and heartfelt wedding held in the chapel of the pines that beautiful spring day in May of 1863.

GOING AVAY QVIETLY

Olaf was busying himself at the new two-seater buggy he bought, with top, mud fenders--and everything. He'd remembered riding with Sig Moen way back that first year he came to the territory, and promised himself someday he'd have such a rig, like Sig had then.

He'd worked hard, saved his money, and now he could share some of the fruits of his labors with his beautiful Marianne. Bessie and Belle, the little feisty bays, would do just fine toting that buggy along, even with the back seat filled to the brim with clothing, foodstuff, pots and pans, dishes, tools, twenty pounds of nails, fuel for the lamps; and just about everything he could think of, including a tin kitchen sink and the pottery comode he knew would come in mighty handy up at their new home. And now, they were all ready to travel.

Marianne came out singing one of her saucy French ballads causing Olaf some consternation, not knowing what the words meant. Then, to irk him further, when stopping, she'd giggle about the foreign words she was singing.

"Now, you'll have to teach me vot those tunes say, Marie, or else I think you're making fun of me," Olaf reminded her.

"Ha, ha, *mon amour,* it says a little French lass never get 'nuff kisses form her big shy beau, and she not lie with him till she gets a hundred moe."

"Then, I'll give you a hundred now and carry you back in the house, my saucy bride of vun veek." He grabbed her and started smothering her with kisses. "I'll show you how shy this big Svede can be," he laughed.

"*Non-non-non, non amour,* I have the feather ticks and pillows all bundled for travel; besides," she snickered, "we not wear em out first week."

They both laughed happily, enthralled with the grand

experience of love-making under divine auspices, now that their union had been blessed.

"Where's Peter Olaf? He'd better come, if we're to get going." Marianne said looking around.

"Don't vurry about him, sveetheart, he's vithin vhistle range. I tell ya, since he got to riding Dancer Girl, he talks to horses just like I do. Yup," Olaf chuckled, "he's a chip off the old block all right."

"Oh, dear Olaf, our life going to be so wonderful. I can hardly wait."

"They say it even gets better. Can you imagine it any better'n this? Lord amighty, ve've vaited a long time." He put his arms around Marianne. "I love you, Marie. You ver virth vaiting for, that's for sure."

"Yes, Olaf, the loneliness of the past seems so far away, now."

Just then, Peter Olaf rode in. "Peter excited enough to go to Papa's great farm. Go soon?" his son asked.

"Ya bet, son. Ve got the rig full packed," Olaf said. "It's a long vay, partner. Ya better go piddle, if ya have to. Ve stop in town first."

"What is piddle?" the boy asked quizzically.

Marianne giggled. "*Toilette. Toilette,* Peter."

As they waited for their son, Olaf detected a worried expression on Marianne's face. Without asking, he surmised she might be leery of crowds after that ugly levee scene only a week before. Perhaps he should forget about a last farewell to friends in town. After all, he'd be back often. On the other hand, it'd be an insult to his brother and close friends who'd come down to say good-bye. They would have to go into the city.

"My darling, don't fret about going into town. There von't be anything unruly, I promise. Ve'll just say good-bye to our dearest friends and then be on our vay to our vonderful free life." he patted her hand. She relaxed.

Olaf and Marianne rode in the buggy while Peter Olaf went alongside on Dancer Girl, an excited and eager threesome. In fifteen minutes they reached St. Anthony Falls, Olaf's old stomping grounds. He thought the place looked strange, void of the usual hub-bub normally present in the town. What was waiting for him at the end of the road, he wondered.

"I think I smell a mice," Olaf said. "Vie, they could shoot a bullet down the street and vouldn't hit anything. It's mind-boggling, I tell you."

Marianne and Peter Olaf looked confused, reacting to Olaf's concerns. Soon they reached the suspension bridge that would take them across the Mississippi River to the new milling district and the big hotels that graced that side now-a-days. Half way across all pandemonium erupted! Boom! Boom! Boom! The big cannon roared from the end of the bridge. The team shied! Olaf struggled to get the bays settled down. He was more amazed seeing his son control Dancer Girl like a real expert horseman.

Then, there was the crowd-hundreds and hundreds of people he knew.

"My Lord, Marie, I'm flabbergasted beyond vords," he babbled. "Vot kind a folderol is this anyvay?" It was obvious the celebration was in his honor; people lining the street and applauding when he appeared.

Marianne, at first looked frightened having never seen anything like the tribute her big Swede was receiving. When seeing the likes of Gustav, Jenny, Matilda, and Olaf's associates from Burbank Company, she relaxed and primped with pride over the honor being bestowed on her husband.

Modest Olaf now grinned his huge toothy smile. "Marianne dear, I'm embarrassed, but...my...this is the nicest thing ever happened to me."

"Olaf, these people love their great frontiersman, and want to show it. Why not stand up so they see you better?"

"Aw, I feel kind a foolish. But, vell...all right...here goes." When he stood up in the open buggy he drew wild cheers, of course.

"Ha, ha," brother Gustav shouted. "We surprised you, bror."

"Did you have anything to do vith this tomfoolery?" Olaf questioned.

"Not me," he said innocently, a hog-eating grin on his face.

Jenny ran over and handed Marianne a pan of goodies. "Just a few treats for the road. Sweets go good when traveling."

"Oh, for heaven's sakes!" Marianne said, then added politely,

425

"How nice of you, Jenny. Thank you much."

Olaf echoed Marianne's sentiments, and added; "Ve'll sure get things in order ven you two come up vith our livestock in two veeks. And Gus, I sure appreciate your offer to help build our cabin. Damn nice of ya."

Moving down the street, the brothers and their wives shouted pleasantries until the crowd totally drowned out their conversation. Everybody called out words of endearment. "Have a wonderful life." "We're going to miss our great hero." "Come back and visit us soon."

Peter Olaf didn't know what to make of things, having never seen anything like it in all his life. He just grinned at the goings on.

Olaf knew he couldn't stop and talk to people, which he sure wanted to do, but there were many more down the street to wish them well. His jaw dropped when he saw a platform had been set up where the Pioneer Brass Band was tootin' away with rousing marching music.

Burbank's teamsters, their wives-and children, waved excitedly as their hero's buggy approached, touching Olaf's heart.

"Holy heifer dust, Marie, I'm gettin horse marbles in my eyes."

Everybody was in one happy mood. The noise was near deafening.

"Hey, Big Swede, thanks for that stove you won for my wife," Nels Augustine shouted, remembering Olaf's winning the arm wrestling match that Nels had bet on.

"Friend Swede, we heard you are married to a real queen. She sure is pretty! Handsome son, too!" Wagoner Dahlheimer yelled.

"Ja, Swede, show her off some, so beautiful she is. Ja, Ja, Ja!" the teamsters shouted. "We can't see your bride, have her stand, Swede."

While Olaf had a great smile on his face, Marianne blushed shyly. Olaf reached down, and though being timid, she allowed him to help her to a standing position next to him. One tumultuous roar of approval went up, and the applause for his beauteous mate made Olaf's chest billow aplenty.

Olaf kept his ponies moving but more and more people wanted to come up and give their favorite frontiersman a slap on the back and a handshake.

The band was getting loud now, as the honored guests pulled up in front of the dignitaries on the band stand. The big Swede was in his glory and began swaying to the tempo of the music, much to the pleasure of the crowd. Marianne was aglow, seeing how the masses doted on her, and Peter Olaf. Peter didn't know why, but such a tribute he'd never ever forget.

There they sat, the three most prestigious citizens of the community; Governor Ramsey, J. C. Burbank, and Matilda Washburn. They were surrounded by flags and banners, one saying, "OUR HERO -- BIG SWEDE, OLAF OLSSON."

Of course, the governor, seizing upon the moment, figured to gain some political hay on the coattails of the Swede's popularity, waved frantically for the crowd to quiet down so he could give one of his silver-tongued orations. Folks reached up to shake the hand of their legendary frontiersman, wanting to extend personal greetings.

Finally, Olaf and his queen sat down in the buggy to hear the governor.

"My good friends, it is my humble honor to dedicate this day, 'The Big Swede Memorial Celebration'." Everybody cheered. "It behooves me to render praise on this giant of a man who blazed trails for our thousands of settlers, daring to penetrate the great wilderness, so you and I could enjoy the multitude of fruits this great land offers..."

The speech went on and on, and Olaf and Marianne watched as Matilda mouthed good wishes, "God's speed" and "I'll miss you, Olaf." Burbank raised a fist, smiled and winked, "Thank you. Thank you."

Olaf mouthed back thank yous to both. And similar expressions were exchanged with Sig Moen and John Blakely, and their families. Olaf had established a love affair with a whole lot of people in the great Northwest.

The turnout was complete. The big Swede chuckled to himself when spotting Mrs. Higgenbottom and her friends of temperance. Seemed like they often shadowed the big bachelor, finding him on occasion, in slightly intimidating situations. This time, they weren't giving the 'naughty, naughty' finger, but a little wave, indicating they'd miss him.

Olaf hadn't heard much of Ramsey's speech, but when he spoke of Indians, and Swede's strong commitment to them, Olaf's ears perked up.

"I am truly sorry I didn't listen to you as my trusted confidant, for if I had, the many misunderstandings between the white man and the red man could have been resolved. Though we have banished them, I am most delighted to tell the Big Swede we are reinstating many honorable Dakota-we'll be inviting more back. As a tribute, I have designated a Dakota honor guard, now serving the State, to lead our Great Hero to the West."

Olaf was not one who needed praise and flattery for his accomplishments; his inner goals were built on the satisfaction of having done good and kind deeds for his fellowman. Whatever the task, he strived to do his best, like improving the lot of the Indian. So, when the applause went up as eight proud Dakota braves rode in-in full regalia-raising their right arms high, palm forward, in salute to Swede, he felt richly rewarded.

The massive gathering of friends followed and waved farewell to the great legend of the frontier as he departed for the West with his beloved bride and handsome son. The Big Swede smiled, reflecting on the dreams he had as a boy in Sweden, to escape the grips of indentured poverty, go to America, and settle on some fine farmland with a loving family of his own.

Ah, how beautiful life had become.